"This calm, quiet book contemplates the spaces between worlds and hearts, reality and… elsewhere. Tristane takes its place alongside Viriconium and the Dream Archipelago as one of the great creations of British literature."
**Dave Hutchinson, author of BSFA Award-winning *Europe in Winter***

"A heart-rending novel about being believed, being trusted, and the temptation to hide the truth. Of people going missing, and their incomplete stories. A generous book, it leaves the reader looking at the world anew. Dizzying stuff."
**Anne Charnock, author of Philip K. Dick Award finalist *A Calculated Life***

"Beautifully told, absorbing, and eerie in the best way – I was left contemplating its images of alienation, connection, and parasitic threat days after I had finished reading it."
**Yoon Ha Lee, author of Hugo and Nebula Award-nominated *Ninefox Gambit***

"Astonishing and brilliant, the best thing this immensely gifted writer has yet done."
**Adam Roberts, author of *The Thing Itself***

"Combining mystery, psychology, fantasy and science fiction with cool, stylish assurance… a genre-busting treat."
**Lisa Tuttle, author of *The Mysteries***

"A superb portrayal of the bond between sisters in a world of ever-shifting realities. Allan weaves a line between the familiar and the profoundly strange with effortless skill and assurance."
**E. J. Swift, author of *Osiris***

"A startlingly original and deeply affecting journey into the otherworlds of grief and its afterlife, *The Rift* is a marvel."
**James Bradley, author of *Clade***

"An intricate and empathetic journey into the feeling of not belonging. *The Rift* examines what it's like to inhabit a house, a city, even an alien landscape. Then it asks – how do we know those places? When are we accepted, and when does that place become home? It's a deep and powerful novel, speaking to those of us who see the world and yet struggle, in flux, to be a part of it."

Also by Nina Allan and available from Titan Books

the RACE

# the RIFT

## NINA ALLAN

**TITAN** BOOKS

To Matt, ... ve

The Rift
Print edition ISBN: 9781785650376
E-book edition ISBN: 9781785650390

Published by Titan Books
A division of Titan Publishing Group Ltd
144 Southwark Street, London SE1 0UP

First edition: July 2017
1 3 5 7 9 10 8 6 4 2

This is a work of fiction. Names, characters, places, and incidents either are the product of the author's imagination or are used fictitiously, and any resemblance to actual persons, living or dead, business establishments, events, or locales is entirely coincidental. The publisher does not have any control over and does not assume any responsibility for author or third-party websites or their content.

A CIP catalogue record for this title is available from the British Library.

Printed and bound in Great Britain by CPI Group (UK) Ltd, Croydon CR0 4YY

# the
# RIFT

# The Before

Selena became friends with Stephen Dent the summer before the summer Julie went missing. Stephen Dent lived on Sandy Lane, four or five doors down from where Selena and Julie and their parents lived. He taught mathematics at Carmel College, although Selena didn't know that until later. The first time Selena saw Stephen he was getting off a bus. She noticed him because of what he was carrying: a transparent plastic bucket with a large orange fish swimming in it. Selena watched the man go into his house and then she went into hers. A couple of days later she saw him again, buying a packet of straight-to-wok noodles at the Spar shop at the bottom end of Pepper Street. Selena was there with her sister Julie. Julie was buying a glittery lipstick and Selena was buying a pop magazine but they were mainly looking for an excuse to get out of the house. The summer of Stephen Dent was also the summer that Selena's parents almost split up. Julie and Selena weren't supposed to know about that, but it wasn't difficult to work out, not so much because of the shouting as because of the silences that descended when the rows were over. The sisters assumed it was their father who was having the affair. They held long intense discussions all that winter and spring about who he might be sleeping with, without coming to any definite conclusions, and only finding out months afterwards that it was not Raymond Rouane who had gone off the rails, but Margery.

For Selena, the most memorable thing about that time was that she and Julie became close again, almost as close as they had been when they were younger, giggling and whispering in corners and finding any and every excuse to be alone together. Selena felt overjoyed at this development, almost enough to be secretly grateful for the disaster that had prompted it. She had felt Julie's growing away from her not just as a loss, but as a punishment. The reinstatement of her sister's affections seemed like a miracle.

Not that it lasted. But for the first part of that last summer they were tight as drums, thick as thieves, close as conspirators. The memories flowed together in Selena's mind still: the smells of baking tarmac and cracked lawns, the particular stillness of those evenings, mauve shreds of twilight collecting in the mouths of alleyways and shop entrances as it began to get dark, the charred scent from their neighbours' barbecues. Neither of their parents seemed to care what time they came in at night, or even notice until they got back that they'd been away.

Stephen Dent was two people ahead of them in the checkout queue. Selena nudged Julie in the ribs.

"That's him," she said. "The fish guy."

"What fish guy?" Julie said, too loud.

"Shut up." Selena spun around to face the door. She did not want the fish man to turn and see her, to imprint her upon his memory. He was tall and slightly stooped, and his hair was going grey, a detail that contrasted oddly with the eye-burning Day-Glo orange of his Adidas trainers. He stood out from the crowd, Selena thought, as people who are loners or misfits tend to do. Julie glanced at him once in an offhand manner then appeared to dismiss him. At one time, Selena would have bumped her in the ribs again and whispered: "*Alien.*" Alien-spotting was a game they used to play all the time, back when Julie was fourteen and Selena was twelve and they were both obsessed with *The X-Files.* Anyone they happened to see who was wearing odd clothes or acting strangely, they would raise their eyebrows knowingly then race around the corner and collapse into giggles. Selena remembered sometimes laughing so hard there were tears in her eyes. She didn't believe these people were aliens, not really, but a part of her felt excited by the possibility that they could be. What she enjoyed mostly was the closeness with Julie, the way they didn't even have to look at each other to know what the other was thinking. The laughter bubbling in their chests, threatening to burst out any minute, like the alien in the movie *Alien*, only without all the blood.

At some point during the months following her fifteenth birthday, Julie stopped being interested in aliens and began spending most of her time alone, or with friends from school Selena didn't know. Even now, during the delicious, unexpected weeks of their renewed intimacy, Selena was afraid to ask Julie if she thought the fish guy might be an alien in case Julie had decided that aliens were permanently off the menu. One false step and Julie would tut and turn away and it would be half an hour at least before things were all right again.

They watched *The X-Files* on video that summer, sometimes, if Julie was in the right mood, but it wasn't the same. Which was a shame, because the fish guy – Stephen Dent – was such a perfect alien. There were the trainers, for a start, which now Selena came to think of it were exactly the same shade of orange as the fish in the bucket. Then there was the contrast between his scrawny, schoolboy's body and his wiry grey hair. He looked like an alien who had taken over the body of a child, a core *X-Files* concept if ever there was one, and now Selena had no one to share it with.

She watched the fish man as he paid for his noodles and then headed for the door. As he passed by her their eyes met, just for a moment, and Selena found herself thinking how sad he looked, how lost. She often wondered if it was that first glancing eye contact, their mutual recognition, that made it possible for them to become friends so quickly, later.

He told Selena he had moved up north from Stoke-on-Trent. His flat – his maisonette, actually – was an identical copy of the bottom two floors of the Rouanes' house. Selena found it mildly unsettling, to step inside Stephen Dent's home and find the same arrangement of rooms and hallways and dado rails as in her own. She knew perfectly well that if her mother had known about her visits to Stephen Dent's flat she would have put a stop to them, but Margery didn't know, she had no idea, and so the visits continued. Selena knew nothing about Stephen Dent's history until after he was dead. She liked to sort through his books, which were piled three-deep on the shelves in Stephen's study, or the dining room as it was in Selena's house. Stephen's books seemed to be in no particular order: novels stacked next to dictionaries, mathematics textbooks intermingled with biographies of Dickens and Einstein and Chekhov, and an opera singer called Farinelli, a castrato who was the star of Handel's operas.

"How do you remember where anything is?" Selena asked him.

Stephen laughed. His laugh was strained and dry, more like a cough than a laugh, as if he found the idea of laughter embarrassing and had invented a new sound to replace it, the way the newspapers would replace swear words with a row of asterisks. "I just do," he said. "Actually, it's easier. When you shelve books in alphabetical order you stop noticing them."

Selena didn't believe him at first, but she found it was true. Stephen's books were more interesting to look at because you could never predict what you were going to find. And the strange thing was that in spite of the random arrangement it really wasn't difficult to remember where a particular book was, if you needed to find it again. Selena soon learned that the book about black holes was shelved next to the tragedies of Aeschylus, that the *Collins Guide* to British Butterflies could be found tucked in next to Old Possum's Book of Practical Cats.

The only books Stephen Dent kept in order were his books on koi carp. Selena's favourite was a long, heavy volume in both Japanese and English, with a colour photograph of a different fish on every page. Selena learned that koi carp were just ordinary river carp that had been selectively bred for colour. There were more than a dozen named colour varieties: kohaku, taisho sanke, showa sanke, tancho, chagoi, asagi, utsurimono, bekko, goshiki, shusui, kinginrin, ochiba, goromo, hikari-moyomono, kikokuryu, kin-kikokuryu, ogon, kumonryu. There was even a name for koi that didn't fit exactly into any of the other categories: kawarimono. Stephen taught her how to write some of the group names in Japanese characters, which were called kanji. She found the kanji fascinating because they seemed to add up to more than themselves, containing many shades of meaning within the one precisely intricate set of pen-strokes. So different from English letters, which were exactly what they said and no more.

The fish Selena had seen Stephen carrying off the bus in the plastic bucket was a taisho sanke and her name was Takako.

When Selena asked Stephen how come he knew Japanese, he told her he'd spent a year in Osaka, teaching English. "I lived with a family called the Shiburins. Mr and Mrs Shiburin were both teachers. I never became particularly close to them, but I didn't know my own parents that well, either."

The Shiburins had a daughter, Hiromi. She was nineteen. "Did you fall in love with her?" Selena asked, knowing that the answer was obvious: of course he did. He was still in love with her when he came to live in Lymm, almost thirty years later. Stephen showed Selena a photograph of Hiromi, who had been a round-faced, gently smiling young girl with her dark hair cropped in a straight line across her forehead. Something about her made Selena think of Peter Pan, and she wondered if this was because in Stephen's eyes at least Hiromi would never grow up. She would always be as she was in the photo, even though in real life she would be a woman now, with children of her own maybe, children the same age as she was in Stephen's picture.

"Did you stay in touch?" Selena asked.

Stephen shook his head. "Hiromi's father wouldn't let her. He said she was too young to think about a relationship. He made her promise not to write to me and said that if I wrote to her he would confiscate my letters. I think he was afraid that if we kept on seeing each other she might have wanted to move to England. He hated the thought of losing her."

Stephen learned everything he knew about koi carp from the Shiburins. Hiromi told him that individual koi might live for a hundred years or even longer. One of the Shiburins' fish, a classic kohaku named Nero, had originally belonged to Hiromi's grandfather, who had been given it as a coming-of-age present by his parents.

"All the fish loved Hiromi," Stephen said. "I liked to think they saw her as a goddess." He laughed again, that odd choking sound. When Selena asked him if he'd ever loved anyone else, after Hiromi, he didn't answer. He acted as if he hadn't heard the question and perhaps he hadn't. Selena didn't feel that she could ask it again.

Stephen's back garden was much longer than the Rouanes' and he kept it immaculate. It was laid out in the Japanese style, with neat sections of gravel and narrow paved pathways, drooped over by the elegant spindly trees with five-pronged red leaves that Selena had seen in the set of Japanese prints on Stephen's living-room wall.

"They're Acers," Stephen told her. "Japanese maple."

At the far end of the garden lay Stephen's carp pond. There were twelve koi in all, ranging in age from three to twenty-five. Stephen had taught them to feed from his hand. Selena found them beautiful but a little unnerving. The oldest fish, Katsaro, was older than she was, and would probably outlive her. Katsaro knew his own name, and came gliding to the surface of the water when you called him. Selena couldn't decide if she found this spectacularly impressive or just creepy. It had never occurred to her that fish might be capable of thought, of remembering words, but Katsaro offered proof that they were. Selena couldn't escape the idea that he was watching her.

Selena learned that Stephen taught maths, but other than that and his time in Japan she knew nothing about his life before she met him and the truth was she wasn't much interested. She thought it was sad that Stephen was still pining for a relationship that had ended thirty years before, especially since she had an idea that the feelings had been much stronger on Stephen's side than on Hiromi's. Selena felt sorry for him in a way, but the main reason she kept visiting Stephen was because he made her feel special. Stephen's flat, so intriguingly stuffed with books and Japanese knick-knacks, gave her an escape hatch, somewhere to go where no one would question her, and that was not seething with thundery reproaches and unspoken resentments. She liked to sort through the books in Stephen's study. She also enjoyed sitting beside the carp pool while she gave Stephen the lowdown on the latest school feuds and teacher outrages, who was in and who was out and who was an idiot. She found Stephen easy to talk to, chiefly because she knew that anything she happened to tell him would remain their secret. She avoided the subject of Julie almost entirely. Selena had the feeling that Julie knew about her visits to Stephen but had decided for whatever reason not to say anything.

As the summer passed its halfway mark and the new school term approached, Julie had begun to drift away again. This second desertion hurt even more than the first, because Selena sensed that this time their separation would be permanent. Her friendship with Stephen Dent was small recompense, but at least it was something.

The idea that Stephen might have done something wrong – that he had been suspended from his job in Stoke-on-Trent, that one girl's mother had accused him in open court of being a dangerous fantasist – would have seemed incredible to her, like something from the tragedies of

Aeschylus. To Selena at fourteen, Stephen Dent, with his greying hair and stooped shoulders, was already an old man.

Almost exactly one week before Stephen killed himself, Selena emerged from the front door of Stephen's maisonette just as Julie was stepping off the bus outside their house.

"Befriending the aliens now, are we?" Julie said.

"Infiltrating," Selena said, and grinned. She felt simultaneously sheepish at being caught and gratified to the point of stupidity that Julie had acknowledged their old enthusiasm, even in passing. She felt a pinprick of guilt also, for having somehow betrayed Stephen, but consoled herself with the thought that he would never know.

From what Selena heard later, it appeared that someone in Stoke had sent a newspaper clipping to someone in Warrington, and the rumours had begun to circulate from there. Stephen, who had come north in the hope of making a new start, was not going to be allowed to forget his past. Even though the courts had acquitted him of any wrongdoing, even though all Stephen wanted to do was earn his living and read his books and tend his koi carp.

One night in late September, some local youths shimmied over the back wall of Stephen's garden and poured a bottle of disinfectant into the carp pond. All twelve fish died, of course. Selena didn't find out about it until the evening of the day it happened, when she called in on Stephen as usual on her way home from school. Stephen came to the door distraught and weeping, barely able to speak. He put his arms around Selena and held her, his whole body trembling. The embrace went on for what seemed like ages and the longer it lasted the more uncomfortable and out of her depth Selena felt. Stephen had never touched her before. This sudden demonstration of affection was both unwelcome and completely unexpected.

He smelled fiercely of sweat, as if he'd been running, or was going down with the flu. He kept repeating Selena's name, as if he believed it could save him somehow. When he told her what had happened, Selena felt a deep-down horror, the kind that twists your guts and makes you feel sick. She had no idea what to say. She could offer him no words of comfort, because there were none. Selena wanted to leave the maisonette and never go back. She felt her refuge had been spoiled, violated by an action so unspeakable she didn't want ever to have to think about it. She would have liked to pretend the carp pool had never existed.

For the first time in a long time, what Selena wanted most was to be at home.

"They poisoned a whole world, don't they realise?" Stephen said, when at last he was able to let go of Selena and talk about it. He made tea for them both, his hands still shaking. "Just imagine if someone pumped the Earth's atmosphere full of cyanide – imagine the terror, the agony. That's what those boys did to my beautiful carp. And for no reason." His voice trembled, and he began crying again, this time more quietly.

Even when Selena finally managed to extricate herself and go home – she made an excuse about a non-existent friend of her father's who was coming to dinner – she immediately began to worry about how she could possibly avoid having to see or speak to Stephen Dent in the future. That night she had a nightmare about the fish. She dreamed she came downstairs to pick up the post and found one of the koi carp on the doormat instead, flapping on the coarse brown bristle with its pink gills heaving, and no water to put it in. She woke with her heart racing, still wondering about how long she could put off visiting Stephen without it becoming obvious that she was avoiding him.

As things turned out, that wasn't a problem she had to deal with. When Selena arrived home from school that afternoon she found two police cars and an ambulance parked in the street outside. According to her mother, someone a few doors along had committed suicide.

"He'd been in trouble at work, apparently," Margery said. She didn't elaborate, and Selena never found out if she knew who Stephen was or what his history had been. Selena felt shocked and empty and sad. She kept thinking of something Stephen had said to her the day before, about not wanting to live in a world where people could kill innocent creatures and get away with it. The idea that he had meant it literally had not crossed her mind. Did this mean that Stephen's death was her fault, that if she'd believed him more she might have done something to persuade him out of it? The thoughts troubled her, but she didn't dwell on them for long. Too much had happened that summer already. She wondered what would become of his books. Stephen hadn't mentioned relatives, not even once.

\* \* \*

There was police tape outside Stephen Dent's house for a while, and then a For Sale sign. Selena never discovered who bought the place, and nor did she try to. By the Easter of the following year, the whole Stephen Dent episode had begun to take on the texture of unreality, a strange interlude that had spun itself out of the backwash of the other unpleasant things that had been happening at the time. Three months later Julie went missing, and Stephen became relegated to what Selena soon came to think of as the Before.

She did not think of him again for many years.

## 1

Selena had been in The George with Laurie and Sandra all afternoon, celebrating Laurie's promotion and bitching about some madam muck in Sandra's cordon bleu class and inevitably going over the Johnny saga for the millionth time. She'd thought she might be able to get through a couple of hours without any of them broaching the J-word, but then Laurie asked if Selena had heard from him and so of course that was it: another round of beers, another hour gone. Laurie and Sandra meant well, she knew that, but Selena had reached the stage where talking about Johnny was becoming tedious instead of cathartic. Walking back from the pub, she kept kicking herself for letting the subject get dragged up again. She made a resolution: the next time anyone mentioned Johnny she would say he was out of her life for good and that the subject was closed. By the time she arrived outside her house she'd come to the conclusion that the situation was her own fault anyway. She should either tell her friends how she really felt or stop egging them on.

Laurie and Sandra were as bored with the subject as she was, probably. As she fumbled her key into the lock,

Selena found herself wondering if they ever talked about her behind her back. *Stupid bitch, why can't she get over it? He was a dick anyway.* She smiled to herself because in a sense it was funny, and because for the moment she didn't care much either way. What she wanted was coffee, and Marmite sandwiches, and whatever was the least worst option on TV.

The phone started ringing more or less the second she stepped inside. Her first impulse was not to answer it, because she'd had enough talk for one evening, and no one ever called her on the landline except for telesales. She picked up mainly to stop the ringing, also because what if it was her mother calling, or Vanja, telephoning to ask if she'd open the shop for her the following morning? Vanja made this request so often Selena wondered why she didn't just put Selena down for Monday earlies on a permanent basis. It wasn't as if Selena ever gave her grief over it.

If it wasn't Vanja it would be a call centre. They could piss right off.

"Hello," Selena said. She pressed the receiver against her ear, listening for the familiar hiss that would confirm that the call was being processed through an automated switchboard. Laurie once told her she always slammed the phone down when she heard that sound, she didn't even wait for anyone to speak, but Selena always found she couldn't do that, she could never not feel sorry for the person at the other end. She wondered how often call centre employees got sworn at per day, on average. Laurie had once worked in a call centre. Selena would have thought that might make her more sympathetic, but apparently not.

"Selena?"

That voice. Selena's heart knocked, as if she'd been caught eavesdropping.

The caller wasn't Vanja, Selena knew that at once, but she recognised her all the same, or at least she thought she did – she knew her voice. Someone from way back, she told herself. An echo, rising up through the mists of time like a memory you can't quite grab hold of but that still churns around inside your head like a captive ghost. *Her*.

The beer-fuzz dissipated almost instantly, lifting off in a rush like a flock of starlings, leaving the surface of her mind feeling vulnerable and exposed. Raw and pink, like the tender, newly formed skin you find under a scab.

Who was it? Selena knew full well who it was, only she didn't. The same feeling you got when you ran into someone familiar out of context, and couldn't think for the life of you who they were.

The caller knew her name, though, she'd spoken it aloud. Selena hesitated. She leaned her head against the wall next to the phone. She thought about saying "wrong number" and putting down the receiver. The idea was tempting but ultimately void – whoever this person was would just call back. "Hello," she said again. She hoped the caller might say something else, give her a clue.

"Selena, it's Julie."

Selena's first, split-second reaction was that she didn't know anyone called Julie and so who the hell was this speaking? The second was that this couldn't be happening, because this couldn't be real. Julie was missing. Her absence defined her. The voice coming down the wire must belong to someone else.

A prank call. There had certainly been enough of them, at the time. Selena listened to the faint shhh-shhh-shhh of the open phone line, the more distant background hum of the fridge. There was a pain inside her skull, an entity. She tried not to concentrate on it, not to give it houseroom. She was holding her breath and her lungs hurt. She stared at the perforations in the inverted plastic cup of the telephone receiver, knowing that if she breathed out there would be a rushing, a susurrus. The person at the other end would know she was there.

"Please don't put down the phone," Julie said.

"Julie?" said Selena. She found she was listening to her own voice, trying to memorise the sound of it, as if it were a recording she was hearing and not the real thing.

The police had said that if there were prank calls they should be notified immediately.

Whoever heard of a prank call after twenty years?

"No," Selena said. Like: no, this isn't happening or no, I don't know who the fuck you are but you're not my sister or no, just no. Pick one.

"I know how this must sound," said Julie. Selena laughed, a bright, shallow, tinny sound, like balls of scrunched-up aluminium foil being rattled around in the bottom of a plastic cup. I sound like a laughter track, Selena thought. Someone making noises at something that isn't funny, but trying to get a laugh out anyway because they know it's expected.

*I know how this must sound.* Like imagine that someone died, and you went to their funeral. You opened the cards and answered the letters, said thank you for the flowers. You saw time whipping past your windows like a thick blue fog.

Twenty years later you picked up the phone and suddenly someone's telling you it was all a joke.

Ha ha, very funny. Now piss the fuck off.

"Who is this?" Selena said. Then silence, a blank space so loud Selena could almost feel the hurt in it. She could hear her own teeth chattering, as if she'd just found out about something awful and was about to cry. Things she heard on the news affected her like that, sometimes. Missing children and railway accidents, house fires, the kind of bottomless everyday tragedies she couldn't talk about because if she even opened her mouth to mention them she knew she'd burst into tears.

You're too soft, you are, Sandra had said to her once.

So far as Laurie and Sandra knew, their friend Selena Rouane was an only child.

"It is me," Julie said. Her words sounded faint, like an afterthought, as if having her existence exposed to doubt had shaken her belief in it.

"You don't," Selena said.

"Don't what?"

"Know what it sounds like. You don't know me."

"I meant to call sooner, honestly. I know your number by heart."

"How did you get this number, anyway?" Selena made a point of keeping the landline ex-directory. Because of the call centres, mainly. Fat lot of good.

"Mia Chen gave it to me. I told her I was a friend of yours, from college."

"So you're spying on me now?"

"Calling Mia's not spying. She's in the phone book."

"I haven't seen her in months." Selena remembered the way Mia had looked at Dad's funeral: the gorgeous suit she'd been wearing, her own tongue-tied awkwardness. How do you tell someone you're pleased for them without making it sound as if you resent the hell out of their success?

Dad had always liked Mia. He'd be sad if he knew they'd fallen out of touch.

Selena wondered if Julie knew their father was dead.

"Julie." Trying it out again just to hear the sound of it, the sound of Julie's name in her mouth. Selena tried to remember the last time she'd called her sister by name, spoken it to her instead of about her, and found she couldn't. You never called people by their names, not usually. Not unless you were annoyed with them, or trying to attract their attention on the street.

Was she willing to believe this was Julie, even for a moment?

What if she gave credence to this woman's story, and it turned out to be bullshit?

"Have you spoken to anyone else?"

"No. Selena—"

"What was the name of that glove puppet I had? You know, the racoon."

"You mean Mr Rustbucket?"

Julie spoke the name without hesitation, without missing a beat, the kind of corny scene that crops up in the movies, when the missing spy or twin or whoever has to prove their identity by giving the answer to a question that no one else would know. And who would know about Mr Rustbucket, other than Julie? Selena felt a wave of nostalgia for the stuffed toy, a plush replica of the cartoon racoon in *Deputy Dawg*, hero of the ongoing epic she and Julie had invented called the *Dustman Chronicles*. Mr Rustbucket, who had been around forever and was suddenly gone. What had happened to him, exactly? Selena couldn't recall.

"You remembered," Selena said.

"Of course I remembered. Do you still have him?"

"No. I must have left him behind somewhere." Selena felt close to tears, a huge compacted weight of them, like a concrete block, crushing her chest. "Have you told Mum you're back?"

"No, and I'd rather we didn't, not yet anyway. I'd like us to get to know one another again. Is that OK?"

"What happened, Julie?" Selena saw the question as she heard herself speak it, a flashing road sign on an icy motorway: SLIPPERY SURFACE or DANGEROUS CORNER or DANGER AHEAD. If she could see the question flashing she knew that Julie could, too. They had always been close that way, even when they hadn't been, those years when Julie had shut her out of her life almost completely.

The question wrapped itself about her throat like an icy scarf. The closer the coils the colder she felt.

"Soon," Julie said. "I'll tell you everything. I promise."

"Where are you?" asked Selena. "I mean, where are you now?"

The question felt more possible than *where have you*

*been*? It occurred to her there was a room somewhere with Julie in it, Julie holding a telephone and speaking into it. Were her shoes on or off? Was she seated or was she standing? When this conversation was over would she walk calmly into her kitchen and begin making supper?

It was impossible to think of Julie existing anywhere, except in the newspapers.

"I'm here, in Manchester. Have you got a pen?" She gave a street address on Palatine Road, also an email address and a mobile number. "I'm right by the Christie Hospital. I'm working there – in Outpatients. Do you know where it is?"

"Of course. How long have you been back in Manchester?"

"About eighteen months. Well, six months in this place. I was living in Altrincham before but this is better for work."

Why now, Julie? Selena thought but did not say. Her throat felt constricted, swollen around the unspoken words as if someone had punched her there. She's been here all this time, she thought. All this time, without calling, or writing. I could have walked past her on the street and never noticed. Perhaps I already have.

Why now, Julie?

Did you hate us that much?

"Can we meet?" she said at last. The words seemed to hang and twist in the open air. If you blew on them they'd tremble, she thought, like leaves caught in a spider's web.

"That would be great," Julie said. Selena heard her exhale, her spent breath rushing down the line towards her like a gust of wind. She was afraid I'd refuse to see her, Selena realised. Serves her right. "I hate the telephone. The telephone's awful."

"When?" Selena said.

"Tomorrow evening?" Julie named a place in town, a brasserie near The Dancehouse. It stayed open late, Selena knew, because of the cinema. She and Johnny had eaten there a few times. It was nice. "About six o'clock?" Julie added.

"It might have to be six-thirty. Depends what time I get off work."

"Whoever gets there first can grab a table."

"Fine," Selena said. "Bye, then." She felt like laughing aloud. How ridiculous it was to have to say something, when there were no words that fitted. She kept the phone pressed to her ear, listening for the click that would tell her Julie had disengaged. She didn't want to be the first to hang up, she realised, in case this turned out to be it, the last she'd hear from her, that awful clichéd *brrrrrr* sound and then nothing. She stared at the piece of paper with Julie's address on it, the back of an envelope, something she'd torn off for scrap paper because there was nothing else to hand. What had been in the envelope to start with she couldn't remember. A credit card offer, probably, long since recycled.

Belatedly Selena realised the phone had gone dead.

She sat down on the floor with her back to the skirting board. She cradled her head in her arms, pressing her forehead hard against her knees. Closer to the ground, she felt better immediately. She briefly considered falling asleep, right there in the hallway. It was what her body seemed to want, although she knew she shouldn't give in to it. She needed to eat, to pick herself up, to get through the evening.

At least Vanja didn't call, she thought. She got up off

the floor and went through to the kitchen. She would make sandwiches, cheese and Marmite, the same sandwiches she'd been looking forward to when she came through the door. The world had moved on since then, just a bit, but that didn't mean she had to be cheated out of her sandwiches.

An image came to her of Mrs Dennis, who had worked as a dinner lady at their school for more than twenty years: Mrs Dennis in cartoon form, passing a plate of sandwiches through a hatch marked 'yesterday' to a monitor in a dining hall labelled 'tomorrow'. Selena found the image amusing, though she doubted Mrs Dennis, who'd been strictly no nonsense and eat your veg, would have found much to laugh at.

Mrs Dennis had made Julie cry once, Selena remembered. Julie always called her the Menace after that.

*Antiques Roadshow* was on the TV. A woman with a prominent mole on her right cheek and oversized Elton John spectacles with purple frames was being told the value of a gold broach that had originally been given to her grandmother as a confirmation present. The woman was wearing floral dungarees, and looked forcefully cheerful in a way that suggested her life hadn't always been easy, that her grandmother's broach was something of an exception to the rule. What a charming piece, said the resident expert. I estimate its value at five hundred pounds.

Not in Manchester, thought Selena. You must be having a laugh. Vanja really would have laughed her head off, if she'd been watching, only she wouldn't be. Vanja never watched anything on TV except soap operas and cop shows. Apart from her husband Vasili's illegally imported Dutch porn, that is.

I love the pornos, Vanja once told her, rolling the 'r' vigorously and with enthusiasm, like a small but difficult object being trundled downhill. I find them relaxing. Better than comedy. Mostly, Vanja said, porno *is* comedy. She laughed. Vanja had a way of laughing that made you feel you'd taken part in something illegal.

The woman in the dungarees was smiling and saying thank you. She looks a bit like Mrs Dennis, Selena thought, the Menace with a wilder dress sense and a kinder smile. She watched the programme through to the end. After the closing credits, someone came on to do the weather. Selena muted the sound and closed her eyes. Her headache had diminished but was still vaguely present, a tangle of greyish wadding behind her eyes. The gas fire ticked. Selena got up from the sofa to close the curtains and then sat down again.

She had been thinking that everything had changed, but was that really true? In the world beyond the curtains, Julie had been present already, a physical fact. The only difference between today and yesterday was that yesterday Selena hadn't known that, and today she did.

If the world beyond the curtains had contained Julie all along, the world inside Selena's head had been a lie.

Partly a lie, anyway.

Contaminated by lie-stuff, like rust on metal.

Mr Rustbucket, thought Selena. What happened to you?

She would never have given the raccoon away intentionally. Perhaps Julie had taken him with her when she went. Selena drew her legs up on to the couch and curled on her side. She had no idea she'd been asleep until she woke three hours later, her right arm stiff with pins and needles from where she'd leant her head on it.

The television was still on, still mute. There was a police procedural playing, the one that was set in Cornwall with the posh detective. Vanja preferred the American shows, with guns.

Selena switched off the TV and headed for bed. It was quite early still, but turning her mind to anything else felt out of the question.

## 2

Julie disappeared on a Saturday.

Selena had often thought about how if her sister hadn't gone missing, that day would have been erased from her memory. Or not so much been erased as simply faded, merging into all the other, similar days that offered no particular reason to be remembered. As things were, she could recall it in every detail with a knife-edged clarity. Even that wasn't right though, she realised. It was not the details she remembered so much as the details as she had remembered them later: for the police who first came to the house, for the woman officer who interviewed her later about Allison Gifford, for herself, as she went over each moment of the day in her own mind, searching for something she knew already would not be there. How could it be there, when it hadn't been there the last time or the time before that?

That elusive clue, that *salient detail* the detective sergeant kept referring to that would lead them to Julie.

Salient meant protruding, sticking out. The problem was that the more Selena went over that Saturday the more smooth it seemed, the details flowing along in order like lines from a story she'd recited so often she knew it by heart.

Nothing stuck out, nothing protruded, not even the details that had seemed important at the time.

She thought about how it might be if she could return to that day and live it through again, if she would notice things differently, or notice different things. As it was, what she remembered mostly was feeling pissed off. She knew she couldn't say that to the police though, because the pissed-offness had nothing to do with Julie and was therefore irrelevant. In fact she didn't remember much at all about the Saturday morning, only that she had got up late because it was the summer holidays, that she'd sat around in her dressing gown for a couple of hours, eating Sugar Puffs and watching kids' TV, until her mother had finally snapped and ordered her to get dressed.

"Do you have to slum around like that, Selena? Go and put some clothes on. You're wasting the day."

What Margery meant was that she was inside when she could be outside. But Selena felt her mother was missing the point. She remembered drinking milk straight from the bottle, the smooth warmth of the kitchen tiles beneath her bare feet, the back door hanging open because Dad had gone out to fetch the paper and left it like that. Dad liked the fresh air, even though he never said so, unlike Mum who kept the door closed in spite of always droning on at her to get more exercise.

The morning sunlight: still, dappled and pooling on the living-room carpet. TV shows she was too old for but still adored. The sheer, untrammelled luxury of time in hand.

Selena got dressed, tugging on the same jeans she'd worn

the day before together with a T-shirt from the pile beside the bed, clothes that Margery had laundered and folded but that Selena hadn't found the time or inclination to put away yet. She gave her hair a cursory comb-through then went back downstairs. She had no idea where Julie was at that point – in her room, probably. Julie tended to come downstairs before anyone was up, make herself some toast and coffee and then retreat back upstairs. Selena couldn't remember the last time they'd eaten breakfast together as a family, even in term time. Julie seemed to exist in a world of her own these days. She was sometimes so difficult to be around that Selena felt almost afraid of her. She found it was generally safer to keep out of her way.

Selena went into the kitchen and opened the fridge. She felt bored, but not disastrously bored. She was just thinking about calling Mia and seeing if she wanted to go to the park when Margery came in from the garden. She looked like she was in a mood, but then she usually was.

"Stop poking about in there, Selena, it's almost lunchtime. If you're looking for something to do you can go to the Spar for me and pick up some Nescafé. We need the *Radio Times* as well if they've got any left."

Selena made a grunting noise, a sound pitched midway between assent and complaint. Actually she didn't mind. A walk to the Spar was fine by her, telephoning Mia could easily wait until after lunch. She decided to go the long way – round the back of the allotments and across the recreation ground. By the time she was home again, Mum was setting out the knives and forks. She'd made a big bowl of pasta salad, and there were granary rolls from the bakery. Julie was already seated at the kitchen table. She was reading a book, and didn't even glance up as Selena came in, just swung her legs back and forth inside the struts of her chair. Her hair had fallen forward, forming a kind of tent around her face. Selena watched as her sister speared individual pieces of pasta with the tines of her fork and fed them casually into her mouth, her eyes never leaving her book the whole time.

Mum's expression was like a truckload of concrete but she didn't say a word, Selena guessed because she knew that if she did it would end in a row. It was probably her annoyance at Julie that made Margery go off on one when Selena asked her about the school trip to Alton Towers. Selena hadn't been looking for an argument – it was happening before she realised it, Selena complaining that everyone in her class was going, that she'd been looking forward to the outing all summer, Mum telling her to stop badgering her, she wasn't sure yet if they could afford to pay for it. Selena would just have to wait and see.

"You can take that look off your face, for a start," Margery added. "You definitely won't be going if you don't stop whining, I can tell you that right now."

Selena felt the sting of tears, of resentment, of regret at setting off down a road she'd not intended to take. The day was spoiled now. Not just spoiled, but polluted. When she dared a glance at Julie, hoping for some small gesture of commiseration, she saw her sister staring blankly ahead of her, her face a treacherous mask of studied neutrality. Selena felt like striking her, pummelling her with her fists until she stopped being such a prig.

Selena got up from the table, refusing to look at her

mother, who was clearing plates. Later she would replay Julie's non-look over and over, hoping to find a clue and not finding anything except her usual self-absorption, which was so habitual with Julie by now it had become her new normal. Selena slouched upstairs to her room, wishing she'd phoned Mia before lunch as she'd originally intended, because then she'd have a genuine reason for leaving the house.

If she called Mia now it would look as if she was making a point. She didn't want to give her mother the satisfaction.

Selena stayed in her room for about half an hour, trying and failing to work up the enthusiasm for purging the clutter under her bed. Finally she opened her door, listening to see if Julie had come upstairs or gone out but there was no sign of anyone. She waited a couple more minutes just to be safe then crept downstairs to the living room and switched on the TV. There was a film just starting, *Ring of Bright Water*. At the first advert break, she tiptoed through to the kitchen and grabbed a packet of Hula Hoops from the stash in the larder. She returned to the living room and closed the curtains, firstly to stop the sunlight reflecting off the television screen and secondly because she knew it drove Margery mad to see the curtains pulled shut during the daytime.

She opened the Hula Hoops and sat down on the floor, her back resting against the sofa. She was beginning to feel better. When the film came back on, Selena gave herself over to it entirely, the tight feeling in her chest gradually dispersing as the story took hold.

At some point she heard Julie come downstairs.

"I'm going to meet Catey," she called. The sound of her voice was unexpectedly loud, even with the TV on, and for a moment Selena thought Julie was talking to her. She was about to shout something back when she heard her mother's voice, coming from the front office by the sound of it. Selena hadn't known she was in there. She was too far away for Selena to make out what she was saying, and when Julie answered from further along the hallway the sound of the TV meant she couldn't hear her properly, either.

A moment later she heard the front door open and then slam shut again. Julie going out, she supposed. Selena forgot about the exchange almost as soon as it had happened. It was only in the small hours of the following morning that it occurred to her to wonder why Julie had bothered to inform their mother she was going out. Normally, and especially recently, she would simply have gone. As the minutes ticked by, and then the hours, this small detail of Julie's behaviour began to seem more and more strange, more and more *salient*, although Selena knew this was probably only because it was night, and Julie still wasn't home.

This was what they were all still insisting at that point: Julie wasn't missing, she just hadn't come home yet. When the switch occurred Selena couldn't have said precisely, although she guessed it was probably around the middle of the following day.

Selena wanted to explain about the salient detail and then thought better of it. It didn't seem so salient, when you put it into actual words. Also it sounded mean about Julie. She decided it was probably safer to keep quiet.

* * *

*Ring of Bright Water* was sad, much sadder than she'd expected. Selena hated films where animals died. *Watership Down* had upset her so much she'd had to pretend to have a stomach ache, just to stop Mum asking what was wrong. She pressed her eyes shut against the tears, feeling furious with herself and glad at least that she was alone. She turned off the television and was about to go back upstairs when her mother came out of the office and asked her if she knew where she'd put the form for the Alton Towers trip.

"I've had a look at the bills and they're not so bad this month," Margery said. "We can send the money off this afternoon, if you like."

She didn't hug Selena or anything but that was normal. Of the two of them, Dad was the hugger. But Selena could tell her mother was sorry they had argued – she knew from the way Margery had obviously been waiting for her to come out of the living room so she could talk to her. Selena said thanks and then went to find the form, which she knew was in a pile of exercise books and other garbage up in her bedroom.

"We're having coq au vin for supper," Margery told her when she came back. Another peace offering. Selena put on a pair of flip-flops and wandered along to the recreation ground, half-thinking she might find Mia there, but mainly just wanting to be outside in the open air. There were some lads up on the field, kicking a ball about. She imagined swooping in amongst them, catching the ball in a violent header, swooping out again. There were boys and there were boys, she thought. The louts on the pitch with their half-grown bodies, their flaming cheeks and foul mouths, they seemed like kids to her. As members of the opposite sex they didn't interest her at all, though she found she liked watching them. There was a freedom – a fury almost – in the way they ran and yelled and kicked that she secretly envied.

The lad she fancied was called Ethan Crossley. He ran cross-country instead of playing football and he was in the chess club. Some of the back row boys in Selena's form called him the Freak. He had knobbly knees and a bad blazer. Selena knew that so far as Ethan Crossley was concerned, she didn't exist. Ethan was in love with Maisie Honeywell, who thought he was a div. What losers guys were.

She kicked a stone out on to the path and then angled it back again. The day was still warm, though not as hot as it had been. The summer was passing. She made a pact with herself to start on her room-purge tomorrow morning at the latest.

Julie wasn't home in time for supper. Margery spooned Julie's portion of coq au vin into a bowl, then covered the bowl with foil and put it back in the oven to keep warm. She was annoyed but not dangerously so – she'd had enough of family arguments for one day, Selena could tell. Once the washing-up was over and Julie still hadn't come in, Margery went out to the hall and phoned up the Rowntrees. Catey's mum Ginny answered. She said Catey wasn't there, she'd gone to a barbecue at someone called Linsey's house. Catey's dad was going to collect her later on.

"She said they'll drop Julie back when they fetch Catey," Margery said. "She could have let me know."

"Are you sure she definitely said she'd be home for supper?" said Dad.

"She said she'd be back by six, I told you."

"Well, maybe this barbecue thing didn't crop up till later. You know what they're like."

"That's what I mean. She could have phoned." Margery made a tutting noise, although it was easy to see she wasn't bothered, not really, not now she knew where Julie was. She made coffee for herself and Dad, and an ice cream soda for Selena, and the three of them sat on the sofa and watched *Stars in Their Eyes*. Mum complained about the programme constantly, was always on about how ghastly and commercial it was, though she never missed it if she could help it and that night was the final. Dad was supporting the Whitney Houston lookalike but Margery and Selena much preferred Sandra Cosgrove, who was covering Eddi Reader. The Marti Pellow man won in the end. Selena thought he seemed a bit of a jerk, or maybe it was just that Marti Pellow seemed a bit of a jerk, but it was a good evening anyway, just her and her parents together and nobody hassling her. No one mentioned Julie, though Selena could tell her mother was thinking about her from the small movement she made every time a car went past, craning her neck slightly to look at the curtains, as if the act of looking would make this car the one that would bring Julie home.

None of them were, though. At twenty past ten the phone went. Mum went to answer it, not running exactly but moving quickly with her shoulders thrust forward, as if she was worried that if she didn't hurry the phone might stop ringing before she got there. The caller was Catey Rowntree. She told Mum she was home, and that Julie had never been at the barbecue.

"Do you mean she left early?" Mum nodded, listening to the muffled voice of Catey Rowntree at the other end and twisting the telephone cord between her fingers, something she consistently told Selena not to do because it weakened the wire.

"Thanks, Catey," she said in the end. "You will please call me immediately if you hear from her?" She nodded again, then said goodbye and put down the phone.

"Catey says she hasn't seen Julie all day," Mum said. They were all standing in the hallway by then. Margery normally hated people listening in when she was on the phone, but she hadn't seemed to notice, not this time. "She doesn't remember them having an arrangement to meet, either. Ray, I'm worried."

"Who's that girl she's friendly with at college?" Dad asked. "Lucinda?"

There was a flurry of back-and-forth about what Lucinda's surname was, then Mum remembered she had Lucy's number in her address book anyway, from when Julie went to stay the weekend with her just before Christmas.

"It's a bit late to phone," Mum said. "But I suppose it can't be helped." It was getting on for eleven by then. Under normal circumstances, Margery would never have telephoned anyone after nine o'clock unless there was a prior agreement.

The phone was answered almost immediately and after

a brief misunderstanding a woman with an Indian accent informed Margery that the family were away on holiday.

"They left last weekend," she explained. "I'm Meesha's sister. I thought that was her calling, actually. I'm looking after the house for them while they're away."

"Sorry to bother you," Mum said. She replaced the receiver. Her mouth was set in a hard line.

"Something's happened, I know it," she said. Her eyes, Selena noticed, had a curious glassy hardness to them. They seemed not to be looking at anything.

"I'm sure there'll be an explanation, love," said Dad. "She's lost track of time, that's all. You know what kids are like at her age."

"Not like this, not Julie." She turned to look at him then quickly glanced away. Selena couldn't remember the last time either of them had called the other *love*, not in her presence anyway.

"Are you sure she said she was coming home?"

"Of course she did. I told you before. I'm not stupid."

"Don't let's get upset, Mae. We need to think this through properly, work out what's happened."

"I heard her tell Mum she was going to Catey's," Selena said. "I heard her."

Both Ray and Margery looked at Selena as if they'd forgotten she was there.

At twenty past midnight Margery Rouane called the police. The duty officer said she shouldn't worry too much at this stage – it was still early days – but they were going to send a car round, just in case.

## 3

Selena fell asleep surprisingly quickly. She woke with a jolt in the small hours, convinced she'd been having a nightmare, although what the nightmare had been about she couldn't recall. She lay quietly in the dark, staring at the green fluorescent display on her beside clock radio and wondering if Julie might also be awake, and thinking of her. She drifted into a kind of half-sleep, and the next time she opened her eyes it was already light. It was raining out, but not too hard. Selena washed and dressed, trying not to think about Julie but thinking about her anyway: how she was feeling, what she was doing, what time she started work. What she looked like, even. She imagined Julie showering and having breakfast, the same as she was doing, the two of them mirror images of each other. Did Julie live alone, or was she with someone? Julie had always been a loner, but then so had she, and she had lived with Johnny, for a while.

You got out when things started to get serious though, didn't you? she thought. Easier to shoo him halfway around the world than to let him into your life on a permanent basis.

A psychiatrist might say that losing Julie had made her suspicious of permanence, afraid of embracing it, doubting of its existence, even. Perhaps it was true, but then again perhaps it was shit. A convenient excuse, a get-out-of-jail-free card.

Not that it mattered now, anyway – Johnny was gone, racing monster trucks around a private circuit in Kuala Lumpur. Selena hoped he was happy. Really she should call him, clear the air, but she was nervous of doing so because she was worried it might make things worse.

Selena arrived at the shop just after eight-thirty. She made a point of getting in early on Mondays, even when Vanja didn't ask her to – Vanja's weekends had a habit of overflowing, though Selena suspected this was mostly down to Vasili. Selena guessed that Vanja's husband had affairs – men like him always did. Whether Vanja minded she had no idea.

She unlocked the door and slid back the shutters, disabled the triple alarm – beep-beep-beep-*thrum* – then set it to standby. Selena remembered the time a year or two back – Christmas week it had been, Vasili was away on business in Amsterdam – when she and Vanja had been for a drink together after work and ended up holding a drunken competition to see who could disable and reset the alarm in the fastest time.

It was more complicated than it sounded, because there were three different sets of numbers to remember. Selena won, easily. Vanja kept putting the third set of digits in back to front, and would have had the police turning up if Selena hadn't keyed the correct numbers just in time.

"Oh my fucking God," Vanja had screeched. Her laughter bounced off the surrounding buildings like shards of shrapnel. "You would make a top-level thief, Selena, the absolute best. We mustn't tell Vasili, or he'll want to hire you. Hire you or have your ass killed, whichever." Vanja shrieked with laughter again, grabbing at Selena's arm in an effort to prevent herself from falling over.

Once they were finally inside the shop, Selena had brewed coffee for them both in the back office. Vanja had sobered up more or less immediately, her incoherence perhaps more affectation than inebriation.

Vanja was different when Vasili was away: more serious, more reflective, though she would invariably try and conceal it. Hence the after-work binges, the manufactured bouts of drunken hilarity.

"If you could live your life again, what would you do?" Vanja said, suddenly earnest in that way she had, what Vanja jokingly referred to as her Russian soul. "I'm not talking about fantasies, I mean if you could know yourself from the beginning and plan things differently. You wouldn't be working here with me, I'm sure."

"I don't know," Selena said. "I like working here."

She'd met Vanja completely by chance, when Vanja came into Leggett's to buy cosmetics. Selena had succeeded in sourcing a discontinued line of a particular mascara, and Vanja had reacted with surprise and an unconcealed delight which Selena would come to learn was characteristic of her.

"Most people can't be bothered over the little things, you know? Good business means caring about the details. You should come and work for me. I bet I'd pay you better than these arseholes."

She lowered her voice on the last word but not by much. Selena laughed. The idea that someone might walk in off the street and offer you a job seemed bizarre to her – she didn't even know what nature of business Vanja was involved in.

"I don't think I can," she said, and smiled, hoping she didn't sound too rude. She found herself drawn to Vanja, who wore knee-high Doc Martens with a plain black jersey dress that was obviously couture. She was clearly used to speaking her mind and Selena liked that, too. But she had worked for Leggett's department store since leaving college. She was used to the routine, even if the endless bitching between departments sometimes drove her crazy.

"Take my number anyway," Vanja said. "In case you change your mind." She handed Selena a business card, white with silver lettering: ALMAZ. Selena stashed it away in her purse, relieved that the conversation had taken place out of the earshot of Sandra, who was busy serving a customer at the other end of the counter.

A week after Vanja's visit to Leggett's, Selena found herself taking a detour past Almaz during her lunch hour. It turned out to be one of those high-end jewellery emporiums you expect never to go inside: situated in a grubby side street in the northern quarter, the exterior paintwork was rubbed and chipped in what appeared to be a deliberate contrast with the merchandise in the window. The watches and jewellery on display were all without price labels, and Selena remembered something her Aunt Miriam once said: if you need to ask the price you probably can't afford it.

The idea of handling the gemstones on a daily basis felt oddly alluring, not to mention escaping the escalating war between the post room and fourth floor admin back at Leggett's.

Two days later, Selena telephoned the number on the Almaz business card and told Vanja that if she'd been serious about the job, she would like to know more.

"Oh my God that's amazing," Vanja said. "When can you start?"

"Don't you want to interview me first?" Selena asked.

"Only if you want. I don't care about interview, though. Not when I like someone."

Selena's first sight of Almaz's back office, the piles of trade catalogues and art books and dirty coffee cups, left her with the feeling of having arrived on another planet. She thought of Leggett's – the new staff toilets, the accounts office with its jealously guarded, individually styled work stations. She wondered if Vanja kept her tax records up to date, if she cared even the tiniest damn for such minor inconveniences as the Inland Revenue.

The combined contents of the three double-locked floor safes looked valuable enough to purchase a small European principality. The computer, with its ancient and discoloured big-box monitor, wasn't even switched on.

"You'll soon get the hang of things, I'm sure," Vanja said. She broke off what she was saying as the shop doorbell rang, one of the old-fashioned jangling kind that sounded as if it belonged to a village sweetshop. "Come," Vanja said, steering her out of the office and into the shop proper, a narrow, boutique-like space with polished mahogany counters and a ruby-coloured deep-pile carpet that looked as if it might have been filched from a casino. A woman was standing just inside the doorway in a coppery Aquascutum raincoat with clumps of flickering diamonds in her ears. To Selena, she looked like a minor film star of the silent era. She would not have believed with any certainty that money like this – shipbuilding money, shipping-line money – still existed in Manchester, that such connections still flourished. Most of the money that walked into Leggett's was newer, brasher, swiftly earned and swiftly spent, only to pour forth somewhere else, pasting the pavements and storefronts with that grab-it-now Manchester energy that pummelled you senseless through the course of an evening then dropped you legless into a corner to sleep it off.

The woman in the Aquascutum coat looked as if it had been quite a while since she'd sat slumped in a nightclub lavatory puking her guts.

Vanja approached the woman, her distracted diffidence replaced immediately with a courtesy so professional, so perfectly poised between warmth and respect that Selena found the transformation almost mind-altering. It was as if the woman's intrusion had triggered a biological process, something akin to metamorphosis, or the constantly shifting colour patterns of the chameleon.

Selena watched as Vanja talked the woman through her requirements – a graduation present for her granddaughter – and then began laying out items of jewellery for her inspection. Vanja handled the various pieces – a jade and ruby broach, a gold locket with a diamond escutcheon, a series of gemstone rings – with a casual confidence. She seemed to have an uncanny instinct for noticing when the woman's interest began to wane, moving the redundant item quickly aside, replacing it with something else, something other, something to make the woman forget that she had been, however temporarily, bored.

Only once, when the woman seemed about to decide on an amber and onyx writing set, did Vanja assert her own opinion. Selena noted the expression of pity on her face – for the unknown young woman, perhaps, who had dreamed of a sapphire ring and ended up with an ostentatiously expensive pen set instead.

"I don't think that's quite right for Zoya, do you?" she said. "It's been in stock a while, anyway."

Selena tried to imagine this girl, this Zoya, a shinier if more prosaic version of her grandmother, eyes narrowed and hair upswept, a degree in marketing or economics or world domination poking casually from the outside pocket of her leather documents case.

She would have plenty of pens already. She would want the ring.

"Do you think?" the woman said, the gems on her own fingers trembling with renewed uncertainty. Vanja was showing her another ring, a piece she'd most likely kept back for precisely this moment, a platinum band set with an oval-cut tinted stone that Selena thought might be a topaz but that Vanja identified a moment later as a yellow diamond.

"It is rather unusual," Vanja said, drawing the word slowly from between her lips as if she'd only just thought of it. "Which is nice, don't you think, for a young person? And of course the platinum makes the whole piece lighter and more modern. Less of an antique?"

The merest hint of a question mark, just enough to suggest that the customer, whilst being discerning enough to recognise the value of antiquity, would also be sensitive to the tastes and needs of a somewhat profligate yet nonetheless adored and therefore forgivable younger generation.

"I think I'll take it," said the woman. "Yes, I will." Grudging, then suddenly agreeable, the decision that had been arrived at firmly her own. The remainder of the transaction did not take long, and was carried out with minimal reference to the sum involved, a sum that seemed to Selena incredible, the proverbial king's ransom, enough to buy a car with. A used one, anyway.

Zoya owned a car already, no doubt.

Selena was amazed to find the woman had been in the shop for almost an hour.

"You think you can handle these people?" Vanja said once she was gone. Her expression was teasing yet also serious. Selena realised that if there was to be an interview at all, then this was it.

"You know a lot about diamonds," she said. She felt foolish for stating something so obvious, yet it was the knowledge of Vanja's, carried so lightly and utilised so keenly, keenly as a fencing blade, that had most impressed her.

"I know it because I love it," Vanja said. "And you can

learn – learning is easy, if you have the desire. The main thing is can you handle these people, because some of them can be bitches, but you must love them anyway."

Selena knew about difficult customers – you couldn't work the Leggett's cosmetics counter ten Christmases in a row and not – but in the items of jewellery Vanja had shown to the film-star woman, the opaque duality of Vanja herself, Selena had glimpsed something she did not know, had scarcely guessed at and wanted to learn more of. On her way home she stepped into Waterstones and purchased a basic guide to gems and minerals. Later that same evening she read about the Mohs scale for measuring the hardness of precious stones. She read that the yellow colouring in the diamond Vanja had sold to the Aquascutum woman came from impurities in the diamond's structure, in this case nitrogen.

*Lattice, crystal, allotrope, cut*: new words like incantations, spells. Selena remembered chemistry lessons in school: sweltering afternoons of abject, sleep-inducing boredom alleviated only by the outrageous misdemeanours of Michael Robson, the class clown, who had gained instant notoriety and closet hero status by once, at the end of a particularly gruelling double-period on polymers, setting light to a gas tap.

("The headmaster's office, Michael. *Now*.")

Gemmology: the study of gemstones. She had not known until that day that there even was such a word. Selena could barely remember the two years she'd spent at college – years that were miserable mainly because she could never explain to herself why she'd enrolled on an English course in the first place. Because English was what Julie had been intending to study? Because her other A level results had been so poor she was out of options? Either, or neither, or both. She'd dropped out of the course before she was pushed, come back to Manchester, landed the job at Leggett's in less than a fortnight. She'd felt relieved to the point of tears to have somewhere to be, something to do, money at the end of each month that would pay her rent.

She knew her mother was disappointed in her, mainly by the fact that the subject was never mentioned. Selena didn't care much. For a long time the act of survival – of negotiating the world under her own steam – felt good to her, and unexpected, and achievement enough.

This though – the discovery that chemistry could glisten, that it could make people's eyes flash with pleasure and greed, that it was in the world, that the world was made from it.

It was a long time since learning something had made her feel excited. Not in an abstract way, but in a spine-tingling, visceral way that felt as if it might make an actual difference to her actual life.

Selena gave in her notice at Leggett's the following morning.

Would a life she had chosen have panned out better than the life she had found? Selena sometimes thought about returning to college, enrolling for evening or part-time study, but she had not done so. Was it inertia that held her back from the decision, or fear? Was it possible that twenty years later she was still allowing her ambition to be curtailed by something that had happened to someone else?

Or was that, like her rejection of Johnny, just an excuse?

She sometimes wondered what kind of a person she would have been had Julie never existed in the first place.

"Go on, then, what would you have done?" she had said to Vanja the drunken evening they'd played the alarm game.

Vanja had shrugged then gulped at her coffee, which was still steaming. Selena had no idea how she was able to drink it so hot. "I'd like to be a cop," she said. "And not married to Vasili. Can you imagine?"

She spluttered, then shrieked once more with laughter, then closed her eyes.


Vanja finally turned up for work at around ten-thirty. She seemed preoccupied, quieter than usual.

"I need to make some phone calls, so," she said, then disappeared into the back office. From her behaviour, Selena knew she shouldn't disturb her unless it was absolutely necessary. She busied herself with the window displays until a customer came in to ask about engagement rings. He was dressed casually in black Levi's and a hooded sweatshirt, probably in computers by the look of him. He seemed shy at first, and very young, though whether this was down to him being the only customer in the shop or just the emotions aroused by the purchase Selena couldn't tell.

"What does your fiancée do?" Selena asked. She wanted to put the customer at his ease but she was also interested.

She liked finding out about people. Her secret sales weapon, Vanja laughingly called it. But the fascination was real.

"She writes code." The young man seemed to relax marginally. "She's one of the best coders I know. Her name's Justine."

Selena showed the young man twenty rings at least, knowing almost from the start that she would guide him towards the deeply coloured square-cut emerald set in white gold. The ring was very plain, and would not have been to everyone's taste, but the young man – Stefan Risos – enthusiastically affirmed that Justine would love it.

Selena completed the transaction and Stefan Risos left the store. Shortly afterwards Vanja emerged from the back office. She seemed more energised, more like herself. When she asked Selena if she wanted to take her lunch break, Selena said she'd sooner just pop out and pick up a sandwich.

"I was hoping it would be OK if I left early today," she said. "I've arranged to meet someone."

"Yeah, sure. Anyone special?" Vanja folded her arms across her chest expectantly and grinned. She enjoyed gossip almost as much as she enjoyed alcohol.

"Just a friend," Selena said. "Someone I was at school with. I've not seen her in years."

Vanja looked disappointed. She had liked Johnny, Selena remembered, fancied him a bit, even. Once when Vanja was drunk she'd told Selena she must have been mad to let Johnny go off like that.

"He was a nice guy," she had said. "Kind. You don't often get kind."

Selena suspected the main reason Vanja had ended up with Vasili was because she found it difficult to be alone. She bought a panini from Café Cyprus and walked back through the arcade. Less than four hours to go now, she thought. An image came to her: herself and Julie as flashing green telltales on a radar screen, beeping closer and closer together until they collided. Boom. Like one of those movies from the nineteen-eighties about nuclear war.

Selena tried to imagine what it would be like to live in a world where everything was the same as it was in reality with one exception. There was no electricity, say, or no computers. How different things would be, in ways you wouldn't think of at first, how even the small things would change.

Selena had been living in a world where she believed her sister Julie was dead. Finding out she was alive was like a miracle – like the lights coming back on after a twenty-year power cut.

It changed everything, surely?

You don't know it's her yet, she thought. You don't know anything. She took the last bite of her sandwich, threw the paper wrapper into a waste bin. She thought of Julie the last time she'd seen her: elbows on the kitchen table, hair hanging down like curtains in front of her face.

Had she known she was about to disappear? It didn't seem possible, but then neither did her return.

It was almost always young people who went missing. There was a space, for a time, where they had been, but then after a while the world slid closed and carried on without them.

Because it had to, Selena supposed. The windows of

Almaz sparkled in front of her like a blizzard. She always felt comforted by how old diamonds were, how curious it was really that they should be here: in this storefront, in this city, in this world.

## 4

The last time she'd been to The Dancehouse she'd been with Johnny. They'd seen that Ryan Gosling film, *Only God Forgives*. Kristin Scott Thomas had died in it, violently, her hair spreading out behind her as she slid down a wall. Selena couldn't remember if Ryan Gosling survived until the end of the film or not. They'd crossed the road to the brasserie still talking about the movie, reliving bits of it, as Johnny liked to do. He'd loved the shoot-up scene outside the restaurant, that crazy cop.

Didn't the cop have an axe or something, or was she just making that up?

What Selena remembered most about the film now were its dominant colours – red and gold.

The brasserie was always busy, especially after work. There would be plenty of people around and Selena was glad. People and light and chatter, stuff going on. Exactly the kind of venue you might choose to meet an old school friend. I've not seen her in years, she'd said to Vanja, just to see how it sounded. She'd asked Vanja if she could leave early because she wanted to make sure she could get to the restaurant before Julie arrived. She wanted to try and pick Julie out from the crowd before she had to speak to her.

On her way there, Selena found herself thinking about all the articles she'd read in magazines and the programmes she'd seen on TV about people who'd been adopted going to meet their birth parents for the first time.

I knew it was my mum the moment I set eyes on her, one guy had said. I don't know how – I just knew.

Perhaps that was true for some, but what about the rest, all those long-lost sons and daughters, standing on railway platforms or waiting in brasseries just like this one, thinking, *Oh God I think that's her*, and then it's just someone else's aunt?

A portly, nondescript woman in a mid-length houndstooth coat and a burgundy beret, clothes the woman believed were smart and not too old-fashioned but that were really just the standard-issue outfit for mistaken aunts, or for mothers who always looked ten years older or younger than they really were.

How awful it would be, to make a mistake, to hug the wrong person. *Goodness, how embarrassing, I'm so sorry.* Selena remembered a story Laurie had told about going to visit her brother and his wife in Scarborough, about six months after the birth of their second child. I walked into the kitchen straight from the car, Laurie said, and there was this woman standing there, this fat woman with short hair. I was looking at her and thinking who the hell are you, am I supposed to know you or what? I was just about to ask her where Cindy was – my sister-in-law, I mean – when suddenly I realised it *was* Cindy. She was huge, Laurie kept saying. *Huge*. The last time I saw Cindy she was literally half the size. I honestly didn't recognise her. I hugged her hello just in time, only I couldn't stop thinking how ghastly it would have been if I'd said: *where's Cindy*? Can you even imagine it? I could feel myself blushing redder and redder, like a bleeding traffic light, so I just kept on hugging her, hoping the blush would go down and she wouldn't see.

Oh my God, Sandra said. She was laughing so hard there were tears in her eyes.

I'm not joking though, she was huge, Laurie said again.

Selena was laughing too, she couldn't help it, though mostly it was Laurie who'd set her off, the way she told the story, not the thought of Cindy whom she'd never met and whose fatness wasn't funny, especially since the woman had just had a baby.

Might Julie be huge? Selena couldn't picture it. She could only imagine Julie the way she'd last seen her.

She sipped her cappuccino and gazed out at the street. She felt sick with nerves, though she didn't care to admit it, not even to herself. She watched the people instead, counting sheep, she thought, looking for Julie while pretending not to, pretending simply to be there, like everyone else. Her eye was caught by a woman in a red zip-up coat passing by just outside the window. She was tallish and vaguely dishevelled, her medium-length dark hair shot through with grey. It was certainly possible that Julie's hair would be grey now, although Julie would never wear red. She preferred neutral colours: grey or khaki, charcoal, black – or at least she used to. She had once owned a purple hoodie, there were photographs of her in it. Selena assumed her mother still had them. The woman in the red coat pressed the traffic light button, waited until the lights changed and then crossed the road. Selena kept her in view until she disappeared into the crowd. She glanced at her watch: six-ten. By six-fifteen she began to wonder if anyone was coming, if the whole thing had been a hoax, after all.

Who would do that though, what would be the point?

Perhaps Julie had chickened out.

More likely there was no Julie. Selena finished her coffee and looked down at her phone. Nothing. She could feel herself sweating, the clammy moisture coating her neck and underarms. The warmth of the café, so welcome when she first arrived, was becoming uncomfortable. She made up her mind that if Julie still hadn't turned up by six-thirty she was leaving. She glanced towards the street door, which was made of glass with a brushed steel push-bar. There was someone outside looking in, a woman in a dark coat. Selena saw her raise her hand to her hair, as if she was using the door glass as a mirror, which she probably was.

A second later she came inside.

Our eyes met, Selena thought, across a crowded room. The worst kind of cliché, she understood that, which unfortunately didn't prevent it from being true.

She was thinner in the face than Selena remembered, but her hair was the same mid-brown colour – no grey. She was wearing a shapeless duster-style overcoat that looked almost identical to one she'd owned at the age of fifteen or thereabouts. She wore no spectacles, but the way she looked about herself – her head pushed forward slightly, tortoise-like – made Selena wonder if she was growing short-sighted. Leather satchel, no nail polish. Black biker boots with an elasticated top section. Typical Julie.

A group of art students came in behind her, all wearing dark Levi's. Julie stepped to one side, glancing around her, then began moving in the direction of Selena's table. She didn't hesitate, or even pretend to, as Selena felt sure she would have done herself if their situations had been reversed. As she came closer she even speeded up a little.

"Sorry I'm late. My bus got caught in traffic. I was afraid you might leave."

She pulled out the chair opposite Selena and sat down, slinging her bag on the seat beside her, unbuttoning her coat. Selena watched her in silence, thinking how dramatic it would be in a film, this scene, she could see it exactly: Thora Birch and Keira Knightley playing ordinary, or Pauline Quirke and Lesley Manville if you wanted to get real. *Where the fuck have you been, you selfish bitch. All these years and not a dickie bird. Dad went mad because of you, did you know that? No, I don't suppose you did.*

[*They sit in silence for some moments. JULIE stirs sugar into her coffee. SELENA breaks off the end of her flapjack but does not eat it.*]

JULIE: You're looking well.
SELENA: Are we going to talk about the weather now, as well?
JULIE: I don't know what to say. I'm sorry.

SELENA: You can't honestly expect me to
   believe you?

JULIE: Believe me about what?

SELENA: I don't know. That you were kidnapped,
   or held hostage, or whatever other excuse
   you're about to give me for disappearing off
   the face of the flipping Earth.

JULIE: I wasn't going to say any of that.

SELENA: What, then? Did you really hate us
   that much?

JULIE: Do we have to get into this now? Can't
   we just talk? I've missed you, Selena.

SELENA: What do you expect me to say to you? I
   don't even know if you're really my sister.

JULIE: Who else would I be?

SELENA: Honestly? I have no idea.

"What's wrong?" Julie said. "You look as if you're laughing."

"No," Selena said. "This is all just so strange."

"Weird," Julie said, simultaneously. She smiled, a feeble kind of half-smile, falling away towards the end. It made her look different, older, Selena thought, although she felt certain that this was Julie, because how could it not be? The woman looked like Julie, of course, so far as Selena could tell, but it wasn't just that. This went deeper than sight. It was – a feeling. Growing up alongside someone made you aware of them – their smell, their mannerisms, their whole way of being – in ways you couldn't even name.

Sight alone told you nothing. The last time she'd seen

Julie, she'd been seventeen. The woman in front of her was – what? Thirty-five? Forty? An untidy, rather nondescript woman in a grey wool coat. She could have been anyone. You could put her in a police line-up with ten other similar women and any one of them could have been Julie.

How embarrassing it would be, not recognising your own sister. It wasn't even as if Julie had put on weight, not like fat Cindy.

Should I hug her? Selena wondered. It's what you do, isn't it? It's what they do in the films, anyway.

It felt awkward though, with the table between them. She imagined her coffee cup going flying, smashing to the floor in a violent cacophony of broken china and cappuccino foam. No thanks.

"I'll get us some drinks," she said instead. She went up to the counter and ordered two more cappuccinos. At some point she realised her knees were shaking. "Can we get some food, too?" Selena said to the server. "There are no menus on our table."

"Sorry about that," said the guy. "I'll fetch you a couple over when I bring your coffees."

None of this feels real, Selena thought. As she turned to walk back to the table, she caught sight of herself in the CCTV over the counter, her eyes locked on her eyes, rabbit in the headlights.

She's my sister. She remembered Mr Rustbucket. She has to be.

Already that other world – the world without Julie – seemed a million miles away.

* * *

"How long have you been working at the Christie?" Selena asked.

"About eighteen months," said Julie. "It's just an admin job. It's fine for now, though. What about you?"

Are you working? Selena supposed she meant. Who are you, what have you made of your life?

"I work in a shop, in town," Selena said. "We sell fine jewellery. It's interesting. We get some interesting clients, I mean."

"Oh," Julie said. Her indifference was palpable, although knowing Julie, Selena reckoned her reaction would have been the same if she'd told her she was a top-flight lawyer who drove a Jaguar, like Mia Chen. Selena had forgotten the painful power of Julie's self-absorption, the way it could reduce you to nothing in less than a second.

What had she expected? That Julie would be different now, patient and caring, with a Mother Teresa smile? A memory came back to her, so powerfully it was like being struck in the face with it: herself at thirteen, overflowing with excitement because an essay she'd written about *Blake's 7* was going to be printed in the school magazine. Julie's indifference, so cold and so complete it made her wish she'd never told her about the essay in the first place.

She was just the boring younger sister: irrelevant.

Was that how Julie still saw her?

"You know Dad died?" Selena said. The words were out before she realised she meant to say them. A retaliation, she supposed, for Julie's selfishness, the only thing she could think of on the spur of the moment that might get to her. Her own cruelty surprised her. She watched Julie's face, studying it in detail for the first time since she'd walked into the café. The mention of their father had provoked a reaction, at least. Julie had aged, Selena saw that now, more than she'd realised at first, more than Selena.

Like pressing a button and sending time forward. The things we normally never notice, because they happen so slowly.

"Of course I didn't know," Julie was saying. "How could I?"

"I just thought," Selena said. The awkwardness between them, like some ghastly blind date. The wishing you could wipe the tape and start again.

"I don't know anything," Julie said.

"This is all going wrong, I'm sorry."

"Don't be." Julie suddenly reached across the table and grabbed her hand. "I thought I'd never find you, Selena. I don't mean now, here in Manchester – that was easy – I mean before."

Her fingers, stiff and cold, like winter twigs. The physical contact so unexpected it was almost shocking.

"Can you tell me where you've been? Please?" The words so plain and brown, like clothes moths, Selena thought. The kind you find fluttering in the back of the wardrobe, the kind that eat your life away if you don't get rid of them.

"Not yet. Can you live with that, Selena? I'm not trying to hide anything, I just want us to be ourselves for a while, to get to know each other again. Do you think we could do that? It would make things – I don't know, so much easier."

She made her speech in a rush, as if she'd rehearsed it. She tried a laugh, a small one. It didn't catch.

"Can I ask you how you are, at least? Is there anything I should know about?"

Julie shook her head. "I'm fine in myself, honestly. Things are – complicated. I can't believe I'm here, that this is really you."

You and me both, Selena thought. She squeezed Julie's fingers. Julie squeezed back.

"How did Dad die?" she said quietly.

"He had a heart attack, about eight years ago. But he'd been ill for a while." If Julie could withhold information then so could she. Dad wasn't the point at the moment, anyway. Dad could wait.

"And how's Mum?"

"Mum's fine. She's living in Heald Green now."

"Shall we order the food? I'm starving."

So was Selena, she realised. They both went for the chicken with couscous, and Selena found herself thinking about the coq au vin, the meal their mother had made and that Julie never ate.

It's her own fault if it's ruined, Margery had said.

The scent of mushrooms, dense and woody. Mum must have thrown Julie's portion away at some point, though Selena couldn't remember when that had been.

The food came. Julie seemed immediately more relaxed. She chatted about her job at the hospital, people she'd met there, her rented flat on Palatine Road.

"I was lucky to get it," she said. "The woman who owns it moved in with her boyfriend. She gave me first refusal. The rent's not bad, either."

"What made you come back to Manchester?" Selena said.

"The rain." She forked another piece of chicken into her mouth. "What's your excuse?"

Julie grinned, a real smile this time, and Selena realised something important: for the people she'd been talking about – her work colleagues at the hospital, the woman who owned the flat, the people who knew her in the life she was living now – Julie was ordinary. She had a birthday and hobbies and friends like everyone else. She was the woman who worked at the Christie, in the patients' records office. None of them would have a clue she'd been a missing person, a family tragedy. Not unless she'd told them, which Selena doubted.

Which Julie was the real one? Theirs, or hers?

Perhaps the need to know everything for certain was a selfish need. Selena thought of the people you saw on TV chat shows, distraught husbands and wives who'd gone searching through their partner's pockets and emails and credit card statements and wished they hadn't.

If you don't want to know the answer, then don't ask the question.

So Julie guarded her privacy. Was that so strange? They barely knew each other.

"Would you like to come round?" Julie said. "To the flat, I mean. We could go for a walk, or something."

"I'd like that," Selena said.

"What about Saturday?"

"Saturday's fine."

Outside on the street, they hugged. Selena caught the scent of Julie's hair: slightly bitter, damp from the rain, familiar since forever. Julie felt tense in her arms, almost rigid, and for the first time Selena found herself wondering – truly wondering – what her sister had been through.

## 5

In the November of 1996, Greater Manchester Police arrested a self-employed plumber and electrician named Steven Jimson, initially for a stolen passport, although as the investigating officers soon discovered that was just the beginning. Jimson, who was nicknamed the Barbershop Butcher on account of the logo – BARBERSHOP PLUMBING – on the side of his van, was eventually sentenced to life imprisonment on three counts of murder and five counts of violent sexual assault. Jimson had been running a tin-pot illegal courier operation alongside his plumbing business, ferrying knocked-off stereos and packages of cannabis and – occasionally – exotic reptiles all over Europe. He had also been using his van as a mobile murder venue. Jimson was from Stockport originally, but he had friends in Warrington and was often in the area, which was what led police to develop the theory that Julie might have hitched a ride with him.

For the first two months of 1997, media interest in Julie's case spiked again as speculation mounted and newspapers vied with each other for an advance lead on the story they now saw as inevitable: that missing teenager Julie Rouane had been the Barbershop Butcher's fourth victim.

The story never broke, though. Steven Jimson insisted he'd never spoken to Julie, never so much as laid eyes on her, and there was no evidence to prove otherwise. Julie was still missing and no one was any the wiser as to what had happened to her.

The police made just two arrests in Julie's case: Allison Gifford, and the man named Brendan Conway who was supposed to have been acting suspiciously in the vicinity of Hatchmere Lake on the evening Julie disappeared. The papers christened Conway 'the dog-walker'. Selena remembered the newspaper photographs, the endless TV coverage followed by the media freefall that followed once it was established beyond all reasonable doubt that Brendan Conway was innocent.

At the time, the images of the man in the brown anorak had given her nightmares, though as she grew older she had come to feel disgusted by the media's treatment of Conway, who had learning difficulties, and whose only crime was to be seen walking his dogs in the woods at his usual hour.

The final, definitive sighting of Julie had not been anywhere near the lake, in any case, but in their local Spar shop. Beena Gupta, who worked there, confirmed to police that Julie had come into the store at around three o'clock.

"She bought a Twix bar and a can of 7-Up," she said. "Or Tango. It might have been Tango. Yes, she was by herself. She didn't say anything, she just handed me the money and then left. No, she didn't seem worried, she seemed OK, just normal really. I don't know if I ever saw her before. We get a lot of kids in here. Some of them steal things, occasionally, but she wasn't the type."

From a selection of photographs of teenage girls, Beena Gupta identified Julie immediately and without hesitation.

They had given the police Julie's most recent school photograph, Selena remembered, because it showed Julie's face in close-up, although it didn't resemble her, not really, what school photo ever does? Selena only had to think of her own from the same year, her face horribly shiny and covered in spots – that was how she remembered it, anyway. She'd loathed it so much she kept trying to think of ways she could avoid taking it home, like telling Mum the school lost the negative, or that someone had nicked it – that Scott Maidy git, he'd pinch anything.

She'd gazed at Mia's photo with a kind of rapt envy: the smoothly parted hair with its silver hair slide, the flawless skin.

Julie looked like a war child in hers, angry and staring, not as bad as Selena's spots but not great either. Julie never said anything, but she hated that photo, Selena could tell.

It's not a good likeness, Margery had said to the detective sergeant at one point. She tried to give her another photograph, one of Dad's candid shots, Julie sitting at the kitchen table and looking off to one side. Her mouth was slightly open, and there was a small crease between her eyebrows. Selena couldn't remember when the photo had been taken, exactly. It looked like Julie, though.

This is a lovely photograph but it's not so clear, the policewoman had said. She took it away with her anyway, although so far as Selena could recall it had never been used: not in the papers, not in the news broadcasts, nowhere. It was always Julie's school photo they showed, the surly-looking adolescent with her hair hauled back off her face like she was in borstal. Selena felt a thrill of horror each time she saw it, thinking what if it had been her instead of Julie?

It would have been her picture plastered everywhere, the awful one, the one she'd thought of chucking in a puddle on her way home from school. She'd have gone down in history as a bratty teenager with greasy hair and bad acne.

Hatchmere Lake was what the papers referred to as a local beauty spot, part of the deciduous woodland and protected greenbelt that had once been the private hunting grounds of the Earls of Chester. Dad sometimes used to take them there at weekends when they were kids. They'd built camps in the undergrowth, taken turns with Dad's binoculars, ostensibly to identify birds but actually to spy on people down by the water. They'd once run into two men – fishermen, they'd claimed, although there was no sign of any rods or buckets or other fishing paraphernalia anywhere nearby – who had told them a story about a catfish so enormous it broke a man's leg.

"It's true, honest," said the younger one. He had a shaved head, and marks in the crook of his elbow that looked like needle scars. Then the older one had asked Selena if she wanted to see his dick, so they'd run away.

It was scary, only not really, because they'd known Dad was within yelling distance, easily.

"Did you see it?" Selena had squealed.

"Don't," Julie said. She hugged herself and shuddered, making a *brrr* sound. "They're *aliens*."

On the car ride home, Selena asked Dad if it was true that there were catfish that could break a man's leg and he said yes.

"Wels catfish, they're called. They can grow up to six feet long in some places. You won't find them that big in England, though. The water's too cold." He told them that most of the really big catfish lived in the Mekong Delta, in Vietnam.

Neither of them mentioned the man and his alien dick. At the time Julie went missing, they hadn't been near the lake for at least a year, more like two. Selena knew of several incidents that were supposed to have happened out there, the kind of rumours that get passed around at school, becoming more dramatic and more unpleasant with each retelling. Most of them weren't even true, probably, but Hatchmere still wasn't the kind of place you'd choose to go alone.

But what if Julie hadn't been alone? That was what the police seemed to be hinting at, anyway. They asked Selena dozens of questions, over and over: had Julie been unhappy at school, unhappy at home? Did Julie have best friends, boyfriends, enemies? Had Julie ever stayed away overnight without telling anyone where she was? They seemed particularly keen on knowing what kind of mood Julie had been in when she left the house.

"In your own words," said the detective sergeant – DS Nesbitt, who reminded Selena of Etta Tavernier from *EastEnders*. "Anything you can remember, anything at all. Don't worry if it sounds like a small thing. Small things can be important. Would you say that Julie was sad that day, or was she happy?"

"She was just normal," Selena said. She told DS Nesbitt about being in the living room watching TV when Julie left the house, about hearing Julie call out to Margery that she was going to meet up with Catey Rowntree. Selena liked DS Nesbitt, who sat so still and spoke so calmly, and if Margery hadn't been there in the room with them she would probably also have told her how strange she thought it was that Julie had made such a big deal about telling their mother where she was going.

As things were, she felt awkward about mentioning it. What do you mean, Julie never tells us anything? she imagined Margery saying, once DS Nesbitt and DC Simpson had left the house. You know that's not true, Selena, so why say it?

Selena couldn't see that it mattered much. Everybody already knew that Julie didn't meet up with Catey, that she never intended to. The information was hardly ground-breaking. Best to keep quiet.

The most crucial time in a missing persons case is the first forty-eight hours. That's what the police said, anyway. In Julie's case, the first forty-eight hours brought dozens of reported sightings – hundreds. What made the police focus on the Hatchmere sightings particularly was that three entirely unconnected witnesses – a mother of two young children, a passing motorist, an elderly couple – all phoned in descriptions of Julie that put her in the same place at roughly the same time, wearing clothes that were similar to those she'd actually been wearing when she left the house. Two of the witnesses – the motorist and the elderly couple – even mentioned the red backpack she'd been carrying, a detail that had deliberately been omitted from the police description.

The call for witnesses who had been in the vicinity of Hatchmere village on the afternoon and evening of Julie's disappearance also yielded more than a dozen sightings of the same man: a tall, unkempt-looking individual wearing a brown or grey cagoule, or anorak – this in spite of the high afternoon temperatures, which the Met Office estimated at around twenty-eight degrees – and accompanied by two large dogs. Several of the witnesses correctly identified the dogs as Irish wolfhounds. Most also mentioned the man's manner, which they variously described as odd, suspicious, erratic, evasive and nuts. Loitering with intent, said one. I deliberately speeded up to get away from him, said another.

He scared me, said a third, a young woman named Marie Evans who at twenty-one years old was just three years and eight months older than Julie herself.

There was a massive police search for Brendan Conway – the more scurrilous of the tabloids insisted on referring to it as a manhunt. As it turned out, Conway lived with his aunt in one of the tidy new bungalows close to the centre of Hatchmere village. Conway walked his wolfhounds in the woods every day, he said, sometimes twice a day, if it wasn't too hot. The dogs liked being near water, and there was plenty of open space for them to run.

Brendan Conway wasn't much in the habit of watching

the news. He knew nothing about a missing girl. Nor had he seen the police photofit images of himself: a ghoulish stranger in a hooded raincoat and with a blank expression. He probably wouldn't have recognised them if he had.

When the police took Brendan Conway into custody, his main concern was for his Irish wolfhounds, Billy and Bessie. His aunt couldn't walk them, he said. She'd had a heart attack the year before and didn't get out much.

He was worried the dogs wouldn't understand where he'd gone.

Conway's evident distress over being parted from his canine companions earned him brownie points later with the same journalists who'd been busy casting him as a possible murderer only days before. The dogs ate better than Conway and were in fine condition. In the end, even the nastier and more salacious of the local rags were forced to admit that Conway was innocent, a victim of police harassment, a local hero.

Brendan Conway was allergic to sunlight. He wore the mackintosh to protect his skin, which blistered badly if he didn't cover it. His face was scarred with pockmarks, from childhood acne and from what Conway quaintly referred to as slips of the light.

"I go out once it's dark, mostly," he said. "But it's not fair on the dogs, is it, not all the time? They enjoy the sunshine."

\* \* \*

Mum cleared out Julie's room over the course of a weekend, a fortnight before contracts were exchanged on the Sandy Lane house. Selena offered to help but Mum said no, she'd do it herself, she wanted to.

"If there's anything you want to keep now's the time to say so," she added. Dad had already moved out by then, first to Mirlees House, then to the flat Mum had helped to find for him on Didsbury Road, ten minutes from where Selena was currently renting a bedsit in a large Victorian house not far from Didsbury Park. Selena believed that at least one of the reasons Mum finally decided to move was that Dad still had a key to the Lymm house, and Margery didn't quite have the heart to ask for it back.

Dad was always coming over on the bus while Mum was at work. Often she'd come home and find him sitting at the kitchen table reading the paper, as if the divorce had never happened. He also liked to go and sit in Julie's room. He would look at her books or else sort through her things – the stuff on her desk or in her bedside cabinet, even the clothes in her wardrobe. There was something in the way he did this that made Selena uncomfortable, and she knew it drove her mother up the wall.

"He wouldn't be doing this if she were still here, would he? He wouldn't even be in her room without her permission."

Selena had grown so accustomed to her mother not talking about Julie that on those rare occasions when she did it seemed almost indecent. In contrast with Raymond Rouane's all-consuming obsession, Margery's mourning had been a savage and solitary affair, seldom witnessed and never spoken of.

Margery had found her husband's compulsion to talk, to relive, to hash over impossible to deal with, Selena now realised – more impossible than his breakdown even, his brief but searing encounter with full-blown madness. Madness was a disease, after all, something you could treat with drugs and monitor in hospitals. Grief could never be healed, so best not to mention it. Ray Rouane would handle the objects in Julie's room – a silver photo frame containing a picture of Julie and Selena together at Whitby Abbey, a porcelain horse with gilt shoes that had been a present from his sister Miriam – with the kind of reverence that might be afforded to archaeological relics, souvenirs of a vanished civilization. This was what they were, in a way – relics from the Kingdom of Julie, now submerged so far in the past it was dangerous to visit.

Julie herself had lost interest in these trinkets years before she went missing. They were there in her room by default – bits of junk she'd have cleared away by herself if she'd been bothered. In the first weeks following her sister's disappearance, Selena used to sneak away to Julie's room quite often – not to go through her things like Dad did but simply to be there, to sprawl on the bed, to work her way in under the duvet and imagine how furious Julie would be if she came home suddenly and found Selena in her room, the *inner sanctum*, humming along to Julie's Björk CD like she owned the place.

She imagined Julie's rage as a bonfire, and herself dancing in the embers and laughing with the sheer uncomplicated joy of having her back.

For Mum, it seemed as though clearing Julie's room was her way of finally saying goodbye. For most of the past five years, everything had been about Dad: Dad losing his job, Dad having his breakdown, Dad driving around the countryside like a lunatic. The room-clearing was between Mum and Julie. Selena picked out the photograph of Whitby Abbey, the china horse, a wooden pencil box with a sliding lid that had been on Julie's desk since the dawn of time. She also took a piece of Julie's clothing, a maroon sweatshirt with a large appliquéd owl on the front that she had always lusted after. By some miracle, it still fit. Even if she never wore it, Selena didn't like to think of the sweatshirt ending up in the wardrobe of a stranger.

Once Selena had finished choosing, Margery boxed up Julie's books and the rest of her clothes and took them to Oxfam. Everything else she put into bin bags and drove to the dump.

"Aren't you going to tell Dad?" Selena asked.

"I can't, Selena. Be reasonable. You know what he's like."

Selena did know, and although she felt some misgivings about tricking Dad, because what else could you call it, she had to concede that Mum was right. If Ray had known what they were doing he would have insisted on having every last article packed up and transported to his flat, which was becoming a hoarder's paradise as it was.

Mum saved some stuff back for him, though: the leather suitcase from under Julie's bed and everything that was in it, the two photo albums and her diaries, a stack of her school exercise books and project folders – all the things Dad would have picked out first, if he'd had to choose.

By the time Ray next came round the job was done. Selena never found out how he reacted when he found out, because she wasn't there.

## 6

"Tell me what happened with Dad," Julie said. "Please, Selena. I want to know."

"He was in hospital for a while," Selena said. "You know, the Walsey? It's closed down now."

Julie nodded.

"He seemed OK at first," Selena went on. "He was the one bucking everyone up. Demanding answers, making lists, giving interviews, even though the police said it would be better not to. He reckoned the more information people had, the more likely it was that someone would remember something. Or let something slip, whatever. We had no idea he'd been let go from Croyde's, not for ages, not until Larry Kraefsky came round to see Mum, asked her how Dad was taking it. Dad had been bunking off work for days at a time, apparently. Not telling anyone, just jumping in the car and driving around. There was one time he drove all the way to Guildford and back, just because of some news report. Larry gave him three official warnings but in the end he had to fire him. He couldn't afford to keep him on, I suppose, not like he was."

They were in Julie's flat, part of a three-storey Victorian

terrace less than five minutes' walk from the Christie hospital. Julie's flat was on the ground floor. The two reception rooms had been knocked together to form one large living space. French doors opened on to a chaotically overgrown back garden.

"Alisha offered to have it cleared, but I like it like this and so do the birds," Julie said. "In summer it's like a jungle."

"Don't they mind? The people in the other flats?"

"They don't have access. It's nothing to do with them."

Selena gazed around the living room. Two corduroy-covered sofas, a glass-topped coffee table, TV and DVD player, a retro 1950s sideboard and rug, a large and colourful abstract painting in a stainless steel frame. The effect was striking – if the flat was being featured on one of those interior design shows they'd call it eclectic. Selena found she could not see anything of Julie in the room, but what did she know? "It's nice," she said.

"It's Alisha's stuff mostly. I said she could keep it here. You should have seen the dump I had in Altrincham."

"How long were you there?"

"Not long. About a year. Look, I'm sorry about Dad. I can't believe it, really. It's hard to take in."

"It was years ago." Julie, she wanted to say. Years ago, *Julie*, the way you stressed a person's name sometimes just to get at them. Nearly ten years ago, and where were you? Dad might still be alive if it wasn't for you.

The kind of outburst you dream of giving way to but never do, not unless you're in a soap opera. What purpose would it serve, anyway, what would it change? What could

Julie know of what they had been through as a family, the three of them? How could she explain her father's decline to someone who hadn't been there, who hadn't witnessed Ray's transformation from one kind of person into another kind, the two Rays so different in outlook and temperament that the only way to accept the new Dad was by completely letting go of the Dad he had been?

Margery had not been able to do that, which was why they'd divorced. Not because of some stupid affair, but because it seemed inconceivable, suddenly, that the two of them had ever shared a life together in the first place.

"Dad never stopped hoping," Selena said. Never believed you were dead, was what she meant, only the word didn't seem appropriate, somehow.

*She's dead, don't you realise?* Mum screaming at Dad, screaming that Julie had probably been dead even before they realised she was missing. Soon after they found out Dad had been fired, that was. The only time Mum had lost her temper.

Selena hadn't thought about that scene in years.

"I'm sorry," Julie repeated. She sat with hunched shoulders, staring down into her coffee cup, and all Selena could think was that she couldn't be sorry, not really, or she would have come back sooner. Not for me. But for Dad. *Dad.*

What would he have done with this moment?

Perhaps it was better that he had died before.

Before he could be disappointed?

"I don't know if I can deal with this," Selena said. "I need to know what happened. I feel as if you don't trust me."

I feel like I'm going crazy, she almost said, but didn't,

because she wasn't sure if it was even true. Mainly she felt pissed off – pissed off, because here she was again, after everything, still tiptoeing around Julie's feelings, afraid of losing her. She couldn't remember ever having *demanded* anything of Julie – such demands had become impossible, forbidden. There had been the years of their togetherness, and then the rift – the great casting out, as if their closeness had been nothing, had never existed.

She was damned if she meant to go through that a second time.

"If I tell you now you won't believe me," Julie said, so quietly that Selena almost didn't hear her.

"What do you mean?" Selena said. Her own voice sounded harsh to her, harsher than she would have expected or even imagined. "Why shouldn't I believe you? You're here, aren't you? You're here because you want to tell me – you wouldn't have come back at all otherwise."

Selena put down her coffee cup. Her palms were sweating, she supposed with anger. She closed her eyes, imagining her anger opening above her like a parachute, like a great red flower, like the trumpet attached to a gramophone only much, much bigger.

Like a foghorn, blaring.

When she opened her eyes again she saw Julie was crying. The tears oozed slowly from beneath her eyelids, like globules of glass.

"I'm sorry," Selena said, only she didn't feel sorry, not yet, not exactly. Or if she did then there was something mixed in with the sorrow: something red. "This is all so new still."

"For me, too." Julie rubbed at her eyes with the back of her hand. "Do you remember before I met Lucy? You and I were so close then." She sniffed, pulled a tissue from her jeans pocket, blew her nose. Lucy, whose aunt had answered the telephone the night of Julie's disappearance. What Selena remembered most about Lucy Milner was her hair, which reached to her waist and which Lucy always wore in a plait. The police had questioned Lucy, as they had questioned all Julie's friends, although Lucy hadn't even been in the country at the time. Lucy's mother worked as a doctor in Calcutta, or somewhere. Selena wondered what had happened to Lucy, where she was living. Why Julie had brought her up now, she had no idea.

"Shall we go for a walk?" Selena said, changing the subject. "I think it's stopped raining."

"That would be perfect. We can go to the park. It's not far." Julie balled the tissue and stuffed it back in her pocket. "Thanks, Selena."

The park was wintry and mostly empty, the concrete pathways strewn with fallen leaves. They walked slowly along, side by side, as if they came here often, Selena thought, as if they were used to walking there together, as if walking there together was something they enjoyed. She wondered how they might appear to outsiders, if they looked like sisters.

"I wish I'd known," Julie said. "About Dad, I mean. I know it sounds stupid but I think I expected everything to still be the same."

"It's not your fault," Selena said. "Things would have

changed anyway. They always do." A statement that was both true and not true at the same time. Julie had split the world in two when she went missing, a divide so stark you could almost see it, if you thought about it, like a fork in the road.

They walked on for a while in silence. Selena wondered how she would feel if Julie were to disappear from her life again, as suddenly as she'd returned. She felt surprised at how painful it was, the idea. Something about the empty park, the rain, the sense that you could live your life and die and still know nothing about anything.

What if knowing only made things worse? Perhaps it was better to remain in the dark about what had happened. There was an argument for not pursing it, for ignoring the fork in the road, and moving on.

Selena had read about a crime that happened in America, a case in which a young woman named Sharon Wade was kidnapped by a lumberjack and carpenter, Caleb Hatcher. The abduction was carried out with the collusion of Hatcher's wife, Mary.

The kidnap occurred in a small town in California called Mile Ford, an old cowboy settlement that had worn itself away almost to nothing, a gas station and a general store and a strip mall, a railway crossing on the way to elsewhere. Sharon Wade was used to hitchhiking. She thought she knew when a lift was safe and when it might not be. She felt fine about getting into Hatcher's pickup because she could see Mary already inside, sitting in the front seat beside Hatcher with her nine-month-old baby Alicia in her lap.

Sharon Wade was kept in captivity for seven years.

There was a documentary about the case on the Internet. The programme featured interviews with members of Sharon's family and with Sharon herself. Sharon sat very still with her hands in her lap, while an interviewer asked her questions about what had happened to her. Selena was struck most of all by Sharon's calmness. You could never have guessed from looking at her the disastrous and horrific turn her life had taken. She was softly spoken, a quiet woman. She answered each question politely and in some detail. She still seemed wary though, as if she was fully expecting the interviewer not to believe her.

The documentary was typical of its kind: sensationalist and subtly manipulative, a slick montage of photographs and witness statements and coercive music. Selena felt uncomfortable watching it. She found she was especially uncomfortable with the way Sharon Wade was being questioned. Not with the questions themselves, but with the fact that Wade had been questioned at all. They should leave her alone, she thought. She doesn't need this. Sharon Wade was the kind of woman – pleasant-seeming, unobtrusive, tastefully dressed – you might pass by in the local supermarket without a second glance. The language she used in answering the questions was simple and factual, the same kind of language Selena imagined she would have been taught to use on the witness stand. Yet the longer Selena listened to her the more she gained a sense of Sharon as a person apart, a woman so changed by her experience that even if she lived to be a hundred and twenty she would never see the world or be able to live in it the way her friends did, or her neighbours, or her family.

There would always be that gap. As Sharon attempted to explain the ingenious system of mind control Hatcher had used to keep her enslaved – how even on the one occasion she had been allowed a family visit, she had felt utterly bound to him – Selena gained the impression that Sharon Wade no longer cared if people believed her or not. They could believe her or think she was lying, that was their choice. It wasn't her job to prove her story either way. Sharon's energies were directed elsewhere, largely towards helping other women who had found themselves in similar situations.

Selena felt sure that Sharon felt bound to these women in ways that could never adequately be explained. Not to those on the outside, anyway.

Sharon didn't blame anyone for what she had been through, not even Hatcher. Hatcher was *over*, serving a hundred-year prison sentence for kidnap and rape. Simply reporting that fact would be revenge enough. All Sharon wanted now, Selena imagined, was to breathe clean air, to be able to walk along the street without being pointed at, to not have to give people reasons for her existence.

Documentaries really were the new freak shows, Selena thought. Freaks could still be paraded in public, so long as you could get them to sign a contract beforehand.

Sharon Wade had been made to sign a contract, authorising her enslavement to Caleb Hatcher. Every day for seven years, people had driven past Hatcher's trailer on the outskirts of Mile Ford, not having a clue about what was going on inside. Selena found it difficult even to think about. What made it even harder was knowing that Julie might have been through something similar, with Steven Jimson maybe, or someone like him. Almost in spite of herself, Selena began to read up on other cases, women and girls and occasionally young men who had been captured like butterflies, then kept in basements or specially designed strongboxes or abandoned buildings. One particular girl – Selena remembered hearing about her escape on the news – had been imprisoned for more than a decade.

For the most part, the men who perpetrated these crimes carried on as normal: working at their jobs, having drinks with friends, going on holiday. No one had anything special to say about them. It was as if anyone might be capable of such things, anyone at all.

Selena found herself returning again and again to the single black-and-white photograph of Mary Hatcher, who had made a bargain with her husband Caleb: stop torturing me and I'll keep your secret. Mary's eyes seemed both cunning and terrified. They made Selena think of the dog Johnny had adopted, a yellowish, dingo-like creature that had been beaten so badly by its former owner that it was afraid even to accept food. In the beginning it would snap at Johnny's hand the instant after the meat was in its mouth. The rescue centre warned Johnny before he took the dog home that it might never be one-hundred percent trustworthy. Johnny said he was OK with that, he didn't have kids, after all, but he did have patience.

The first time the dog licked his hand after taking its food, Johnny had cried.

In the end it was Mary Hatcher who went to the police. Mary was granted immunity from prosecution if she agreed to testify against Caleb. Selena did not like to think of the nightmares she must still have.

The terrible thing was that in some ways, Sharon Wade had more in common with Mary Hatcher than she did with her own sister, Charly.

The women who returned from the dead were offered counselling. Some of them spent extended periods in residential care, where specially trained medical staff taught them how to readjust to the world outside. It wasn't just the media that were a problem, but the things society at large decreed to be ordinary: paying bills, looking for work, spending the night alone in your apartment with all the lights off. What struck Selena most forcibly was how few of the women felt able to return home to their families. In some cases, they refused even to meet with them.

Maybe it was better to think of Julie-now as a different person. Someone who'd come into her life only recently, and whose relationship to Julie-then was largely irrelevant. Selena had memories she shared with Julie-then, that was true, but it would be a mistake to see those memories as the key to understanding Julie-now.

Could she say that Julie-now was really her sister, even?

The questions circled in her head, never finding solace. Julie must ask similar questions of herself, all the time, Selena thought. Perhaps there were no right answers.

* * *

Selena felt distracted at work, which was unlike her. Normally she found being in the shop – the familiarity of it, the sameness – a powerful antidote to outside stress. Like when she'd been trying to make up her mind about Johnny, for example. In the weeks following Julie's return she felt increasingly distanced, increasingly *compromised*. She even found herself getting impatient with customers – something that had rarely happened to her before.

There were gaps in her life, she realised. She hated terms like survivor guilt because they seemed too convenient, too fashionable almost – and yet she could see she'd been living in Julie's shadow, that was obvious, or the shadow of her disappearance, whatever.

She'd never blamed herself for Julie's fate, exactly – but wasn't it true, at least in part, that she'd denied herself the right to the life she might have lived otherwise because of it?

College had seemed pointless – or rather she hadn't seemed good enough.

The idea of selecting a future, rather than simply accepting the future that was offered, seemed – what? Selfish, inconsiderate, immoral even.

She'd felt she was lucky to have a future of any kind.

Even Johnny – had she refused to go with him to Kuala Lumpur because on some level she believed she had no right to be with a person she loved because Julie would always, however you looked at it, be alone?

The questions coursed through her mind, swiping at

its confines, like flies in a jar. She forgot things, overran her lunch break. She hoped that Vanja would not notice, but of course she did, because Vanja noticed everything. She seemed convinced that Selena's spell of absent-mindedness had to do with Johnny, or rather the lack of Johnny, and for once Selena was content to let her think what she liked. At least it stopped her asking difficult questions.

One evening, about a month after Julie's return, Vanja announced she was kidnapping Selena for a girls' night out.

"What about Vasili?" Selena said. She knew he didn't like it if Vanja came home late.

"He's in Berlin," Vanja said. "Stuff him, anyway."

Selena sensed there was more tension even than usual between Vasili and Vanja. She had no idea what was going on, and preferred to keep it that way. She knew Vanja wouldn't tell her even if she asked – she would either make something up, or shrug off her concern by saying Vasili was an arsehole, which Selena knew already. Vanja had always made it clear that Vasili was her problem, that the best way Selena could help her was by not asking questions. Selena had always been happy to keep her side of the bargain, though she sometimes wondered if this was cowardly of her, an unspoken and selfish desire not to be involved.

What if Vanja was in actual danger? Selena remembered something Sharon Wade's sister Charly had said in the TV interview about Sharon's home visit, about knowing her sister was in trouble but being afraid to do or say anything, in case her interference made the situation worse.

Wasn't it equally likely that Charly had kept quiet

because she didn't want to be involved, either? Selena had to admit it was at least a possibility.

Later, in Podolsky's – a wine bar so retro it was like stepping through a portal into the 1950s – Vanja handed Selena a small leather casket, wrapped in red tissue paper. Inside the casket was a bracelet, one of the Rina Marks line that Selena particularly admired. Rina Marks worked with found metals – natural ores, hand-polished stones. Each of her pieces was unique, off-kilter in a way that Selena found most attractive. "They are rash, but they work," Vanja had said, when she first introduced the line. Selena had once heard Vasili refer to Rina Marks's jewellery as an ugly mess, which only made her covet it all the more.

"I thought you needed cheering up," Vanja said. "You see that metal there?" She pointed to one of three metal ingots, which depended, like silver teardrops, from the bracelet's main chain. "That's meteorite silver, a unique allotrope. No silver on Earth is like it. I should tell you that it's very, very slightly radioactive."

"Where would you get meteorite silver?" Selena said. She found the idea entrancing, though improbable. She hoped it was true.

"My friend Nadine. Nadine Akoujan, she's a xenometallurgist. She lives in London. Sometimes, you know, people offer her things for sale, and then she offers them to me and I offer them to Rina. Good business all round."

"A xenometallurgist?"

Vanja nodded. "She has a specialist knowledge of minerals and metals that are not from Earth. You would like Nadine, you should meet her sometime. She has a little daughter." She paused. "She has always been a good friend to me. She knows what it is like, to live in exile. Sometimes, you know, I think this is what makes her so interested in the space metals. The thought that this silver, too, is in exile from its home." She tapped the silver teardrop, making it swing. "Don't you think that's sad?"

Selena snapped the casket closed, embarrassed. The bracelet's value was equal to three full months of her salary or thereabouts.

"I can't accept this," she said.

"You have to," Vanja replied. "I wrote it off against tax. A charity donation. If you don't take it that will mean I've made a false declaration, which could mean deep scheisse. Deep, *deep* scheisse with the tax apparatchiki. Do you want to land me in jail?"

"Vanja," Selena said. "Thank you." She felt close to tears, not just because of the gift, but because of the ways in which Julie's return had made her feel more alone even than she had before. She watched Vanja as she went to the bar: the way she walked – something between assured and casually contemptuous – always filled her with delight and a mild stripe of envy. She knew Vanja had suffered trauma – the exact nature of which she did not like to guess at – and yet here she was. *Here I am, people, so fuck you hard*. Her walk insisted upon it.

When Vanja came back with the drinks, Selena told her it wasn't a friend she'd been meeting from work the other week, but her sister.

"Sister?" Vanja said. Her eyes opened wide in comic-book surprise. "I never knew you had a sister, why didn't you tell me?"

"She's been away," Selena said. "I haven't seen her in years."

"Fuck," Vanja said. She swirled the ice in her Stolichnaya, making it clink. "If my sister bitched off like that I'd want to kill her, not go for a drink with her."

"Is your sister still in Russia, then?"

"I don't have a sister. But if I did."

"She didn't go off, exactly. She's been ill."

"Oh," Vanja said. She was thinking loony bin, Selena could tell, the words so clear in her mind they might as well have been printed on her forehead. No, my dad was the mad one, Selena thought. She felt like laughing, though it wasn't funny, how could it be. It was the relief, she supposed, the relief of telling someone at least a part of the truth.

Admitting to someone out loud that Julie existed.

"She's much better now," she said. "I had a postcard from Johnny the other day," she added, as a kind of reward. Vanja's attention was captured immediately, as Selena had known it would be.

"Yeah? What did it say?"

Selena closed her eyes, trying to imagine the illusory postcard: the blue glare of its skies, like they'd been spray-painted, its glittering high-rises, the sugary-white, perfect contours of its spotless beaches.

What might Johnny say? That he was fine, that he was missing her?

"He has a new sponsor," she said. "He seems excited."

"Bastard," Vanja said. "You should send the fucking thing back, pretend you've moved."

## 7

Their father's death had been sudden, but no one could pretend it was exactly a surprise, either. Raymond Rouane died of a heart attack, but everyone knew this had simply been the defining moment, something official you could put on a death certificate. What Dad died of was burnout: ten years labouring under the obsession that had defined his grief, that had usurped grief to become an end in itself, both the product of his nervous collapse and the cause of it.

Julie's disappearance had revealed their father as a different person. The Dad of the Before had been faintly boring, so predictable and so dependable it was more or less impossible not to take him for granted. A straight-home-from-work dad whose past had become obliterated by his daddish present and could not now be excavated. He brought no friends with him into his marriage. The only clue to what he had been before he became their father resided in a single black-and-white snapshot, a twenty-year-old Ray Rouane with his hair slicked back and sitting astride a motorcycle.

To his daughters, this image had been equally an object of wonder and of secret ridicule.

As a child, Selena always felt closer to Ray than to

Margery, the kind of closeness that remained unspoken because it was so obvious.

Margery was spiky and closed and inclined to moods – more like Julie, Selena realised now, than either of them would have cared to admit. Some years after the divorce, Margery confided in Selena that the main reason she'd had to leave Ray, finally, was that he was no longer the man she'd married. Her admission made Selena feel sad, not because of the divorce – she knew by then that for her mother at least, any other option had become untenable – but because of her increasing realisation that her father had probably been trapped in the wrong life all along.

After Julie went missing, Ray became increasingly solitary, reticent in a way that was quite unlike his old reticence, prone to flights of the imagination that somehow reminded Selena of the man on the motorbike, the boy in the photograph, the teenage tearaway who had somehow morphed into her father.

Selena remembered the day he died, her mother telephoning her at Leggett's, something she would never do unless it was an emergency.

"It's Ray," she said, as soon as Selena came on the line. She never called Dad Dad any more, though occasionally she would refer to him as *your father*. "He's had a heart attack. I'm sorry, Selena. If you want to see him you'd better come now."

Neither of them used the word dead, Selena remembered, though it hung unspoken in the air between them, suspended in the telephone wires. Margery asked if Selena would be all right getting a taxi, and Selena said yes.

They were keeping Dad in a side room. One of the nurses, or it might have been a ward assistant, asked Selena if she would like a cup of tea. Selena said no, she wanted to see her father. When Selena asked her mother why Dad was on a trolley and not lying in a proper bed, Mum said it was because he hadn't actually died in the hospital.

"He was dead when they brought him in," she said. "There was nothing they could do for him."

DOA. Dead on Arrival – that's what they call it, what they write in the notes. Dad's eyes were closed, and there was stubble on his cheeks. Selena thought of those stories you hear, about how a person's hair and fingernails keep on growing after their death. She wondered if they were true or just urban myths. Dad's arms lay still by his sides, and Selena noticed he wasn't wearing his watch, a detail she found strange, because he never took it off usually.

The top button of his shirt was missing. Perhaps it had sprung free when they tried to resuscitate him.

She could hear a loud humming sound. She couldn't work out where it was coming from, then realised it was the air conditioning. They must have turned it up high, she thought, to keep the room fresh.

It came to her that this was the last time she would see her father's face, ever.

"Can I touch his hand?" she said to Mum, then touched it anyway. Ray didn't feel cold, or warm, or anything, really. Selena thought of those scenes you always see in TV hospital dramas – *Casualty* and *ER* and *Holby City* – the relatives standing around, holding hands and weeping over the body.

She realised with a kind of amazed relief that there was no point in such scenes, that they were completely wrong, because the person on the trolley was already gone, so gone it was impossible to get your head around. You might as well be crying over a life-size plastic model of your father, for all the sense it made. Or one of the styrofoam cups the nurses brought you coffee in.

Raymond Rouane died in woodland close to Hatchmere Lake. His body was discovered, ironically, by a man out walking his dog. It was late October. The forest pathways were less frequented during the colder months, especially during the week. The pathologist's report said that Dad had probably been lying there for several hours. There were no signs of what the police liked to call foul play, it was just a heart attack. It had been raining, and for Selena this was the most upsetting detail of all: the thought of her father lying there dead while the rain fell on him, the moisture seeping through his clothes and no one there to even lay a blanket over him.

She and Mum cleared out Dad's flat together. Margery decided the only sensible solution was to hire a skip.

"There's so much rubbish here," she said, which was probably Mum's way of apologising for suggesting they chuck the bulk of Dad's possessions straight into landfill. Selena couldn't think of a reason to argue with her – not a good one, anyway. Looking at Dad's stuff brought it home to her, how *inanimate* it all was, how useless, how it needed Dad's presence to make sense of it. How the things you own become trash from the moment you die.

In Dad's case this was doubly true. All the furniture in the flat belonged to the landlord, and Ray's actual possessions – clothes, TV, kitchen equipment, the few bits and bobs he still had from his sister Miriam – could have been fitted into the corner of one room, and yet the space was full nonetheless, stuffed to bursting with the books, magazines, newspaper clippings and computer printouts he had accumulated during his ten-year search for Julie and the truth of what had happened to her. The printouts and clippings alone filled three large filing cabinets.

An ocean of information, and only a fraction of it directly related to Julie, or to her disappearance.

Dad had books on real-life missing persons cases, alien abduction and UFOs, unsolved murders, true lives of the serial killers, astrology, spiritualism, Aleister Crowley and the Golden Dawn, animal spirit guides, Madame Blavatsky, ley lines and haunted houses, biographies of famous detectives, forensic science and toxicology, criminal psychology, the underground subcultures of Manchester and Glasgow, genealogy and something called false identity syndrome. Selena couldn't help noticing that the books Dad acquired became more and more obscure as time went on, and that there were always more of them than there had been on her previous visit.

From time to time, Ray Rouane had become involved with various fringe societies – UFO clubs and spiritualists, mainly – but these liaisons never lasted for very long. Dad always fell out with someone, sooner or later, and generally made his presence unwelcome.

Selena had once heard one of Ray's drinking buddies from The George call her father a cussed old bastard, which she supposed he was, or at least had become. The Ray Rouane from the Before had usually been the last person in the room to express a contrary opinion.

During his final years, Ray and Selena had become close again. Selena ate lunch with him in The George most Sundays, and they had taken to sharing an Indian takeaway at least one night of the week, usually in front of one of the cop shows Ray liked. At such times it was possible to believe he was normal, that he was Dad again.

Selena had always been careful never to involve herself in his fantasies, his unshakeable belief that Julie was alive somewhere, that there was a definite truth to discover. That did not stop her envying him the strength of his faith, the fact that he had something he believed in, full stop.

She could never have explained it to Margery and nor did she try, but Selena always secretly preferred the new Ray to the old.

They ended up throwing most of Dad's stuff on the skip. Unlike Julie's, Dad's clothes weren't good enough to donate to Oxfam. Selena rescued Miriam's china dog, the partner to the horse with the golden shoes that had once been Julie's. At the last minute she decided to keep the two books on false identity syndrome as well as another that claimed to be a comprehensive study of alien abduction testimonies. She filled a large cardboard box with assorted correspondence and press clippings, as well as Julie's old diaries and photo albums. Margery raised her eyebrows but said nothing. Once the skip had been hauled away they cleaned the inside of the fridge and the oven and hoovered. Mum said she'd drop the keys off with the landlord on her way home.

The flat was let again in less than a month – the landlord had a waiting list, probably. Selena wasn't entirely sure why she'd saved the books and letters, only that it seemed important – for Dad's sake – to keep something. She shoved the box as far back in the understairs cupboard as she could, then mostly forgot about it. The idea of going through its contents appalled her, as if in doing so she might stumble upon more layers of Dad's madness, deeper layers she hadn't known existed.

Perhaps it's all rotted away in there, Selena thought. Crumbled into dust. Her mind filled with images of scuttling silverfish, the desiccated carcases of house spiders. She dragged everything out of the understairs cupboard – the vacuum cleaner, an ancient amp she was storing for Johnny, other junk she didn't even want to know about – and uncovered the box, fuzzy with dust and cobwebs, BRILLO stamped on its side in capital letters approximately the same shade of purple as the soapy, foamy stuff that came out of Brillo pads themselves.

Did Brillo pads even exist still? They were probably illegal now, banned on grounds of health and safety by EU officials. *Alien artefacts.* Selena grinned to herself, knowing how much Julie-then would have loved a box like this. She remembered how she'd gone on and on about that time capsule thing they'd made on *Blue Peter*, insisting that she and Selena make one too, using one of those giant family-size ice cream tubs as a container. Can I put in my maths homework? Selena had pleaded. Stop it, Julie had said. This is serious.

They never made the capsule in the end. Selena couldn't recall why not – Julie had most likely run out of enthusiasm. Only here was Julie's own time capsule, untouched for nearly a decade, a small section of the past, undoctored by the passage of passing years. Selena reached forward, inserting her upper body into the cupboard, tugging the box forward on the gritty floor and into the light.

Seeing it again made her think of Dad suddenly, the day they'd cleaned out his flat, and she felt like crying.

*The Refuge*
*Warner Road*
*Sittingbourne*
*Kent*

*Dear Mr and Mrs Rowan,*

*You won't know me, and I thank you for taking even the time to read this letter. My whole existence has been a lesson in learning to accept the hurt and injustice that comes with the affliction of being routinely disbelieved, of having my words* twisted against me, of being pursued, both verbally and physically, as a servant of Satan. As one privileged with the guardianship of a specific gift, I have, I hope, learned to accept such misinterpretations and misrepresentations as a part of being chosen, as the Christian martyrs have been forced to endure before me. It is in this spirit of acceptance and open-heartedness that I write to you now, offering my services and guidance as a child of spirit parents, who through their patience and benign watchfulness have initiated me into the domain of the unseen.

I have seen your daughter Julia. I have seen her crying out for you in the mist, holding out her hands for succour, her aching feet seeking the right path home to you, and failing. I have spoken with Julia and I know she is sincerely sorry for the missteps that have led her away from our world and into the meantime. I feel certain that if I can only win your trust, as her Earth-parents and good guardians for the duration of her Earthly childhood, we can, by working and seeking together, lead her back to our domain, and to the light.

You will find my telephone number here below. If you cannot as yet find the security in your hearts to speak to me in person, please feel confident in writing to me at the above address, and together we will find the right way to proceed.

With blessings and sincere hopes for your wellbeing,
Sister Maria, of the comradeship of Girda,
dame goddess of death's armies.

\* \* \*

*3 Clelland Avenue*
*Bondi*
*NSW*

*To my former mother and father,*

*This is to let you know that I am well, and alive, and in full possession of my mental faculties. I am writing to inform you that I shall not be returning to what you call home, the place I have come to think of as a prison, and that this is the last time you will hear from me. I no longer think of myself as your daughter. I am living contentedly here in Australia, as far away as I could travel from my past unhappiness, among people who know me properly. You don't need to worry – I have not informed anyone of the crimes you committed against me, and do not intend to do so. I have no wish to bring the old unpleasantness and bitter memories into my new life, and in time I hope to forget they ever happened.*

*I wish you well, insofar as I am able to do so, given the circumstances, and insofar as people like yourselves are able to understand the term. I hope that in time you will be able to see the reasons for your suffering, and make new lives for yourselves without me to hinder you.*

*Yours sincerely,*
*Julie Matherson (Mrs)*

\* \* \*

*You don't need to know my name, though you can call me
Saviour if you are of the kind that needs a name to know
a person. Your daughter was not a virgin before she died.
Neither was she a virgin before she came into my comfort,
which makes her a fruit rotten on the vine, and best disposed
of, lest more of the common herd be thus contaminated. One
bad apple, or so they say, though when the world is riddled
with rotten apples, plentiful as maggots seething in a barrel,
the situation is pointless anyway, and there is no solution,
save the stamping out of individual vermin for the momentary
pleasure of seeing them, trampled and squirming, die
underfoot. I plugged her mouth with rags and then I skewered
her, first with my rod, then with the poker, hot from the fire,
for does it not say in the Bible that fire is refining? For he is
like a refiner's fire and he shall purify the sons of Levi, shame
though they be Jews, and your daughter Julie-Ann, whose
name must surely count as an anagram of Judas, did scream
loudly and, we can only hope, loudly enough to cast out her
demons, as Christ cast out the demons from the leprous man
on the road to Galilee. Her remains are scattered. You will
never see her again. You would not know her now, even if you
could find her, which you cannot.*

There were seven hundred and ninety-eight letters in all.
Most had been written during the six months immediately
following Julie's disappearance, but there were some,
printouts of emails mostly, that dated from just a couple of
weeks before Ray's death. The Julie of these letters had run
away because she was pregnant, because she'd found God,

because she'd been raped by one of her teachers, because her father was a secret paedophile, because she wanted to start a new life with the Mennonites, the Tuaregs, a communist commune in Birmingham, because she'd learned the truth about the end of the world. She'd become a sex worker, a croupier, a car thief, a poet living in Mexico City, a lap dancer working in a hostess bar to pay the bills. She sent letters from Hackney and from Arbroath, from Sydney and Naples and Cambridge, Massachusetts. She had been sighted in Athens and Dublin and Malibu and Austin, Texas, on the platforms of metro stations in Tokyo and Barcelona. The Tokyo letter even included a photograph, a blurred Polaroid of a girl or young woman in a belted mackintosh and tatty-looking lace-up plimsolls. Her face was turned away from the camera, staring up at the lighted display screen. Dark hair bunched around her collar, a white plastic carrier bag dangled from her left hand.

Who was she, Selena wondered, where had she been going? The words on the LED display screen, though they appeared in both English and Japanese characters, were too blurrily indistinct to make out, though the plimsolls were so exactly of the kind Julie might have worn that Selena almost found herself being persuaded that the figure was her sister.

Here were the crank letters the police had warned them about: the hoaxers, the deluded well-wishers, the people claiming to be Julie or to know where she was. A small number of the letters contained such obscenities Selena felt sick reading them. Most though were simply *wrong*: fabrications and falsehoods, just stories really. They were troubling to read, but essentially harmless, when you came down to it, if you could ignore the disturbance of mind that had driven the sender to write them in the first place.

Some seemed so heartfelt, so impassioned that Selena almost felt sorry for them, especially since it was obvious, usually from the first line, that these correspondents, whoever they were, had no personal knowledge of Julie whatsoever. Many had not even bothered to familiarise themselves with the most widely distributed details of her disappearance. They were desperate to be heard, that was all. So desperate to be noticed they would do anything to attract attention, even for a moment.

DS Nesbitt had told them to ignore the hoax letters, to hand them straight to the police without reading them. We know they can be really upsetting for families, she said. At least this is one thing we can help you with.

Margery would have obeyed DS Nesbitt's instructions to the last word, Selena knew. She would have dismissed the crank letters, as the police had advised, as the ravings of social inadequates. Dad though – he had clearly read the lot. Not just because he was convinced the police were missing important clues in their search for Julie, but because he was curious. Curious about these alien minds, reaching out to his, no matter how distorted their perceptions.

And there was always the chance that one of the letters might have contained something important. Ray Rouane would have read and reread them, searching for that vital link, that web-fine interface between imagination and reality. Further down in the box Selena came upon a world map, its folds brittle with age, which her father had used to record the postmark location of every single piece of the hoax correspondence. As an accompaniment to the map he had invented a key, a complicated colour-lexicon in which the sender's address as well as any other locations mentioned in the letter were arranged in a distinct hierarchy.

The intense care that had gone into the creation of the chart rivalled or even surpassed the obsessiveness on display in the letters themselves. The whole business was crazy, Selena knew that, yet she felt a rush of love for her absent father nonetheless, who unlike the police and the crowds of well-wishers, the TV reporters and the journalists, had retained his staunch belief that *something could be done*.

There were other things in the box: bus timetables, photographs, more maps. There was also a folder of correspondence with the police – not DS Nesbitt this time but another officer, a DI Nelson who Selena couldn't remember ever meeting. The letters on her father's side – Ray had taken carbon copies of all of them – had become increasingly incoherent and rambling, whilst DI Nelson's had become more and more terse until finally a letter came, signed not by DI Nelson but by someone in the Greater Manchester Police public liaison office, informing Ray that no further correspondence could be entered into at this time, and enclosing a form for filing an official complaint.

This last letter had been sent more than five years after Julie's disappearance. Selena replaced it in its envelope together with the complaints form and put it back in the folder. There was too much stuff here, too much to do anything but skim the surface. It was like stumbling upon a tomb, in a way – one of those ancient Egyptian burial chambers, only filled with letters and stories instead of golden goblets and ceremonial jewellery.

She remembered when she was a child, seeing a documentary about the Tutankhamen exhibition at the British Museum, people queuing around the block to see it, which she remembered thinking was creepy even at the time. She couldn't see what difference it made, that Tutankhamen had been dead for thousands of years – it was still his stuff, wasn't it, his private possessions? The thought of people lining up to gawp at the artefacts made her feel weird.

There were those who believed the archaeologists who opened the tomb had brought down a curse upon themselves, upon the world too, maybe. As a child, the idea of a curse had seemed exciting. Less so now.

Perhaps the past really was better left buried. Selena wondered what she was doing, looking through this stuff, what she was, in fact, looking *for*.

You'll be getting like Dad, if you don't watch yourself, she thought.

Perhaps it was just that she missed her father more than she realised.

## THE DRAGGING OF HATCHMERE LAKE: AN INVENTORY OF ITEMS RETRIEVED

Die-cast model fire truck, Tonka D4879 (1)
Bicycle, Raleigh, girl's model, blue (1)
Batteries, AA, AAA, 5AMP (558)
Baby doll, Mattel, 'Tiny Tears' (1)
Boots, shoes, trainers, assorted (67)
Diver's flipper (1)
Jam jars, sauce bottles, assorted glassware (133)
Vauxhall Corsa, white (1)
Domestic cat, skeletal remains (2)
Domestic dog, Labrador retriever, skeletal remains (1)
Domestic dog, Staffordshire bull terrier, skeletal remains (1)
Sewing machine, Singer, treadle operated (1)
Food processor, Kenwood (1)
Portable stepladder, aluminium (1)
Portable television (2)
Computer monitor (3)
Shin bone, part, human, male (1, pending further
investigation)
Television aerial (1)
Buttons, buckles, zips, clothing embellishments, metallic (109)
Diver's chronometer, Solaris (1)
Wristwatches, assorted (28)
Earrings, post, clip, sleeper (53)
Jewellery, metallic, assorted (38)
Tupperware sandwich box, contents £350 in used notes (1)
Hairbrushes, combs assorted, metal, plastic (25)

Music centre, Sanyo (1)
Sony Discman (1)
Hedge cutter, Bosch (1)
Marbles, glass, porcelain (63)
Camera, Kodak Instamatic (2)
Pyrex serving dish, large oval (1)
Dustbin, metal (1)
Mattress, single, pocket sprung (1)
Beer bottles, Beck's, Grolsch, Peroni, assorted other (56)
Drinks cans, food tins, aluminium (387)
Soda siphon, large, glass (1)
Guitar, electric, Fender (1)
Lawnmower/strimmer, Flymo (1)
Compact discs (67)
Minidiscs (5)
Cassette tapes (127)
Child's plastic telephone, Fisher Price (1)
Mobile phones, Nokia, Samsung, Motorola, assorted (34)
Inflatable dinghy, vinyl (1)
Inflatable lilo, vinyl (1)
Cotton reels, wooden, plastic (24)
Garden secateurs, wire cutters (5)
Garden shears (1)
Garden rake (1)
Spade, steel (1)
Wading boots, rubber (1)
Coffee maker, DéLonghi (1)
Spectacles, pairs of (4)
Spectacles cases (3)

Die-cast model cars, miniatures, Matchbox (33)
'Slinky' child's spring toy (1)
Thermos flask, plastic (2)
Thermos flask, aluminium (1)
Fish tank/aquarium, plastic (1)

\* \* \*

### *Warrington Guardian*, 26th August 1994

Following the excavation of several tonnes of assorted artefacts and detritus from the waters of Hatchmere Lake, Delamere, in the continuing search for missing teenager Julie Rouane, it was unanimously agreed by members of Delamere Parish Council that the lake should become the focus of a major clean-up and renewal programme, to take place over the course of the following twelve months. 'As a leisure and relaxation area for families, a base for numerous local sporting activities as well as a site of considerable scientific and ecological interest, the lake and its environs are vital to the people of Hatchmere, Delamere, Warrington and its surrounding villages,' said Mrs Susannah Baylis, parish councillor. 'We cannot allow environmental pressures, most specifically the illegal practice of fly-tipping and dumping, to degrade our precious natural resources in such a manner as has recently been highlighted.' When asked specifically about the missing teenager, Mrs Baylis stated that this was a police matter and beyond her remit, though she commended Warrington and Greater Manchester Police, who jointly masterminded the Hatchmere excavation. 'Whatever there is to be found, I feel confident of the abilities of our police in finding it,' she stated. 'As I understand it, investigations are still very much ongoing.'

## 8

"Do you remember that story Dad told us, about the giant catfish?" Selena asked.

"The Destroyer of Worlds," Julie said. "It wasn't Dad who told the story though, it was that guy in Mia's maths class, the one who was always on about toxic sludge. Luke, I think his name was." She laughed. "He thought the lake was radioactive, that there was some kind of government cover-up, don't you remember? He said he was going to gather all the information he could find and then go to the newspapers."

"I don't mean that one. I mean the catfish in the Mekong Delta. Dad told us about them, that day we went to the lake and that bloke with all the piercings tried to show us his cock."

Julie frowned. "I don't remember that. Not at all. When was it?"

"It doesn't matter. It was ages ago." It was strange, Selena thought, the way the subject of time had become touch-sensitive suddenly, like a bruise that wouldn't heal. Selena knew she was testing Julie, trying to catch her out even. Talking about the catfish – about the guy with the piercings

– had mostly been a way of talking about the lake. The list of items retrieved from the water had been written in longhand, in black biro, almost like a shopping list, on both sides of a sheet of paper torn from an A4 notepad. Selena hadn't recognised the handwriting. It definitely wasn't Dad's, she knew that for certain, which made her wonder how it had ended up in the Brillo box with all the other stuff.

The article from the *Warrington Guardian* had been attached to it with a paperclip, together with a brown envelope stuffed with photos of what Selena could only assume was Hatchmere Lake. Some had been clipped from newspapers, others were camera snapshots, plus a whole bunch of undeveloped negatives.

Selena guessed that at least some of the blurry landscape shots, snapped from different vantage points around the lake, had been taken by Ray. But there were others, photos that looked as though they'd been taken from *behind* the section of yellow tape the police had put up. The objects in these pictures – a filthy-looking stub of bone, the rusted carcase of a drowned saloon car, the skeleton of an umbrella – were obviously part of the inventory that had been dragged from the lake. The images had a sharpness and clarity that made Selena feel pretty sure they were police property.

Had Dad paid for the photos, or stolen them? She would once have found the idea of her father stealing anything preposterous, but not any more. Where Julie was concerned, Ray had clearly become capable of anything. The snapshots of the lake, together with the letters to DI Nelson and the handwritten list of excavated artefacts, were proof, if any were needed, of the way that the stretch of murky water had taken over his mind, nudging all other obsessions aside until in the end Hatchmere possessed his thoughts almost entirely.

Both DS Nesbitt and DI Nelson had been at pains to stress that the Hatchmere Lake search was simply one line of enquiry among several. Assume too much, they warned, and you run the risk of blinding yourself to other possibilities.

For Dad though, it was all about the lake – the lake and the acres of woodland that surrounded it. So far as Ray was concerned, Julie had been there and something had happened and that was that. He'd been determined to prove it. He had died trying.

Julie talked about the lake as if it was no big deal, no more and no less significant than any other subject.

"Have you ever been back there?" Selena asked her.

Julie looked surprised for a moment and then shook her head. "No," she said. "Why would I?"

Selena decided that like her father she would read through every one of the seven hundred and ninety-eight letters in the Brillo box. She wasn't sure what this might achieve, but she did it anyway. She gave each letter a number, marking each envelope with a round, easy-peel sticker, and entered the numbers into a notebook she had purchased for the purpose. Against each number she entered the date of the postmark, the date on the letter, if there was one, the name of the sender, if a name had been given, and their address. In the absence of an address, she entered the postmark location instead.

As an activity it was oddly calming, even in spite of the content of some of the letters, and Selena wondered if it had been this, after all, the sense of bringing order to a chaos that could not otherwise be rationalised or accepted, that had made her father adhere so faithfully to his obsessions.

For Ray, reading and cataloguing the letters had been a way of keeping Julie alive, of keeping her present, even while she was absent.

Like talking to ghosts.


Selena knew the letter was from Julie the second she saw it, because she recognised the handwriting. Handwriting was peculiar in that way: when you read it, it was almost as if you could hear the person speaking. The envelope was greyish with ingrained dust, the paper slightly furry to the touch, which was what happened with paper if you over-handled it. There was a grease spot on one corner. It looked like a fingerprint. Selena wondered whether it was in fact Julie's fingerprint, or just a random mark.

The letter was postmarked COVENTRY. The date on the postmark was 23rd March 2003, eighteen months before Dad died, more or less. The ink was still quite dark. There was no return address on the back flap, though there was one on the letter inside: 18 Coundon Road, Coventry.

It was letter #492.

Dad –

I'm writing to tell you I'm OK, and that I'm sorry for everything you've been through, you and Mum and Selena. I wish I could have been in touch earlier but it just wasn't possible. I don't expect you to understand, or to forgive me – after all this time I'd understand if you never wanted to see me again. But whatever you might think, and no matter what anyone else might tell you, I truly am sorry, and I do miss you, very much. I would love it if we could meet, just to see each other again. I hope you'll at least think about it. Anyway, now you know. You can write to me at this address. Could you do that? Even if it's just to tell me you received this letter.

I love you, Dad. I hope you're well.

Julie

Even without the handwriting, the letter would have stood out. It was so different from all the others, those hundreds of outpourings, the confessions and revelations and accusations. Julie's letter was different because there was no explanation and no story, just an apology. Very few of the other letters had included apologies.

The only mystery was why Dad had ignored it.

Perhaps he didn't. Maybe he was in touch with Julie all along and never said.

It barely seemed possible, though in keeping Julie's existence a secret, wasn't that exactly what Selena was doing herself?

She made up her mind to confront Julie about the letter, to ask her straight out.

"I found this," Selena said to her, two days later. "Did you send it?"

She slid the envelope across the table. She tried to make the gesture seem unimportant, an afterthought.

Julie glanced down at the letter. She made no move to touch it, to open it, although why would she, Selena reasoned, when she knew damn well what was inside?

"Where did you get this?" Julie said. Her eyes seemed very bright, and for a moment Selena was convinced she was about to cry.

"It was in with some things of Dad's, stuff from his flat. I meant to sort through it all after he died but I never got round to it. I thought it was time."

Julie was silent for so long Selena was beginning to think she wasn't going to say anything. Damn you, Julie, she thought. You can't have everything your own way. If Julie's intention was to make her feel like a bitch, she was succeeding, though in the matter of the letter at least she was determined to get an answer.

It had been a simple enough question, after all.

"I was scared," Julie said in the end. She drew in her breath, slowly, let it out again. "Dad wrote back. Just a note. He said it didn't matter where I'd been or what had happened, all he cared about was that I was all right. He asked when he could visit. He said he'd come as soon as I was ready. He was so – Dad, even after all that time. I felt – I don't know, paralysed. Then I lost my nerve completely. I knew that if I didn't write back, Dad would probably come and look for me anyway, so I moved house."

"You moved house?"

Julie nodded.

What do you mean, you lost your nerve? Selena wanted to say. She found she couldn't bear to think about what it must have been like for Dad, to have come so close to finding Julie and then losing her again.

Had he died happier, knowing she was alive, at least? Or had he even believed that the person who had written to him was really his daughter?

His death at the lakeside suggested he hadn't, or at least not completely, that he was still looking.

In the weeks since Julie's return, Selena had grown so used to having her around that she – Julie-now – had more or less expunged her memory of Julie-then. From time to time she thought about how terrible it would be if Julie-now was not the real Julie after all, if her sister was still out there somewhere, suffering or alone, or just dead, as everyone except her father had always believed. In spite of the increasing amount of time they spent together, Selena could not help suspecting that the new intimacy between herself and Julie was a surface thing, a kind of photocopy rather than the original. She was reminded of the summer her parents almost split up, the summer she and Julie had become close again, only not really. Selena always had the feeling that Julie was using her, that she was biding her time.

Waiting for the summer to end, so she could go back to ignoring her, back to her real life. She had the same feeling now.

The one question she could never answer was what would anyone have to gain by being Julie, by pretending? People who did that kind of thing in the movies were always after something. Usually it was money, but there were other reasons too: status, acceptance, revenge. Julie-now showed no signs of wanting revenge. Indeed there was something about her – a vulnerability – that sometimes made Selena want to shake her, not from anger but from fear. Fear that whatever had happened to her might happen again. She knows nothing about the world. Perhaps she just wants a family.

Selena needed someone to talk to, and in the end she confided in Vanja, because there was no one else, she thought at first, only realising later that Vanja also happened to be the person she trusted most. In the old days it would have been Johnny, but contacting Johnny now would just add to the confusion. Speaking to Laurie or Sandra felt out of the question.

Telling Vanja was a risk, but Vanja knew all about risk. Vanja was the number one master of keeping her mouth shut.

"You remember I told you about my sister?" Selena said. It was after closing and they were cashing up. The street door was locked. Selena had just switched the phone over to voicemail.

"Your sister who's been ill?" Vanja put down the bag of coins she had been counting, immediately attentive. Her instincts were so sharp, like a hawk's, like a raptor's. She knew when to wait for information to emerge, rather than trying to rip it out of its hole. Try telling Laurie anything and you'd be waiting half a day for her to shut up before you could do it.

"Her name's Julie. She hasn't been ill exactly, she's been…" She paused. *Missing*, she thought, testing the weight of the word in her head before speaking it aloud, the way you might test the weight of a stone in your hand before skimming it across the water.

"Missing? Like, for real?"

Selena nodded. "She disappeared when she was seventeen. I was fourteen at the time, almost fifteen. Anyway, she turned up suddenly, completely out of the blue, about three months ago. She doesn't want anyone to know. That she's back, I mean. Not even our mother." She paused. "It all feels really weird."

"Are you sure it's her?"

The central question, the only question, just like that. For a moment, Selena inwardly debated not answering, pretending she hadn't heard what Vanja had said. But then wasn't this what she had wanted of Vanja all along, that she should ask that question?

"I don't see how she can't be," Selena said at last. "She knows things – about our childhood, stuff only Julie could know. She looks like Julie." She paused. "I can't think of any reason why she wouldn't be."

Vanja shrugged, then began tapping figures into a calculator. "I don't know, but people do all kinds of weird shit. You know about Anna Anderson?"

Selena shook her head.

"She's a woman who climbed out of a river in Berlin just after World War One. Claimed she was the Russian Grand Duchess Anastasia Romanova – you know, the girl that got shot along with the Tsar and the rest of his family. The thing is, Anastasia was just a child when she was murdered, so who knows what she would have been like, later on? Even now there are still people who believe Anna Anderson was telling the truth. She's dead now," Vanja added. "They've done DNA tests and everything." She jabbed a final figure into the calculator. "You OK?"

"I'm all right. I feel bad though, because of Mum. I keep thinking she should know."

"Not your decision to make, *milaya moya*. If she is really your sister, she has the right to decide for herself who she wants to speak to. You can tell her to go to hell if you want to, but telling your mother? That has to come from her."

"I know you're right."

"The truth always comes out in the end though, like it did with Anastasia." Vanja rested her chin on her hand. "I always wanted a sister. But then I hear something like this and it reminds me of all the women I know who do have sisters and wish they didn't. They can be such bitches."

Selena laughed. "Julie isn't a bitch."

"What do you call this, then? Laying all this shit on you?"

Vanja scooped up the cash bags and took them into the back office. Selena let down the window shutters then went into the office herself to collect her bag and coat. Speaking to Vanja had made her feel better, but she was no further forward.

"Any time you need to talk more, you let me know," Vanja said. She was kneeling in front of the cash safe, peering into the dark rectangle of its interior as if she'd forgotten for the moment what it was for. "You owe her some questions, I think."

"Maybe."

On her walk to the bus stop, Selena found herself remembering the story Laurie had told about her sister-in-law, how Laurie hadn't recognised her because she'd put on weight. Selena hadn't had that problem with Julie, because Julie looked the same, only older. But was that really true? Had Selena taken one look at Julie and decided to trust her, because it was easier to believe what she said than to ask awkward questions?

I'll never know, Selena thought. It's already too late.

Two a.m., and the phone started ringing. Selena woke instantaneously from a deep sleep, so convinced the caller was Julie it was as if she could already hear her voice at the other end. I must have been dreaming about her, Selena thought. She grabbed for the bedside extension. She couldn't remember the last time she had used it. To speak to Johnny, probably, before he went away.

The sound of Johnny's voice on the line was like déjà vu.

"Hey," she said.

"It's OK to call now, isn't it? It's not too late?"

For a second Selena imagined she meant them: their breakup, his departure, whichever of the two was supposed to have happened first. Then she realised he was talking about the time.

"It's twenty past two, Johnny," she said. "In the morning."

"Oh Jesus, Selena, I'm sorry. I'm still crap at working it out. I'll call back tomorrow."

"I'm awake now," she said. "Don't worry. How are you, anyway?"

"Good," Johnny said. His voice floated out of focus slightly, and Selena knew it was because he was turning his head away from the speaker, glancing back over his shoulder the way he always did, his eyes on the traffic, the street, the storefronts, the women, whatever. "It's forty degrees here."

"Amazing," Selena said. She tucked the telephone receiver in between her cheek and the pillow, closing her eyes as she listened to Johnny gabble on about his new sponsor and the flat he was sharing with someone called Ryu, one of the track engineers, she thought Johnny said. It didn't matter, she was never going to meet him, it was just nice to hear Johnny's voice, the same as before, the same as it had always been, minus the tiny salient detail that he wasn't here.

"What's going on with you, anyway?" he asked at one point.

"Nothing much," she said. "Just Vanja, you know, the shop. I'm still thinking about doing that geology course with the Open University."

"You should," Johnny said, and Selena thought yes, she should, if she enrolled within the next six weeks she'd be in time to begin the foundation course next October, although it seemed a long time since the subject had been uppermost in her mind.

If you had a conversation with someone and they didn't know about something, could that mean that in a way the thing hadn't happened? It was an interesting idea. She curled on her side, still listening to Johnny, and at some point she must have fallen asleep, because the next thing she knew she was awake again, with the telephone still pressed to her cheek and the wheezing, high-pitched hum of a dead line keening into her ear.

It was half-past five, not quite light. Selena replaced the receiver, wondering for a horrified moment if she was going to end up being billed for a three-hour call to Kuala Lumpur, then remembering it had been Johnny who called, not her, that he must have realised what had happened and hung up.

# A Voyage to Arcturus

**[The Return: notes for an essay on Peter Weir's *Picnic at Hanging Rock* by Julie Rouane, Film Studies A/S dissertation portfolio, Priestley College, Warrington, December 1993]**

The story told in the movie is very simple: on St Valentine's Day, 1900, a group of girls from an exclusive boarding school in southern Australia are taken to visit a famous beauty spot, an area of prominent limestone formations known as the Hanging Rock. They picnic at the base of the rock, and read each other's valentines. At some point during the afternoon, four of the girls ask permission to examine the rock closer to. While the rest of the group and their teachers fall asleep in the sun, Miranda, Marion, Irma and Edith climb through the tunnels and crevices that make up the rock formation. Some hours later, one of the girls, Edith, runs screaming from the bushes. Her legs are scratched and she is missing her shoes. There is no sign of the three other girls, and one of their teachers, Miss McCraw, is also missing. A week later, Irma is found in a cave, high up on the rock. She is alive and unharmed, but has no memory of what happened to her, or to the others. Miranda, Marion and Miss McCraw are never seen again.

There are two main subplots, one involving Sara, an orphan who holds a particular attachment to Miranda, the other involving Michael Fitzhubert, a young man staying nearby who develops an obsession with the missing girls. The main focus of the film though is always the mystery: *what really happened?*

One of the first things that struck me about the film was the way the people seemed so uncomfortable in the landscape. In spite of the extreme heat, the headmistress of the school, Mrs Appleyard, tells the girls they must not remove their gloves until they are clear of the village – she doesn't want 'commoners' to see them behaving in an unladylike manner. When Irma is found, her corset is missing and everyone is obsessed with whether or not she is still a virgin. "In England, young ladies like that wouldn't be allowed to go walking in the forest. Not alone, anyway," says Michael Fitzhubert. Michael Fitzhubert is dressed like Little Lord Fauntleroy in top hat and tails.

The only character at ease in the outback is Bertie, Fitzhubert's valet, also an orphan and – unknown to us at first – Sara's brother.

The figures of the young women move stiffly like dressed-up dolls against a background of flagrant, uncompromising wilderness. We feel the heat, we hear the squawks of kookaburras, catch the movements of lizards and insects from the corner of our eye. The wilderness Weir shows us does not conceal its dangers, its strangeness. We can see those dangers clearly – more even than seeing, we feel – but for Mrs Appleyard and her pupils there is no danger in red rock and flyblown grassland, only discomfort or, worse still, impropriety.

They are horribly unprepared for the encounter.

The rock boulders are like great grey Easter Island faces. They watch without caring as the women climb, the men search. It is as if the women *must* climb the rock, the men must follow.

Marion, Irma and Miranda are shown as special, charmed. As Miranda turns away from us for the last time, the sun outlines her head in gold, like a halo. Mademoiselle de Poitiers, the French mistress, refers to Miranda as "a Botticelli angel". In fact the three missing girls are just normal young women with nothing special about them except the fact that they come from rich families. It is their money that sets them apart from Sara, who is bullied and patronised and finally rejected because of her poverty. Sara is a much more interesting character than Miranda, because of her defiance and her desire for escape – she reminds me of Helen Burns in *Jane Eyre*. Mrs Appleyard is also an interesting character because the person she pretends to be is so different from the person she really is. In reality, her control is an illusion. She is a depressed alcoholic who longs to escape the life she has made for herself. Her terrible behaviour towards Sara arises out of her despair over the power she once had, and is now losing.

IRMA – the Irma who returns to the school *is a*

*different person*. Her apartness is highlighted by the way she is dressed – all in red, in contrast with the rest of the girls in their drab school uniforms. Only a small amount of time has passed, yet Irma suddenly seems a world away: distant, removed, *adult*. Her former classmates turn on her like a pack of feral children – like the boys who torment Piggy in *Lord of the Flies*. They resent her separateness from them, even as they reinforce it. They are desperate to know what happened, yet we fear they will not believe a word she says, that the simple act of being set apart by experience has turned them against her forever.

One of the most interesting things about the film is that many people still believe it is based on true events.

1

You won't remember this – you were too little – but for a while – I was about seven when it started, I think – I was terrified of black holes. I'd seen part of a science programme on TV – *Horizon* probably, or *The World About Us* – describing how nothing could ever escape a black hole, not even light. There was an animated diagram, showing what might happen if a planet were to get sucked into a black hole's event horizon, and a map of our galaxy showing where astronomers believed black holes might be located. Gaping empty spaces, patches of nothing, the lairs of monsters. I kept seeing that planet being dragged towards the point of no return and the idea petrified me so much I couldn't bear to talk about it. What frightened me most was that no one seemed to care. Thousands of people – millions – would have seen the television programme, and yet life was going on as if nothing had happened.

For my Christmas present that year, I asked Dad if I could have a book on astronomy. I told him I wanted to learn about the planets in our solar system, but really I wanted to find out as much as I could about black holes. The book I was given – *Hutchinson's Junior Encyclopaedia of Space* – was full of beautiful colour images and photographs: the Earth from the Moon, the rings of Saturn, the Milky Way. There was a pull-out map of the solar system, showing how far each of the planets lay from the sun, and a set of diagrams showing you how to identify the constellations. Towards the end of the book there was a short chapter called 'Black Holes and Other Unexplained Phenomena'. I read it straight through at top speed, then again more slowly, hoping and not quite daring to feel reassured. The book said astronomers believed that black holes were actually stars, but turned inside out: collapsed suns that had become so magnetically powerful they pulled everything into their force field, including whole planets and other suns.

The book said the chances of a black hole entering our solar system were a trillion to one.

A trillion to one was huge, but it could still happen. A couple of days after Christmas I finally plucked up the courage to talk to Dad about it. When I asked him if he thought we were in danger, he laughed and ruffled my hair.

"The nearest black hole is more than twenty thousand light years away from us," he said. "Can you imagine how far away that is?"

I couldn't, and that was the problem. Twenty thousand was a large number, but it was still finite. In bed at night, I imagined the black hole careering through outer space like a vast typhoon. For a long time – thousands of centuries – it would be too far away to notice, or even to think about. Eventually though, it would come, and we would begin to feel it. Just a minute tug at first, but still a presence.

Mountains will fall, I thought. All those mountains and wars and centuries, all for nothing.

It seemed unutterably sad to me. I could not imagine how the world could continue, in the light of it.

I know you won't believe me, but I'm going to tell you anyway: on Saturday July 16th 1994, I travelled from the area of woodland around Hatchmere Lake, near Warrington, Cheshire, to the shore of the Shuubseet, or Shoe Lake, an elongated, slipper-shaped stretch of water not far from the western outskirts of Fiby, which is the smallest and most southerly of the six great city-states of the planet of Tristane, one of the eight planets of the Suur System, in the Aww Galaxy.

How I came to be there I cannot tell you. Cally's brother Noah believes there is a rift – a transept, he calls it – something like an enlarged pore in the void between Earth and Tristane that allows objects and occasionally people to travel instantaneously from one place to the other. Noah has a theory about Hatchmere Lake being a four-dimensional photocopy of the Shuubseet, a kind of cast of it, like one of those ready-formed plastic pond liners you can buy in garden centres. He reckons that if you photographed both lakes from the air they'd look identical, like Rorschach blots of each other, but when I asked him why that would matter he couldn't explain. Something about twisted vortices. Makes me wish I'd paid more attention in physics really, but the Frog was such a bore. Did I ever tell you about the time I fell asleep in his class – I mean *actually fell asleep* – and Catey had to stab me in the arse with her compass to wake me up?

Cally says I was born on Tristane, that my life on Earth was a dream, a fugue state, something my brain invented to help me recover from what happened at Sere-Phraquet, though when I ask Cally what did happen, she refuses to tell me. She seems to think the memories will return on their own, when I'm ready to deal with them. Until then she thinks I'm better off just living from day to day.

Everything I know about Tristane I know from books. Cally's books mostly, also a school history primer I picked up in one of the street markets in Gren-Noor. The book was faded from use, and from sunlight, but I grew very fond of it. I wish I'd kept it with me.

Paper has a slightly different texture on Tristane, because it's made from julippa pulp, I suppose.

Nothing is like you think it is, Selena. Nothing at all.

Now at least you know why I haven't spoken to you openly until now. You've probably been thinking it was just me, just Julie being her usual self-obsessed, self-important self. But honestly? I just couldn't bear the thought of seeing that look in your eyes, the look that said, *Oh God, what the fuck is she on?*

You know that moment in almost every horror movie you'll ever see, when the main character comes dashing out of the woods, or the haunted house, or the cellar or wherever, gibbering some insane story about a monster or a psycho or a secret passage leading straight into hell? There are all kinds of variations on that scene, but the one thing that's always the same is that the person who gets told the story never believes it. You sit there watching and thinking what an idiot, can't he see she's telling the truth? You're almost glad when the idiot character wanders off and gets munched by the monster, because really they should have trusted their friend in the first place.

What if it were you though? In real life, I mean? What if your best friend came rushing up to you outside Sainsbury's and said, *They're coming, they're coming!* Would you even consider believing them, even for a second?

Of course you wouldn't, because who would? Instead, you'd begin to convince yourself you'd seen the signs, that you'd seen this coming. That your friend hadn't been the same since they'd hooked up with that arsehole you warned them against – Gavin or Gary or whatever his stupid name was. That *they'd changed*.

There are Wels catfish in Hatchmere Lake, but not giant ones. The water's too cold.

I came out of the woods by the lake. It was the most perfect afternoon, the sunlight spinning through the trees like torn-off bits of tinfoil, the blue water shining under a blue sky like an image on a postcard from Switzerland or Italy. *This place is heaven, wish you were here*. A far cry from Manchester, anyway. My legs were shaking. I couldn't understand how this place – this world – could exist at the same time as my journey in the van with Steven Barbershop. The two realities seemed to repel each other, the way magnets do, when you place the matching poles end to end and try to force them together. I stared at the lake, the kids dicking around playing British bulldog, the two old guys with their fishing rods, and

I could feel the unreality pushing at my senses, building up inside my head like some sort of dust. My saliva turned bitter suddenly, as if I were about to be sick.

I kept seeing his face, that nasty grin of his: *Steady on, will you? The safety locks are still on.*

How could I have been so stupid? Why?

The margin between freedom and destruction is so narrow, Selena.

There was a fallen tree trunk, not far from me, twenty yards at the most. I started thinking that if I could only get to the tree trunk I could sit down on it and wait – wait until I felt better, I mean. Then I could ask someone how to find the station so I could get away from here. I could take the train to Altrincham, catch the bus home. Easy.

I remember moving towards the tree trunk, aiming myself at it, as if it were a target and I were an arrow, an arrow gliding in slow motion like in *Robin of Sherwood*. Just as I reached the tree trunk – I remember reaching out to touch it – it seemed to tip up at one end, *thwang*, like a seesaw, only then I realised it wasn't the tree trunk tipping up, but me tipping over, my legs boneless as pipe cleaners suddenly, like one of those dolls they used to make from clothes pegs on *Blue Peter*.

When you fall down in a faint, the ground doesn't feel hard. It's like falling into bed, or on to one of those rubber gym mats they put down at school. It's not the ground that's changed its nature, but you. Your body loses all inhibition, all tension. You're falling through space so softly and you're not afraid. It's as if you're watching yourself from outside, or in a movie:

*[Julie crumples to the ground. She lies
motionless with her eyes closed. The camera
pans out across the lake. In the distance a
dog barks. The sun dips briefly behind a cloud
and then comes out again.]*

I don't know how long I was unconscious – just seconds, probably, though I have no way of telling. When I came to, I lay still with my eyes closed, reluctant to move. The scent of earth and dry leaves was comforting and I wanted to go on smelling it. Then I realised I was cold, that there was a breeze blowing. The sun had gone in. I wished I'd thought to bring a sweatshirt, only it had been so hot earlier the idea hadn't occurred to me. Then I heard someone – a woman – asking me if I was all right, and I came properly awake.

"Thank goodness I found you," she said. That's lucky, I thought. I can ask her where the station is. I opened my eyes and she was looking down at me, a woman with dark skin and light grey eyes and closely cropped hair. She looked confused, or maybe just worried, and I wondered if I'd seen her before maybe, if I knew her from somewhere.

"Julie," she said. "You could have died out here."

It was only then that I became fully aware of my surroundings. I was still by a lake, but everything was different. The tree trunk was gone, and instead of the footpath leading into the forest there was just bare earth, a greyish, bleak-looking shoreline strewn with pebbles and gravel. Off to one side I could see several small wooden cabins, or shacks, built from planks and roofed over with corrugated iron. Behind the shacks the ground rose steeply towards a line of trees, a bluish-grey forest, vast and faceless, like in one of those depressing films about the end of the world.

I knew something was wrong, but I was still too dazed and disoriented to work out what it was. I'll never get home from here, I thought. I closed my eyes again and pictured stars, constellations so wildly off kilter it was as if the world had slipped sideways and out of orbit. Then I saw blackness, soft as velvet. I let it surround me and for a moment felt warmer, wrapped in the dark.

"Get up," the woman said. "We need to get moving." She put out her hand to help me stand, and I took it without thinking. Her fingers were warm, a detail that convinced me she was real. She took off her coat, a dun-coloured parka. "Put this on," she said. "You must be freezing."

I pulled it on over my T-shirt. It had a sour smell, like horse hair, but the warmth, after feeling so chilled, was an immediate relief. I smiled. I still couldn't bring myself to speak, but the woman seemed to accept that and didn't press me. "Come on," she said. "It'll be dark soon."

"What's your name?" I whispered finally. "Where are we going?"

"I'm Cally," she said. "And we're going home."

Kayleigh, I thought, remembering Marillion, the lie I'd told Steven Barbershop about me liking the band. Had I dreamed this woman up, I wondered, out of the confusion and terror of what had just happened?

No, I thought. It's too cold to be a dream.

I pulled Cally's jacket more tightly around me.

Hatchmere Lake in winter can feel desolate and miles from anywhere. It is as if, as the seasons turn, the forest turns inward towards its other self, its shadow self: Shoe Lake, close by the city of Fiby, in Tristane's arid and rather chilly southern hemisphere.

What I remember most about the afternoon of July 16th 1994: the piercing blue sky, the whirr and click of fishing lines, the sounds of children playing British bulldog. I remember a man in a long grey mackintosh walking two Irish wolfhounds, a woman in a patchwork skirt, rubbing sunscreen into the arms and cheeks of a girl in a wheelchair.

Cally has long, narrow feet and delicate hands. As we made our way along the foreshore of Shoe Lake, I remembered walking with Lucy at dusk past an old factory yard somewhere in the backstreets of Manchester: the iron gates chained shut, a warehouse looming, semi-invisible, out of the darkness, a single light in an upstairs window where no light should have been.

"I don't like this," Lucy said to me. "I think we should go."

That was when I remembered when I'd first seen Cally: the night I went to see *Schindler's List* with Allison Gifford. Afterwards, on the street outside Allison's flat, a woman had stopped and asked me for a light.

"I don't smoke," I said to her.

"That's OK," she said. We both stood there for a moment,

just looking at each other. I remember thinking it must be the night for weird things happening because I was sure I recognised her from somewhere, even though at the same time I knew I'd never seen her before in my life.

"Cities live and die, like everyone else," Cally said to me. Months later this was, in one of the waterfront cafés in Gren-Seet. "Their lifespans are longer, that's all."

We walked along the lakeshore for what seemed like ages. The going was uneven, but not strenuous. There was a taste of dusk in the air, and when we finally turned away from the lake most of the light was already gone from the sky. Cally led me towards a small expanse of gravel and dirt, a kind of parking area. Scrubland, dotted with narrow copses of scrawny-looking trees, extended in all directions. Leading off from the car park was a rough dirt road. A vehicle stood waiting, a high-sided cart, harnessed to a large brown animal, some kind of donkey. A man jumped down from the driver's seat and came towards us. He had long hair, and wore a hooded fleece. He and Cally embraced briefly, then stepped apart.

"I found her," Cally said. "Down by the fishing shacks."

"She can't keep running off like this, Cay, it's ridiculous. And dangerous. You should make her see a doctor."

"No," Cally said. "You know what they'll say. They might try to take her in again. I'm not risking that. She'll be fine, Noah. She just needs time."

"And your coat, apparently." He was staring at me, the man,

as if the sight of me was familiar to him and not particularly welcome. There was a look in his eyes, a weariness, and I noticed for the first time how alike they were physically, Noah and Cally. Were they brother and sister?

"She'll be fine," Cally repeated. She took my right hand in both of hers and kneaded it as if she was trying to put warmth into me, traced her index finger lightly across my knuckles. They were grazed, I saw. I'd probably caught them while I was running through the bushes.

"Come on then," Noah said. "Give me your stuff."

Cally handed him the backpack she was carrying, hoisting it carefully from her shoulders. It looked heavy. "Don't bash it," she said. He gave her a look. "Get in," she said to me. "Noah will help you." She placed an arm around my shoulders, steering me gently towards the cart. There was a neat, two-rung stepladder bolted to its side just below the door. Noah stepped up to the driver's platform and then reached out his hand.

"All right?" he said. I took his hand to steady myself and climbed into the cart. Behind the driver's seat was a wooden bench, bulked out with cushions. I settled myself in one corner. In spite of the warmth of Cally's coat, my teeth were chattering. Cally pulled herself into the cart and sat down beside me.

"You're safe now," she said. "We'll soon be home."

"Heesh, Marsia," Noah said. He jingled the reins, and I realised he must be talking to the donkey. The cart lurched and then began to roll forward, its grooved tyres crunching against the gravel.

It was now almost dark. Cally fiddled with something under the bench and four carriage lights came on. They cast a dim yellow glow that lit up the road directly in front of us but not much further. The sky overhead was strewn with stars, vast swathes of them, bright and numerous as sequins sewn into a ballgown. Catey had a dress like that from Monsoon, I thought. She was going to wear it to the prom.

Did the stars seem brighter because it was darker here, or were they different stars? The question scrabbled for a handhold on the surface of my mind and then slid off.

I closed my eyes. The air smelled fresh and damp, the way it does in the Peaks when it's been raining.

I've missed the barbecue, I thought. I imagined them all in Linsey's garden, bopping around to one of Richard Lovell's ghastly Top 40 mix tapes and getting stuck into Catey's vodka punch.

White Czar vodka, she made it from, that lethal paint-stripper knock-off they sold at the Spar.

Who cares when it's just a mixer? Catey always said.

I thought about Catey, the way she would have met me at the door, arms flung around my neck and the warm smell of her, her mother's Rive Gauche cologne and the bubbling up of laughter she could never quite contain.

*Thank God you're here, Ju. Maisie's just been sick behind the greenhouse.*

The scent of lilacs and charcoal and warm tarmac, all of them gone.

## 2

[From *Our Planet, Our History, Our Home: Elementary Studies in the geography, mythology and culture of Tristane and her Golden Satellites*]

Tristane is a big planet. Her land surface is divided more or less equally between the forested region, which has a tropical climate, and the belts, which are cool to temperate, except at the equator, where the temperatures regularly exceed those of the forests. The equatorial belt is arid and stony, swept by vicious dust storms. Nothing much grows there – just the ribbed, boulder-like succulents that are known as water towers, and the rust-coloured, semi-animate lichens that coat the cracks and undersides of the rock formations. Both the water towers and the lichens have evolved to store water.

There is a famous southern legend about a seven-person expedition that set out from Fiby hoping to reach the city-state of Galena, which lies on the boundary with the Wrssin Forest and several hundred miles due north of the equator. The explorers suffered one tragedy after another. Two of them died of heat exhaustion. The others would have died also, had it not been for the moisture and nutrients they were able to harvest from the lichens and water towers. Chalia Bestow's classic novel *The Seven*, written from the point of view of Vesrea, the expedition's horologist, includes extended meditations upon the nature of the equatorial region and its manifold dangers. The Vesrea character describes the landscape of the equatorial region as dangerously hypnotic:

*The rocks soar up. On a clear night they seem to glow, their faces and fissures ablaze, like the windows in the forests of skyscrapers that have sprung up along the harbourfronts of Arcturus, Fiby. Further out into the desert, the rock formations are so dramatic they are almost alive: an army of giants, their mouths fringed with tapering, dagger-like crystals, like the teeth of Gren-Moloch.*

At its extreme north, Tristane is icy, a grey-white wilderness of needle-like rock formations and solid permafrost. There are bottomless, water-filled crevasses, topped with a crust of ice a hundred feet thick. The southern polar regions – the land to the south of the Marillienseet – remains largely unmapped. There are numerous legends among the belt settlers as to why that is, although Tristane's early geographers mainly put it down to the practical difficulties of crossing the mountains, which act as a natural cordon for the entire area.

The twin temperate zones known as the belts lie to either side of the equatorial desert. The southern belts are slightly narrower and a great deal less fertile. The population is sparse and mostly nomadic. What towns there are retain the feel of way stations, temporary halts on the journey from the southern mountains to the northern forests.

The fashion that once existed for large-scale explorations of the southern regions has largely died out, although this seems only to have increased the public appetite for expedition memoirs, the more doomed the better.

The more doomed the better, Cally says. She showed me a book she owned, a beautifully illustrated volume called *Last Vestiges* that reprinted an ancient saga of the southern belts, set alongside textured monoprints showing the artefacts found at the abandoned base camp of the Linder Traas expedition. There hadn't been much to retrieve: some scrimshaw buttons, a pair of gutting scissors, two hunting knives, a sealskin mitten, a waterproof survey map that covered the part of the journey they'd already completed, a library copy of Shomer Narlep's *Testament*, protected inside a Ziploc wallet.

Of Linder Traas and his comrades themselves, no trace was found.

"How can that be?" I asked Cally.

She shrugged. "No one really knows what's out there," she said. "Probably they just starved, though."

*Testament* was supposed to be the true story of a Noors palaeontologist who came from beyond the mountains to settle in Fiby. She claimed there were still southern felids living in the Noors mountains, though of course no one in Fiby believed her, Cally said. Most people thought the book was a fake anyway, though that did nothing to stop it becoming a bestseller.

\* \* \*

Cally has a cousin who went to live in Davis, a small mining town in the northern belts, about halfway along the northern railroad between Galena and Twin. That's a long way out from the city, Cally said. She hasn't seen her cousin Lila since she left Gren-Noor.

"What made her go?" I asked.

"Teachers make good money in the belts. And Lila always wanted to travel."

Many months later, Cally told me the real reason Lila went north was because she was in love with Noah. "She asked me if I'd give him up," Cally said. "I felt like punching her stupid fair face, only her eyes were already puffy from where she'd been crying. I told her it was pointless her making a drama out of it, Noah and I were already cleaved, she'd have to get over it. Two weeks later she was gone." She paused. "It's so cold up there in winter, much colder than here. Some of the settlements are two days' travel from one another, even by cutter. I can't imagine what it must be like, growing up in one of those places."

Lila has a child now, apparently, a daughter of eight.

"What's her name?" I asked.

"Cathrin. Cathrin Noa."

"Is Lila married, then?"

"I suppose so. Someone she met out there, I think. Another teacher."

She was trying to sound as if these things didn't matter to her, but I could tell they did. Cally and Lila had grown up together, they were like sisters. Cally showed me a photo of the two of them together when they were children. Lila was lanky and shy-looking, with fine blond hair, like corn silk.

"So pale," Cally said. She briefly touched her fingertips to Lila's photographed face. "Her father was a Noorsman."

I wondered what it had been like for Lila, having to travel thousands of miles from where she'd been born to live in one of the block-built, slate-roofed miner's homesteads I'd seen only in photographs. Having to bring up her child there.

I wondered if Noah had known about Lila being in love with him. When I asked Cally if she had any photos of Lila as an adult she looked at me strangely.

"You should know," she said. "You helped me clear out her place."

I turned away from her, half in frustration, half in fear. These odd statements of hers still unsettled me. We'd go along for a while as normal, and I'd think she'd stopped pretending, then suddenly and out of nowhere she'd come out with another one. I couldn't get used to them, I suppose because they made me doubt everything I believed I knew – about my life and what I thought had happened in it, about who I was, even.

Cally kept insisting my memories would return but every day I'd wake up, still me, still knowing I was from Warrington, Cheshire, that Cally and Noah and Fiby didn't really exist.

**[From *Our Planet, Our History, Our Home: Elementary Studies in the geography, mythology and culture of Tristane and her Golden Satellites*]**

The people of the northern belts are mainly farmers, or miners. The belts are rich in mineral deposits of silver, copper, lumia, platinum and coal. Most belts settlements are small- to medium-sized. They are based mainly around work, although there are also theatres, reading houses and racing tracks, with regional festivals drawing crowds of many thousands, especially in summer.

Dwellings in the belts are built low to the ground and close together as extra protection against the mistrals and winter snowstorms. Over the centuries, the people of the north have striven to attain economic parity with the city dwellers, though their overall way of life remains strikingly different.

Tristane's forests are hot and wet. Around fifty percent of the forest trees are julippa, and it is the julippa's bark and resin that yield the soft, pliable material of the same name. Julippa is the most versatile natural substance on the planet. In its raw state it is similar to rubber, but it can be easily processed to form hard and soft, brittle and flexible variants of itself. Julippa is strong and extremely durable. Almost anything can be made out of it, from picnic cups to modular housing units to entire sewerage systems. Julippa processing and manufacture forms a central strand of economic activity in all the six city-states.

There are six greater city-states on Tristane: Seiolfar, Argene, Galena, Julippa, Clarimond and Fiby. As well as the city-states themselves, there are several dozen semi-autonomous satellite cities, varying in size from the vast underground metropolis of Staerbrucke, a protectorate of Clarimond, to the scattering of village-states that flank the northern shores of the Marillienseet and fall under the jurisdiction of Fiby.

The Marillienseet is the only true ocean on Tristane: a vast expanse of brackish water that covers roughly one-third of the southern hemisphere. The northern forest regions are criss-crossed by great-rivers, some of them several miles across in places, and there is also the Norraspoor, the giant inland lake that defines the landscape of southern Argene. There are many thousands of natural braes, tarns and freshwater lakes throughout the northern belts, as well as the network of artificially constructed canals known as the skein.

The oldest of the six city-states is Seiolfar, founded some fifteen thousand years ago by plainsfolk travelling westwards through the belts, a straggling line of pushcarts and water barrows and camp dogs and great-oxen. Some say that Seiolfar's founders were miners in search of new silver deposits. Others insist they were farmers, driven from their homelands by a succession of especially brutal winters and rainless summers. Most likely they were both. Seiolfar's first buildings were a cluster of wooden shacks, built around a larger central meeting house constructed from julippa beams. The meeting house was later rebuilt in stone, becoming what would eventually be called the first praesidium. By its fifth century the city was growing more rapidly, upwards and sideways and downwards, eating up hundred-mile swathes of forest in its advance.

A century after that, Marin Clair, a great-descendent of one of Seiolfar's original founders, gathered together a band of like-minded fellow citizens and headed south along the forest boundary until they came to the Norraspoor. It was here that they founded what would be the new city-state of Argene.

Argene has always seen herself as a rival to Seiolfar, both

economically and in terms of ideology. The city-state of Galena, which lies to the north-west of Seiolfar and deeper into the forest, is Argene's closest ally. In terms of her politics, Fiby is closer to Seiolfar, though geographically she lies closer to Argene.

Julippa is the largest of the city-states, a vast, overheated citadel surrounded entirely by forest. Julippa forges alliances pragmatically, although traditionally she has preferred to stand alone. Julippa, grown high and mighty through the limitless, inherited fortunes of the great plastics dynasties, has been a pioneer of advanced communications technologies.

Clarimond is similarly unaffiliated, though her isolated position, just beyond the forest's northern boundary, makes the city similar to Fiby in both climate and outlook. Clarimond was the site of the first interplanetary communications centre at Mel-Niki. Even though all known space travel between Tristane and her sister planet Dea ended several centuries ago, Clarimond, like Julippa, still prides herself on her technological accomplishments.

Clarimond's southern railway station, whose colonnades are made entirely from toughened lead crystal, is widely celebrated as one of the artistic and architectural wonders of the world. Cutters entering the Grand Terminus make their final approach over the Fennc Bridge, a granite and titanium structure which is a uniquely grandiose feat of civil engineering in itself. The bridge's support plinths, hand-carved with more than ten thousand sigils from the Antrobus Cantor, stand at more than two hundred metres in height, and are still judged by certain scientists at the Lyceum to be a logistical impossibility.

## 3

Cally and Noah live in Gren-Noor, which is a suburb of Fiby, five or six miles outside the city wall. Their home is a single-storey timber-frame casa with a stable yard and half an acre of vegetable patch. Noah, who is an algebraist, works mainly from home. Cally divides her time between Gren-Noor and the studio she rents in Tarq, one of the more affordable central districts of Fiby proper. Accommodation in Tarq is cheap because of the factories. A lot of artists are based there.

"It's good for Noah and me to spend time apart," Cally said. "We're so close it's too much, sometimes. We can't hear ourselves think."

In four out of the six city-states, sexual relationships between siblings are legal, even if they are frowned upon. When I explained how things are here, she stared at me hard, the way she did when she was trying to work out if I was being serious or not. When she realised I meant what I said she shook her head.

"That's inhuman," she said. "Why would you invent something like that? What would be the point in such a law?"

I mumbled something about genetics, and she shook her

head again. "Who said anything about children? Anyway, that's what gene therapy is for."

She told me it was accepted in Fiby that brother-sister marriages would occasionally produce children, that children might be desired even, but that any such couple who did produce offspring would be looked down upon socially unless the foetus was fertilized in vitro and genetically adjusted.

Cally and Noah never wanted children. It wasn't about sex either, Cally said, not any more, not for a long time. Mostly it was about memories. She and Noah had known from puberty that they would make their connubial promises each to the other.

"Our memories are genetically bonded," she said. "That's something you never have with an outsider. I wouldn't feel right with anyone else. Not for living together."

I understood what she meant, some of it, anyway. I remembered a conversation I'd had with Lucy about her cousin Jaina who lived in Kolkata. Jaina had been promised in marriage since the age of twelve. Her fiancé was the son of a friend of her parents, a paediatrician who had done part of his training alongside Lucy's mother.

"Jaina could have said no, if she wanted," Lucy explained. "But she's met this man several times now and says she likes him. They write to each other all the time when he's in London. I think it's romantic."

I thought it was weird, like choosing a husband from a Littlewoods catalogue. But the more I thought about it the more I wondered if it was any more peculiar than promising to spend the rest of your life with someone you happened to meet on holiday or at the school disco. A lot less, probably. At least Jaina and this doctor guy would know from the start they had things in common, family connections, support from both sets of parents. What did Catey have in common with Richard Lovell, apart from the hots for him?

Remember when we were small, Selena, the worlds we made? I was happy then, at home in the world in a way I've never been since. Perhaps it was my dis-ease with the world that lost me my place in it.

I slept so soundly that when I woke it was at least a minute before I began to regain my memories of the day before. I was lying on a pallet bed, covered with a woollen blanket in a narrow, box-like room with plank walls and high ceiling beams. The room smelled pleasantly of wood resin. I could see my clothes – the jeans I'd been wearing, the grey T-shirt and grass-stained trainers – folded and placed neatly together on a chair in one corner. There was a wooden chest, a high shelf with what looked like a clock on it, only the numbers seemed different somehow.

I wrapped the blanket around my shoulders, then stood up and went to the window. It was daylight outside, though barely. The mist-blurred outlines of nearby buildings, the bare expanses of dirt lots beyond. A rutted yard and pockmarked road, low-lying, scruffy-looking scrub vegetation. From somewhere further away a low booming, followed by a higher, keening sound. A klaxon of some kind, or an alarm? Perhaps a factory whistle?

A sense of displacement crept over me, of being utterly and completely lost in a way that surpassed any normal understanding of the word. Vast and vertiginous, for a number of seconds it consumed me utterly, and I felt I would faint from it. I didn't, though. I closed my eyes. When I opened them again a moment later it was all still there.

The idea that there was still a present day, a July 17th 1994, a Sunday morning on which Mum and Dad were worrying their brains out and calling the police – these things seemed so far outside the bounds of possibility suddenly that it was not simply as if they could not be happening, but rather as if they *never could have happened*, as if the world in which they might have happened had been a fabrication, nothing but a conjuring trick. Folded paper and playing cards, a swiftly palmed coin.

What seemed most real to me in those moments? *You*, Selena. However far away you were in space or in time or in some other dimension I had no idea of, I knew you were out there somewhere. For a second, I could almost feel us touching and that meant everything. It meant that in spite of the impossible thing that was happening I was able to retain a sense of who I was.

Let's see how we go, I thought. I rubbed the weave of the blanket gently between my fingers. Rough, coarse fibres, rust-coloured. Someone made this, I thought. Someone spun the fleece, carded the wool, wove the cloth. A real thing that exists, even here. Simple facts, but of the kind that can sometimes help to salvage your sanity.

In describing the blanket, I was describing a world I could recognise, a world I could live in.

Warm blanket, red wool.

Let's see where this leads, this ball of yarn.

I put on my clothes, then lay back down on the bed with the blanket over me. I watched the day grow brighter against the wall.

Cally said: "You do know where you are?"

I shook my head. "No," I told her.

"You're speaking, anyway." She sounded relieved. She gave me breakfast, something like porridge. I wolfed it down. I realised I hadn't eaten since lunchtime the day before. What did we have? Tomato soup or pasta salad? I couldn't remember, and I felt like I needed to remember, isn't that strange? I thought about it until there were tears on my cheeks, but it still wouldn't come.

"Do you remember where you're from?" Cally said.

"Lymm. It's a village near Warrington, in Cheshire. That's where my parents live, anyway." I knew it was a stupid answer, or at least not the answer Cally was looking for. I don't know how I knew that, but I did. Cally fell silent. She was sitting beside me at the table. The table was wooden, with metal legs. The bowl containing my porridge was made of terracotta.

"Warrington? Is that somewhere in Noorland? Beyond the mountains?" She hesitated. She had no idea what I was talking about, I could tell, yet she seemed not to want to come out and say so.

Because she thought I was crazy, probably. That's the rule with crazy people, isn't it, don't get them worked up.

"The Pennines, you mean? They're not that high though. Not like the Himalayas."

"The Himalayas?"

"You know, Mount Everest."

"I have never heard of such a mountain." Cally was frowning. "We are in Gren-Noor, in Fiby, capital of the southern provinces. The city's hieroglyph is a harp in silver. This is where you were born."

I shook my head again, more slowly. I felt like an idiot. I also felt frightened. This woman seemed convinced she knew me, yet she said nothing of our one and only meeting, in Manchester, outside Allison's flat.

Something made me not want to mention it either, in case she denied it had even happened. "Are we in Sweden?" I said instead. "Or Denmark? It feels very cold here."

"I don't know these places." She pressed her hands together, entwining her fingers, and then stood up. "Let me get the atlas and you can show me." She left the room.

A few moments later she returned with a book, a bundle of stitched-together papers really, parchment-like and dishevelled-looking, like those notebooks made from handcrafted paper you can buy in Paperchase. Cally moved aside the porridge bowls and placed the book on the table between us. She opened it near the front.

"This is Tristane," she said. She swept her hand across

the open pages. I could see two images, twin circles, bright with colour, green and grey and sand. The images looked hand-tinted, like pages from *The Book of Kells*.

Each circle represented half of a world, I realised. I could make out land masses, forests, the jagged edge of a coastline. Which coast, though, which land masses? Nothing about the drawings made any sense.

"It's beautiful," I said.

"Here is Fiby," Cally said. She pointed to a greyish blotch, irregular in shape, like a patch of mildew on a damp cellar wall, in the bottom left-hand quadrant of one of the circles. I looked more closely and saw the place name printed across it – F.I.B.Y. – in darker grey capitals. The blotch of Fiby rubbed up against a larger blotch, blue instead of grey and clearly an ocean, or perhaps a large lake. There was a strange word printed across it – *Marillienseet* – and a tiny delicate engraving of a fish.

There were other blotches on both of the circles, one of them red as the red spot of Jupiter, the others grey, or greyish-green, like the blotch of Fiby. A planet, circled by bands of russet and ochre and sage, like a china marble. Which planet, though? I remembered the geography module I'd studied for GCSE, the maps and diagrams showing continental drift and volcanic activity and the ancient, gigantic continent of Pangaea. Could this be Earth, but at a different time? The idea made sense in a way, but not completely. There were no cities in Pangaea, no people. Pangaea was just glaciers and mountains, covered in dense Carboniferous forest and surrounded by ocean.

"Is Tristane the name of a continent?" I said to Cally.

"Continent? Continent is a word for placidity, plain sailing. Tristane is the name of our planet, of course." She seemed to hesitate, then reached out to take my hands in both of hers.

"It is all right, Julie. Don't try to force it. Everything will come back to you."

"I don't understand," I said.

"I know you don't, but don't worry. You've been through a lot. These things take time. The only thing that matters is that you are safe."

I nodded. The feeling of vertigo, of hideous displacement, had returned. None of this should be happening, and yet it was. I was alive, though. I was still breathing, I could still think.

Nuna, Rodinia, Panottia, Pangaea. The last four supercontinents. Those first weeks in Fiby were terrible, really, in spite of Noah's forbearance and Cally's kindness. Once the truth of what had happened to me began to seep through, a rift seemed to open in my mind, a rift between the universe I appeared to be living in and the one I understood. I found that running through the names of Earth's ancient supercontinents, repeating them like a mantra, like the lines of a poem, would sometimes help me to fall asleep at night. Laurasia, Gondwana, Laurentia, Siberia, Baltica: names that were code for a past as deeply lost as I now was myself. Curled in the red woollen blanket, I would try to recall every detail I could about those geography lessons

– not just the names of the supercontinents, fracturing and dividing like cosmic amoebas through the passage of aeons, but the names of my classmates too: Phoebe Evans and Nuria Ahmed, Sonny Soames and Joel McPherson, Tiger MacFadyen and Honey Pugh – Honey Pugh with her tiny round glasses and diamond nose stud, her arm curved possessively around her exercise book, the entire left-hand page covered not with the names of the supercontinents and their geological lifespans but with an intricate cartoon: our teacher Clarence Denbeigh to the absolute life, his shock of silver hair drawn to look like a lion's mane, 'Clarence the Cross-Eyed Lion' printed in exquisite Gothic capitals on a placard around his neck.

Honey Pugh, and her onyx propelling pencil. Clarence Denbeigh, who had a false leg and no left hand because of thalidomide. His voice though was a marvel: soft yet at the same time booming, the voice of an actor on the stage at Stratford-upon-Avon. Each time he opened his mouth to tell you about grain yields in the Ukrainian bread basket you found yourself imagining him reciting *Hamlet* or *Macbeth*.

Sunlight streaking across the linoleum floor and bouncing off the gold trim of Honey Pugh's propelling pencil. The wavery line of white dust beneath the blackboard. The traffic cone on top of the stationery cupboard, confiscated from one of the Brier brothers two terms earlier and now a part of the furniture.

Clarence Denbeigh, drawing Pangaea on the blackboard with a stick of white chalk. Etching in the fault lines, showing us how and where the rifts will develop.

In the classroom, it is always summer. If I think about it hard enough, I can be there again, my head swimming with sunlight and boredom, resentment and the desire to escape.

Nuna.

Laurasia.

Panottia.

Pangaea.

Marvellous, like the names of Greek goddesses. Fierce clods of cake-coloured earth in a steel-grey sea.


For a while, I was frightened to go outside unless Cally was with me. I was afraid people would see me and *realise*, that they would point and yell in unearthly voices, like Donald Sutherland at the end of *Invasion of the Body Snatchers*, unmasking me as an alien, running through the streets in droves as they hunted me down.

When I eventually explained these fears to Cally, she just laughed.

Gradually I became used to the homestead, and the stable yard, the lots and packed-dirt roads immediately surrounding it. I spent most of the time in the casa, reading books, the histories especially, and Cally's atlas, her holographic *Gazetteer of the City of Fiby*, which came in its own carrying case, marbled julippa with silver clasps, the moving images updated every day from some central database. I learned by heart the names of the districts: Gren-Noor, Gren-Seet, Sisqueena, Murleet, Tarq, Justina, All-Noor, Preet, Callanoor, Suut-Lina, Jon-Tarq, Semmeq. Also the larger fishing ports of Summa, Noorq, Purl and Marilly, the disorganised sprawl of satellite towns along the eastern seaboard, settlements that had sprung up as trading outposts or way stations between one larger settlement and another and had later become permanent, micro-economies founded on scrimshaw or pearl fishing or wrack harvesting and housing those too poor or too rich or too disaffected to pay residency taxes or employment licence to the city proper.

These were the places that haunted my dreams. I told myself that if anything went wrong with Cally and Noah – if they grew tired of me or threw me out, or if they too turned out somehow not to exist – then I could find my way to one of these frontier communities and at least survive, waiting tables in one of the bars, or sweeping the floors in a factory or studio. I could get by. I soon learned that in the port towns you didn't need identity papers, that all you had to do was say you were Noors and your word would be accepted.

The Noors were said to live beyond the mountains. Occasionally small clans or even lone individuals crossed into Fiby and remained there. They tended to keep themselves to themselves, took unassuming jobs, spoke little and asked few questions.

Cally had a book about a Noors poet named Olla Wurock. Wurock had lived in the port town of Serp for twenty years, working in the canteen of one of the open-cast silver mines. She wrote poems and stories about her journey to Fiby and about her life in the port, mixed in with Noors myths and legends, anecdotes about her family and the close friend she'd been forced to leave behind. Eventually, Olla

Wurock became famous, and even consented to interviews occasionally, though she never gave up her job at the canteen.

Her poems started out very simple, but became increasingly complicated and obscure, filled with strange imagery and threaded through with Noors words and phrases that I had to look up in the glossary at the back of the book.

I recognised something in them, though. Something of my own desire to escape from one life and into another, the horrible aching need to make something happen.

## 4

I was so furious at Mum for her affair. What got to me most was who she'd had it with, that odious Bill guy, that sales rep. I know if I asked her straight out she'd probably tell me she didn't choose Bill, it was just that Bill happened to be available and she knew he fancied her. Seducing Bill was easy and – because she didn't actually give a stuff about him – having a fling with Bill didn't pose any risk. Not much of a risk, anyway. She knew Dad wasn't vindictive.

Having an affair with someone she cared about would have opened up the possibility of being hurt – a possibility she would have found unacceptable.

You don't know this, Selena, but once when Mum was at work and not long after the whole Bill thing came out in the open, I went through that cupboard in her office, the one where she kept all those photos and diaries from before we were born, from before Dad, even. I told myself I was just checking to make sure she wasn't seeing Bill still, but that wasn't it, or not the whole of it, anyway. The truth was I wanted to find out who the hell Mum really was.

I don't think I've ever had a proper conversation with Mum, not once. She was so competent a mother in all the practical ways, and I suppose that's what you mainly notice when you're small: that your school uniform is washed and folded and your favourite flavour of crisps is in your lunchbox.

When you're a kid you live so much in your own world you barely think of adults as having lives, even. When I realised that Mum lived mostly behind a screen – a screen of efficiency and reasonableness designed to hide every trace of her real personality – it was like playing the alien game all over again.

Who was the alien, though? Her, or me?

Mum had stuff in that cupboard not just from before she was married but from when she was still at school. Copies of her school magazine, a souvenir mug from Blackpool Tower, an empty perfume bottle (Worth's *Je Reviens*), a collection of old postcards, all of castles. Some of the postcards had writing on: sloping copperplate script, remarks about the weather in Scotland or the difficulties of obtaining Marmite in Munich. One of the school magazines featured an essay by Mum, in which she talked about searching for old postcards in junk shops in Scarborough and York.

*It is as if I travel back in time, just for a moment*, she wrote. *Holding the postcard in my hand, I can share a fraction of a life that isn't mine.*

The essay – 'Paper Treasures' by Margery Hillson – revealed to me a girl whose imagination was the biggest part of her.

What happened?

Between the ages of sixteen and twenty-one she kept a regular diary. I read some of it, then stopped. Her words, her ideas, the things she wrote about reminded me so much of myself I felt terrified suddenly, scared I would turn into her, with her reasonable husband, her reasonable job at the local medical centre, her two mostly reasonable kids with their blasted lunch boxes (wholemeal bread, not white, and always a Granny Smith apple and a Penguin biscuit).

If those things had happened to Margery Hillson they could happen to me.

I searched for evidence of Bill, not because I cared but because it felt more legitimate. Mum had shagged Bill, after all – didn't I have a right to know if that was still going on? There was nothing – nothing I could find, anyway – and I can't say I was surprised. Mum ended up more bored with Bill than she was with Dad. What I did find was a whole stack of letters from someone named Tony. Like the diaries, they were embarrassing to read. Not because they were full of sex or filthy language or anything like that, but because they seemed so full of love. Not the obsessive lust any randy teenager might feel for their first sexual partner, but love for Mum, for Margery Hillson, for the girl who collected antique postcards and kept a diary and hoarded old perfume bottles.

Tony wrote from Macclesfield where he lived and went to college, and then from a town called Champaign, Illinois, where he was doing some kind of advanced summer course in computer science. He talked a lot about how much space there was in America. *It makes me feel I could achieve anything*, he wrote.

Reading Tony's letters gave me the oddest feeling. It was like watching a film, the kind you know is going to end badly but you keep watching anyway, because you can't not. You're drunk on sadness and in any case, the sadness is OK because it's not happening to you.

And it turned out to be exactly like that because the letters just stopped. The final one was dated just over a year before Mum and Dad got married.

There were no clues in the letter about what might have happened. I wondered if maybe he'd died, this Tony, had a car crash or something. Or perhaps he'd met someone else, out there in Champaign, Illinois: a fighter pilot or a coffee waitress or a cowhand, *someone*. I was desperate to know, desperate in the way you get with soap operas, when there's a good storyline brewing.

I could hardly ask Mum though, could I?

I couldn't confide in you, either. You were only fourteen.

I didn't know what I wanted, and that was the problem. I didn't have a clue.

You remember Perdita and Rhiannon James? Catey used to call them the piano twins. They were allowed to leave school early on Wednesdays because of their special lesson at Chetham's and they always, *always* came joint first in the summer essay competition and usually the maths marathon as well. Lucy was kind of friends with Perdita. She told me once – Lucy, I mean – that the twins had to sit down and do their homework literally the moment they finished supper, and that if either of them scored less than eighty percent in an exam they were both grounded for a week. Not that it made much difference – they were more or less grounded anyway because of all the extra homework and piano lessons.

I thought it sounded like being in prison. I remember saying to Catey that I would have run away from home if it had been me. What I didn't tell Catey was that at the same time I envied them. I envied them their godawful pushy parents and their book allowance and their residential summer schools. I don't mean because of the money that was being spent on them. I envied the feeling you always had when you were around them, that Rhiannon and Perdita would grow up to be something, that they had life sorted.

It was the same with Lucy, too. Lucy didn't have piano lessons but she knew from the age of ten that she wanted to be a doctor, like her mother. How she knew was a mystery, but she did. She felt the doctor-force within her, I suppose.

I think of Olla Wurock, scrubbing down the tables in the works canteen, then going home to her poky apartment above the net lofts and writing a poem about ice on puddles or a flower seller in the market in Serp.

You wouldn't mind scrubbing tables, would you, if you knew that later on that evening you were going to write a poem?


When I first came to Fiby I used to think about those letters of Mum's all the time. I kept wondering what had happened to Tony, how different Mum's life might have been if they hadn't split up. I wanted desperately to talk to her about it, even though I knew full well that it would never be possible.

Talking to Mum about Tony would mean admitting I'd broken into her cupboard, that I'd searched through her things. That wasn't the only reason, though.

I've forgotten that Bill guy's surname, isn't that weird?

The south side of Fiby is defined by her proximity to the ocean. On clear days you can smell it: a sharp and tangy aroma that is vaguely reminiscent of ginseng. When the weather is overcast, which is most of the time, the atmosphere clings, dampening your hair, leaving salty deposits on your skin and clothes. Whereas the other five great city-states of Tristane have expanded outwards in concentric circles, Fiby has grown sideways and backwards, flowing away from the ocean and into the belts. The northernmost districts, a hundred miles or more from the waterside hotels of Gren-Seq, from the wharves and warehouses, the walkways and piers and cafés of the Seide Arrondy, are so different from them in character it is almost as if they are part of another city.

The cobbled lanes and grand piazzas of the Seide Arrondy eventually extinguish themselves in the factory yards and chimneys and looming sandstone edifices of the Tarq district. Cally's studio is in one of the refurbished whale-meat processing plants close to the central arm of the main tramlink. The whole of the ground floor area has been given over to the City Library of Maritime History. Cally originally found the studio through a friend, Alix, who worked as a copier in the library's archive.

Cally is an urban cartographer. She makes maps of

derelict buildings and districts within the city's enclave and especially under it. The city-states are so vast, it is easier if you imagine them as small countries: thousands of acres of buildings and parkland, biodomes and industrial complexes and sub-dorms and cultivation arcs, tram and sub-tram networks and civil protectorates that take days to cross. If cities on Earth are like giant anthills, the city-states of Tristane are termite mounds of unimaginable proportions.

Change sweeps through them in waves, favouring one area with sudden, inexplicable popularity while sweeping another into financial chaos, planning stalemate, political upheaval, social disfavour or cultural disdain. As new neighbourhoods spring up, older districts may be abandoned entirely, only to be reclaimed a decade later as the height of bohemian chic, or simply as somewhere you can rent an apartment for less than half of what you'd pay in an adjoining quartier.

The abandoned places can be dangerous, but they are also fascinating. Dereliction brings an aura of mystery along with the misery, Cally says. She once suggested she made her living from chasing ghosts.

Freak weather events are not uncommon in Fiby. A century ago, an underground river overflowed its channel, flooding a large part of the eastern subterranean district of Pershore. Thousands died. Cally was commissioned to map the Noor-set bazaar and its adjoining courthouse, both completely submerged. It was a lucrative contract, Cally said, because it was dangerous, mainly – no one knew exactly what was down there. She trained with a pearl diver from Marilly, who taught her how to use the breathing equipment, but she still found the job onerous.

"I felt panicky the whole time, even with an air cylinder," she said. "It's so dark." She shuddered. She told me that most of the bodies were still down there, because the praesidium had decided it was too expensive to recover them. An Atlantis of hollow-eyed skeletons, still trapped in their homes.

Cally's job involves miles of walking, every day. Most cartographers use distance-scanning equipment these days, she says, but she prefers to go on foot, taking photographs and collating measurements, listing street signs and advertising hoardings and the ancient place markers put down in the early centuries of the city's foundation. Later, in her studio, she uses urban planning software to transform the data she has collated into accurate maps. These maps can then be licensed to publishing companies, to the praesidium's central intelligence archive, to the city constabulary, to commercial investors, whoever is interested.

Cally likes to call herself a scavenger, a waste merchant, collecting together the parts of the city that have been forgotten. She said she knew where to look for me that last time because she'd been telling me about a contract she'd landed, to collect data on Urfe Station, which is only accessible on foot now and miles from anywhere. She reminded me I'd always been fascinated by the old radio transmission headquarters, by what had gone on there, why the decision had been taken to shut it down.

"You were obsessed with that place," Cally said. "I mean, completely." She frowned. "You should never have tried to get there on your own, though. You know no one goes near the lake, not in winter. You could have frozen to death out there."

[From *Our Planet, Our History, Our Home: Elementary Studies in the geography, mythology and culture of Tristane and her Golden Satellites*]

Of the four planets in the Suur System capable of supporting life, only Tristane and Dea are known to be inhabited. Dea is much smaller than Tristane. The planet began to be colonised shortly after the founding of the third praesidium. For many centuries, trade and cultural links between Tristane and Dea were strong and mutually beneficial, with a regular shuttle service between the two planets as well as widely accessible public radio and later digital communications networks. Following the establishment of the sixth praesidium and in the wake of the armed conflict between Argene and Julippa, all private and commercial navigation between Tristane and Dea was suspended. The technology that enabled it became corrupted, and was eventually lost.

"They said it was the war that stopped the shuttle flights," Cally explained. "There was a fuel shortage. Prices went sky high and never came down again. That's what they taught us in school anyway. The reasons seemed stupid to me. I've never been able to understand why people aren't more curious about it."

Urfe Station itself continued to function for another

hundred years. Although messages could be and were still passed between the two planets, bumping their way across the sky on the backs of radio waves like children speeding down a snowy hillside on a toboggan, the station's function and importance was gradually eroded. What had once been a hub of interplanetary communications eventually became a one-way broadcasting studio for light entertainment programmes, recorded concerts and the occasional radio play.

By the time Urfe Station closed for good, even the entertainment broadcasts had mostly ceased.

"It was as if they'd stopped listening," Cally said. "Don't you think that's weird?"

"Not if there was no one there to listen," I said.

Cally frowned. "That's what you said before," she said. "I don't know what you mean, though. How could all those people just disappear?"

"I don't remember," I said. How could I remember something I'd never said?

There was something, though. A shard of terror, lodged in my mind, a splinter of knowing.

Like a white van.

Like a black hole.

Things I didn't want to think about, or even acknowledge.

If you stand outside in the darkness and look up at the sky, Dea is barely visible. She is closer to the sun than Tristane, but she is still far away. You need a telescope to see her in any detail. Cally showed me some old nitrate prints of the Vester

Wall on Dea, and the great waterfall at Jerrefus. The Vester Wall is a natural rock formation that extends across the planet's surface for two thousand miles. Scientific textbooks claim that Dea is a more dynamic planet than Tristane, which means that volcanic activity on Dea during her prehistoric era was more violent and caused more far-reaching changes, both to the planet's atmosphere and to her surface terrain.

Dea's landscape is more diverse and more extreme as a result.

"It's supposed to be beautiful there," Cally said. "The mountains especially."

She said something about a new government initiative, a lobby group that had been set up with the aim of re-initiating contact and eventually travel links with Dea, but it's not something anyone ever talks about.

Not openly, anyway.

It's as if everyone knows, deep down, that there's something to hide.

What if there are things I don't want to remember? Not what Cally says – the events at Sere-Phraquet, whatever they were – but something to do with my old obsession, Urfe Station?

Why else would I have tried to return there?

When I asked Cally what I did before, who I was before I became ill, she laughed and said I was as lazy and full of dreams as any other seventeen-year-old.

"You were about to start college," she said. "You were going to study languages."

I was about to ask her what happened to Dad, why I wasn't living at home any more, but suddenly I realised I was afraid to. I didn't want to hear what she might tell me.

The final shuttle transport from Dea returned to Tristane with only half of her crew. Among those that did return was a senior aeronautics technician named Linus Quinn. In Quinn's luggage were his journals: factual accounts of his travels, mostly, as well as a long, fragmented memoir of his friendship with a naturalist named Eduard Farsett and his wife Elina. Quinn's account contained numerous references to a deadly parasitic isopod he called the creef. Quinn insisted the creatures described in his journals were real, although when people asked him if he had proof he was unable to provide any.

No one believed Linus Quinn, in any case. He was a difficult man, and solitary. He suffered from mood swings and a form of depression that made him prone to hallucinations. He claimed his ability as a technician, which by all accounts was considerable, was the by-product of a psychic affinity with inanimate objects.

Now that Quinn could no longer travel into space, he took off for the mountains. He left his journals with his sister Jianne, who had suggested Quinn might raise some funds by having them published. She took them to one of the more independently minded publishing houses attached to the Greater University of Galena, who agreed they were of interest, although they were careful to stress that it was highly unlikely that Quinn or his sister stood to make much money from them.

Chance proved otherwise. A critic from one of the more popular tabloids got hold of an advance copy, referring to it in his review as a novel. "Quinn's desperate, terrifying narrative will leave no heart unmoved," he enthused. The publisher's small print run soon sold out, and after a short interval the book was repackaged as fiction and became a bestseller. *The Mind-Robbers of Pakwa* was thought of as a minor classic for a while, although today it languishes in obscurity, of interest mainly to those scholars who have chosen to make Deani literature their speciality.

I was six when Urfe Station was decommissioned, although the main transmitter wasn't shut down for good until some years later. As a child, I barely knew the place existed, but later, after I read Quinn's journals, it became an obsession. Cally told me that it would be a challenge even to get close to it, but the difficulties only made me more determined.

Urfe Station had not been occupied since the transmitter was dismantled. It was just an empty building, and officially derelict. As far as Cally knew from her contacts in the cartographers' union, the site was unguarded. Guards weren't the problem, though. The station perimeter lay some fifty kilos beyond the city boundary, the final section of the route a lengthy hike over rough terrain. It was not difficult to imagine getting stranded, or injured. You could break a leg shinning over a fence, for example, or climbing in through a window. If that happened then no one would find you. It would be a death sentence.

Do you remember the time we went to Cannock Chase, Selena? You would have been six, I think, or maybe five, so perhaps you don't. What people mostly think about when you say Cannock Chase are the murders that happened there in the 1960s. Dad took us there to show us the ruins. I remember we walked for what seemed like ages, then suddenly there they were – the ruins, I mean – a massive chunk of house sticking up from the ground. I remember thinking at the time that it looked as if a giant had torn the place apart with his bare hands, then dumped the pieces anyhow, like sections of a ripped-up cereal box.

The section I remember seeing was a corner piece, three storeys high, tall windows like empty eye sockets. It was covered in ivy, with young saplings growing inside the walls, the kind of landmark you'd think would be visible from miles off, only it hadn't been, not the way Dad brought us, it seemed to come out of nowhere.

Dad told us the house had once belonged to an earl.

"They knocked it down after World War One," he said. "This is all that's left."

We played around in the leaves, digging for treasure. I was obsessed with finding treasure, with the idea of uncovering things, things that had once been secret, I suppose. I remember I found some shards of pottery, a green cup handle and the edge of a plate, cream-coloured with an ear of corn painted on it, dark blue. I remember that piece of china so clearly it gives me goose bumps just thinking about it. When I started to look up information about Cannock Chase the other day I was half convinced I would find the entire memory had been a fabrication, that there never had been a house there and us playing in the ruins and the pieces of pottery were all in my mind.

The house was real, though, Selena. It was called Beaudesert, and was once the ancestral home of the Marquis of Anglesey. As I read about the break-up of the estate, the sale and eventual demolition of the house itself, I could feel my heart thumping in a kind of ecstasy. This memory at least was real. It had not betrayed me.

Beaudesert was supposed to have been levelled, destroyed completely. The only reason the ruins remained was that the company in charge of the demolition went bust before the work was finished.

When I asked Cally if she'd gone ahead with the contract to survey Urfe Station, she told me she had. "The money was too good to pass up," she said. "Because of the weather conditions, mainly. I had to camp there overnight. Bloody freezing." She shivered. "I wouldn't fancy going out there again, I tell you."

"What did you find?" I asked. I was trying to sound casual, as if I didn't really care now, either way. "Anything?"

"Letters, mostly," Cally said. "There were thousands of them."

Not letters with envelopes and stamps, but voice messages sent from Dea by radio or satellite, transcribed by the station's wireless operators, filed away in Ziploc folders and then just left. Cally said she found a whole storage room stuffed with these folders at Urfe Station, with messages dating back as long as ten years before the facility was finally closed.

"Why did nobody pass them on?" I asked her. "Don't you think that's strange?"

Cally shook her head. What she meant was that she didn't know. She told me about the half dozen or so pirate radio stations that used to broadcast to Dea during the final years the transmitter was in operation, piggybacking off the main signal at Urfe and beaming out music, chat shows, private telephone calls, whatever people felt like sending.

"They weren't illegal exactly," Cally said. "It was more like no one cared."

Once the main transmitter shut down, the pirate stations perished – their technology wasn't advanced enough for them to continue.

"Can you imagine how it felt for people on Dea, being cut off like that?" Cally said quietly. "The suddenness of it."

Like being cast adrift, I thought but didn't say. *Alienated.*

There was a friend of Noah's, Errol Maas, who used to run one of the old pirate radio stations from the back room of a scrimshaw cooperative in Purl. Maas's great-great grandfather had been born on Dea, Cally said, and Noah seemed to think he still had relatives there. Errol Maas had left the city some years ago, but Noah had an address for him, in the gold-mining town of Red Cloak, which lay some five hundred kilos to the east of Seiolfar beyond the city wall.

"I've often thought I'd like to speak to him," Cally said. "I'd like to ask him what happened, why he thinks they shut down the transmitter. He was there right up to the end. He must know something."

"What do you think happened?" I asked.

Cally was quiet for a long time. Her eyes seemed sad, or full of doubt, the emotions visible upon her face like small, swift eddies in a pool of water. "You know what Noah believes?" she said in the end. "He thinks something went wrong on Dea, something the praesidium doesn't want anyone to know about. That's why they stopped the transports, as a kind of quarantine. Then they shut down the radio station as well, so no one would find out. I'm not saying I think he's right," she said. "But I read some of those messages. They were awful, Julie. Those people knew they'd been abandoned. They were saying goodbye, mostly."

## 5

Soon after I arrived in Coventry, I started working behind the counter at Southam's, a chemist's just ten minutes down the road from the bedsit I was renting on Coundon Road. Six months later I landed a job as a doctor's receptionist. Dr Kapur kept on at me to go back to college, to do an evening class at least, but every time she tried talking to me about it seriously I changed the subject. I felt nervous of meeting people – of being around other people, even. I was afraid they'd realise I was different, that they'd mark me out as a freak, but that wasn't the only reason. The world should have felt familiar to me, but it didn't. I felt overwhelmed, every day, by the strangeness of everything. I was convinced that everyone already knew I was an alien, that they were only waiting for me to fuck up so they'd have definite proof.

Things weren't so bad when I was at work, because I had something concrete to do, a set of rules and procedures that gave each day a definite shape. Without rules, I felt naked. As a kind of test for myself, I began taking driving lessons. The lessons gave me something to do outside of work, but I still felt safe – safe, because the driving instructor would never need to know anything about me aside from my name and how well I was able to follow the rules and procedures I was paying him to teach me.

I passed my test first time. I felt pleased, but also disappointed. Passing the test meant the lessons were over, that I would have to look for something else to do in the evenings on Tuesdays and Thursdays. The week seemed empty suddenly, as if someone had died.

I bought a car, an ancient Ford Anglia. It had been well looked after, and still functioned smoothly. It came fully serviced. For a while, the Anglia was the only friend I felt I could trust. The car gave me freedom, even if that freedom consisted mainly of driving out of the city and into the flattish Midlands landscape, a landscape whose most outstanding feature is its lack of drama.

I liked to walk by the Coventry Canal. I wondered what it might be like to live on one of the narrowboats, their greenish, gleaming exteriors like the tidily folded wing-cases of large beetles, but felt held back by my lack of expertise. Who would help me to fix the engine if something went wrong?

Instead, there was my room above the bookies, Ladbrokes, its windows riotous with plunging green horses and featureless riders. The room was furnished with a fold-down bed and a fridge, a compact Baby Belling cooker and grill. I liked the room because it felt like mine, but still I was always nervous as I walked back from work, wondering if today would be the day I returned to find Dad standing there, waiting for me outside the betting shop. He would insist on bringing me home, and I could not come home. The thought of being back in Lymm terrified me more than the idea of being snatched back to Fiby.

You probably won't understand that. It's hard to explain.

There was someone, for a while. Her name was Lisa. I met her early on, while I was still working in the chemist's. She came in to buy a support bandage for her ankle. She was limping, favouring her left foot, and I asked her if she thought she should see a doctor. I don't know why I spoke to her. I wouldn't have done normally, I would have sold her the bandage she asked for then let her leave.

I think it was maybe because she reminded me of Cally's cousin Lila. I'd only seen Lila in a photograph, but I could still see that Lisa was like her: the fine fair hair, the slightly convex forehead, like the back of a spoon, the preoccupied expression, as if she were focussed on something in the far distance, or inside her head.

"Don't worry, it's nothing," she said. "It's an old injury. It flares up sometimes, that's all. I probably just need a new pair of trainers."

She spoke in an offhand manner, as if she'd known me for ages and didn't feel like finding the time to explain something she assumed I already knew. She added that she went running every morning. Her wake-up call, she said.

"Where do you run?" I asked.

She named a nearby park. "Perhaps I've seen you there," she said. "I'm sure I recognise you."

I laughed. "I don't think so," I said. "I've never been into jogging. I doubt I'd make it to the end of the street."

"Oh." Her voice dipped, disappointed, and then immediately brightened again. "You should give it a go. You might find you enjoy it."

"Maybe," I said. I rang up her purchase. She paid with a five-pound note. After she left I did something weird: I swapped her five pounds for one from my purse, so I had her note and mine was in the till. I was careful no one saw me make the switch. I didn't want anyone to think I was stealing money. I wanted that note, though – something she'd touched, something we'd touched together. I didn't even know her name at that point.

The next day during my lunch break I visited a sports shop in the nearby shopping precinct and bought myself a tracksuit and a pair of trainers. I felt as if everyone was looking at me – those sports places always make you feel like an idiot, don't you find? – but I felt light-headed with triumph when I came out. One small battle won, though it was another three days before I plucked up the courage to put on the tracksuit and go to the park.

I didn't see Lisa. There were plenty of other people, though – dog-walkers, joggers – and I quickly realised there was no need for me to worry about looking conspicuous. Lisa had said she went running every morning, but she hadn't mentioned what time. There was a chance she wasn't running at all at the moment, because of her ankle. I managed one slow lap of the perimeter and then I went home. I ought to have felt depressed, but I felt elated, just to have done something different, something I would never have thought of trying on my own. I went the next day and then the next, enjoying the sensation of having a purpose. It was the same as with the driving lessons, I suppose.

On the fifth day I caught sight of Lisa, running towards me along the diagonal stripe of asphalt that ran through the main part of the park, away from the football pitch and the three tennis courts you had to put your name on a list for if you wanted to use them. It was a shock to finally see her again, I think because I'd more or less convinced myself I never would. I geared myself up to run right past her, prepared to pretend I was there by chance, a nobody, no one she'd recognise, anyway. What had I been thinking, that she'd see me and stop, remembering? That we'd strike up a conversation, become friends?

She caught sight of me – I saw it happen – raised her hand.

"Hi," she said. She sounded pleased. "You decided to come, then?"

Decided to come, as if we'd had an appointment, as if she'd been expecting, maybe hoping to see me, as I had her.

"I'm giving it a go," I said. "I'm not very good yet."

"Keep it up. You'll soon get better." We did a lap of the park together. She was obviously running more slowly than she was used to and I felt self-conscious, terrified I'd slip over or get out of breath or faint from exhaustion or something. As we came back round towards the gates I told her I had to go, that I'd be late for work if I didn't. It was true, although I felt desperate to get away in any case, to leave before I managed to make a fool of myself.

"Will you be here tomorrow?" she asked. I nodded and said I supposed so. Four days later we arranged to have coffee together after work. There weren't that many coffee places – not back then, not in Coventry – so we ended up meeting in the cathedral refectory. I'd not been into the cathedral before that – I'd never had a reason. As I sat at a table in the corner, picking at a slice of lemon cake and waiting nervously for Lisa to arrive, I thought about how this was the first time I'd met anyone in a public place since my return to Earth.

[From *Our Planet, Our History, Our Home: Elementary Studies in the geography, mythology and culture of Tristane and her Golden Satellites*]

Among the most renowned public buildings in Fiby are her temples, their gorgeously painted interiors illuminated by whale-fat candles and kerosene lanterns, their tiled floors strewn with richly embroidered prayer cushions. The temple refectory is usually kept open night and day. Many of the more spectacular temples are several storeys underground, with lift access. On viewing the hundred-feet-high central atrium of the Trehia Leviatan for the first time, the anthropologist and travel writer Pers Lilyane confessed to experiencing a sensation close to vertigo.

"At street level, the Leviatan is invisible. Those unaware of its existence would certainly pass it by without stopping. It is only once you are inside that the scale of the structure becomes apparent. The peculiar disjuncture between the magnificent vastness of the interior and the knowledge that to all intents and purposes the Leviatan has no readily provable exterior existence gives rise to the feeling – part awe, part anxiety, part childlike astonishment – of verily being in the presence of the divine."

Fiby is an agnostic state. There are temples to the city herself, to the mountains that shield her from the worst of the winter ice storms, to the great-whales and ichthyosaurs, the megalodons and leviathans that serve her livelihood and provision her trade and found her legends. Worshippers might come to think, and sit, and light candles, to sample the fish chowder and millet bread served in the refectory, where refreshment is invariably excellent and cheaply priced. Mostly they come to pay allegiance to Terezia Salk, who founded the first Temple of the Leviatan after being rescued from rough waters by a fishing craft off the coast of the harbour town that is now named Marilly. This was before the first annals of the city proper were even encoded, and Marilly was just a scattering of fishing huts and a central eating place.

Silver medallions of Terezia Salk can be purchased in most of the temples in Fiby. The practice of worshipping her as a saint is discouraged, but still widely perpetuated.

Have you ever been to Coventry Cathedral, Selena? The remains of the old temple sitting in the shadow of the new, a ghost of itself, a memory carved from stone. The new building is constructed from red sandstone. It is deliberately angular, deliberately novel, nothing like the old cathedral. You would think a structure like that would be ugly, a modern monstrosity, but it's not, it's beautiful, especially inside. The building seems so aware of what it's there for, it's as if it can speak. When I first went inside there was an organ playing, someone practising for a recital later on that evening. I'd never heard organ music before that, isn't that stupid? Well, only on television, at the end of *Songs of Praise* while we were waiting for *The Borrowers* to come on, or else at Christmas, Mum watching the carols from King's on BBC2. I remembered the sound of the organ as a kind of low droning, like someone trying to hum a tune through greaseproof paper.

When you hear an organ being played for real it's completely different. Earth-shattering, like the voice of God, if there were a god, which there can't be, can there?

I sat on one of the benches at the side and listened. I thought of Terezia Salk, the saint who was fished out of the water by shark-hunters close to Marilly. When I stood up to go through to the refectory I saw there was a place near the altar where you could buy candles and then light them. I decided I'd light a candle for Terezia Salk, who was worlds away and who had most likely been dead for thousands of years.

The organ was still playing, and I thought of the great ichthyosaurs, plunging through the icy waters of the Marillienseet. There is a painting in the Othar Gallery in Fiby, not far from where Cally has her studio, that shows Terezia Salk riding on the back of a silver-sheened leviathan, her arms clasped tightly about its scaly neck, her black hair streaming. I breathed slowly in and then out again, filling my nostrils with the scent of candle wax and stone, the sulphurous aroma of a hundred tiny dancing tongues of flame.

For a moment, it seemed to me as if the rift were about

to open again, that all I had to do was step forward into the music and I'd be gone.

That tomorrow I would wake up in my room in Gren-Noor again, the muddy stable yard outside my window, the bald sun rising over the ocean like a blowtorch.

"Sorry I'm late," Lisa said. "There were customers. You know what it's like."

"You're not late," I said. I'd been trying not to check the time. Lisa worked in a garage, as a car mechanic. When she first told me I felt something go click inside, a cold, sick feeling I couldn't explain, like a nasty little door closing, or opening. It was only later I realised it was Steven Barbershop I'd been thinking of, Steven Barbershop, who'd told me his ex-bandmate Jonno worked in a garage. A posh garage, he'd said. Jaguar.

Lisa worked in a car repair workshop on the city's eastern outskirts. She was the only woman there. When I asked her what that was like she made a face, then shrugged. "Most of them are all right," she said. "At least they are when they're by themselves. I get on with my work, mainly."

I sensed there was more, but I didn't push it, not then. Months later, Lisa would tell me that one of the other mechanics, an older guy named Charlie, had once started pestering her for a date. When she refused he'd tried to get her sacked.

"The boss told him to pack it in," Lisa said. "So I was lucky, I suppose. He's got two daughters. The boss, I mean. His wife's from Pakistan." Her voice trailed off, the way it did when she was still thinking something over. I asked her how she'd first got into mending cars. She said it was a summer job that started it, working behind the counter in a petrol station.

"And I like mending things," she said. "I always have."

I thought we could be happy, and for a time we were.

Lisa came from a small village in Fife. Her parents still lived there, she said. She'd not seen them in almost ten years.

"We're exchanging Christmas cards now, at least," she said. "I suppose that's a start."

She smiled, raised an eyebrow to show me she was all right, she was able to joke about it, though I could tell she was upset. She'd come south with her first girlfriend, someone she'd been at school with. A woman who worked in the local supermarket had seen them holding hands outside the cinema and told Lisa's mother.

"Her face when I got home," Lisa said. "It was like she'd decided to forget who I was."

"Are they religious, your parents?"

"Not really. Not so's you'd notice."

I told Lisa I'd had an affair with one of my teachers. That it had been in the papers, that the teacher had lost her job and my parents had thrown me out. I felt sick while I was telling her – not because some of it wasn't true, the bit about Mum and Dad throwing me out, I mean – but because I knew I'd never be able to tell her why I'd lied.

I think that's when I realised we could never be together, not properly. There would always be that distance between us.

"Any brothers or sisters?" she asked.

"A brother," I said at once. "He's still at school, though."

I invented him on the spot, a lovable tyke with a mop of dark hair and a habit of daydreaming. A brother I knew I might never see again but still loved anyway. "I'll always love him," I said, just to try out the words. I found them so convincing I could feel tears starting.

"I'm sorry," Lisa said. "I shouldn't have asked."

"It's OK," I said. "I wanted to tell you." I knew she wouldn't ask about my family again and I felt relieved. Afterwards I wondered why I hadn't told her the truth – why the annoying fake brother with the curly hair and angel eyes when I had a sister who actually existed?

*Her name's Selena. She's three years younger than me but we've always been close.*

I could have told her stories then. Real stories, about us.

Perhaps that's why I didn't. I didn't want to remember you, Selena, because I wasn't ready. A fake brother I could cope with, but not the real you.


Do you remember that film we saw about those girls in Australia who go missing, *Picnic at Hanging Rock*? We watched it together – I'm pretty sure it was during the summer of Mum and Bill. We watched so much TV that summer it was like a drug. For me it was, anyway, the only thing that muted my anger, that let me float above my own existence, at least for a while. It was an odd film, because you never found out what happened. To the missing girls, I mean. Even with the one who came back, you never found out.

There's a scene where they take her back to her old classroom to see her friends. They're sitting there like a load of statues when she's brought in, all those rows of silent schoolgirls behind their desks. The girl who went missing looks so different from them already, she looks so much older. For ages no one says anything. They just sit there, staring, like the birds strung out along the telephone wires at the start of *The Birds*. Then someone calls out: "Tell us what *happened*?" and it sets off the rest of them. The girls are screaming at her, yelling, leaping up from the desks to surround her. They're not like schoolgirls any longer, they're like an angry mob.

The missing girl – Irma – cowers away from them. She covers her face with her hands, and for a moment you think the others might really tear her to pieces, they really might.

## 6

[From *The Mind-Robbers of Pakwa: A True Account of a Friendship, and a Journey Taken,* by Linus Quinn]

There was a researcher I knew, a man named Farsett. He and his wife had spent many years in the field, returning to Silver only infrequently to stock up on supplies. Farsett and I got along almost from the start, I suspect because a man who makes his home in the wilderness and a man who spends his life suspended between one orbit and another would be bound to have attitudes in common. Farsett's wife, Elina, was a woman I might have killed for, had I met her first: level-thinking and loyal and with an intelligence so keen and so impartial you might find yourself quailing before it, and yet still comforted, if that makes any sense.

I still dream of her some nights, although the question of what became of her has made a hideous mockery of such dreams, rendering them more hopeless than they were to begin with, which was completely.

The closeness between Elina and Farsett (Farsett's given name was Eduard, although I never found reason to call him by it) was of a kind similar to that unbreakable, frequently unfathomable sympathy between a twinned brother and sister, only with the heat of sexual intercourse between them they were likely closer still. The idea of bringing discord between them would have been obscene. I felt lucky to name Farsett as a friend – for he accepted me as such upon our first meeting – lucky to know Elina, to accompany them on occasion into their elements, their beloved hinterlands, to have my imagination tortured by frequent, lewd and entirely fabricated intimacies with Elina, such intimacies intuited by her at least a little I fear, yet sweetly and, I hope, swiftly forgiven.

Not since my boyhood friendship with Rachid, who died of the Yellows, had I dared to think of enjoying the kind of togetherness I enjoyed with the Farsetts. Aside from my bond with the ships, it was my chief delight.

As a life's vocation, being on the ships suited me in its entirety. The life is hard, they warned me. No one would expect you to serve for more than a decade, and the retirement pay is good after even five years. Among the shuttle crews, a decade stood as a shorthand for legendary service. I served for twenty-five years, past legendary into ornery, through ornery and into lunatique. I accepted the accolades, the shakes of the head, the cold shoulder, the steadily rising credit balance of my untouched deposit account. So far as the money went, I barely thought of it. I was simply being rewarded for what I excelled at, which seemed a natural expression of the laws of commerce.

Being alone. Being alone and not wishing it otherwise. Having no friends but the glittering internal circuitry of the craft I nursed.

*Bettina Alis*, with her faulty light cells. *Parsen's Glory*, with her flooded cargo hold and malfunctioning energy-renewal systems. *The Clairmont Wren*, with her tendency to overcompensate during re-entry. I loved to imagine them as rash leviathans, these machinecraft I managed: their wilfulness, their anger, their depressions and exaltations, the ecstasy of their wild trajectories when they were flying right, their patched and fire-scarred hides rippling in the blackness, like the silverfish skins of their ocean cousins plumbing the bottomless depths of the Marilly Chasm.

For much of the time they barely spoke to me but sometimes they did. Occasionally they'd cleave to me, my goddesses. Guiding them swooning to earth I would faint with desire.

The steel and the girder, the anchor and the crystal, the reactor and the thrusters and the engine oil.

The eye, the hand, the muscle, the heart, the blood.

I am not of the kind that would spend half a lifetime warring with other, dissimilar mindsets over the rightfulness or the veracity of their convictions. What would be the point, when things are as they are, no matter what any of us might think or be inclined to believe? But not to share what I have seen, and my conclusions about its significance, would be a dereliction of my duty as a human being, and one I would not bear lightly upon my conscience.

I am an engineer, not a biologist, and with only a layman's knowledge of Dea's ecology, a hiker's enthusiasm for the geology and natural history of that same planet. I know I am unlikely to engage the attention of those readers who are more particularly informed. I can write this memoir, though, this account of our expedition to the ghost-settlement of Pakwa and of what I saw there. I can write of what happened to Elina, and what Farsett did afterwards. I can *report*, the way an engineer should, paying attention to detail and the clearest interpretation of that detail, all this without forcing his captain's hand, or seeking to advise his captain except in providing information of sufficient quality and quantity for the captain to come to their own conclusions in their own good time.

You, my reader, stand in place of my captain. I shall make my report to you, neither falsifying nor exaggerating nor seeking to soften the fact of the matter. For when can softening the fact of the matter be a good route to take, save when the situation is past hopeless, and some final crumbs of comfort might be offered, in good conscience, to palliate hard truths?

I am writing this in the hope that the outcome is not yet hopeless. I hope and trust that my captain, who is wiser no doubt than I am, or why else are they captain, may yet determine a means of averting catastrophe.

Of course it was Farsett who told me about the Chelina ruins, the patterns of broken-down rock, of smoothed shale and engineered plateaux, situated in the mountains close to the Ancelly cave system, and which some students of Deani palaeontology, including himself, had taken for evidence of human habitation from a previous era. Until he showed me the survey maps, the drawings and photographs he and Elina had amassed from previous field studies and, during my next secondment, the stones themselves, I had firmly believed, along with most others of my generation, that Dea was a virgin planet when we first made landfall there, ten centuries before my birth or even earlier.

Farsett, with a firmness of conviction that was unusual with him – Farsett always seemed to relish asking questions far more than he enjoyed delivering answers – thought otherwise. The idea of publishing a definitive study of the ruins and all they implied had, over the course of some years, become a passion with him.

"There were people here before us, Linus," he said to me. "All the evidence points to it. I believe it is our duty as scientists that we do our best to discover what happened to them, don't you?"

If I am honest, I could not see that it mattered much. People come and people go. Perhaps it was Tristane that was settled from Dea, and not the other way around, as is commonly believed. But if this happened to be true, then what of it? The discovery might count as interesting, but as to its practical importance, I could not grasp it. I would have said as much to Farsett, but he seemed so convinced, so *enamoured* of his theory that it seemed callous to question him. And I cannot deny that the idea of seeing the ruins for myself appealed to me. I was curious to learn more of the planet. The knowledge that Elina would be travelling with us only added to my enthusiasm.

When I suggested that I accompany them on one of their trips, Farsett agreed at once. He seemed delighted, delighted that I should be interested. The fact that I was a layman, of no more help to him in making his findings than a tourist, did not appear to deter him in the slightest. Of course, our journey to the Chelina ruins, in the diesel-fuelled buggy that Farsett himself (together with Faro M'wule, lately deceased) had engineered for the traversing of larger tracts of difficult terrain, was not the first such expedition I had undertaken with the Farsetts, though it was without any doubt the most ambitious. I hoped at least I would be of some practical assistance, for example if there were problems with the buggy. Farsett responded he had no doubt of that, but that this was not the reason they were pleased to invite me.

"You're our friend, Linus," he said. "It's good to have you aboard."

There are those who believe in the gift of foresight, who have journeyed to the Noorsmen, who are said to possess it, in hope of initiation. As for myself, I am inclined to believe in the phenomenon, if indeed it exists, not as a gift but as a curse. I am not of a religious tendency, but as a native-born southerner I honour Terezia Salk, the same as anyone. If I were to thank her for anything in particular, other than the decades of safe passage among the stars, then it would be for the years I spent in ignorance of what we encountered at Pakwa, the Farsetts and I, and of the papers Farsett would press upon me for safekeeping, the last time I saw him.

I would like to say the years of our friendship are still sacrosanct, innocent of their ending, but alas! they are not.

When I asked Cally about the way she shelved her books, the map books and histories jostling side by side with novels and travelogues and lives of the poets, she looked at me strangely, as if my question came as a surprise to her.

"I've arranged them that way since I was a child, you know that," she said. "No book is completely true or completely a lie. A famous philosopher at the Lyceum once said that the written word has a closer relationship to memory than with the literal truth, that all truths are questionable, even the larger ones. Anyway, it's more interesting. When you shelve books alphabetically you stop noticing them, don't you find?"

"I've never thought about it," I said, although the longer I thought about it, the more it made sense. Categorisation is a kind of brainwashing. How do you know which books will turn out to be important to you, until you've encountered them?

*The Mind-Robbers of Pakwa* was one of those books everyone at school was into suddenly, the kind you bolt down in a single night and then press on your friends, insisting they read it immediately because you can't not talk about it. I don't know now who started the craze – just that it happened. I wasn't even among the first wave of readers – they were postulants mainly, final-year students studying sixteen hours a day for their Lyceum entrance examinations, high as kites on adrenalin and sexual frustration. They made a big deal of how important Quinn's novel was as a cultural artefact, how *significant*, but I suspect they were mainly interested because of the shagging. Once the lower forms got hold of the book their secret was out. For most of us that read it, Quinn's writings were our first encounter with such explicit material. I lingered over those pages, I suppose, the same as the rest of them, but my interest in Quinn's sexual fantasies was secondary to my growing obsession with what he claimed Eduard Farsett had discovered in the Ancelly cave system. The book terrified me, but I couldn't stop reading it. I also found myself identifying with Quinn as a narrator. I enjoyed his disregard for convention, his misanthropy, his habit of describing machines as if they were alive.

"Was he real?" I asked Cally.

"Quinn was real, yes. Look him up if you like. He has an entry in the GAE archive – that's the Guild of Astronomical Engineers. He was the serving chief engineer on the *Silver Sword* when she made the final crossing from Dea to Tristane."

"Was any of it true, though? The stuff about the ruins?"

"It's true that he knew Eduard Farsett, I do know that. There are papers by the Farsetts in the Grand Geography, at the Lyceum. They wrote about insects, mostly. New species were being discovered on Dea all the time, which is probably why they wanted the placement, even though it meant years away from home. Elina Farsett died out there – a rare kind of haemorrhagic fever. Most people think Quinn's story grew up out of that, a kind of nightmare reimagining of what really happened. He was strange enough in the first place. Watching Elina writhing in agony must have sent him over the edge." She paused. "You do know he wrote about spaceships as if they were people?"

[From *Tristane in Wonderment: A Book of Beasts and Mythologies through the Centuries*]

A fully adult creef is as large as a man and sometimes larger, but has the uncanny ability to sequester itself, to fit itself into a space that is many times smaller. The creef's singularly durable exoskeleton can contract itself in the manner of a concertina, one section sliding over another as in a series of closely aligned metal plates, thus allowing the creature to slide through a narrow aperture – beneath a doorframe, for example – or to secrete itself inside access ducts or wall cavities or any one of a hundred similar spaces that at first glance would appear several times too small for the containment of so large an animal. Thus a room or storage space that on first glance appears empty of parasites may in fact be swarming with them.

Even an adult creef moves quickly, with the rushing, surfing gait of a silverfish or centipede, covering a large distance in a relatively short span of time, sweeping themselves undercover at the first intrusion of light or extraneous sound.

If there is no human host to hand, creef at any stage of their life cycle – egg, nymph or adult – can switch into deep hibernation, a state that mimics death so closely it will often be mistaken for it. Creef can survive in such a state for as long as a century and perhaps much longer. A rise in the ambient temperature or significant alteration to the surrounding air currents – both reliable indicators of human activity – will bring adult creef to breeding readiness within a matter of weeks. The creef are parthenogenetic – any adult individual is capable of producing fertile eggs and larvae.

The adult creef is impervious to cold, radiation and extremes of heat in excess of a hundred degrees centigrade. It can survive full immersion in water for extended periods, perhaps indefinitely. Creef are able to ingest and neutralise many poisonous or radioactive substances. The only sure way of killing them is to blow them apart.

The creef's particular method of parasitism is insidious, uncanny, and possibly unique. Once ingested, or otherwise absorbed into the bloodstream of its human host, the creef egg or larva begins an immediate process of organic bonding with the host's bio-material. The bond takes place at the sub-atomic level, gradually parasitizing and then dissolving the host's internal organs whilst using the host's skin and muscle structure as a secure 'container' for the process of metamorphosis to be brought to fruition. This process might suitably be compared with that which takes place inside the chrysalis of a moth or butterfly: a complete tissue breakdown, followed by a radical restructuring in advance of the emergence of the new organism.

First-stage creef larvae are waterborne. Ideally, the adult creef will lay its eggs in or close to running water, although clean still water would be an acceptable substitute. If the water source dries up unexpectedly, unhatched eggs will lie dormant until a viable water supply is re-established. The free-swimming larvae are small – approximately the size of a grain of wheat – and may enter the host body in a variety of ways, including accidental ingestion or through any bodily orifice including flesh wounds or even a deep skin abrasion. The initial stages of metamorphosis are slow – it may be many weeks before the host or the people around them begin to notice symptoms. The preliminary signs of infection – forgetfulness, an increased tendency to fatigue, a slow response to vocal stimuli, a heightened sensitivity to cold, a dislike of bright lights or loud music – may often be confused with unrelated conditions such as dementia or other brain diseases.

As the process of assimilation continues, however, the

host's human personality will become increasingly erratic and compromised. Infected hosts will begin to lose cognitive awareness of themselves as distinct individuals. They will fail to recognise others, even members of their own family or close social network. Self-identification as a human being will become degraded or distorted. Once brain, organ and bone dissolution reaches its advanced stage, the host will finally become comatose. Life signs will appear to cease until such a time as metamorphosis is complete. This stage may take anything from two days to three weeks, depending on prevailing external conditions.

Finally, the now-brittle human 'shell' is shucked off, revealing the fully grown adult creef, a semi-aquatic isopod whose appearance might best be compared with the pelagic trilobite, or with a very large woodlouse, or pillbug. A newly hatched adult will become reproductively mature within a period of one to three months.

The discarded human skin is glasslike in appearance, and as easily shattered, having been fully converted to silicon during the metamorphosis.

Any medical or surgical intervention at any stage of the assimilation process will almost invariably result in the death of the host. Although the process of metamorphosis from human to creef can sometimes take as long as eighteen months to complete, the biological identity of the host becomes compromised within a few hours of infection. Creef bio-material spreads rapidly throughout the human system at a micro-level, and is ineradicable. Full metamorphosis is best prevented by euthanizing the host and cremating the body.

Whether the creef are sentient is not fully known. It should be noted that suicide rates among first-stage infected hosts are surprisingly low. Rather, hosts have been observed to become secretive and reclusive, emotionally distant but with a rarefied sensitivity in matters of hearing, touch and smell. Before transforming, hosts will become intent on seeking out a 'safe place' in which to complete their metamorphosis. Hosts prevented from accessing their sanctuary will occasionally become violent or distressed, though for the most part they remain tractable and finally mute, perhaps in an instinctive attempt to pass unnoticed.

## 7

I liked Allison Gifford. I went to a coffee bar with her once after class, where we talked mainly about my coursework. The next day she came up to me in the corridor and asked if I'd like to go and see *Schindler's List* with her. She said we could go for a meal afterwards, if I had time. There was an essay competition she wanted to tell me about, something that was being organised by the *Warrington Guardian*.

"I think you stand a really good chance of winning a prize," she said. "We can pop back to my place and I can give you an entry form."

I said maybe, I wasn't sure, and I thought that would be that. I did feel flattered, that out of all the people in our tutor group it was me she was paying attention to and not Shauna Wainwright – Shauna, who was taking extra English lessons after school to help her get into Oxford and whose dad was running for parliament or something. At the same time I found her difficult to talk to. I was always afraid I was going to say something stupid, that she'd realise her mistake and want nothing more to do with me. She seemed different from the other teachers, probably because she was part-time and didn't get sucked into the departmental bitching the way the rest of them did. Also, you didn't have to sit an exam for her course, so it didn't matter so much if you happened to miss a week. The course was called Life Writing, although Allison said right from the start that no one should feel under pressure to write about their own lives if they didn't want to. Memoir was just one of the directions we might choose to go in, she told us, but it wasn't the only one. The point of the course was to find out what most interested us, and write about that.

"If you want to research your grandmother's family history then that's fine," she said. "But if you'd rather write about nuclear disarmament then that's OK too."

Allison told us she used to work as a journalist, in London and in Manchester and for a year in Beijing. Now she was back in Manchester for good, teaching in two sixth-form colleges and in a women's prison.

I couldn't understand what would make someone want to listen to a bunch of Warrington school kids all day when they could be conducting secret interviews with political dissidents in China. "What happened?" I asked her. This was when we were at her flat. I suppose it was cheeky really, coming out with such a personal question when I barely knew her, but she didn't seem to mind. She laughed, the kind of laugh that said she'd been asked this question a bunch of times already and she was used to it.

"Someone close to me died," she said. "I came back for the funeral and realised I was tired of travelling. It does happen, you know."

"I can't imagine it," I said, although I wasn't sure if I

meant I couldn't imagine growing tired of travelling, or what it would be like to have someone you loved die like that, when you were on the other side of the world and probably didn't even hear about it until it was over.

Would the dead person even seem real any more?

Every time I think of Dad now I think of Allison too. I wonder if she was as scared as I was, coming home.

When I asked Allison what it was like to teach in a prison, she said it wasn't really all that different from teaching in school. "The people inside don't want to be there, and they're convinced the teachers know nothing." She laughed again, properly this time. "They're right though, we don't. Most teachers are just muddling along, the same as everyone else. The one thing I can say to the women in there is that most of the reason they're on the inside and I'm on the outside is down to chance. We can't always control what happens in our lives, but we do have our voices. We can talk about our experiences. Our anger too, if we want. The idea of talking about their lives is very new to some of these women. No one's ever given much of a damn what they feel or think, you can tell. Some of the best writing I've ever read has come out of prisons." She paused, resting her cheek upon her hand. "There's something about it though, something evanescent. You can't always harness that kind of energy. With some of them, letting out the anger is like striking a match. It flares up so brightly, but afterwards there's just the charred remains, no fire, nothing to build on. It's as if they don't know how to imagine a future, or else they've forgotten. It's a shame."

I listened, filled with nervous excitement and a strange

kind of horror. The thought of any prison was terrifying to me, even the kind of prison Allison worked at, where there were colour TVs in all the rooms – no one called them cells, according to Allison – a gym and a library and open grounds you could walk in by yourself. Imagine being locked up, I thought to myself. You'd never get over it.

When I read about Allison being arrested, the first word that came to me was *chance*, the same word Allison had used to describe her relationship with the women prisoners. Allison was in custody for just forty-eight hours before being released on bail, but for weeks and months afterwards she was forced to endure more police interviews, court appearances, harassment by the media and – eventually – a forced resignation from two of her jobs. The women's prison stood by her, but both of the sixth-form colleges made it obvious they would prefer it if she left.

In some ways she'd have been better off staying in prison for a while. At least the papers wouldn't have been able to get to her there.

I felt my own anger flare up, like a struck match. Was what happened to Allison Gifford my fault? I remembered – though I hadn't thought of it in years – the small living room of her flat, overflowing with books and the large number of objects she'd brought back with her from her various travels: a soapstone Buddha, a silk wall-hanging showing a dragon hovering in the summer sky above old Nanking, a tailor's mannequin, covered in pin badges, that Allison said had belonged to her best friend in college.

Things, beautiful things. I longed to touch them all.

Because they were new to me and I was curious, because no one knew I was there except me and Allison.

That sense of no one knowing, which is the opposite of prison, that strange feeling filling the room when we were in it together. Allison sitting next to me on the corduroy sofa and then ten minutes later getting up and moving to the armchair opposite, a battered old thing with a chintz cover that looked as if it might have belonged to someone's gran.

"There's more room this way," she said, and smiled, and though I felt immediately more comfortable I was disappointed too. All I could think as I nibbled on one of the lemon sandwich biscuits Allison had put out for us to eat – not that Allison ate any – was *I bet Lucy would be jealous, if she saw me now. I bet you anything you like.*

Afterwards, on the street, I stood looking up at the sky and thinking *thank God that's over*, breathing in the black night air and wondering what it might feel like to have just been released from prison – would you be frightened or would you be ecstatic or would you mostly be confused, like I was now?

There was a light in the sky, I saw it quite clearly, a small flash, like a meteor speeding overhead or some other unidentified flying object. Aliens, I thought, which made me want to laugh. I was so busy gawping up at the sky I almost walked right into the woman with the dark skin and long hands who was also standing there, outside on the street, looking up.

"Oh, sorry," I said. Mumbled, really. I saw she had a blue streak in her hair. Cool.

"That's OK," she said. "Did you see that?"

She was talking about the UFO, of course – what else?

"Weird," I said. I glanced up again, briefly. "It's gone now."

She took a pack of Marlboro Lights from her jacket pocket. "Got a light?"

"I don't smoke. Sorry," I said, wishing for a moment that I did smoke, simply because that would mean I'd have a lighter on me. I'd lean across and flip the wheel, touching the flame to the end of her cigarette, our heads momentarily closer together in the dark.

"No worries," she said. "See you, then."

She seemed to hesitate, and I waited also, wondering what else she might say, but after a moment she turned away from me and moved off down the street.

See you, I thought. I tipped back my head and gazed upwards into the darkness, hoping I might catch another glimpse of the alien spacecraft, but no such luck.

How far had she come to see me? Was she checking that I was OK, or was it all just chance?

"The way you write," Allison said to me. This was before, when we were in the coffee shop. "It's very honest. Very fearless."

I told her that couldn't be true, because I was scared of everything: nuclear weapons, sharks, bringing dogs' mess inside on my shoes, talking to people I didn't know, thinking about the future, my sister dying, my best friend going to college to become a doctor, drowning, fire, murderers, getting lost at airports, forgetting my name, life, the universe and everything and especially black holes.

"Why are you frightened of black holes?" Allison asked.

"I just am," I said. I didn't feel like explaining. It was too stupid and too terrifying.

"I'd like to see you write an essay about that. Do you think you could?"

I said I would try. Allison smiled. She touched my hand, just for a second, and that's when I first noticed that feeling between us, something sweet and sour at the same time, like salt and vinegar crisps, or someone scraping their fingernail across the blackboard. If I'd known what was going to happen to Allison because of me I'd never have gone to her flat, never watched *Schindler's List* with her, never had coffee with her either, probably.

I don't think Allison knew about Lucy or even laid eyes on her. Lucy's A levels were in Chemistry, Biology, Physics and Advanced Maths. She never went near the English department – she had no reason to. Lucy never said anything to me about the problems I was having, trying to make up my mind which courses I should apply for, for university, but I had the feeling she was annoyed at me for being so indecisive. She must have thought I was an idiot. It was all right for her, she knew what she wanted. I bet no one in the history of the world ever got criticised for wanting to be a doctor.

I remember Lucy telling me about some girls in the village her mum came from, or her gran, I can't remember which, how some of those girls weren't allowed to go to school because their dads or uncles or whatever were against it. How a woman Lucy's mother still wrote to was beaten and locked inside for two weeks for trying to sneak into a maths lesson. "There were men in the class," Lucy said. "Her father went mental."

She was upset talking about it, I could tell. I made a face, and said it was a good job her mum married an Englishman then, wasn't it? Lucy didn't speak at all for a moment, then she said it wasn't that long since women hadn't been allowed to graduate from Cambridge University.

"They could go to lectures but they weren't awarded degrees," she said. "That was only fifty years ago." She sounded more hurt than angry. I didn't know what to say. Lucy never normally talked about India much, or her family there, and I never asked her. India was one of the things I was scared of. Because I didn't understand it, and because I was afraid it might eventually take Lucy away from me.

I think Lucy was trying to tell me that for some people, deciding to become a doctor was the scariest, most dangerous thing you could choose to do.

Cally's family were from Purl originally, an affiliated coastal township some two hundred kilos to the east of the city, a sprawling, low-rise suburb of overhead tram lines and kitchen gardens, fish markets and scrimshaw factories and the Jara-mira julippa works.

"What's it like?" I asked her. I was curious. If I could picture Purl at all, I imagined it to be a bit like Barrow-in-

Furness, where one of Catey's aunts lived. Catey was dragged off there every now and again to spend wet weekends traipsing through the grounds of Furness Abbey, or hunkering down in fish-and-chip shops with her rowdy cousins. Catey said the place was a dump and I was lucky I never had to go there but I secretly envied her. Barrow's bleakness was appealing to me, the acrid scents of salt and blistering iron.

"There's nothing there, really," Cally said. "Just the factory." Her father owned and managed one of the scrimshaw workshops. Cally didn't mention what her mother did, and I had the feeling they didn't get on, although she never said so specifically. Once, when Cally was away at the studio, I took down one of the large albums containing her prentice pieces, maps she'd drawn when she was younger, before she became a licensed cartographer. The maps were immensely detailed, beautifully drawn, but even I was able to see that they weren't to scale. Many of them were of Purl, which turned out to have a *castello* and a labyrinth as well as the allotments and the julippa factory. I was surprised. Cally had given me the impression that Purl was a windswept, primitive place, almost entirely without culture.

I was still poring over the pages of the album when Noah came in from the yard. Noah never spoke to me much usually, and I alternated between feeling convinced that he disliked or disapproved of me in some way, and rationalising that he never seemed to speak much to anyone. He was a gaunt, untidy man. He looked so much like Cally it was unnerving, although it was difficult to believe he was only a year older than her. I felt uneasy around him, not because I believed he wished me harm, but because I found it difficult to tell what he was thinking.

I turned in my seat as he entered the room. We stared at each other.

"I was just having a look at Cally's old maps," I said. I was gabbling slightly. With Noah, I always felt I had to give a reason for what I was doing. He made me feel like a waste of space, the same way Mum did sometimes. I smiled. Noah didn't smile back, though once again I had come to realise that this was simply the way he was.

"Cally loved Purl," he said. He had an abrupt way of speaking, like an engine suddenly coughing into life. "She wouldn't tell you that, though." He came closer, leaning over my shoulder and turning over the pages of the album until he came to some images near the back, not maps this time but drawings in pencil, lots of them. Wooden shacks, a stone jetty, three squarish clapboard structures I thought might be drying sheds. There were other things, too – an animal that looked like a porpoise, or a dolphin, the elongated head of a creature I didn't recognise at all.

"Our father used Cally's designs in the workshop," Noah said. "They were very popular." He drew his finger gently along the margin of the right-hand page. "That's an amber shark. You have heard of it?"

I shook my head, bemused. This was the most Noah had ever spoken to me.

"They're dangerous beasts. I remember my father telling me about one that came ashore when he was a child. It was old, and sick, and would have died soon anyway. There are fragments of its skeleton still, at the shrine to Terezia Salk at the end of the harbour."

"In Purl?"

"In Purl." He pronounced it 'pawl', with an odd twang that made it seem to me for a moment that he and Cally weren't related at all.

"If you liked it there so much, why did you leave?" The words leapt out of me like errant fishes, slippery and wet. I couldn't remember ever asking Noah a direct question before. He stepped back from the table, put both hands behind his back.

"I wanted to be an astronomer, you know? I wanted to learn about the stars." He balled his hands into fists. There was real anger on his face. I'd never seen him like that before. I was surprised, and a little frightened. Just for a moment he reminded me of Steven Barbershop.

"Why didn't you, then?" I said. "Become an astronomer, I mean?"

I was trying to keep my voice steady. I didn't want him to know that I'd been afraid. I didn't expect him to answer – he seemed to be speaking more to himself than to me. I was mistaken, though.

"Because I happened to love my sister, and refused to lie about it. You won't know this, because Cally never speaks of it, but our mother disowned us. She said that if it hadn't been for my sister's selfishness and my idiocy, I would have cleaved with Lila, and our family would have been spared the disgrace we seemed determined to inflict on them. None of this is true. For me to cleave to Lila when I knew there was no possibility of happiness for her would have been abominable. And Cally and I – we are not the first, we won't be the last, and not all families are so determined in their devotion to convention. Our decisions and actions have no bearing on our mother's standing. Yet she preferred to disown Cally, and disavow me. We came here to Gren-Noor because these matters are of no account in the city. But without my mother's sanction I could not attend the Lyceum in Galena, as I wished to. And so here we are."

I wasn't sure what he meant by needing sanction. I knew of the Lyceum – Cally had mentioned it often enough – but as to why Noah would need his mother's permission to attend, I had no idea. I thought perhaps it was not permission exactly, but something equally important: money, or sponsorship. Not exactly an alien concept, even on Earth. Better to find out from Cally – asking Noah straight out felt like asking for trouble. The whole subject was clearly a problem for him, even now, years later. I didn't want to make matters worse by displaying my ignorance.

"What about your father?" I asked instead.

"What about him? Our father has his own troubles. He mostly solves them by going fishing."

I laughed. I couldn't help it.

"That's par for the course with fathers, I should think."

"Par for the course?"

"Typical. What you would expect."

"Par for the course then, yes." It took me a moment to realise he was smiling.

"I miss my dad," I said. I realised it was true.

"I'm sure you do." His expression was hard to read. I sensed he was trying to goad me but didn't know why. My continued presence in his home must be difficult for him, I could see that, but there was something more behind it, I could tell. Was it simply because I was young, as he had once been, and seemed equally determined to squander my chances? Because he thought I believed, as young people do, that time is endless and therefore unimportant?

I tried to imagine Noah as a young man – his lip curled, contempt in his eyes, no grey in his hair. Had he sworn at his mother, taunted her as a slave to convention, called her bluff? It was easy to imagine, because it was easy to see that Noah then had been pretty much the same as Noah now. Except for his bitterness against the world, which had curdled inside him and fractured his will.

It was easy for me to see myself in him. If the same was true in reverse, then his anger was understandable.

"Is there no chance you could study astronomy on your own?" I suggested. "From books, I mean. There are many great scientists who never went to – to the Lyceum."

"I read every book as soon as it is published. But to progress – to have your work noticed – you need the Lyceum. They have the best equipment, the best telescopes. And unless you are one of their number they don't give a damn."

I fell silent. For the first time I wondered what life was like for Noah and Cally when they were alone together. Did they speak of these things, or keep them hidden? Did they know one another so well there was no need? I turned back to Cally's album, opening it at random – at the Labyrinth of Purl, where in Cally's angular, not-to-scale drawing the streets of the township narrowed and narrowed, drawing in upon themselves until they became straitened passageways, mere cracks between the buildings, so constricted you would need to squeeze yourself flat against the stones to pass through them. I wondered if the labyrinth was really like this, and what it was for. What would be the sense in making a part of the town all but impenetrable?

To contain a minotaur, I thought, and felt a twinge of alarm, even though I knew the idea was ridiculous.

"Have you ever read that novel by Linus Quinn?" I asked. "*The Mind-Robbers of Pakwa*?"

Noah raised his eyebrows, questioning, then sighed.

"Must we play this charade again? Of course I have read it. Every schoolchild has read it. It is a popular horror story."

"You mean you don't think it's true?"

"What is truth? Tenets that are true for one person are blatant lies for another. Or amusements. A game. You do understand the concept of dramatic irony?"

"Of course. But Linus Quinn didn't sound as if he was joking." It was the chapters about Elina I was thinking of, the horror of what happened to her, Quinn's agony at being forced to witness it. And Farsett as well, of course, the way he too seemed to change, although in his case it was science and not the creef that made a monster of him. Quinn insisted it was grief that altered his comrade, but I don't think even he believed that.

*This man who was once my friend*, Quinn said at the end. Was that Quinn excusing Farsett for what he did, or

Quinn saying that Eduard Farsett was no longer his friend?

We can argue about that for centuries, but we will never know for sure.

"I agree," Noah said. "It does not read like a joke." He gazed at me steadily, his eyes a curious gunmetal grey that seemed to absorb light rather than reflect it. Cally's eyes are grey too, but of a lighter shade. "Most people will insist that the creef are a fable, the product of a disturbed mind, or else the fruit of a nightmare. But there are others prepared to believe what Quinn has written." He fell silent. I waited for him to continue. I found I was unable to rid myself of the idea that he was testing me in some way. "There are those who believe all human life on Tristane originates from Dea, that the ruins at Pakwa are not ten thousand years old, as Farsett conjectured, but closer to one million. That a once mighty civilization was turned to dust by this pernicious insect, that the last survivors sought refuge on Tristane, that they hoped to rebuild here everything that was lost. There are books, stories, articles. I can show you, if you are interested. Some of them will try to persuade you that the mind-robbers became extinct along with Pakwa. Others will insist that the creef are still rife on Dea, that we must remain vigilant."

"And those who believe this…?"

"Are close to power. Many of them, anyway. How else would our links with Dea have been so thoroughly severed?"

"But that was centuries ago. Because of the war."

"So we are taught."

"But you believe it was deliberate – a conspiracy?"

He laughed, a startling crack, like a branch breaking.

"What I believe, for what it is worth, is that whatever measures were taken, were taken too late. They are among us already – they are bound to be. We traded with Dea for centuries. It is impossible to think – ludicrous, almost – that in all that time there was not one contaminated water tank, one infected deck steward. If the creef exist they are here on Tristane, and it is only a matter of time before what finally happened at Pakwa happens here also."

He strode to the window and then back again, as if trying to allow me time to assimilate his words.

To let their iciness paralyse my veins, like poison darts.

"We are a big planet," he said, more quietly. "Much larger than Dea. But size does not guarantee immunity. Not forever."

"You don't believe that," I said. My voice was trembling slightly, and I was filled with the same panic at being held captive that I had experienced in the van with Steven Jimson. I think it was then that I began to realise all over again what the creef really were: a black hole, spreading through the fabric of the universe like an ink stain. If there really were rifts in the fabric of space – potholes in time, like the one that brought me from the shores of the Shuubseet to my bedroom in a house in the village of Lymm, near Warrington, Cheshire – then why should not the creef make use of them also, make use of them as stepping stones from one naively acquiescent civilisation to another? Whether by accident or conscious design, it hardly mattered. No world would be safe, not forever. Not even ours.

"Don't I?" Noah said. "Why not?"

"Because no one could live with that knowledge. It would be unbearable."

He laughed again, more softly this time, a wisp of wind flickering through the carcases of fallen leaves. "The things I hoped for in my life are lost to me already. I live from day to day. I look out for Cally. We have our love, or what is left of it. Sometimes when the night is clear I harness Marsia and drive out into the wilderness so I can look at the stars. I think about what I might have been in another life. Perhaps it is another life that they offer, these monsters, have you thought about that?"

I didn't answer. The idea occurred to me – the obscene idea – that Noah was infected, that he was beginning to turn, like Elina Farsett, into something else.

"You don't believe that," I repeated. I gulped. My throat felt dry. "Why is no one doing anything?"

"For something to be done would first mean gaining an admission that a danger exists. Whole generations, whole dynasties of political power have been founded on the assumption that the ruins at Pakwa are simply the remnants of an abandoned settlement on an abandoned colony. If you think such an ironside can be turned around so easily, then you do not know politics. I for one would not waste my life on such a fruitless endeavour. Not that some have not tried. My old comrade Erroll Maas, for instance. And your father."

"What do you mean?"

My whole body felt cold, the tips of my fingers as numb as they had been the night Cally and Noah brought me home from the outlands to Gren-Noor. I felt the numbness and

I thought again of the sensation of resistance, of negation, that results from trying to force together the two like poles of two magnets. A reality that denies itself. It is difficult to explain or to describe.

"Your father, Radar Farquharson, who perished beneath the wheels of an ironside at Sere-Phraquet? You remember him, surely? You were there when he died." He hunkered down, putting his face close to mine. I could feel the ebb and flow of his breath, grazing my cheek. "Officers of the city guardia recorded an accident, but anyone who knew Ray Farquharson knows it was merely fate catching up with him. Too many questions, too many enquiries, too many late-night agitations with troublemakers like my old comrade, Erroll Maas. Your father was not dangerous, not to the praesidium. But there were those who clearly thought it prudent not to let him become so." He stood up, backed off. "I am sorry. My sister believes you should be sheltered from these truths until your mind recovers. I believe that is so much flummery. I have been watching you, Julie. I think you know – you remember – more than you admit. You need to face the facts. Your life is passing you by."

"And my mother?" The numbness had spread to my lips. It was as if someone else spoke the words. I did not feel them leave my body.

"Margery? She is at home, in Tarq. Your rejection has broken her heart, though she will not say so. Why do you think Cally spends so much time at the studio? She reports to her on your progress three times daily." He paused. "Would you like a glass of water?" he said. "You look pale."

He crossed to the sink and turned on the faucet, filled a beaker. The beaker was made of glass, and had a heavy base. As Noah handed me the glass, the water inside caught the light from the window. Its circular surface flashed, like a winking eye.

"It is good and cold," Noah said, and although I'd drunk water from the tap hundreds of times, I found myself wanting to dash the beaker into the sink.

*First-stage creef larvae are free-swimming, approximately the size of a grain of wheat.*

The water was clear, of course – there was nothing in it. I put my lips to the rim of the glass and took a long swallow. I felt better at once.

It's just some stupid theory, I thought. Like the black hole thing. Three trillion to one.

## 8

Lisa and I were good for a while, but it didn't last. How could it, when I kept the truth of myself hidden from her?

"I feel like I don't really know you," Lisa said to me, more than once. This was near the end of our time together, when things were beginning to get difficult. I knew she'd leave eventually, or else I would – it just hadn't happened yet. "It's as if you decided to cut me out, right from the start."

In a way she was right, but it wasn't for any of the reasons she probably thought. Mostly when you try to hide something from someone you love it's either because you feel guilty or because you're afraid they won't believe you. You're scared some important aspect of your relationship is going to get broken and you'll do anything to prevent that, even if it means breaking it yourself, in another way.

None of that was true with Lisa. If I'd told her what I'm telling you now, she would have tried to believe me, and even if she couldn't bring herself to go all the way in that, she would have accepted my story as part of me, an odd part that needn't do us any harm, even though she most likely wished it didn't exist. The reason I didn't tell Lisa had nothing to do with trust. I knew I could trust her, but I didn't want to. I thought that if I pretended none of it had happened, then it really wouldn't have. I wanted to inhabit a world where the lies I told Lisa were true, a world in which I'd come south to escape my troubles and to make a new start. A new start with someone exactly like Lisa.

If I could make Lisa believe this version of me, then would not this version, in some crucial sense, be real?

There's a woman I know, an IT technician at the hospital. Her name's Jenny, she's worked there for years. Soon after I first started at the Christie, Jenny went to South Africa to visit her eldest son, who runs a vineyard there. Jenny had been saving up for the trip for ages. She and her closest friend – a radiography nurse named Sheila – were always talking about it: all the things she was going to do there, all the places she hoped to see.

While Jenny was away in Cape Town, Sheila had a massive stroke and died. It came completely out of the blue – there was nothing in Sheila's medical records, no family history of any kind. It happened one lunchtime, in the hospital canteen, which was lucky if you think about it, although there turned out to be nothing anyone could do for her.

Sheila died on the Thursday after Jenny left, and the following Wednesday a whole load of us went to her funeral – anyone who wasn't on shift, basically. The day after, another Thursday, the first of Jenny's postcards arrived: a view of Table Mountain, and a short note, telling us about her flight and her safe arrival. Someone pinned it to the office notice board, the usual habit. I couldn't help wondering about the other cards Jenny might have posted at the same time.

There would have been one for Sheila, definitely, sent to her home address, with a private joke maybe, or a more personal message meant for Sheila alone. The following week another postcard arrived, a photograph of antelopes this time, antelopes in the veldt. Jenny mentioned a barbecue she'd been to, and a half-day safari. She sent her love to everyone, then added a PS – *just in case my card to Sheila didn't arrive* – with a mobile phone number.

The postcard got pinned to the notice board next to the first one. A couple of hours later someone pinned something else over the top of it, over them both, the announcement of a departmental meeting or something similar. There was no more room on the notice board, probably, but there was another reason too: a growing sense of discomfort, of horror, really, at the way the world seemed to have split itself in two.

In Jenny's world, Sheila was still alive, looking forward to Jenny coming home so they could go out to dinner somewhere special and catch up on news. In our world, Sheila was dead and cremated, already a part of the past. I thought about using the mobile number Jenny had given to call her and explain what had happened, just to send a text even. I didn't though – I didn't want to spoil her holiday. Either that or I was simply a coward.

On the day Jenny was due back in the office I called in sick. The next time I saw her, she knew everything. She looked ten years older. People kept whispering about how she seemed like a different person.

\* \* \*

I started having nightmares, more and more. I would dream I was back in Gren-Noor, in the room with the wooden ceiling and the red-tiled floor. I felt I was in a prison cell, or some other place I knew instinctively I couldn't get out of. I would listen to Cally moving about in the room beyond, certain and terrified that she was changed in some way, that if she came into my room and saw me I would be destroyed.

"What's going on?" Lisa asked, after I'd woken up three nights in a row with my heart hammering, my limbs bathed in sweat. "What's wrong?"

"Nothing. Just a bad dream," I replied. I lay there in the dark beside her, resting my hand on her shoulder, feeling the warmth of her skin and trying to steady my breathing. As soon as it was light, she got up to go for her run. I'd stopped running soon after Lisa and I started dating – getting up so early, especially in winter, seemed like too much of an effort – but there were times, plenty of them, when I wished I hadn't, when I thought about how good it would feel to be outside, to see the brightness creeping into the sky, a sky that, though I knew it was infinite, seemed so comfortingly present, reassuringly *real*, a shield against whatever lay beyond.

All those puffy grey Coventry clouds, scudding along, just being themselves.

"Have it if you want, I think it's ugly." Cally paused. "It was Lila's."

"How come you have it?"

She made an open-handed, dismissive gesture: *who*

*cares?* "It was with the rest of the stuff she left behind in her apartment. We had to get rid of most of it. We didn't have room for it – not here. Noah said we should keep some of it though, the personal stuff, in case she asked us to send it on later. She never did, though."

The pendant was about two inches long, a teardrop-shaped lump of crystal in a silver surround. The surround was an elaborate cacophony of tiny forms, angels or devils all clustered together like in those creepy German woodcarvings in that museum Dad took us to in Nuremberg. The figures all had tails, hairless and squirming, tangled together like mouse tails. When I touched the crystal's surface I was surprised to find it felt soft, giving way very slightly beneath the pressure of my fingertip. I wondered if maybe it wasn't crystal after all, but some sort of plastic. It was cold though, whatever it was, and very heavy. I touched it again and felt the same sensation of rubberiness, although when I looked at the spot where my finger was pressing the tip looked flattened, as if I were holding it against a windowpane or the curved glass surface of a beer bottle.

It was only when I held the pendant up to the light that I realised there was something inside it, something embedded in the heart of the crystal like a fly in amber. A spindly-legged creature, with narrow wings and body, like a daddy-long-legs. Amazingly, it appeared to be moving, swimming in slow motion within the bubble of its transparent prison. After staring at it for a minute or two I came to realise that the creature was locked into a repeat cycle, the same half a dozen movements endlessly reiterated. I found its jerky, spasmodic rhythms close to hypnotic, like watching the same ten-second sequence of a David Attenborough nature documentary. The insect was semi-transparent, barely there. When I turned the pendant against the light at a certain angle the creature seemed to disappear entirely.

"It's a silverwing," Cally said. "You find them close to water. They're very common. To make these pendants they freeze them in time for half a second. It's supposed to represent eternity."

"How do they do that?"

Cally shrugged. "No idea."

I wrapped my fingers around the pendant, enclosing it in my fist. The thought of the silverwing performing its endless swim-cycle made me feel queasy. Did the creature know it was in there? It was only an insect, I understood that, but even so.

"Why did Lila leave it behind, do you think?"

"I don't know. Maybe it held bad memories for her."

It was obvious from the way she said it that Cally had no wish to discuss the matter. It occurred to me that Noah might have given Lila the pendant, as a keepsake maybe, as a gesture of farewell. I'd said nothing to Cally about my conversation with Noah, and I couldn't imagine that Noah had, either. Even so, nothing had been the same since. Cally seemed preoccupied and more reserved towards me generally. No matter how much I tried to tell myself I was imagining things, I couldn't get rid of the idea that she was fed up with me being around all the time and wished I would leave.

Noah on the other hand seemed easier in my presence.

He spoke to me as little as ever, but the next time Cally was away at the studio, he asked me if I'd like to go on a night-drive with him and I agreed.

We piled Marsia's cart with blankets, filled a hamper with food and two large thermos flasks of coffee.

"We should leave before nightfall," Noah said. "If you want to see the stars, we need to get beyond the city boundary. It's not dark enough otherwise."

We followed the coast road for what seemed like hours, then Noah drove the mule inland, into a wasteland of scrub and criss-crossed dirt tracks that Noah said were called baranye, or giants' footsteps.

"There's a Noors legend," he told me, "about the giants who marched north from the mountains, seeking the forests. These rocks are what remain of the dust storms, churned up by their boots."

"What are they really?"

"Solidified lava, probably. No one knows for sure."

The sky above us was rich with stars. Not the vain little pinpricks of light I was used to seeing from our back garden in Lymm, but whole armies of them, whole armadas, clustered together so thickly in places and so brightly it was difficult to look straight at them.

Alien suns, I thought. Each and every one of them.

"There is Dea," Noah said, and pointed. The planet hung low in the sky, and was the colour of hearthlight.

"Do you think they're watching us?" I said. The idea – that there might be people up there, looking down – seemed both miraculous and terrifying.

"I don't know," Noah said softly. "Probably."

He gazed up at the blazing sky, his face rapt, as if he'd never seen such a sight before that night.

By the time we arrived back in Gren-Noor it was almost dawn. I offered to help Noah with the mule, but he said there was no need. I went straight to my room. I pulled the blinds half-closed then undressed and climbed into bed. I found I was exhausted, too tired for sleep.

When Noah came to my room about half an hour later I felt no surprise. He stood in the doorway, not saying anything. His hair was down, and in the shreds of colourless morning light filtering in through the blinds his face looked oddly ageless, like the face of a statue. I drew back the bedcovers, and after a moment Noah closed the bedroom door behind him and began removing his clothes. His ribs jutted squarely, like a dog's, and there were some purplish scars, or perhaps they were burn marks, on his left shoulder.

I was curious, I suppose. He was in me more or less as soon as he lay down, breathing hard in my ear, his prick stiff and uncomfortably bulky as a piece of wood. I moved beneath him, trying to shift his weight. I thought about Linus Quinn, all those nights he'd lain awake in his tent, listening to Eduard and Elina Farsett making love, Eduard with his little grunt, Elina making no sound at all until the very end. Quinn had grown so used to their ways that those nights, at first an agony, had quickly become his secret pleasure.

*I knew Farsett's sounds, his movements, his whispered*

*endearments so exactly I came to believe that in those moments I actually became him*, Quinn had written. *As I immersed myself in the rhythms of their coitus, I could almost bring myself to believe I could feel Farsett's rasping, incendiary breathing leaving my throat, the savage pressure of Elina's knees as they gripped my sides.*

*Such that when we came to climax, we were truly three, and not a lonely two*, Quinn continued. As Noah quickened his movements, I turned from thoughts of Quinn to thoughts of Elina – Elina Farsett, her veins already swarming with alien enzymes, the process of irreversible change already begun. Her cries, which for the first months of her transition had been especially intense, branding the skies above the ruins of Pakwa as with the death throes of stars.

How long did she and Eduard continue having intercourse, I wondered, after they began to realise Elina was changing? Did Farsett fear his wife's condition might be contagious, or did he not care?

I imagined him, courting uncertainty like an addiction. Noah's buttocks jerked, and he cried out. Elina's fingers, deep within me, relaxed their grip, the sweat glittering along her hairline like droplets of dew.

Noah left, and I fell into sleep. I dreamed I was floating above the city on some kind of transparent pillow. I pressed my face to its see-through surface and looked down. Below me I could glimpse a labyrinth of tiny houses, like the ones Cally had drawn on her map of Purl. There was also some kind of scrap yard, piled high with the rusting carcases of strange machines. I knew the machines weren't real: they were painted in bright enamels, and looked like toys. *Croftson's Meat Merchants*, read a sign at the entrance. Suddenly I was on the ground and walking into the Spar. I went to look at the magazine rack but the shelves were filled with packets of frozen vegetables instead. As I turned to leave the shop, I saw someone outside the window, looking in. I jumped inside my skin, which jerked me awake. Instead of the wooden beams I saw a pockmarked ceiling, patchworked with damp stains. On the wall beside the bed a faded print of pink roses hung in a cheap gilt frame. I could hear traffic passing by outside, the muted roar of a motorbike. When I crossed to the window and looked out, the stable yard was gone. In its place was a city street, lined on either side with tall terraced houses and parked cars.

In my hand was the silver pendant. The gemstone at its centre was bluish and cloudy, like a piece of rock quartz.

The silverwing was gone. If it had ever been there in the first place.

My rucksack lay on the floor at the foot of the bed. My mouth tasted dry and faintly furry, as if I'd drunk too much alcohol the evening before. I tried to remember how I'd got here, but all I could think of was the endless sky over the belts to the west of Fiby, the stars strewn over the blackness like a box of sequins, spilled across a carpet the colour of night.

## 9

I remember July 16th 1994 as a hot day. I spent most of the morning in my room, reading. I couldn't face anyone, to be honest. It was more than a week since term ended, and all I could think about – still – was the row I'd had with Lucy over Justin Mitchell. Neither of us had been prepared to admit it was Justin we were arguing about, and of course it wasn't really, it was us. But Justin was the breaking point, the symbol.

The thought of Justin and Lucy made me sick. I don't mean that in the way people normally mean it, as an expression of disgust, but really, literally, as in I'd actually thrown up once, in the girls' toilets, just from imagining them together. That's the kind of state I was in. I had these pictures of Justin inside my head. I don't know if you'll remember him even, Selena, but he was beautiful, that was the only word for him: half boy, half angel, with that wispy-curly hair he wore tied behind his head and those incredibly long, almost entirely colourless eyelashes. He looked like a girl almost, an impossibly gorgeous one, and when I thought about him with Lucy there was always a girl's body under his clothes when he took them off.

I can't remember what Lucy and I said to each other,

not all of it anyway, but I know it was awful. It was as if we were digging around in our heads, searching out the most hurtful, most unfair accusations we could think of and then just flinging them out there, like coils of barbed wire, for the other one to trip on and get snarled up in. You've seen that Italian horror movie, *Suspiria*? Like that.

Three days after it happened I went down to the phone box next to the Spar and tried to call her. She wasn't there though, she was spending the summer with her mum's family in Calcutta. Lucy had told me about the trip ages ago but with everything else that was going on I'd completely forgotten about it. A woman answered, someone whose voice I didn't recognise but who turned out to be Lucy's mum's sister. She was looking after the house while they were away. I was so confused I forgot to ask her what date they'd be back, which made the whole thing worse. I had no idea how I could contact Lucy even. I kept writing her letters then ripping them up. I felt so awful it still makes me unhappy to think of it.

There was no one I could talk to. The thought of Catey finding out? Just no.

I made myself come downstairs for lunch. I knew Mum would make a scene if I didn't, and anyway, I was hungry. I don't remember much about it except that there was an atmosphere brewing. Mum and Dad must have had a row or something. I'm not sure I ever told you how much I hated the way things were at home after Mum's affair, everyone trying to pretend everything was normal, all of us knowing it wasn't. There was no way things were ever going to go back to how they were before. I often found myself wishing they'd split up at the time and had done with it. The more I thought about it, the less I could understand why they'd ever got married. They had nothing in common. Mum should have been running a country or a vast business empire or something. Dad – do you remember that photo of him on the motorbike, how ridiculous he looked? I don't think he ever had one clue about what he wanted to do with his life. That's how he ended up with Mum, probably.

Once lunch was over I told Mum I was going to meet Catey but really I was just desperate to get out of the house. I knew Catey was going to a barbecue at Linsey Fanshawe's house. She'd called me the day before and asked me if I wanted to go with her and I'd said maybe I'd come over later, but I didn't really feel like it. I knew Richard Lovell would be there, and the thought of having to watch him and Catey pawing each other all evening was more than I could stand. Richard was all right really but the way Catey seemed to deliberately drop twenty IQ points the moment he walked into a room drove me insane. You could see it happen, like a screen coming down. Her voice would change. She'd lose all interest in whatever we'd been talking about and start making flirty jokes about French knickers or who might have got off with whom on the college French trip. I hated that she could do that to herself. It made me feel like ripping things to pieces.

At least it would be somewhere to go, though. It was either the barbecue or bus into Warrington and hang around the shops. Not that I had any money to buy anything. I supposed I could always walk along by the canal, down to the old Transporter Bridge and back – the iron gallows, some people called it, the cranes rearing their heads against the sky like worshippers, like dinosaurs. I think cranes are really the dinosaurs of the modern age.

You look out over Manchester or Warrington sometimes and think the apocalypse has already happened. That should feel awful but it doesn't. In a strange way it's a relief.

There was a van parked outside the Spar shop. The van was white, with a logo on the side, a dripping tap with BARBERSHOP PLUMBING printed in capital letters in a circle around it. I thought what a weird name, makes it sound as if they only do plumbing for barbershops. Or maybe they go in for close harmony singing while they mend their toilets or put in their boilers or whatever they do. The idea made me giggle, which made me notice the sunshine, which was killing but still amazing, like having hot butter poured over your skin. I felt the urge to take off my sandals, to feel the heat of the paving stones soaking up through the soles of my feet, to walk through the streets like that, free of everything.

I thought maybe I'd go to Linsey's barbecue after all. I'd lie in the grass and drink rum and coke. At least no one would get on my case. Who gave a stuff about Richie being there anyway? Certainly not me.

Or maybe the guy's surname was Barbershop, I thought. I couldn't seem to let the subject drop. Jimmy Barbershop, Kevin Barbershop, *Sebastian* Barbershop. I almost spurted out saliva thinking about that one, the way you do when you need something to be funny, funnier than it really is, just so you can laugh out loud and let the crap go to hell. And perhaps Sebastian really was his actual name. It was at least possible. *All* things were possible, I decided. The idea made the world feel suddenly larger than I'd imagined.

Just as I came level with the van, someone came out of the Spar, a tall guy with long, curly grey hair and a black Motörhead T-shirt. He walked around the front of the van and into the road, unlocked the door on the driver's side.

Sebastian Barbershop, I presume, I thought, which really did almost make me laugh out loud, even though the guy was less than ten feet away from me and would definitely have heard. I could feel myself going red. I turned my head away, pretended to look through the Spar shop window, but he'd already seen me.

"What's so funny?" he said. The kind of question that could have sounded aggressive, but it didn't. He made it seem as if he wanted to share the joke.

"Nothing," I said. "It's the name on your van, that's all." Even now I couldn't say what made me tell him the truth. The relief of being out of the house, the sunshine, the fact that I was finally feeling OK about going to the barbecue. I think I just wanted to hear my own voice, communicating, talking to someone – even this guy with the grey hair, a total stranger but who I could tell was a bit of an arsehole, even then. He had a look about him, that sly look. The look of a man who lies out of habit, because he can.

The sky overhead was so blue that if you stared up at it at a certain angle it looked white.

"It's the name of a record label me and some of my mates wanted to set up," he said. "Barbershop Records, I mean, not Barbershop Plumbing. The band didn't make it big enough, surprise, surprise. We still play the odd gig on the weekends, though. You know Status Quo?"

"Are they still going?" I said.

He looked bemused for a moment, then laughed. "Nice one," he said. He opened the driver's door. "What's your name, then, when it's at home?"

"Selena," I said. God knows what made me say that. I felt queasy in my stomach suddenly, the way you do when you know you've forgotten something, something vital, only you can't remember for the moment what it is. It was like I knew something bad was going to happen, even then, while I still had the chance to stop it. It would be easy to stop it, too – easier than not. All I had to do was go inside the Spar shop and hang around the magazine racks till he drove away. And he would have to drive away. It would look weird if he didn't, someone would notice. Once he was gone I'd head over to Catey's and we could go to the barbecue. I could watch Richie frigging around with the firelighters while Catey made encouraging noises. Ooh, my hero.

Maybe that's what did it – the thought of Richard Lovell parading around in his shorts, thinking he looked like Tom Cruise or something.

"You want a ride, Selena?" said Sebastian Barbershop.

"Where to?"

"You tell me." He grinned, looking pleased with himself in a way that made my skin crawl. I pretended not to notice.

I remember asking myself, what's a thing someone like me would never do? The answer came back immediately: get in that van.

It would be an adventure, I decided, a gas. The kind of escapade you kick yourself for afterwards because *anything* could have happened but of course nothing did. Not this time, anyway.

"You can give me a lift into Warrington if you want," I said. "I was going to catch the bus."

"Shift yourself, then." He got into the van himself, then leaned over to open the passenger door. "It's a bit mucky in here." He brushed an empty cigarette carton off the passenger seat and on to the floor. "Make yourself comfortable."

I climbed in and slammed the door. The inside of the van stank of cigarette smoke. The rear compartment was divided off from the cab by a piece of dingy orange cloth, ripped in several places, heavily marked with what looked like coffee stains or engine oil. I settled myself in my seat and clipped on the seatbelt. There was still time for me to change my mind, to get out of the van, but all I could think was what an idiot I'd look if I did. Not to him, but to myself.

"Got any of that Barbershop music, then?" I said as he started the engine.

"Seriously? You want to hear us?"

"Why not?"

He leaned across me to open the glove compartment. He smelled of cigarettes, and sweat, and greasy hair. "What's your name, anyway?" I asked. I realised he hadn't said, not even when I told him my own name, or rather yours. I was still thinking of him as Sebastian Barbershop. A large part of me wanted to go on thinking of him that way. To know his real name would be to admit that he existed, that this was actually happening. I shouldn't know his name, because I shouldn't have spoken to him in the first place. Or got into his van.

"Steve."

"Steve what?"

"Steven J. Rockefeller. What's it to you?"

He extracted a paint-spattered cassette tape from the jumble of rubbish inside the glove box and inserted it into the van's stereo system. For a couple of seconds there was nothing but the sound of the engine, then music blared out, a formless mass of guitar feedback with a man's falsetto warbling along over the top.

"Is that you?" I said, and he nodded, but I didn't believe him. There was something familiar about the sound of the voice and I wondered if I'd heard it before, at Catey's perhaps, or on the radio late at night, which has always been my favourite time for listening to music. They put on such obscure records you never know what you're going to hear next.

I wondered why Steven Barbershop had been so touchy over his surname. The only thing I could think was that he didn't want me to be able to identify him later. To look him up in the phone book, maybe. As if. He could take his paranoia and stuff it right up his rectum.

Rectum, I thought. Catey's swear word du jour. Barbershop turned to me and grinned, all straggly hair and pointed nose. Like a wolf, or a coyote on the prowl. How corny is that?

"This is our own stuff. Not the crap pub gig stuff. Like it?" We were on the main road by then. Other vehicles were passing by in the opposite direction but they didn't slow down, why would they? We were on the dual carriageway in less than five minutes.

"It's all right," I said. "My sister would be more into it, probably."

"What kind of music do you like, then?"

"I don't know. Indie stuff. Suzanne Vega. Joni Mitchell."

"Johnny Mitchell? Never heard of him."

"She's Canadian."

"I can't stand that hippy shit."

How do you know it's hippy shit if you've never heard of her? I thought. I felt something turn over inside me. I think it was then that I began to realise – to actually believe, instead of just kidding myself – that Steven Barbershop was playing a game with me, as I was playing a game with him, when I'd lied about my name, only now the rules had changed. I've told myself, over and over, that if he'd stopped the van at that point – at a petrol station, say – I'd have got out, phoned Dad, stood by the pay area until he came to fetch me and who cares what a moron I might have looked.

But would I have, though? To step out of the van would have meant admitting that I was frightened, that I believed I was in danger. And that couldn't be true, because stuff like that only happened to stupid people, or characters in the movies.

I've wondered since, how many people have ended up in serious trouble because they've refused to trust their instincts, their gut. The gut is rarely mistaken when it comes to sensing danger. The mind, on the other hand? The mind often doesn't know what the hell it's talking about.

"I like other music, too," I said. "I like Marillion." It was Catey who liked Marillion, but the side effect of that was that I'd been subjected to their albums many millions of times. Catey knew the entire lyrics to *Misplaced Childhood* by heart. She thought *Misplaced Childhood* was a work of genius. I thought she was bonkers. Marillion was just a bunch of guys with guitars, after all, guys in too-tight trousers who obviously fancied themselves. I quite liked 'Kayleigh' but otherwise I couldn't see what all the fuss was about.

"Prog rock," said Steven Barbershop, "is for poofs."

When he veered off to the left instead of taking the turn for Warrington I pretended not to notice. I knew if I asked him where we were going that would be it. It would be like that moment in *Little Red Riding Hood* when the wolf stops pretending to be the grandmother and shows its true nature. There would be no way back from that – for the wolf, I mean. Once you've decided to go for it there's no room for mistakes. You can't go for being a monster, and then pull back.

I wondered how it would feel, to know you were about to kill someone. Would a monster feel excited by its victim's terror, or sick to its stomach? Sick at the thought of the things it's going to have to do before its prey stops screaming.

I knew my only hope was to keep playing the game.

I gazed out of the window at the traffic and asked him about his mates, the ones who'd been in the band with him. "What are they doing now?" I said. "For work, I mean?"

"Matt's a lorry driver now," he said. "And Jonno's a

motor mechanic. He's working at some posh Jaguar garage in Northwich."

"Do you enjoy being a plumber?"

"It pays the bills. Gets me out of the house, anyway." His eyes stayed fixed on the road. I thought maybe if I kept my nerve, that might give him time to go back on it, to decide not to. It was such a lovely day, after all, exactly the kind of day you'd want to spend driving around in your van with your music on and the windows down. He could tell himself it had been a mistake, a joke even, something he'd wondered about but never considered actually doing. Not seriously anyway, not for real. There was a chance he was as frightened as I was. If he could only find a way of getting himself out of it, we might both be OK.

We were heading into the real countryside by then. Sunlight filtered downwards through the trees. Narrower roads led off from the main one, carving pathways into the forest like treasure trails, like in *Hansel and Gretel*. It looks like paradise, I thought. Maybe anywhere would look like paradise when you believe you're going to die.

"It's so green out here, isn't it?" I said.

"I thought we'd ride around a bit. You don't mind?" He turned his head to look at me, just for a second. His eyes looked blank and cunning at the same time. Reptilian, I thought. But then reptiles are born that way, aren't they, they can't help being cold-blooded. I shook my head quickly, then went back to staring out the window.

"This is great. I wasn't doing anything this afternoon, anyway."

We seemed to drive for miles. The cassette of the band music finished. When Steven Barbershop turned it over, *Elvis: The Love Songs* came flooding out. I recognised the album because Dad had it. It was odd to think of a man like Steven Barbershop having music like that in his van. Perhaps the tape was his dad's, I thought. Even Steven Barbershop had to have a dad, somewhere.

After about half an hour's driving I spotted a brown tourist sign for Delamere Forest and Hatchmere Lake. I remembered our picnics by the water, the stories Dad liked to tell us – about how some of the trees there had been alive in Henry VIII's time, about the giant catfish that lived in the mud at the bottom of the lake, the huge pike that would eat anything that got in their way. When there was no more food left, the pike would eat each other. I remembered one of our Eng Lit classes right before the end of term, before I had the argument with Lucy and everything was still mostly OK. Miss Willoughby handed round printouts of a poem by Ted Hughes. The boy in the poem – Ted Hughes himself, probably – goes fishing for pike at night beside a ruined monastery. It's pitch black out there, and you know what it's like at night, you start thinking strange things. The boy begins to wonder what else might be in the lake, besides the pike, and even though he's terrified he can't bring himself to leave. It's as if he *has to know* what's down there. He can't let go.

The poem was really creepy, actually. Miss Willoughby asked Shauna Wainwright to read it aloud to the rest of the class. When she'd finished Miss Willoughby asked us what we thought it was about. Everyone sat there in silence. Then Sophie Ridout, who was down for the Oxford entrance with Shauna Wainwright, put up her hand and asked if the pike was actually a metaphor for evil, a way of showing how the weak are always exploited by the strong.

"When he talks about the baby pike, in the aquarium," Sophie said. "There are three of them at first, but then the two smaller ones get eaten by the larger one. I think Hughes is trying to tell us it's a dog-eat-dog world."

"Pike-eat-pike world, more like," said Ali Blasim, and everyone laughed. Ali fancied Sophie, had done for ages, and everyone knew it. Miss Willoughby waited for the laughter to die down, then said that Sophie's answer was very interesting, and did anyone else have any other ideas. The discussion became quite lively after that. Derek Morris said he thought the poem was about secrets, about going fishing for stuff you had no business knowing.

"That's why he's scared, Miss. He's worried about what else might be in the water. That's what I think."

Derek Morris was always top in history, but he never normally said anything in English lessons. A murmur went round the class, then someone said what you mean like Godzilla and everybody started laughing again. At the end of the class, Miss Willoughby said she wanted us to write down our thoughts about 'Pike' as part of our summer English project. I folded the photocopied sheet into four and stuck it in the back of my exercise book.

So far as I knew, it was still there. I decided Steven Barbershop was more like a pike than a wolf. His mouth was like a pike's anyway, cold and narrow, with just the edge of a tooth showing when he smiled.

"We could go for a walk," I said to him. I thought about saying I'd been to the lake before, with my dad and sister, then decided against it. I thought it might be a bad idea to let him know I even knew where we were. He hesitated. I could see the thoughts going through his mind, ideas being channelled, like the wheels clicking slowly round inside a clock. If he said no, he'd either have to give a reason or not give one. Either way it could be dangerous, because it would mean admitting to both of us that I was in his power. I thought about asking if we could go back now, because it was getting late and I had a barbecue to go to, but that seemed impossible. The barbecue itself seemed impossible, an entertainment for other people but not for me.

The thought that I might never see Catey again: an idea so strange it was barely graspable, a thought that was full and empty at the same time, like that sculpture of a house that was made from concrete, poured inside a real house and then left to set.

A ghost house, it had looked like – I'd seen it on the news. The council knocked it down in the end. I imagined running my fingers over the concrete, absorbing the people and the rooms and the time, like peculiar vapours, through the pores of my skin. Steven Barbershop was driving more slowly, looking for somewhere to stop, perhaps. There was no one around, just the odd passing car. I wondered if any of the people in those cars would remember having seen us, later.

"There's nowhere to park," he said. He was pretending to

sound pissed off, pretending we had no choice except to keep driving. I could feel my heart speeding up. I found I could picture it: a cherry-coloured, fist-shaped mass at the centre of my chest. Adrenalin being pumped into my bloodstream in a broken, Day-glo line of tiny green arrows.

"Yes there is," I said. "Look." I tried to sound nonchalant, tried to sound like I didn't give much of a damn either way, either stop or drive on, no big deal. I pointed through the windscreen and it was true, there was a place, he could see that at once. A shallow lay-by, not so much a car park as a place where cars could be parked. As if to prove the point there were a couple of vehicles there already, a beat-to-shit Cortina and a Volkswagen camper van that looked as if it would have trouble making it as far as the local Tesco's.

Steven Barbershop began to pull over, and I began thinking about what I might do once I was outside. He would have to let me outside, I realised – we were right on the road here, another vehicle might swoop past at any moment. The thought of being in the open air was making my head spin, but I couldn't dwell on it, daren't, not yet. The idea was still mostly an abstraction, still beyond my reach. The van's tyres made a scraping sound against the dry earth. I knew I couldn't run, not straight away. Too much of a risk. As Steven Barbershop removed the key from the van's ignition I tugged down on the door handle. Nothing happened.

"Steady on," he said. "The safety locks are still on." He grinned, pike tooth gleaming, then flicked a switch on the dashboard. The look on his face made me realise what I should have known all along: that I'd been a prisoner from the moment I decided to get into the van. I couldn't have escaped even if I'd tried.

I tried the door again and this time it opened. The feel of the ground beneath my feet made me elated, almost high. I knew I mustn't let it show, not in my face, not in my behaviour, not even a little. I scuffed the earth with the toe of my trainer, rolled a stone around. "Come on," I said. "Let's see what's down here."

I began walking towards the woods, past the rotting camper van and on to a pathway, half hidden between the trees, scattered with fallen leaves and small drifts of gravel. I knew that even now Steven Barbershop must already be wondering what the hell had happened, how come I was out of the van, with him tagging along behind me like a first-class moron. He must have known he'd blown his chances. Only not quite yet.

"Where are you going?" He sounded pathetic. The distance between us was increasing gradually but he was still there, still following. He seemed bound to me somehow, I could feel it. As if we were tied together by a piece of elastic and it was down to me to snap it, snap it clean through and without letting myself be bounced right back to him, a dead weight at the end of a bungee rope. I could feel the breath going in and out of my lungs like a visible substance, a silvery dust. I was almost more frightened now than I'd been in the van. It would be so easy to make a mistake.

"I want to see if we can find the lake," I said. I glanced back briefly over my shoulder then carried on down the path. Dried leaves crunched under my feet. I could feel him getting angrier, and I understood that I wasn't real to him, not really, not as a person. I was a thought in the shape of a girl and I belonged to him, the way his other thoughts belonged to him. I should not be getting away, I had no right, I was his secret. He speeded up a little. I could feel him thinking he'd been a prick, such a prick, prick, *prick* to pull over in the first place, that's what had done it, what a devious little bitch I'd been, to con him like that.

I wanted to turn round again, just so I could see how far behind he was, but I didn't dare risk it. I looked further down the pathway in front of me instead. I could just see where it branched off, on to another, wider track that I hoped would turn out to be the path to the lake. Just as I was wondering what to do, whether it was safe to run yet, I saw two people come into view by the intersection, a man and a woman, their heads bent close together in conversation. The woman was wearing a yellow baseball cap. I've never forgotten it. It was like a light going on, a bright blazing 'go' sign. I ran. Ran towards them, the man and woman, trying to look normal and not panicked. The man glanced up as I dashed past. I threw him a smile but said nothing. I was afraid they might not believe me, that admitting there was something wrong might somehow end in me being returned to Steven Barbershop.

Keep them in sight, I thought. That's all. Just keep them in sight. I slowed my run to a brisk walk. I was about ten yards ahead of the man and woman at that point, close enough to hear their voices. I had no idea where Steven Barbershop was, whether he was still following or not, lurking up the path somewhere, hoping I'd trip or run out of running or be delivered back into his custody some other way. I thought it was unlikely, to be honest. The appearance of the man and woman had changed everything. They had changed the world.

I came out of the woods by the lake. I felt thirsty and I felt sick. I was crying, just a little bit. I thought that so long as I didn't completely lose it that wouldn't look too crazy, people would assume I'd had a row with my boyfriend or something. There were more people around now anyway: a bloke with three kids running ahead of him, fighting over a football, two younger women in sundresses, gabbling like parrots, a guy in a long grey raincoat with two massive wolfhounds. He must be boiling in that, I thought. It was the first normal thought I'd had since getting into the van. I was beginning to wonder about what I was going to do, how I was supposed to get home. I knew Delamere station was around here somewhere, but I was afraid to ask anyone in case it turned out to be miles away. They would know I was lost then, and that could be dangerous. I kept walking. No one looked safe to talk to, not even the plump dad with the oversized football shirt and the Jesus sandals. I knew I wasn't thinking straight, but my life seemed to have changed in a way I couldn't explain, not even to myself.

All I knew was that I shouldn't tell anyone. Telling would mean admitting I'd got into Barbershop's van of my own accord, that it was *all my fault*.

And all to punish Lucy, for liking Justin.

That man was going to kill you, Ju, said a voice inside

my head. It could be happening right now. In another world, it is happening. His hands are around your neck. You can still see the light through the trees, but soon it will be gone. There are cuts on your knees and on your face. One of your trainers has come off, and two of the toes on that foot are broken where he stamped on them. You can smell his sweat and his awful breath, stinking of cigarettes. Everything you ever wanted is nearly over. None of it matters. None of it mattered, ever, because it was only ever going to end in this.

I could taste earth in my mouth, and I could feel her terror, and I knew I'd betrayed her. Somewhere in some other time I'd been unlucky, or simply too frightened to know what to do. Because what were the chances, honestly, of a girl of seventeen being able to outwit a creature like Steven Barbershop? I remembered a story that had terrified me as a child: the myth of Theseus and the Minotaur, in which the Minotaur's victims had been chosen by drawing lots. A silk bag full of beads, two-dozen white beads and one black.

I'd drawn a white bead this time, which meant I was safe. But somewhere – next time – another me had drawn the black.

The young woman opens her fist. The black onyx bead, like a miniature time bomb, glows in her palm. Her hair flops damply against her forehead. She is out of breath. She can go no further.

I kept following the path around the perimeter of the lake. I saw two guys fishing, the kids still wrangling over their football, a woman with three small orange dogs trotting at her heels. They're corgis, I thought. Just like the Queen's.

# 'Franziska's Journey'

by

## JULIE ROUANE

*Life Writing A1/36B teaching supervisor Ms A. Gifford,*
*Priestley College, Warrington, April 1994*

On the night of Tuesday 17th February 1920, a Berlin policeman by the name of Hallmann was coming off duty when he witnessed a young woman throwing herself from a bridge into the freezing waters of the Landwehr Canal. Luckily for the young woman, he was able to pull her from the water before she went under. Hallmann then summoned help, and the woman was taken to the nearby Elisabeth Hospital to recuperate. The doctors who examined her found that aside from some minor symptoms of exposure she had not suffered any permanent physical injury from her attempted suicide. Her body, however, displayed multiple scars from earlier injuries. A Dr Joseph Knapp claimed she had been beaten so severely that her jaw had been fractured, and several of her teeth were missing as a result. The deep scarring behind her right ear suggested a bullet wound. There were numerous smaller scars all over her body.

The woman consistently refused to give her name, and refused to talk to anyone about what had happened to her. When asked why she had tried to kill herself, her answers were cryptic. "Can you understand what it is, suddenly to know that everything is lost, and that you are left entirely alone? Can you understand then that I did what I did?" The hospital staff referred to her as Miss Unknown.

She spent most of her time sitting silently on her bed. If a stranger approached she would turn her back, or cover herself with a blanket. In spite of appeals from the hospital, no one came forward to identify her and after six weeks of convalescence she was transferred to Dalldorf, one of the city's asylums for the mentally infirm. On June 17th 1920 she was interviewed by police officers who were anxious to trace possible relatives, or indeed anyone who might know who she was. The officer who interrogated her noted that she had to be restrained before they could photograph her. It was clear that Miss Unknown was desperate to retain her anonymity. She even made faces at the camera to distort her appearance.

Everyone seemed to agree that she was not insane. She knew who she was and why she was in the asylum – she simply did not wish to share the information with anyone else. The nurses who had most contact with her all remarked upon her politeness, her fondness for reading, and her fluency in four European languages. It was to one of these nurses, Thea Malinowski, that Miss Unknown finally revealed her identity. Catching sight of a photograph of the murdered Russian Tsar and his family on the cover of a popular Berlin magazine, she told Malinowski she was Anastasia, the youngest of Tsar Nicholas's daughters. She had survived execution at the hands of the Bolsheviks. She was alive.

The first thing she remembered was waking, bloodstained and half-delirious, under blankets in a peasant's cart. She had been rescued by an officer in the Tsar's own army. He had transported her secretly out of Russia and into Romania, using the jewellery sewn into her garments to pay their passage. There was a soldier, a rape, a child she later abandoned on the steps of an orphanage. Her story was the stuff of fairy tales. "We came through such lonely districts, we had to rest in forests, we travelled so many roads." Eventually she came to Berlin, a lost soul with no identity, no family and no future.

Even though she swore her nurses to secrecy, it was only a matter of days before the news was leaked to the outside world. Miss Unknown is questioned, prodded, adopted, taken to tea. No one can agree on who she is, who she might be, who she is not.

[And this is where we turn the record over, play the other side.]

You were born Franziska Czenstkowska in 1896. Your place of birth was a hamlet called Borowihlas, a rural settlement in what was then Western Prussia. Borowihlas was a farm place, a scattering of homesteads and cattle barns, with a closely knit – you would say incestuous – population of less than two hundred souls. Your father was known to everyone as Anton the Drunkard. Anton married late, almost as an afterthought. His first wife died of complications following pregnancy. His second – your mother, Marianna – was more than twenty years his junior. You cannot imagine what drew them together, and mostly you don't try because it's just the way things are. You are not – quite – their eldest child. A brother, Martin, died before you were born. Was it Martin's death that made Marianna so bitter, so undemonstrative? If you could make yourself believe that it might make things easier, but you cannot. Marianna had her own reasons for being disappointed with life, reasons she never told anyone and especially not you.

A small place and a plain place. Your brothers and sisters seemed to belong there, but you never could. You found the mud and the need, the scraped, awkward, cramped and paltry nature of life in Borowihlas maddeningly depressing. A life reduced to its bare essentials was scarcely a life, especially for someone with the vision to see beyond it. You looked forward to school because it gave you a respite from mud and cooking. The teacher praised you for your fluent reading and your sure grasp of languages. A slim, very nearly good-looking man who had lived in Berlin. When he praised you, you felt happy, not because you cared for him but because in his words you could feel the breath of places that were not Borowihlas.

When Anton drove to town he brought you back dresses. Dresses and white socks, neat little patent leather shoes with gleaming buckles. Marianna was furious at what she perceived as the waste of money. If it's not drink it's this foolishness – how are we supposed to eat this week, tell me that? You stood silently with your eyes cast downwards, secretly laughing. How you hated this dried-up old woman with her hard mouth and stabbing eyes, eyes that condemned you for crimes you could barely guess the meaning of. How you loved the shoes, the pretty garments, the chocolate walnuts in their cellophane wrapping.

My Franny was what he called you. He whispered that you were different, better. His hands on your budding breasts, swelling breasts and then in your fanny, Franny. The salivating combination of lechery and horror. Your friends seemed strange to you now, their interests – their needlework, their grandmothers, that sweet boy Julius who smiled so innocently as he filched their handkerchiefs – so far away so lost so utterly madly gone forever never was. The teacher who once praised you seemed so stolid. If he couldn't guess what Anton was doing, then what did he know? Anton the monster, the drinker, the foul-breathed fucker. How he loved to play cards, to carp crap about his family once being lords, the von Czenstkowskis, if you please, like anyone gave a shit. Anton with his plump, crooked fingers, plucking at the knee socks, the fine white crochet that he himself had bought you on one of his pub crawls. If he can drink, why can't he whore? At least then he might leave you the devil alone. The truth was, your fat and drunken father was afraid to get his prick dirty.

Marianna howled through your nights like a maenad.

Maddened by jealousy by grief by guilt by plain old ugly anger. They call her the witch now, in the village, did you know that? It's her shouting that did it, her pointy-nosed yelling. She had to shout, Marianna, to drown out the gossip, the appalling filth they were spreading, those Borowihlans, lies that couldn't be true they were so terrible, and even if they were, she had to admit you'd most likely led him on. Those clothes, the hoity-toity manners, the speaking in tongues. What would a place like this be doing with a bitch like that? In any case, she knew you were lying. Fat Anton hadn't been up to dipping his wick in donkey's years.

But whores will be whores. And the look she gives you if you try to speak to her, as if you were hen's piss. Spare the rod and spoil the child, that's what your cousins say, and you's a spoilt little madam, you have to admit that, even if they can't help feeling sorry for you, at least a little. Hey, Franny, they yell as they pass by. Give a dog a bone, Franny. The mud is deep and treacly, right where you're walking. The cartwheels whoosh and the dirt flies up. Your prissy white skirts get caught in the crossfire and those cousins of yours, they bust their balls laughing.

The drunken old goat snuffs it eventually – tuberculosis – and Marianna remarries. You are seventeen, and she can legally disown you, which she does. You come to Berlin as one of thousands, farm girls from the provinces, all of them looking for love, money, soldiers, housing. You find work as a housemaid and then as a waitress, but what is this, the life of a servant, no better than the crap you had to endure at home. You're damned if you'll settle for drudgery. The city must have more to offer, even to you.

The men are gone for soldiers, every one, and the factories are taking in women, churning out weapons. And it can be fun in the factory sometimes. The women are mostly girls your own age, they aren't so bad, some of them are friendly and even amusing, in spite of their coarsened tongues, their filthy hands. None of them care for books, but they can sometimes be kind.

A soldier of your own, my maid? All the nice girls love a soldier, especially these days.

Your soldier came, your soldier went, and in the long weeks after his leaving you can still taste his scent, like leather, on your skin and in your clothes. Who was he? You barely knew, and then he was gone, back to the Front and from there – you heard eventually – to his eternal rest. You know the factory foreman will dismiss you if he finds out you're pregnant. What the fuck are they scared of, these men with their cocks, their cocks that make kids and, apparently, saddle a man forever with a fear of women. You'd hate them and their cocks, if you had the energy, but you're just too tired. You find someone – a woman with iron fingers and the closed-door, furious face of Marianna – who says she knows how to fix it but God, it hurts, the iron in her fingers as she shoves it into you, this severance of the then from the agonising now. You try to stand and cannot. You wonder if your soldier bled like this when they bayoneted him. Did they hurt your soldier this much? How foul it is to be poor, you think, and without a weapon.

Back in the factory you are faint and ill. The word hell is not a real word, it's a book word, yet this is hell nonetheless, the heat, the noise, the nausea, the pain in your cunny. You're polishing grenades when one of the monstrous, devious objects slips from your hands. It falls in slow motion then rolls across the boards, a round-thing-trundling-on-wood noise, though nobody hears that, it's too cacophonous, to rambunctious in here, too many people yelling and laughing and working all at once. You stand paralysed, your vision blurring. The grenade strikes the heel of your line-manager, who is everywhere and nowhere suddenly, a hot red mess.

"An accident. A very bad accident. I fainted. Everything was blue. I saw stars dancing and heard a great rushing in my ears. My dresses were all bloody. All was full of blood."

They let you go, but they let you go. You wandered nameless through the streets, seeking asylum. When finally you are sent home again, Marianna says it's pulling potatoes or you'll be out on your arse.

The decision to end it all comes suddenly, one of those mad ideas that can take you over entirely for an hour and then retreat again. What would it be like to die? you wonder. Better than this shit, anyway. As soon as the water takes you, you realise you're mistaken. For once in your life you're lucky. A passing policeman, a Sergeant Hallmann, is there to help.

The best thing about being a princess is that it's a job in itself. You don't have to do anything to be a princess, except exist. You can turn your face to the wall and refuse to answer, if you like. You can gaze at the photographs and count your sisters: the bossy one, the sweet one, the dutiful one. And who are you if not the clever one? You always were.

Did you play with their faces in your mind, as you played with drowning? Their white dresses and winsome smiles, that endless, luminous summer before the war? You never spoke the words 'I am a princess' because you didn't have to. The world needed a miracle, and you, Franziska Czenstkowska, had never been a miracle before.

1

Selena had never suffered from nightmares much, not even when she was younger, not even after Julie went missing. Her dreams were mostly boring – small-scale dramas about getting lost in Sainsbury's or forgetting someone's birthday. They were anxiety dreams, but the anxiety they invoked was commonplace, easily handled.

Hearing Julie's story seemed to change that. Selena's dreams became charged with panic, filled with voices and landscapes she didn't recognise. She would wake from these dreams with her heart racing, her limbs bathed in sweat.

"This isn't Manchester," somebody said to her in one of the worst dreams, a woman with narrow features and wispy red hair. They were standing outside some kind of storage facility – an abandoned factory or perhaps a grain silo. Once she was awake, Selena wondered where these images had come from. Films she'd seen, perhaps. *Five Easy Pieces*. That truck stop at the end. Johnny loved that movie.

The woman with the red hair turned to her and smiled. A thin smile, not unfriendly exactly, more like a warning.

"Manchester's inside," she said. "It's small enough to fit now. Don't you want to go home?"

She kneeled down in the dirt and began fiddling with something: a small metal grille at the base of the silo, held in place by rivets and a bent-over nail. Some of the rivets were so old and so rusted they looked painted on. Unscrewing them would be impossible, even if you wanted to.

"Don't open that," Selena said. Her mind and body were filled with the same illogical terror that characterised her earlier dreams. A sound was rising up from the grille, a distant, high-pitched keening, like the wind over the Pennines, and Selena remembered how she and Johnny used to drive out to the Peaks at the weekends, awful weather usually but there was always a pub to hole up in. They'd play cribbage sometimes, or just read the papers. It was nice.

Somewhere behind the keening sound she could hear music playing. She thought it might be The Pogues.

The red-headed woman straightened up. The grille was still attached to the silo, but the woman's fingers looked battered and crooked. Their tips were covered in blood, or perhaps it was rust.

"It's over," she said. She looked straight at Selena, the smile still pinned to her lips, her hair hanging in ratty strips about her thin face. "You'll have to go in. You know that."

Selena woke with a start then, which was what always happened. She'd never dreamed any of these dreams through to the end, never found out what happened, or what was going on, although wasn't that true of all dreams? The dreams you dreamed through to the end you never remembered.

\* \* \*

On the night Julie told her story, the only question Selena felt safe in asking was about Steven Jimson. The Jimson part of the story made sense at least, although who was to say that even that was true? There were all the old news reports, for a start. Anyone could look them up, if they were interested. Selena had read them herself. She knew them by heart.

"Are you sure it was Steven Jimson driving the van?" she said.

How did you know, was what she wanted to say. How did you know it was Jimson? When did you decide that was the story you were going to tell me – last week, last month or last year? When did you begin researching your own life, Julie?

"I didn't know at the time, obviously. I only worked it out afterwards. Recently," Julie said. Her face was grey with tiredness by then, tiredness and strain, and something else that might have been fear. Fear that she wouldn't be believed probably, although what did she expect? Selena thought Julie might be angry at her question, but if she was she didn't show it. She answered in an offhand, distracted manner that was already familiar from all their other meetings: *Why are you bothering me with this shit when it's so not the point?* "At the time he was just this guy. I only found out his name when I looked online. There was a photo of him. Several. It was definitely the same man." She looked down at her lap. "I was in that van for over an hour, Selena. I'd know his face anywhere."

They were sitting at a corner table in Dido's Diner, an insalubrious but seemingly immortal greasy spoon just off Canal Street that had had its signboard graffitied to Dildo's Diner more times than Selena could remember. She didn't know why the management didn't just decide to leave it like that. It would save a lot of time, and money. Everyone called it the Dildo anyway, so what difference did it make? People liked going there because the food was cheap and not too bad and because the place stayed open round the clock. When Selena went to meet Johnny off the plane after his first interview they'd had breakfast in the Dildo at five in the morning.

For most of the time she was telling her story, Julie had seemed blanked out, in a trance, as if she'd been hypnotised by Derren Brown and then *commanded* to speak. Afterwards, Selena kept thinking how young she'd looked, as if the intervening years had been cancelled out and here at last was the Julie she remembered, her sister the teenage runaway, lost but now found, the mystery of her disappearance finally revealed.

Whatever happened, she isn't the same. She can't be. She looks like she's made of glass. Glass and steel wire.

She wondered why Julie had placed Jimson last in her story, when in fact he was the first thing that happened. It took less than ten minutes to walk from their old house on Sandy Lane to the Spar shop at the end of Pepper Street, but that was all it took sometimes, to step from one world into another. The TV and the Internet were full of such stories, enough of them to make you afraid of leaving the house ever again.

As for the rest of it, she had no idea. A delusion of some kind maybe, a *fugue state*, brought on by her experience in the van with Steven Jimson. She could not bring herself to believe that Julie was simply lying to her, that she had concocted this ridiculous story as – as what, exactly? An excuse for what she'd put them all through? An excuse for Dad's death?

On the whole, the idea that Julie had gone mad was a lot less painful. Selena was used to madness, and in this situation, whatever this situation was, madness as an explanation seemed to make more sense than anything else. Selena realised she was just sitting there, her head hanging, her capacity for listening exhausted. I want to go to sleep, she thought. She remembered when she and Julie were kids, how they would sometimes sneak into one another's bedrooms after lights out, how they would chatter and giggle and freak each other out until one of them or both had fallen asleep. This is the same, Selena thought, only now I'm too old. Too old for *The X-Files*, too old for aliens, too old for this.

They'd managed to find a taxi somehow. It dropped Julie off first, then Selena. There were no dreams that first night, or none she could recall. Selena awoke the following morning feeling surprisingly refreshed, surprisingly normal. At some point during the morning Julie had phoned her at work and asked if she felt like seeing a film when she clocked off, and Selena said yes. She had spent the rest of the day dreading their meeting – she couldn't face the thought of rehashing everything – although in the event all they did was watch the film. It was a romcom, something about a washed-up boxer and the manager of the bar he frequented. Selena found it surprisingly entertaining, though she had to make a conscious effort not to fall asleep.

When the movie was over they had coffee in the cinema

café. Julie asked how her day had been, and Selena found herself telling her about a Russian woman who had come into the shop, one of Vasili's girlfriends, she suspected. Vanja didn't seem to like her much, anyway.

"She was demanding all this stuff on account," Selena said. "She claimed Vasili had put it aside for her. Of course there was no record of it."

"What an arsehole," Julie murmured. Whether she meant Vasili's girlfriend or Vasili himself, Selena couldn't tell. They left the café soon afterwards, with nothing more said. That night, Selena had the first of her nightmares. She waited a day, feeling stunned, then called Julie on her mobile and asked if she'd like to come over at the weekend.

"You haven't seen the house yet," she said.

"I'll come on Saturday," Julie said. "You can give me the grand tour." Selena had thought Julie was being facetious, although she had to admit that Julie did seem curious about the house when she turned up, at first anyway, poking into every corner, taking things down from shelves to look at them, opening cupboards. Selena was surprised how much she minded, though she didn't say anything.

"Your garden's tiny," Julie said, and it was: a paved yard with an outside toilet, squared in behind high brick walls. Margery was always on at her to have the toilet demolished.

"You'd double the size of the garden," she insisted. More than half the households in the row had had their privies torn down, or else converted into garden sheds, but Selena had resisted the idea. It wasn't just the mess and disruption that put her off – the builders forever traipsing into the kitchen to make cups of tea – but the sense that the house needed the toilet, that it would feel bereft without it. The two had been built together, after all, they were used to one another.

In any case, Selena didn't want to double the size of the garden, not particularly, it was fine as it was. The redbrick paving was original – many of the houses on Egerton Terrace had lost their paving along with their privies – and she liked the back wall, with its round-shouldered gate, the kind of gate that looked as if it might lead into Narnia but that actually gave access to the litter-strewn service lane stinking of cats' piss where the wheelie bins were stored.

There was just the one flowerbed, dominated by a monster rose bush, the sort that played dead all winter then flowered – voraciously and, Selena suspected, vindictively – right through from March until the end of October. The blooms were enormous, a raucous yellow. Selena sometimes found herself imagining the rosebush had it in for her: *Thought I was done for, bitch? Well, I ain't done yet.*

The house was hers though, which was all that mattered, the one thing she had that counted as what Margery might refer to as something to show for herself. In a strange way her silent stand-off with the monster rose bush was an acknowledgement of that. *We're in this together, bitch, an' don' you forget it.*

If Selena sometimes felt her grasp on the material world was ineffectual, the rose bush had tenacity enough for both of them.

"The yard's big enough for eating outside," Selena said. "The road's quiet, too."

Julie looked at her strangely, as if she'd said something surprising, although it was more likely that the subject of the house had ceased to be of interest to her. Julie didn't care about the house, or where it was. She was too wrapped up in her own stuff – the alien abduction stuff, or whatever Selena was supposed to believe it was.

[SELENA and JULIE are seated at the table in Selena's kitchen. Selena has just made tea. There is some tension between them, as if each is waiting for the other to speak first.]

JULIE: Why don't you just spit it out, Selena? You're obviously dying to have a go at me.
SELENA: I don't know what to say. What did you expect?
JULIE: You don't believe me.
SELENA: I believe something awful happened to you. Maybe — I don't know — this whole story about being spirited away to another planet is your way of rationalising it. Things like that do happen. I've read up on it.
JULIE: You've read up on it? What am I now, some kind of case history? I don't need therapy-speak. I need to know what you're really thinking.
SELENA: What do you want me to think? You can't expect me to take it seriously, not all that stuff about aliens or monsters or

whatever. And how come everyone on this
so-called planet spoke English? It's like
something out of *Star Trek*.

JULIE: I've thought about that a lot. I think
that maybe they weren't speaking English,
but I could understand them anyway.
Something happened when I went through the
rift. I think I switched over.

SELENA: Switched over?

JULIE: To their language. Cally's and Noah's.

SELENA: Cally and Noah. I'm fed up with
hearing about them. It's like you're asking
me to believe in unicorns. Or the Loch Ness
Monster.

JULIE: You used to, once. You loved all that
stuff.

SELENA: That's completely different and you
know it. We were kids.

JULIE: Adults are just kids who have been
brainwashed into forgetting who they are.

SELENA: It's called growing up, Julie.

JULIE: Is that really what you think?

SELENA: I don't know. [Beat.] I suppose a part
of me feels I'd be letting you down, that's
all.

JULIE: Letting me down how?

SELENA: By pretending to believe this rubbish.
Maybe it would be better if—

JULIE: Now you're going to say you think I

should see a doctor. You weren't like that
with Dad.

SELENA: I was going to say that perhaps you
need help, that you should talk to someone.
Someone outside the family. Is that so
awful? And Dad has nothing to do with this.
Dad was different.

JULIE: Different how?

SELENA: Because what happened to Dad was real.
Believable. There was an explanation. He was
so desperate to find out what happened to you
he'd have latched on to anything.

JULIE: You don't think he really believed
then? He just pretended?

SELENA: How should I know? You have no idea
how bad Dad was. You weren't there. [Beat.]
Sorry.

JULIE: I know they locked him up for asking
questions.

SELENA: No, they locked him up because he was
refusing to eat and we were terrified he
might commit suicide. Anyway, Dad wasn't
locked up. That's not what happened.

JULIE: He sent me another letter, you know.
He said he didn't care how unreasonable my
story was, he would believe me, whatever.
Impossible things happen every day. That's
what he said. I've never forgotten it.

SELENA: Why did you run away, then? You broke

>     his heart, you know. [Beat.] Look, this is
>     getting us nowhere.
>
> JULIE: I didn't run away.
>
> SELENA: Yes you did. Even if everything
>     happened the way you say, every single
>     thing, you could have come home sooner. Soon
>     enough for Dad, anyway. I don't understand
>     why you didn't.
>
> JULIE: Because of this. What we're doing now.
>     I couldn't stand the thought of it.
>
> SELENA: We can't go on like this, Julie. *This*
>     can't go on, I mean, us hiding in corners
>     and pretending everything's normal. I want
>     to tell Mum.

Selena felt surprised at herself for actually saying it – for daring – although the thought had been there in her mind since Dido's Diner. Julie had come to her for a reason – either because she needed someone to talk to or because she was fed up with being alone. Probably it was both. Her need for privacy was understandable, but it was becoming an imposition. If she kept acceding to Julie's demands, would she not be at least partly responsible for her sister's delusions?

Selena had never once pretended to believe in her father's theories about flying saucers and the people – Ray called them passengers – who claimed to have been transported in them. She had always seen her not pretending as a part of her love for him, a sign of faith that the real Ray would eventually be restored.

Pretending to Julie, even for a day, would be like saying her sister had ceased to exist.

They'd been living inside a bubble, she could see that now. But that's what addicts do – they make you complicit in their compulsions. It was time to call a halt, to expose Julie's fantasy of alien abduction to the light. As if it were a vampire. She remembered the scene in *Interview with the Vampire*, Madeleine and Claudia, trapped in the round courtyard as the sun came up, their insides catching fire, their bodies crumbling to dust. Selena sat very still, both hands clasped around her tea mug. She wished Julie no harm – the opposite. She wondered how much damage she'd already done by playing along.

"All right," Julie said. "You can tell her."

Selena stared at her incredulously. She had expected Julie to react to her suggestion with hostility, with outright anger even. Her acquiescence was more shocking than either.

"You're OK with that?" she said at last.

"If that's what you want."

It's for the best, Selena thought but did not say. Already her mind was swimming with doubts, and she could not escape the feeling that she had broken something, some vital marker of trust that she had stupidly refused to recognise until it was too late. She wished she could talk to Johnny, who had a way of accepting things at face value that Selena had been wont to criticise as naiveté but secretly envied.

She remembered a discussion they'd had once, about whether ghosts existed.

"If they exist they'll carry on existing, whether we believe in them or not," he had said. Selena imagined he'd have been equally laid back about the idea of Julie being whisked away to another planet.

*Cool*, he would say, most likely, and the thought made her smile, in spite of herself. There were so many of these stories out there. Would it really be so weird if some of them were true, some of the time?

"Do you still have the necklace?" Selena said suddenly. "Lila's pendant?"

A look passed across Julie's face, an expression Selena found it difficult to decipher. Was it hurt, or just disappointment?

"You want proof? Here." Julie reached down inside the neck of her T-shirt, ducking her head as she drew forth the chain. "I never take it off, usually."

The pendant was large, Selena saw, and teardrop-shaped, exactly as Julie had described it. The links in the chain were large and square, bright as platinum but with a higher sheen. The central stone was smoothly polished, a cloudy greenish-blue, speckled with darker patches, like a bird's egg. There was no sign of anything inside it. Selena thought it looked like a moonstone, or possibly moss agate.

The silverwork around the stone was also as Julie had described – a mass of tiny intertwined figures, satyrs or demons – though nothing she said had prepared her for the virtuosity of what the maker had accomplished, the individual manikins so lithe and so lifelike it was almost possible to imagine that they were moving, crawling over each other in a frenzy of mysterious activity, like ants in the secret chambers of their underground warren.

The pendant felt heavy in her hand, heavier than it ought to. Alien, Selena thought, and then checked herself. She laughed softly without meaning to, wondering where Julie had happened to find such a thing, how much she'd paid for it. The pendant looked valuable – not just an antique, but a rarity. As to its origins, Selena had no idea. At first glance she would have said Indian – something in the fine detailing, the seething liveliness of those strange little figures – but she knew her guess would be wrong. Julie had said the manikins reminded her of German folk art, but that wasn't right either.

The truth was, Selena had never seen anything like it, anywhere, ever. It was ugly, but it was compelling, too. There were people who would pay a lot of money for something that strange. She had a fleeting vision of the woman she'd seen on the *Antiques Roadshow* the evening Julie had first telephoned, the woman with the flowery dungarees and the Elton John spectacles, deferring to the expert with the voluminous sideburns.

See what you make of that, waistcoat man. That should take the wind out of your sails.

"It's very unusual," Selena said. Julie's palm was open, waiting. Selena placed the pendant into it. Her hand felt curiously light afterwards, like a puppet hand being tugged upwards at the end of a string. "Beautiful."

"You don't like it, I can tell," Julie said.

"I do," Selena answered her, although Julie was right, she realised, there was something about the pendant that creeped her out.

"It doesn't matter. I should be going now, anyway." Julie sounded sad, worn down. She slipped the chain back over her head. The pendant disappeared inside her T-shirt. Selena felt relieved to see the back of it.

"We're going to sort this out," she said to Julie. "You do know I care about you?"

"Of course," Julie said. She smiled, but her thoughts were already elsewhere, Selena could tell, worrying away at scraps, tag ends of old memories, the faded rags of time. Selena thought again of Johnny, who enjoyed surprises the way a child did. Johnny had dreamed of racing monster trucks, so that's what he did. He never gave a thought to what others might think, or what was sensible. Possible, even. The only question Johnny had asked himself about chasing his dream was how best to go about it.

Selena tried to imagine Johnny in his new world: the shapes, the colours, the pervasive heat. Forty degrees, she thought. For the first time she wondered if she might have made a mistake in not going with him, as he had wanted her to.

What was so great about her life that she couldn't imagine changing it for someone she loved? What had she been waiting for?

Then she realised that if she had gone to Kuala Lumpur, Julie would most likely never have found her.

The kind of coincidence that only someone with Johnny's love of the ineffable would properly appreciate.

## 2

Selena remembered seeing Allison Gifford on the TV news, a straight-backed, dark-haired woman with a habit of looking away from the camera. She had scant memory of the newspaper articles though, the endless, predatory speculation about Gifford's personal life: the partial breakdown she'd suffered during her final year at Oxford, the death of her partner, the lack of any regular contact with her parents and sister. Selena found it difficult to imagine what it must have been like for Allison Gifford to have her privacy violated like that, to have her rights called into question on the basis of a few unsubstantiated rumours.

Selena wondered who had reported her, who had seen it as their business – their duty, even – to make that phone call.

In the end, the story had run its course and then died down. Going on for a year after Julie's disappearance, a brief article in the *Warrington Guardian* announced that Allison Gifford had resigned from her part-time teaching position at Priestley College and would not be returning in the new academic year. *Gifford briefly hit the headlines last summer when she was arrested as part of the investigation surrounding the disappearance of Priestley student Julie Rouane, the* article stated. *The college authorities have issued a statement affirming that Allison Gifford was an excellent teacher in every way and that her students would miss her. It is believed that Gifford has since moved away from the Manchester area.*

Selena continued her search of the online news archives, surprised by how much of this stuff she had forgotten or simply chosen not to remember. I must have blanked it, she thought. Pushed it to the back of my mind, the way people move unwanted furniture into the spare room and then forget about it. At the time, Margery had done her best to banish newspapers from the house entirely, and yet Selena had sought them out anyway, sneaking copies of the *Warrington Guardian* from the pile that always accumulated in the laundrette she passed on her way home from school, hiding them in the bottom of her bag and then sneaking them up to her room to read in secret, as if they were pornography. She would pore over every article, trying to still the flutter of excitement that would flip up inside her each time she saw Julie's name mentioned and never quite managing it.

She asked herself if this was what it felt like to be famous.

Not that anyone gave a monkey's what she thought or felt. Selena remembered how she had become afraid of mentioning her sister or even speaking her name, caught as she was between the shame of saying something stupid or irrelevant and the horror of accidentally revealing her obsession with the forbidden news stories. The illicit delight she felt in *being important* when she happened to overhear her schoolmates repeating those stories on the playground at break time, saying that teacher of Julie's must have been guilty of something, or why would she have been arrested? Julie and Gifford had been lesbian lovers, that was obvious, they were planning to run away together. Only Julie got scared, that's what happened, and so the bull dyke strangled her with a piece of fishing line, stuffed her body in the back of her car and…

*Dumped her in the lake, didn't she? That's why the police keep looking there.*

What Selena feared most was that in listening to these snippets of gossip she was letting Julie down in some way, that she was maybe even preventing her from being found. She lived in terror of Margery unearthing her secret stash of newspapers.

Above all, she was furious at Julie, for disappearing. Trust her sister to grab the headlines – she would love this. But how can you be angry with someone who might be dead?

## 'A Woman Seldom Seen' – Celeste Adewami for the *Independent on Sunday*, May 2012

'Did I think she was beautiful?' says Allison Gifford. 'That's a question I can't answer. I think beauty is a dangerous conceit, especially when it's applied to people and especially when it's applied to women. Julie was tall, and rather angular. She never wore much make-up, if any, and she didn't dress up. She seemed most comfortable in jeans and trainers, plain T-shirts and jumpers in neutral colours. I don't think Julie disliked her body, she just wasn't bothered about clothes in the way some girls are. She was a private sort of person. Not shy exactly, just cautious. I never had sex with her, whatever the newspapers wanted people to believe. I have no idea if Julie had a love life – she never told me and I never asked. Did I have fantasies? Yes, I had fantasies. Who doesn't?'

The first draft of what eventually became my fourth novel, *Snake in the Grass*, was inspired by the disappearance of the Yorkshire chef Claudia Lawrence in 2009. What fascinated me especially about the case was the way it went cold. For a week or so the news was full of Claudia – her photograph, documentary footage of where she'd last been seen, interviews with members of her family and with her colleagues. But look at the papers a month afterwards and there's nothing.

A large number of missing persons cases are actually resolved fairly quickly. Either the person turns out not to have been missing in the first place, or the police follow a trail of clues, resulting in an arrest and, not infrequently, the discovery of a body. Very occasionally you might hear about the kind of case we all recognise from detective fiction: someone really does go missing, only this time the police are clever enough or lucky enough or simply quick enough to find that person alive.

What we hear less about are what I like to call the real missing persons cases: those individuals who disappear from their lives one day, never to

281

return. Sometimes such a disappearance may be voluntary, sometimes not. In the case of Claudia Lawrence, there was no evidence to suggest she planned her departure, and as I studied the dwindling news reports I began asking myself how many other cases like hers might exist.

What interested me most was what happens next. There is no more news, because there is no news. But what might be going on behind the scenes?

I began reading about as many of these cold cases as I could find, and it was during the course of my search for information that I first came across the case of Allison Gifford, and Julie Rouane. Julie disappeared from her home in the village of Lymm, near Manchester, in the mid-1990s. Her body was never found, nor was anyone ever convicted of her murder or kidnapping. The Rouane case remains a mystery, unsolved. Of the three suspects apprehended and questioned by the police, only one of them, Steven Jimson, turned out to be of significant interest. Several years after Julie's disappearance, Jimson was tried and convicted on four counts of murder, along with a string of violent sexual offences. He is currently serving a life sentence, although he has always vehemently denied any involvement in the disappearance of Julie Rouane.

The other two suspects could best be categorised as innocent bystanders. The first to be arrested, Brendan Conway, was a man in his thirties with moderate learning difficulties. In the hours and days following his arrest, the tabloid news media portrayed Conway as a ghoul, a misfit, the stereotypical dangerous loner who is a menace to society in general and to young women in particular. When Conway was proved to have no identifiable connection with the case, the papers lost no time in recasting him as a local hero, misunderstood by the public and deserving of a wider sympathy. Many photographs of Conway with his two Irish wolfhounds appeared in local papers and on television.

The second suspect, Allison Gifford, was not so quickly exonerated. Gifford, who worked as a part-time teacher at the sixth-form college attended by Julie Rouane, was taken into custody four days after the teenager disappeared. Although all allegations were eventually dropped, Gifford was suspended from her job and faced an onslaught of intensive media scrutiny for weeks and even months following her release. It was rumoured that Gifford had been pursuing an illicit relationship with Julie, and although Gifford always insisted that her friendship with the teenager was entirely innocent, the news editors at the time seemed reluctant to give up the story, fanning the flames of outrage and running a number of interviews with a former male partner of Gifford's. After receiving a particularly offensive series of poison pen letters, Gifford reluctantly decided to sell her home and make a new life elsewhere. She appears to have no online presence, and I was finally able to make contact with her through the English department of the adult education college in the west of England where she now teaches. She informed me she has little interest in or knowledge of crime fiction, but generously agreed to meet with me and answer some questions.

Allison Gifford was thirty years old at the time of her arrest, still in recovery from the death of her then partner and still trying to decide if her move from journalism to teaching had been a good one. Her hair is grey now, but she is recognisably the same person: courteous but bluntly spoken and with a directness of approach to difficult subjects that is unusual. We spend some time talking about the inevitable difficulties of the north-south adjustment before I begin to tentatively ask her about Julie Rouane. I am interested to know if Gifford remembers the first time she saw Julie, if she made a particular impression? I expect a degree of prevarication on Gifford's part, nervousness even, but she answers me as fully and as thoughtfully as she answered my earlier question about leaving Manchester:

'Yes, she did make an impression, but not in the way most people mean it when they say that. People want to believe there was a big attraction, but I noticed her because she was sitting by herself. She was already in the room when I got there, reading a book and fiddling with a pencil. She didn't seem to have any friends, and I made a mental note for myself to keep an eye on her. She had the look of someone who was being bullied, or who had been bullied in the past – a closed-off, watchful look, as if she found it difficult to trust anyone. I remember checking to see what it was she was reading – a book about alien abductions, or flying saucers, not what I'd expected at all. That was something else that made her stick in my mind.'

When I ask Allison Gifford if she thinks Julie was someone who went out of her way to be different, she shakes her head at once.

'Was she seeking attention, you mean? I don't think so, not at all. She seemed very shy the first time I spoke to her. A week or two later I asked her if she wanted to go for coffee. She said yes, but she looked scared, as if she thought she might be in trouble for something. I shouldn't have done it, I knew that even at the time. I'd never behaved that way before, not with a student, although nothing really happened. The newspapers said all kinds of stupid things, but none of them were true. One of those parasites even tried to make a connection between Julie and Jo, although Julie was the opposite of Jo in almost every way. Jo always knew what she wanted. She never compromised and that was part of why I loved her. If I had to use one word to describe Julie it would be restless. She seemed to have no idea of what she wanted, or even who she was, most of the time. There was an energy about her though, an intensity. Like a radio with the volume turned down, only still broadcasting. She said some strange things, Julie. She once told me she'd been adopted, although I was pretty certain that wasn't true.'

Jo was Josephine Adams, a young dramatist Gifford met when the two were both students at Oxford. Adams was diagnosed with leukaemia while Gifford was working on assignment in Beijing. She died eight months later. It was Adams's death that prompted Gifford to give up news journalism and move into life writing. At the time, she says, the change seemed dramatic, a necessary withdrawal from the world, though she has since come to believe that the two disciplines are closely connected.

'The wars between individuals and families are really not all that different from wars between nations. Observe closely enough and you'll see it's just a matter of scale.'

Does Gifford believe that Julie's disappearance might, as some believed at the time, have been connected to problems within her own family?

'From what I could tell, Julie's parents were decent people who cared about her. Julie never tried to suggest otherwise, though it was clear she felt she was different from her parents, that they were conventional and rather dull. She had a younger sister she used to be close to, but they'd drifted apart. She was a typical teenager, in other words. She was still very young. People tend to forget that.'

We talk for some time about our own childhoods, and the way teenagers today seem so much more confident and streetwise than we felt ourselves. Gifford tells me a little about some of the women she has encountered through her prison writing projects, how mature they seem in some ways, how astonishingly naive in others. She is clearly angry about society's attitude to women offenders, passionate in her engagement with their stories.

When I ask her what she believes happened to Julie, she is quick to answer.

'I think she was murdered. She was probably dead before anyone realised she was missing. I remember the night she disappeared as if it were yesterday. I ate Chinese takeaway in front of the television. *Blind Date* was on, then *Stars in their Eyes*. I watched that through to the end then spent the rest of the evening doing some marking. I wanted to get the school work out of the way so I would have Sunday free. Those were the last properly peaceful hours I had for the whole of the next two years. Julie going missing was the worst thing that ever happened to me. Worse than Jo's death even, because Jo's death was private. What happened with Julie left me wishing I'd never met her, never spoken to her, that she'd never existed. Even the act of remembering her seemed tainted, as if I were guilty of something, which I knew I wasn't.

I thought I'd never get over it.'

She pauses, and for a moment I see her as she was in the newspaper photographs: the hurt in her eyes, a sense of isolation that can never be lifted.

'You know the strangest thing about her?' Gifford adds. 'Julie was terrified of black holes. She told me they gave her nightmares. When I asked her why, she said that black holes proved there were a lot of things we didn't know about the universe, and that most of them were terrifying.'

[From *Snake in the Grass* by Celeste Adewami, Macmillan, 2012]

The fear rose up in Angela like damp rising up through the lawn, the kind of dampness that comes on at night, beading the grass stems with dewdrops, with what Angela's sister Agnes used to call fairy piss.

It disappears with the sunrise, Agnes said. Pfff, like ghost breath. That's what the sour smell is, you know, when you open the back door first thing.

Evaporates, Angela had corrected her. And there's no smell anyway. You can't smell fairies.

You can, too. They're all stinky when you get a lot of them together, I bet. Like a nest of white mice.

Did Rowena remind her of Agnes, is that what it was? Angela didn't think so, not at all. Rowena was tall, like her name. Agnes was small and firm and upright as a Russian doll. One of the maths masters at their old school had once referred to Agnes's intellect as terrifying. When their father found out what the master had said, he'd threatened to go up to the school and have it out with the man.

Oh God, Dad, no, Agnes had moaned. Mr James is just a bit of a—

Dipshit? said Angela.

I was going to say unreconstructed nineteen-fifties male, Agnes said.

So your father is a better feminist than I am, said their mother. Why else do you think I married him? She was leaning in towards the hallway mirror, applying lipstick in a shade called Aurora's Dream, a sort of pinkish brown, like dawn light shining on the pointed facades of the ironstone almshouses just off the High Street. Aurora was the goddess of the dawn.

Rowena's hair was strawberry-blonde, a similar colour. Dense and faintly wavy, like some kind of grass crop. Rowena moved around Angela's sitting room on tiptoe, hugging her bag to her side as if she was afraid of breaking something.

You have a lot of books, she said. Angela couldn't help noticing how Rowena's eyes kept sliding off the books and wandering towards the shelf where she kept the things she'd brought back from China, tourist souvenirs mainly and yet they were precious to her, keepsakes from another life. She loved the soapstone box especially, with its entwined dragons. Pinkish, like alabaster.

She wondered if it would be all right to offer Rowena a glass of wine. She had a bottle already opened, a fragrant Chianti, so no one could accuse her of opening it especially. Perhaps coffee would be safer, or even hot chocolate, a child's drink for a child's late night, although the thought of cocoa, with its intimations of crisp bedsheets and plump duvets, made Angela's head spin.

Would you like something to drink? she asked, and

then immediately regretted not replying to Rowena's comment about the books. She could have asked her if there were any she might like to borrow, or simply talk about. Talking about books might make sense of things. Of this, of whatever this was. Asking Rowena back to her flat when there was no reason for her to come here, no reason at all, except that her flat was close to the cinema and Rowena had seemed so upset by the film, there had been tears in her eyes. Angela hadn't liked the idea of her going home straight away. That's what she told herself, anyway, though why she'd invited Rowena to go to the cinema with her in the first place remained unclear.

A student, Angela thought. The kind of thing you read about in someone's discarded copy of the *Daily Mirror*.

I'd love a cup of tea, Rowena said. Her fingers brushed the lid of the soapstone box.

You can pick it up, if you like, Angela said. I bought it while I was in China. She hurried into the kitchen and put the kettle on. The relief of being out of the room, whilst knowing that Rowena was still in the room, made her knees shake. She made tea in the straight-sided china beakers she'd brought back from Copenhagen, modern variants on a Chinese original in Danish porcelain. Rowena would think she was obsessed with China, which she had been once. Still, not to worry, who cared. Two mugs of tea, even though Angela herself would have preferred a glass of wine. Vastly preferred, she would have said. Maybe later. Macaroons on a sky-blue plate. Pretty things, sweet things, she thought to herself, then realised she was sounding like the witch in *Hansel and Gretel*, a difficult image to dispel once it had wandered in.

She returned to the sitting room with the tea things. Rowena was sitting on the edge of the couch, the way you'd sit at your aunt's house, afraid of scrunching the cushions or getting dirt on the seat covers. The soapstone box was balanced on her knees. Angela smiled.

Here's your tea, she said. She placed the tray – beakers, macaroons, the whole shebang – on the low table in front of the sofa. Carved legs in the shape of lions' feet. China again.

Thanks.

Angela went to sit on the sofa beside her, then changed her mind. She sat in the armchair opposite, her eyes drawn – inevitably, unsparingly – to Rowena's drawn-together knees and the dragon box upon them, the long droop of rose-coloured hair, the same colour, almost, as the hair of the girl in the film who had played the accomplice, the weaker one, the girl who'd been ill but who had agreed they should go through with the murder nonetheless.

She hadn't swung the brick but she'd been there when it happened. She hadn't stopped it.

Of all the murders she'd seen onscreen, that had been the worst, Angela thought, because it seemed so real. She reached for her tea.

Are you feeling better? she asked.

I'm sorry. You must think I'm pathetic.

It's my fault. If I'd known the film would upset you so much—

I felt so angry, that's all. They should have left them alone.

The girls? Angela couldn't remember Rowena ever saying so much at once before. Not just in class – in class she was mainly silent – but that time they'd had coffee together in the refectory, she'd barely said a word then, either. Embarrassed to be seen with a teacher? And yet when Angela had asked if she'd like to see a movie with her, Rowena had agreed at once.

*As if she'd been waiting to be asked*, or so Angela had told herself. She wondered now if that was wishful thinking, if Rowena had simply been too embarrassed to say no.

They weren't hurting anyone, were they? Rowena said. All they wanted was to be together. But that's what always happens when adults are scared of something. They try and destroy it.

There were tiny spots of colour in her cheeks. She looked as if she might start crying again.

Life is always difficult for people who are different, Angela said. The newspapers of the time had described the girls as possessed, monsters, daughters of Satan. She wondered if she should share this information with Rowena, then decided to tell her about the soapstone box instead.

I found this in a funny little antiques shop close to the centre of Beijing, she said. It was in the basement of a warehouse somewhere. I can't remember now who told me about it. One of the other reporters, I expect. I wasn't really there long enough to have Chinese friends.

Angela remembered Jing Li, who had been assigned to their office as their official translator: the dark line of her hair against her jawline, straight as a blade, the perfect curve of her throat, like the inside of a shell. It had been a joke between herself and Agnes, how much she'd fancied her. Of course she'd never dared do anything about it, she was far too shy.

I think it's beautiful, Rowena said. I love the dragons.

Have it, Angela almost said, then didn't, because the box was hers and she still wanted it, needed it to remind her of who she'd been when she'd come across it in that unexpected place, half market stall, half junk room. All that teal-blue silk, she remembered, piled up in the corner like old dustsheets.

If she gave the box to Rowena she'd never see it again, never hold it in her hand, small as a pack of cards but twice as heavy. That might not matter now, but it would hurt later, she knew it would. She plucked the box from Rowena's knees and placed it gently on the tea tray, next to the sky-blue plate with the macaroons.

I should call you a taxi, she said.

I could stay here, if you want, Rowena said. She pushed her hair back from her face then let it fall forward again, her cheeks flushed red, as if she'd drunk the Chianti after all. It would be easier for getting to college in the morning.

A little joke for them to enjoy later, once this peculiar, awkward beginning was long in the past and they could laugh about it? God, you were so slow! I thought nothing was ever going to happen.

What about your parents? Angela said.

That's OK. I can tell them I'm staying over with a friend.

Which is exactly what she did, five minutes later, padding into the hallway in her stocking feet, only she was wearing socks, not stockings, an Argyll pattern. Men's socks, they looked like, her dad's, probably. Her feet in those bulky socks. Angela felt she might faint from longing at the sight of them. She sat rigid in her armchair, trying not to eavesdrop. Yeah, Miranda's, she heard Rowena say, but nothing else. She glanced at her watch: just gone eleven. Would they phone Miranda's house, to check? Who phoned anyone after eleven, unless it was an emergency? Why would they, anyway? She was just being paranoid.

Rowena looked different when she returned to the room. *Older*, Angela thought, wished, told herself. There was a light in her eyes that hadn't been there previously. Right, Rowena said. That's them sorted. Shall we put on some music?

Angela fetched the Chianti from the kitchen and they danced. At the time, Angela thought she would remember forever the detailed step-by-step of how it happened – how one minute they were sitting in armchairs drinking tea and the next they were dancing to Hazel O'Connor, their arms draped across each other's shoulders, wine glasses in hand.

Rowena crooned along to the lyrics, laughing when she came to the end of the line, just to play it safe, Angela supposed, just to prove to them both it could still be a joke if either of them wanted it to be. And then that sax riff, spiralling into the night like the bleeding outer edges of the Milky Way.

At least Angela still had a part of her mind left, enough to stop the thing from ending her completely.

There's just the one bed, she said. I'll sleep on the sofa.

It's OK, said Rowena. They'd finished the wine by then, and it was well after midnight. Rowena was beginning to droop. She rested her head on Angela's shoulder, the rucked-up mass of her rosy hair tickling against her nose.

I'll find you something to wear, then, Angela said, and she did, a huge grey T-shirt with a hole under one arm, REYKJAVIK across the front in dirty-white capitals, not the place but an obscure post-punk band from the end of the eighties. Angela had seen their drummer play live once at Ronnie Scott's. Cass had been her name, Cass Reinhardt? Angela loved the T-shirt too much to throw it away.

Rowena removed her jeans and then her jersey, their evacuated tubes dumped in messy worm-cast piles at the side of the bed. Rowena's body was firm, squarish, the bushy mass of pubic hair surprisingly dark. The moment hovered and then passed. Rowena pulled the Reykjavik T-shirt over her head. It reached to her knees. Beneath the faded cloth, the bumps of her nipples were just visible.

Rowena—

It's OK, Rowena said. We were just dancing. She

pulled back her side of the duvet and scrambled in. Angela undressed, facing the wall. By the time she turned back to the bed Rowena was asleep, or at least she was pretending to be.

Angela climbed into bed and switched out the light. She could hear the girl's breathing, slow and deep, see the dark bulk of her shape faintly outlined against the curtains. Angela shifted to lie on her side, then slid her hand beneath her nightshirt and between her legs. Her clitoris felt huge, like a grape. She teased it gently with the edge of her nail, relishing its soreness, remembering the blunt convexity of Rowena's nipples, the dark pubic hair. She penetrated herself, squeezing the insides of her thighs against her hand. She came almost at once, a liquid silence. The rhythm of Rowena's breathing did not change.

Angela dozed on and off for a couple of hours, her thoughts a feverish jumble of disjointed syllables and dream images. A child's first alphabet: beach balls and elephants, a gyroscope, a pair of red velvet slippers with golden trim. At some weird hour she reached sideways to her bedside table and picked up her watch. Five o'clock. She tiptoed to the bathroom, quietly washed her face and then dressed herself in the clothes she'd dumped in the laundry basket two days before. Rowena surfaced at around eight o'clock. Angela made them both coffee and toast, then Rowena said she'd better be going, she had a class at nine.

Urban studies, she said. We're learning about the history of Manchester.

They were the last words Rowena ever spoke to her, at least in private.

*No act of intimacy took place.* When they asked Angela about that night later – at the police station, on the witness stand – that was the story her lawyer said she should stick to, and so she did. She told them she slept on the sofa, and occasionally she convinced herself that she really had. *No act of intimacy took place.* Could dancing to Hazel O'Connor be classed as an act of intimacy? She doubted it. Not by lawyers, anyway. Angela kept the tape of *Breaking Glass*, but she never played it again. Some years later she bought a CD replacement, but she never played that, either.

Selena read *Snake in the Grass* from cover to cover in just a few hours. She was surprised by how deeply she became absorbed in it. There had been a time when she avoided crime stories of all kinds, but especially any that involved a missing person or a lost child. The bit that always got to her was when the police came. The moment when a normal day became something horrific, when the lives of ordinary people became a story for others to read about in the newspapers.

Celeste Adewami's Wikipedia entry said she was a junior BBC researcher who had stumbled into writing fiction almost by accident. She still enjoyed doing research, and liked to base her crime novels on real-life cases. In Adewami's fourth novel *Snake in the Grass*, Rowena Kingston gets abducted by someone she meets by chance in the city art gallery, a man no one seems to know or to have even laid eyes on. The subplot about Angela Craig starts off seeming like a red herring, but turns out not to be. Once she is released from prison, Angela becomes more and more obsessed with Rowena, and with her disappearance. She ends up on the trail of the killer, whose identity Adewami keeps cleverly hidden until the very end.

Selena felt uncomfortable at first, knowing that Adewami had based the character of Angela Craig on Allison Gifford, but after a while she became so wrapped up in the story she stopped thinking about it. She liked Angela's voice, the skewed clarity of her thoughts, the intensity of her inner reflections. It was as if Adewami had been transcribing the thoughts of a real person.

Rowena Kingston though, she was like the blank space in a jigsaw puzzle where the missing piece should go. People talked about her all the time, but everyone seemed to have a different opinion and you ended up not trusting any of them.

No one knew Rowena. Not really.

In Adewami's novel, Rowena's best friend was called Carina Ghosh. Either Allison Gifford never mentioned Lucinda Milner in her interview with Adewami, or Adewami had chosen not to include the material. Julie seemed to think that Allison hadn't known about Lucy, but even if that was true, there had been photos of her in all the local newspapers, both soon after Julie went missing and a year later, when Lucy got into Oxford.

Until she read Adewami's book, the idea of tracking down Lucinda Milner had never occurred to her. Lucy had come to the house a few times, though Selena had barely spoken to her. She had seemed mysterious and vaguely aloof, part of the new life Julie was leading at college, the life she guarded like the entrance to a separate existence. Where Lucy ended up after Oxford, Selena had no idea. The Milners would have moved by now, several times, probably. In the end it was only her certainty that the trail would have gone cold that allowed Selena to dare herself to dial the Milners' old number, still preserved like an autumn leaf, between the pages of an old school exercise book in Dad's old Filofax, one of the artefacts she'd rescued from his flat without knowing why.

A woman answered, and when Selena stammered that she was looking for Lucy, that she'd been at college with Lucy but had lost her address, the woman did not seem surprised, not even mildly. She said it was no wonder Lucy couldn't keep track of her friends, not with all the moving around she went in for.

"Not that I'm not proud of her, but you know, it would be nice if she could decide to stay in one place for more than five minutes," the woman said. She read out a telephone number then got Selena to repeat it. "If you do speak to her, you could remind her it would be nice if she telephoned home once in a while," the woman added. Selena said she would. She thanked the woman and then put down the phone. Her knees were shaking. What's wrong with you? she asked herself. She didn't even know who you were.

A London dialling code. Selena studied the number closely, as if she meant to learn it by heart. Did she really mean to dial it? Apparently, she did. Four, five, six rings, and then an out-of-breath voice: "Hi, Sunita – I literally just got in."

In an initial moment of confusion, Selena thought it was her own name Lucy had uttered – not Sunita but Selena. She hesitated, realised, blushed.

"Hi, is that Lucy?" she said.

"Oh my gosh, I'm so sorry. I thought you were someone else. Yes, this is Lucy speaking. How can I help?"

"This is going to sound weird, coming out of the blue like this, but I was wondering if I could talk to you for a couple of minutes? It's Selena Rouane."

In the moments between dialling the number and Lucy picking up, Selena had found herself wondering if her name would still mean anything to Lucy Milner. It was a long time ago, after all. Lucy had known Julie for what, eighteen months? Two years at the most. There was every likelihood that the drama and horror surrounding her friend's disappearance had faded, had become a distant tragedy associated with childhood, terrifying while it was happening but now very much in the past.

Lucy's sharp intake of breath removed these doubts pretty much immediately.

"Selena?" There was a long pause, long enough for Selena to hear Lucy's expectations of a cosy chat with her friend Sunita go glugging away down the plughole like stale beer. She could almost feel her wondering: had Julie been found? She was dying to ask, Selena could tell, but what if Julie had been found, but dead? Better to let the silence take them both over.

"Nothing's happened," Selena said quickly. "It's just that my dad died, and I've been going through his stuff. It brought back some memories."

"I'm sorry, Selena," Lucy said. She sounded relieved. Not that Dad's dead, of course. Just that it's nothing more – more onerous. A sympathetic ear was all Selena needed. Lucy was a doctor. How hard could it be?

"We never really talked, did we?" Selena said. "I suppose I'm still trying to understand what happened." She was surprised at how easily it came to her, the role of the survivor seeking closure, the victim of a thousand TV reality shows. She wanted to laugh, to become Sunita just for a moment so she and Lucy could have a good snigger at how ridiculous she was, this woman who was prepared to phone up a total stranger in search of answers to questions that should have been asked twenty years ago or not at all.

"I'm not sure how I can help," Lucy said. "I don't know what happened, either."

"Julie never tried to contact you? After she went missing, I mean?"

"Of course not." She sounded shocked, though whether it was the question itself or her for asking it that had prompted this reaction it was hard to say. "I would have gone straight to the police if she had. I wasn't even in the country when Julie disappeared. I was staying with my cousins. You do know that?"

"I'm not trying to blame anyone, please don't think that. I know you and Julie were close, that's all. I thought you might be able to tell me what you remember."

"We were kids." Lucy sighed. "They're not good memories, to be honest. I don't just mean Julie going missing, I mean before that. We were close, for a while, but everything got very intense and that wasn't what I wanted. It was such a relief, to get on a plane and leave the whole mess behind. I honestly believed that by the time I came home in September, things might have sorted themselves out. Having to answer all those questions – being in the paper – made everything worse. I know this isn't what you wanted to hear. I'm sorry."

"That's OK," Selena said. "It was just on the off chance."

"Listen, I didn't mean—"

"No, honestly, I shouldn't have called. It was a stupid idea. I'm sorry for disturbing you."

She replaced the receiver. In the second before it went down, she could hear Lucy at the other end, still trying to say something, still apologising. The sound of her voice had brought it all back – the way Julie had behaved around Lucy, the way Selena had felt invisible when Lucy was around. That hadn't been Lucy's fault, Selena understood that, but she felt a thrill of pleasure in hanging up on her, nonetheless. Replacing the receiver in its cradle without coming to a mutual agreement as to when this should happen. As if she had made Lucy invisible for once, instead of the other way around.

**[Letter from Mrs Lucy Khalil MRCS to Selena Rouane, undated.]**

*I didn't always want to be a doctor, believe it or not. But I did some volunteer work at the hospital where my mum worked and I suppose you could say I got hooked. Mum worked in* obstetrics. She trained in Kolkata. My dad just happened to be out there doing a placement – that's how they met. I had to repeat a year at college so I could get the right A levels. My parents supported me all the way though, which made things easier. Julie never knew I was going to India the summer she disappeared because we'd more or less stopped speaking by then anyway. It was awful when I got back. People kept asking me how I was feeling, making allowances for me for being such a bitch most of the time, but what I was mostly feeling was anger. For ages I was convinced that Julie had decided to run away – she did sometimes talk about it, just skipping town, she called it – and I felt furious she hadn't told me, that she'd left me behind on my own to deal with her shit. I couldn't say that though, could I? Not with them dragging the lake and everything. It was like being gagged.

Even though we had that row, I always believed we'd get over it. Real friendships survive those kinds of setbacks and I thought we had something real, in spite of everything. I think I hated Julie for a while. It was lucky I had the hospital work, because it helped to take my mind off her going missing and how guilty I felt. By the time I was back at college I felt like a different person, which I suppose I was.

The actual fight was about everything and nothing. I'd started seeing someone – a bloke. I was curious, and flattered. Julie was furious. I mean, death-ray furious. She said I was faking my feelings just to get attention and I told her to stop being so fucking jealous. It was awful. I was used to getting into rows with my brothers but this was different. I felt as if I'd just torn my whole world apart. I thought at the time it was all about Julie being queer and me being straight, but it wasn't, not really. It wasn't about jealousy either, or at least jealousy was only part of it, a symptom. There was more of a fundamental personality clash at work, I think. I'm a practical person. If I'm not satisfied with something, I start looking for ways to fix it. Workable solutions, Dad calls them, but Julie didn't believe in workable solutions. She preferred revolution. Burning down the castle. There was an intensity about her. That's what attracted me to her in the first place. But it became oppressive in the end. Depressing. I think my starting up with Justin was a bid for freedom. I knew it was the one thing Julie wouldn't stand for and so I just went for it. Justin and I didn't last out the summer, although he is still a friend, funnily enough.

I'd like to keep believing Julie did run away, that she disappeared through choice, because it's better than the alternative. I can't bear to think of her being dead – murdered – while I was still so angry at her. I still feel uncomfortable about that. Stupid, I know. But if I'm being realistic I suppose that's what happened. She trusted the wrong person, got into the wrong car, who can say? I always thought how appalling it must be for her parents, that the police never managed to find her body. There's something so final about a body. I see dead bodies every day, and the thing I found surprising almost from the first day is how restful they are, how reassuring. When you're dealing with a body there's never any doubt in your mind that what you're seeing is just a shell. Human remains. Whatever was inside it is long gone. I've never once cried over a body because there's no point. But seeing the body – touching it – does help you to focus on the person, to remember them.

*To know they're OK, even. I would always encourage relatives to view the body of a loved one, even if there's damage. That probably doesn't sound very scientific, but it's how I feel.*

*Julie sometimes used to talk about the south of France. She said it was cheap to live there, that we could get jobs as grape-pickers or hotel staff or something. When I asked her what we were meant to do in the long run she said that didn't matter, we'd know once we were there, the important thing was just to leave, just to do it. I thought it was all a pipe dream. I wanted to do my A levels. Some revolutionary I turned out to be. I suppose I should have told the police this at the time, but I didn't. I wasn't trying to hide anything. I just thought it sounded daft, when you said it out loud, the kind of fantasy kids have about escaping their parents and beginning a new life somewhere else. I told the police I had no idea where Julie might have gone, that I hadn't spoken to her since before the holidays. That was almost true, although she did phone me once, the weekend after term ended, which was the weekend before she went missing. She was calling from a phone box, and she was crying. I asked her what she wanted, and when she didn't answer I put down the phone. My whole body was shaking, I don't know why. I felt sorry for her, but I didn't feel like seeing her, not yet anyway. I didn't say anything to the police because I didn't want them to know about our row. I've never told anyone I lied to them, can you believe it? I still feel odd about that.*

*I had no idea about Gifford, not even remotely. Not until it was in the papers, I mean. I was a bit pissed off, actually. I remember wanting to ask Julie how long it had been going* on. *I could hear the words inside my head, how long has this been going on, like a scene from* EastEnders. *I thought that if I had something to accuse her of I might feel less awful myself. It really wasn't a good time for me. I felt sorry for Gifford, though. She must have been through hell.*

## 3

"Don't worry," Selena says. "You'll be fine."

Julie is wearing a dark-green pleated skirt, a jersey top and a pair of knee-high lace-up boots. Aside from the nondescript trouser suit Julie wears for her hospital job, it is the first time Selena has seen her in anything but jeans and trainers. She's trying to look smart, Selena thinks, though mainly she just looks uncomfortable.

"What did you tell her?" Julie asks.

"Nothing much. I thought it would be better to wait until we get there. It'll be fine," she insists again. They have come in Julie's car, which makes the whole enterprise feel strange, topsy-turvy, as if it is Julie who suggested it, although of course she did not and in fact Selena has revealed nothing to their mother apart from saying she'd like to come over for dinner on Tuesday if that's all right, she has some news for her.

Selena knows Margery will presume it's Johnny she wants to talk about, that perhaps Johnny is coming home, that they're not splitting up after all, something like that. Selena tells herself she's kept quiet in order to make things easier for Julie, to avoid making a big deal of everything, and perhaps that's true, but mainly what she wants is to take

Margery by surprise, to get a good look at her expression when she opens the door.

Mum will know at once if it's Julie or not, and that will be proof. Proof that Julie is really Julie and not some impostor. Proof that there is no harm in believing her story, the parts of it that make sense, anyway – Steven Jimson and the flat in Coventry and the woman named Lisa. Julie won't tell their mother about the alien planet, the brain-eating isopods, not a word, Selena would bet her life on it.

As they arrive on the doorstep Julie hesitates. "I don't think I can do this," she says.

"We're here now," Selena says. "You'll be fine."

She presses the bell before Julie can change her mind, then places a hand on Julie's arm, more to prevent her from doing a runner than to offer support. There is a light already on in the hallway. Margery's shape looms at them from behind the glass, a shadowy outline that could be anything, Selena muses, if you didn't know beforehand that it was your mother.

"You're early," Margery says as she opens the door. She's right, they are, Selena realises, because in spite of the various traffic holdups the car has brought them here more quickly than the train. She watches Margery's face closely as she sees firstly that there is someone else here besides Selena and secondly as it dawns on her who this person is. Then it happens, so clearly unmistakable it is like a camera flash: the moment of incredulity, the confirmation Selena has been seeking from the second she picked up the phone and heard the woman who said she was Julie utter her name.

Selena watches the sequence of emotions play out,

freeze frames on a movie screen. Her mother's eyes darting, quick as a bird's and as avidly hungry. Then the negation, the blanket of self-protection pulled swiftly around her: *Do others see what I see, or will they think me a fool? Will we be laughing about this later, or will they?*

"Selena?" Margery says, and Selena realises she is asking her permission – permission to believe in the impossible.

"Mum," Julie says, pre-empting her. She buries her face in Margery's shoulder, her own shoulders shaking. Margery clasps Julie closely and somewhat awkwardly – she has never mastered the art of hugging, never taken to it – and stares over the top of her head towards Selena, her entreaty and incredulity now tinged with just a grain of fury: how long have you known, how could you keep this from me, *do you think I'm like Ray?*

"Surprise," Selena says at last. Her mother does not pass comment and she is glad. The matter is out of her hands now – it is part of the world. She is filled with relief, heady as wine and coloured only slightly by that sense of resignation she felt so often as a child, the sense that Julie was the problem one, the serious one, the important one, that she, Selena, was ordinary and usually in the way.

Who gives a shit, she thinks. She lets out her breath, which coalesces in front of her face, a wisp of pale steam. She misses Johnny, suddenly. The feeling seems to have materialised out of nowhere, along with her breath.

\* \* \*

"You should have warned me, Selena. There's barely enough to go round."

The supper is a dish of lasagne and there's plenty to go round. If Selena had come by herself, Margery would have divided the lasagne between them and put the leftovers in the fridge with cling film over it, for her supper tomorrow. As it is they finish the lot. Julie devours the pasta enthusiastically, wiping around her plate with a chunk of ciabatta. She is telling her mother about her job at the Christie.

"I've been offered a place on a practice management course," she says. "I'm not sure I want to be in admin permanently though. It's not really what I want to do."

"There's no rush," Mum says. "I can help you go over your CV, if you like?"

Selena waits for the shake of the head, the non-committal *mmm* sound that means Julie is about to withdraw from the conversation, but it doesn't come. "That would be great, Mum," she says instead. She is like a different person, an alien. This is the first Selena has heard of the admin course, for a start. She tries to imagine what Julie's CV looks like and cannot do it. But then what is a CV anyway but a fabrication, a levelling down of the self to fit a generalised mould?

"I'm interested in pathology," Julie is saying.

"You shouldn't have any problems switching to lab work," Margery says. "Especially when you have experience working in hospitals already."

Is Julie faking it, Selena wonders, trying on the new personality like the clothes she is wearing? Or is this who she is, after all? Who she wants to be, at any rate – accommodating and trusting, at ease with the world? Selena eats her lasagne and listens, as she might listen to a story read aloud or a play on the radio. She finds the conversation diverting yet also confusing, as if she'd come in halfway through and missed some vital plot element, a buried secret perhaps, or the truth behind one character's relationship with another. Every now and then, Julie attempts to draw her in, to make her part of the conspiracy: *Selena, remember that book we were looking at in Waterstones last week*, or, *You know what you were saying about starting a gym membership?*

Each time it happens, Selena gives some vague answer and wonders what would happen if their mother went out of the room for a moment. If this were a movie, Margery would be the one who looked foolish, chattering brightly away about nothing while the two sisters exchanged meaningful glances behind her back. The reality doesn't feel like that at all. When Selena announces she's going to make a start on the washing-up, neither Julie nor their mother tries to stop her. They're dying to be alone together, Selena realises. She cannot believe how quickly she has slipped back into her accustomed role – the annoying younger sister, forever missing the point or making snide comments.

"Could you put the coffee on while you're at it?" Margery says. "We can have it in the lounge."

Selena begins to stack the dishes by the sink. Once Julie and Margery have disappeared into the living room she puts on the radio, the same small portable that used to be in their kitchen in Sandy Lane. There's a documentary on, something about illegal gangmasters in Morecambe Bay. Selena retunes the radio to an Asian station Johnny used to listen to: fusion music mostly, and an off-the-wall cookery programme that always seems to end with everyone yelling at each other in three different languages.

Other worlds than these, Selena thinks. She has a feeling this is a quote from something but she can't remember where from. *This is Susheela Raman*, says the DJ. *'Nagumomo'*. The music glistens, the woman's voice standing out against its shimmery textures like a wavy golden thread in a swatch of dark silk.

Selena imagines a hot, dust-blown street, music like the music on the radio playing loudly through an open window, a battered flatbed truck honking its horn. Without knowing why, she finds herself thinking of Cally, the mapmaker, the single-storey house with the wooden rafters she shares with her brother Noah in a place called Gren-Noor. Selena wonders where they have come from exactly, these stories of Julie's, so deeply and closely imagined they could almost be real. She stacks clean dishes in the drainer, then runs another bowl of hot water for the glassware and cutlery. She briefly considers leaving, heading for the station without saying a word to anyone. She wonders how long it would be before her mother and sister realised she was gone.

She finishes the washing-up, puts the coffee things on a tray and goes through to the lounge. Julie is seated on the sofa, their mother is sitting in the armchair that abuts it. She is holding Julie's right hand in both of hers. The gas fire is lit. Bluish flames jerk nervously from its fake coals. They are like pictures of flames, Selena thinks, as she thinks every time she is here. An image of what a fire should be like, without really being one.

Seeing Julie and Margery together is a little bit the same.

"Julie's just been telling me about what happened with that ghastly Jimson man," Margery says. She angles her head slightly to glance at Selena then turns back to Julie. "She doesn't want to go to the police and I agree with her. She's suffered enough trauma already. And seeing as that murderer's already behind bars it can hardly matter. The only thing that matters is that Julie is home."

To hear her mother speaking of trauma is like gazing into the artificially generated, perfectly flame-shaped flames of the gas fire. Margery hates what she invariably refers to as psychobabble, the newfangled language of empathy and identity and universal compassion. Normally she would say upset, or business, as in *she's had enough of this business already*. Julie remains silent, her head bent, staring at her hand between their mother's hands as if it were an artefact, a scientific specimen. For the first time, Selena wonders if Julie is acting illegally by failing to notify the police of her return and she wonders why this question has not yet occurred to her. A lot of time and energy has been expended in trying to find her, after all. *Multiple resources*, if you prefer cop-speak.

It could be that they know already, or could know, if they could be bothered to find out. Julie presumably has a bank account, a tax record, a national insurance number. A paper trail so long and so detailed that by rights it should have been the police informing them that Julie had turned up again, rather than the other way around.

Sod them, then, Selena thinks. "It's up to Julie who she tells," she says. She sits down in the other armchair, helps herself to coffee and an almond slice. She should feel angry, she supposes – angry for being relegated, angry for being sidelined so completely that their mother hasn't even thought to ask her about her own part in Julie's resurrection, even though it was Selena Julie turned to first, and not Margery. She should feel furious, and yet she doesn't, she feels uneasy. There is something unreal about what is happening. She could almost be watching it on TV, a scene from one of those treacly afternoon mini-series that were so popular in the nineties: prodigal sons, stolen children, twins separated at birth – high dramas so full of corn, as Laurie would say, there would be enough to feed the five thousand and still have a sack left over.

It is as if Julie and Margery are both acting, playing out the roles that are expected of them and not a single cue missed. Selena finds it strange, just being in the room with them. She tries to imagine what might happen if she were to ask her mother if Julie has told her about the aliens yet, then abandons the idea. The way things are at the moment, she would be the one who ended up looking stupid. Stupid or treacherous or just plain crazy.

Let them get on with it, why don't you? She closes her eyes. The cloying heat from the gas fire is making her drowsy. Margery is asking Julie if she'd like to stay over.

"I won't, if you don't mind, Mum," Julie says. "The flat's easier for work, you see. I'll come over at the weekend though, if you like."

They make plans. Selena can't work out if she's being included or not, and doesn't much care. She tries to imagine a Saturday that is not, in one way or another, bound up with Julie, and cannot do it. Julie has come to dominate her thoughts to such an extent she is stuck on one track, she realises, like someone who has been diagnosed with a fatal illness. It is all but impossible for her to think about anything else.

Half an hour later she and Julie are in the car, heading back into Manchester.

"Thanks," Julie says. She has been silent up till now, so silent that her voice, in the darkness beside Selena, seems disembodied, the word Julie has spoken shorn of its meaning, more a sound than a word.

"What for?" she replies.

"You know."

"For not telling Mum your alien abduction story, you mean? I don't get you, Julie." Selena feels a jolt of the anger she should have felt earlier, a shot of adrenalin straight into her bloodstream. "Why invent all that junk in the first place? What was the point?"

"Because it's true." Julie's eyes are fixed on the road, her face reduced to planes of light and darkness in the wavering yellow beams of the oncoming headlights. It is cold inside the car still, even though the engine has been running for at least ten minutes. There will be a frost tonight, probably.

Selena shivers. "I can't tell Mum, can I?" Julie says. "I couldn't tell Lisa either, when it came down to it. I told you because I had to. I had to know that at least one other person knew the truth about what really happened to me. I can't stand feeling so alone, Selena. Not any more."

They drive on in silence. There is less traffic on the road than when they drove out. The orange lights, the shadows of signposts thrown on to the tarmac, make the dual carriageway resemble a fairground ride. Dodgems for real, Selena thinks. There is something wrong with Julie, she knows that, something bigger than she can cope with, maybe, but whatever it is, she finds it less awful than the idea that Julie has been stringing her along. Stuffing her head full of lies and nonsense and then pulling the rug out.

"It went OK, didn't it?" Julie says. "With Mum, I mean. At least that's over."

"I told you you'd be fine." Selena wishes she could say something more, something reassuring – *we'll work this out*, maybe, or *I believe you* – but she finds she cannot. To promise Julie that she can help her, that she can accept her story, would be like somebody promising to save someone from drowning when they know they can't swim. She can sit beside her in the car though, she can at least do that. The inside of the car is warmer now, a bit, anyway. She tries to picture it from above: a tiny tin vehicle moving at speed along a rubber roadway, the sewn-together moorland beyond, a billion stars above, probably more.

Five minutes after she gets in, the phone rings. The caller is Margery. Selena knows this even before she picks up. Julie won't be home yet, not quite, and who else could it be? Now she'll quiz me, she thinks. The idea that her mother has been waiting to do this all evening after all is simultaneously satisfying and dismaying.

"I'm just checking to make sure you got home safely," Margery says.

"Hi, Mum." She is too tired to take the initiative, she finds. She waits in silence for the onslaught, the teasing out of secrets, of answers. She'll give it five minutes, she decides. Say mostly nothing then plead exhaustion.

"Selena," Margery says. She can hear her mother breathing, Selena realises, the breaths rasping in and out so harshly she can almost see them, fluttering in the dim light of her hallway like panicked moths.

"What's wrong, Mum?" She feels afraid suddenly. This is the opposite of what she's been expecting.

Margery is silent for a moment, then her words pour forth in a rush, a stack of small change spilling from a broken money bag. "I don't know who that woman is, but she isn't Julie." She pauses, still breathing hard, as if she's been running. "I don't want to see her again."

"What are you talking about, Mum?" There is a blankness inside her head, the vast concavity of a phantom sea, trapped inside a whelk shell, pressed hard to her ear.

"That woman," Margery repeats. "I don't want to see her. I don't want to talk to her. I don't want her near me. I can't tell you what to do, Selena, you're an adult, but you should be careful. I think she could be dangerous."

"Dangerous?"

"Yes. These people are, you know, once they get a hold of

you. They take over your life. I've read about it on the Internet."

"Of course she's not dangerous, Mum. She's Julie. I've spent time with her. She knows things no one else could know. She remembered Mr Rustbucket." Tears spring into her eyes. "Why would she pretend? What could she want from us? It's not as if we're millionaires."

"You think I wouldn't know my own daughter? I don't want to talk about this any more, Selena. Not ever." She falls silent and tugs in her breath. Selena knows for certain that she is crying.

"Mum—"

"I mean it. Keep her away from me."

"But you invited her over yourself. Saturday, remember?"

"I won't be here. I'm going to Auntie Janice's. It's already arranged."

There is a long pause and then a click. Her mother has put the phone down. I'm too tired for this, she thinks. All of it. She replaces the receiver in its cradle and goes upstairs to her bedroom. She leans on the windowsill for a moment before drawing the curtains. There is frost on the privy roof, glistening like shards of glass from a shattered mirror.

Jack Frost, Selena thinks. Frost the Magician, Uncle Jack. We're not supposed to believe in him either, but we all know he's real.


Selena telephones Julie the following morning. She tells her they won't be able to visit their mother at the weekend, after all.

"Mum's had to go to Auntie Janice's. She's not well, or

something. Auntie Janice, I mean. Mum says to tell you she'll see you when she gets back. She realised she didn't have your number to call you herself."

"What's wrong with her?"

"Wrong with who?"

"Auntie Janice?"

"Oh." The upsurge of panic subsides. "I'm not sure. Mum didn't say." Selena draws in her breath. "Come over here instead, if you like."

"I'm not sure what I'm doing yet. I'll let you know."

Julie sounds guarded, cagey, as if she knows there's something Selena isn't telling her but is choosing, just for the moment, to ignore the fact.

Wise move, Selena thinks. "Bye then," she says. She puts down the phone, briefly considers calling Janice to check whether her mother is really there or not, then decides against it. Let Janice handle it, she thinks. I am not my mother's keeper. It comes to her that in all the years since Julie disappeared, she cannot recall having a single proper conversation with Margery about Julie, not since she left home, anyway. Their conversations, when they occurred, had centred around Dad: Dad and his illness, Dad and his inability to let go of the past, Dad and the multitude of problems that seemed to surround him.

Since Dad's death it's been mostly their jobs. That, and the weather.

Could it be that at some point they stopped believing that Julie had ever existed?

In Selena's case, her unbelief has made no difference.

She has asked Julie questions, made up little tests – the stuff about Mr Rustbucket, for instance – but she has known in her bones that Julie is Julie, right from the start. Not just from the tone and timbre of her sister's voice, but from the things she says and the way she phrases them. Her pronounced and annoying tendency to disagree, to contradict everything, to pick up on irrelevant detail and use it against her.

Her tendency to be Julie, in other words. Something you couldn't mistake, not even with your eyes closed.

If their mother does not feel it, what does that mean?

Is Margery going crazy, or is she?

Selena goes online and looks up creef. There are no results, of course: just listings for people with Creef as their surname, the suggestion that she meant to search for Crieff, which is either a small market town in Scotland or a slang term she has never heard of for the fold of skin at the base of the penis.

She looks up woodlouse instead, then trilobite, and after half an hour's random surfing she comes across a YouTube video featuring half a dozen sea crustaceans called isopods, rapaciously stripping the meat from the carcase of a tuna fish. The isopods are each around a foot long, pinkish-white in colour and with ovular, segmented bodies. The video commentary informs her that isopods are scavengers, usually found on the sea bed at depths of up to three thousand metres. They are exceptionally sensitive to sunlight and to sound.

The creature's Latin name is *Bathynomus giganteus*.

They look like giant pale woodlice. Selena had no idea

such a creature existed. She watches the tuna fish video several times and then searches for others. There turn out to be plenty, including a bizarre home-produced rock video entitled 'Giant Isopods Ate My Well-Known Brand of Corn Chip', in which a man with long straggly hair in a coloured bandana runs along a beach beating an electric guitar and screaming about a kraken. Selena is pretty sure that a kraken is some kind of sea monster, which the isopods aren't, not really, because they aren't big enough. A monster should at least have the power to destroy a reasonably sized galleon, Selena decides, although a woodlouse the size of a cat, as one of the nature videos describes it, is pretty unnerving.

Selena lies in bed, wondering if it is possible that Julie has become infected with the creef.

Could it be that this is what their mother has picked up on, some subtle alteration in Julie's behaviour – her smell, even – something you couldn't easily describe or even see but that if you knew the person well enough you'd notice anyway? Some kind of psychic aroma?

Psychic aroma my arse, Selena scoffs. I'm getting as bad as Johnny.

Linus Quinn had known that Elina Farsett was changing. He knew even before Eduard did.

Was Julie still Julie, as she had insisted to Margery, or was she turning into a monster? Selena felt light-headed, not so much with tiredness as with unreality. Could unreality be transmitted from person to person like a virus, like a cold germ?

Perhaps that's what happened to Dad. Maybe people would find madness easier to understand, if it were something you could pick up from standing next to the wrong person at the supermarket checkout, or in a crowded train carriage.

Was Julie's madness catching?

But if being around Julie had made her susceptible, then so had trying to pretend since she was a child that those years of Julie's absence had not left their mark on her, that she was really OK.

Selena had been defined by her sister's disappearance, almost as much as Julie had herself.

I'm a cast-off, Selena thinks. Cast off like knitting, like a fishing line, like a pile of old clothes, like a mooring tether. She pictures herself as she has never been: a small girl standing in the round, rocking belly of a rowing boat and freeing herself from the rope that binds her to shore. The boat bobs slowly away across the water. Shoe Lake – the Shuubseet – spreads out around her and for once the sky above it is a cloudless blue.

Selena can see these things clearly. She can feel the alien air, tart as bracken, cool on her face, and suddenly it is as if she has known this landscape all her life: the rocky wastelands that surround the city, the cold vastness of the mountains beyond. It is the life she is living now that is the dream, the deception. A droplet of airborne madness she has inhaled by mistake, the legacy of a stranger she will never know the name of or see again.

## 4

"What was that film we saw?" Selena said to Johnny. "The one where that Scottish guy's stepdad murdered his sister?"

"*The Shoe*," Johnny said immediately. "It was set in Glasgow."

"That's the one," Selena said. "I knew you'd remember. You're brilliant at remembering films."

"Why did you want to know, anyway?"

"No reason, really. I was thinking about it the other day, that's all. I couldn't remember the title and it was driving me mad. Anyway," she said, "how are things with you?"

It was strange getting another phone call from Johnny so soon after the last one. For the first three months he was in Kuala Lumpur she'd barely heard from him. Now, two phone calls in less than two weeks. She couldn't imagine Johnny feeling homesick – travelling was what he lived for. An affair that had gone wrong, then? The idea of Johnny dating someone else made Selena feel like punching him, or at least slamming the phone down. Maybe in time they'd evolve into the kind of relationship where he could call her up and cry on her shoulder about his latest love catastrophe, but that time wasn't yet.

"I've been thinking of coming home," Johnny said.

"What?"

"I miss Manchester. Don't laugh."

"I'm not." She felt relieved he'd said Manchester and not her, although she was bound to admit they were probably one and the same. She felt a rush of gladness at the thought of seeing him – at the thought of their being together again, even for a day – followed almost immediately by the desire to shut the situation down before it got out of hand.

"I don't think you've given it long enough," she said. "This contract – it's what you've always wanted, Johnny. You can't give it up. Not so soon, anyway. You'd be kicking yourself in no time. You have to give things a chance."

"Are you seeing anyone?"

"God, no." What does that have to do with anything? she almost added, then didn't. It came to her that she didn't want to make out as if there was nothing between them any more, not even to prove a point. That wouldn't be true, and it wouldn't be fair on either of them. "That's not what this is about. I meant what I said, that we should leave things as they are for a while, see what happens. That doesn't mean you have to come rushing home the moment you start feeling lonely. I don't think you should."

"And you still won't change your mind? About coming out here?"

She sighed. "I can't, Johnny. There's stuff I need to sort out here. And there's the house."

"We could have a house over here."

"I can't," she said again, more gently. "Nothing's changed."

She paused, listening to the sound of his breathing, and then found herself suggesting they have this conversation again in six months' time. Johnny seemed much more cheerful after that, back to his usual self in fact, joking and taking the piss and telling her about the cool South Korean horror movie he'd been to with his flatmate, the Japanese track engineer.

"Ryu's a total horror nut," Johnny said. "He's seen more films than I have."

He told her they'd been thinking about moving out of the team accommodation and renting somewhere closer to the city centre. "It's a bit of a ghetto, this place," he said. "A bit one-track."

"Ha, ha," Selena said. She hoped she hadn't promised Johnny more than she'd meant to. Moving to Kuala Lumpur would have been a disaster for her, for the simple reason that she had no reason to be there other than Johnny. She admired Johnny for what he did, not just because he was great at it but because he loved it so much.

She wondered how different their lives might have been, if she'd been more ambitious – if she'd nursed a hunger for something, the way Johnny always had with his racing, with his monster trucks. Johnny would never have tried to stand in her way, she knew that, he'd have welcomed it. He wasn't like some of the others at the track, that creep Hoppo Bennister, for instance, who referred to his girlfriend Rose – a senior staff nurse at North Manchester General – as the kitchen staff.

Hoppo had been mad as hell when Johnny landed the Kuala Lumpur contract, and Selena was glad.

What a mess, she thought. Her, she meant, not Johnny,

Johnny was cool. His mentioning the Japanese track engineer made her think of Stephen Dent, the maths teacher with the koi carp, the man she'd befriended during the summer of Mum's affair. No one had known about Stephen Dent, only Julie, who had made certain Selena knew she knew, not threatening her exactly, but simply making it clear that she had the information.

Information that Julie could use to make her life difficult, if she had a mind to. Selena had been the last person to see Stephen Dent alive. She'd spent the following six months tortured by the idea that she'd been to blame in some way for his suicide, that she'd let him down.

Then Julie had gone missing, and her grief over Stephen Dent had taken on the aura of a dream. A selfish private fantasy that was also shameful. She had barely known the man, after all, so how could she grieve for him?

Out of the blue, she found herself wanting to tell Johnny about Stephen Dent, about his hopeless, pathetic love for Hiromi Shiburin, about the horrible way he had died. Most of all about the koi carp, how lovely they had been, how vulnerable to harm.

The way we all are, here in our fish bowl. The whole stupid lot of us.

Selena knew that Johnny would never say, *You mean this bloke killed himself over some dead goldfish?* Johnny would get it, and even if he didn't, he would never take the piss.

Vanja was right. He was kind.

"I should go," she said at last. "We've been on for ages. This call must be costing you a fortune."

She half expected Johnny to argue, but he didn't. Quit while you're ahead. That was Johnny all over.

"I'll call you," he said. "Soon."

After they'd hung up, Selena logged on to IMDb and looked up *The Shoe*. The film was directed by Aislin Warner, and told the story of a young homeless man, living on the streets of Glasgow in the late 1980s. He originally leaves home because he suspects his stepfather of killing his younger sister, although the audience doesn't know that at the beginning. The film opens with the homeless guy, Tony, meeting a woman at the local benefits centre and gradually beginning to put his life in order. He gets a council flat and then a job, even goes back to college part-time to study history.

When anyone asks him about his past or his family, he tells them he was brought up in a children's home. He recounts stories about the other kids there, invents whole lives. Then one day he receives a parcel through the post. Inside the parcel is a child's shoe. The shoe awakens terrible memories in Tony, because the shoe is his sister's.

The film won prizes at several independent film festivals, but although many critics had written positively about the movie, most of the discussion seemed to centre on whether or not Tony was partly to blame for the death of his sister. No one seemed that interested in the alternative childhood Tony had constructed for himself. The consensus seemed to be that Tony had created a false past in order to avoid feeling guilty, or to appear more righteous than he was. Better.

Only one critic, someone called Mark Samphire, mentioned something called false identity syndrome. Samphire argued that the shoe was important not because it proved Tony's guilt, but because it challenged Tony's invented version of reality. The shoe proved that Tony's sister Leanne had existed, even if it couldn't prove – not by itself, anyway – how she had died. Only Tony knew the truth about who had killed her, and once his real past had been revealed to him, he was finally ready to let that truth be known.

"Something's happened, hasn't it?" Julie said. "With Mum, I mean? She's not answering her phone."

"She's still at Auntie Janice's," Selena said. Julie looked at her as if she'd said Margery had emigrated to Australia, or joined MI5, or something.

"Are you going to tell me what's going on, or not?"

"She freaked out a bit, that's all. She needs some time by herself."

"Time by herself with Auntie Janice?"

"You know what I mean."

"What did she say to you, Selena? I know there's something. It was you who wanted me to go and see her, remember? You've been acting strangely ever since we went round there." She paused. "You can tell me, you know. I won't break."

Selena hesitated. "Mum called me the same night, actually, after I got home. She said she didn't believe you are who you say you are. She doesn't want to see you again. The being at Auntie Janice's is real, though. I phoned up to check. I didn't tell you because I think she's being ridiculous and I didn't want to worry you. I'm sure she'll be feeling differently by the time she comes back."

Julie gazed at her impassively. "Is she all right?" she said at last.

"Who, Mum? I have no idea. I haven't been able to speak to her. She's always out when I call. That's what Janice says, anyway."

"So Janice is covering for her?"

"Not necessarily."

"I don't really care, to be honest. I know it sounds awful, but I don't give a stuff what she thinks. It's one less thing to worry about."

They fell silent. Julie's attention was clearly elsewhere. She seemed to have lost all interest in the subject of Mum, or Janice, and maybe that was good. As Julie said herself, it was one less thing to worry about.

"Have you ever seen a film called *The Shoe*?" Selena asked suddenly.

"I don't think so. What's it about?"

"It doesn't matter. Did you mean what you said to Mum, about working in pathology?"

"I think so. I haven't really decided yet. I don't want to go on filing patient records for the rest of my life, but it's hard to think about the future with – well, with knowing what I know. It's like being in prison."

"Prison?"

"You know what happens when someone's committed a crime? They don't even get considered for parole until they start to express remorse for what they've done. But what if you didn't do it? What if the evidence you gave was true all along? You either have to lie, or stay in prison. I know I'm not actually in jail but that's how I feel. If my own mother believes I'm a lunatic, what hope is there?"

Not a lunatic, Selena thought. Just not Julie.

"What if you had proof, though?" she said.

"What do you suggest? March a bunch of people down to Hatchmere, see who gets taken?"

In the film *The Shoe*, Tony Costello starts out by insisting he has no idea why anyone would want to send him a child's shoe, that the parcel must have been wrongly addressed, that there was another Tony Costello, all kinds of excuses. In the end it's his wife, Marina – the woman he meets at the dole office at the start of the film – who forces him to face up to what's happening.

She doesn't bully him though, or threaten him. She helps him to understand that hiding the truth will never let him feel safe in the way he imagines.

"You have the pendant," Selena said. "I've been wondering. Would you let me borrow it, just for a little while? I think I know someone who might be able to help."

The look on Julie's face – a kind of dumb horror, as if Selena had suggested something unspeakable. Like calling the police, say. Telling them she'd been abducted by a bunch of aliens.

"The silverwing is all I have," she said quietly. "If I lose it, I lose everything. I lose who I am."

"I'm not talking about giving it up. I'd like someone to have a look at it, that's all. There's a woman in London – my boss knows her. She specialises in identifying, I don't know, alien metals. She has a degree in it, or something. Vanja will know. If we could get the metal analysed, we might have a better idea of what we're dealing with." She paused. "Vanja's not like other people. She doesn't judge. You can trust her completely."

"What would you say to her?"

"That my sister owns an unusual piece of jewellery and would like to know where it came from."

"I don't know." Julie hunched her shoulders, curving in on herself as if she were cold.

"Vanja won't tell anyone. Not unless you want her to." Selena thought of the various unsavoury characters who turned up at the shop to see Vasili, the seedy-looking men with their expensive leather jackets and bulging back pockets and designer stubble, the elaborate tattoos, Vanja showing them through to the back office with a resigned shrug, flipping them a double 'v' the moment the door was closed: *fucking arsehole, what a knob.* "You'd like her."

After what seemed like an interminable interval, Julie nodded. "Just ask her what it would involve if I said yes."

"I'll ask her tomorrow. And don't worry."

"That's easy for you to say." Julie laughed, then pressed her lips together, trying to make a smile and not succeeding, and Selena wondered if this was how it was going to be from now on: for most of the time she'd be able to convince herself that Julie was coming to terms with whatever had happened to her, that things were returning to normal. Then suddenly and out of nowhere this ground-level fear, like a bomb had gone off.

The way things had been with Dad, in other words. Selena remembered how it had been the last time she'd seen Ray alive. They'd had their usual Sunday lunch at The George, then afterwards they'd played darts with a few of the regulars, mates of her dad's, or half-mates, people he knew by name, anyway. It had been a laugh. Ray had seemed relaxed, happy even. At the end of the afternoon he'd hugged her and mussed her hair like any other father. *See you next week, love*, he'd said. Four days later he'd taken himself off to the lake to search for aliens and had his heart attack.

All that madness, still churning away inside him. Selena had been powerless against it. She'd barely had a clue.

Ray had appreciated her love, she knew that, needed it even. But it had never been enough to make him well again.


"You remember I told you about my sister?" Selena said.

"Not the crazy one?" Vanja opened her eyes wide, faking innocence, then grinned. She was wearing steel-blue eye shadow, as a diversion, Selena guessed, from what looked like the remains of a bruise. Vanja saw Selena looking and grinned again. "What is it you say, I fell down the stairs, or what?" She shrugged. "Don't worry about it, *dushen'ka*, it's not what it looks like. We had some trouble with a guy who was staying with us over the weekend. Vasya had to throw him out in the end. He broke all my flowerpots. Anyway, what's the problem with the crazy sister?"

"Her name's Julie."

"Julie, then. What about her? You're not asking me to

give her a job, are you? We have enough crazy round here with Vasili." She leaned forward on the counter, laced her fingers together and steepled them. She was wearing a topaz ring, a great white elephant of a thing they'd had in stock for several months. Selena had known for some time that Vanja had her eye on it, probably because it was so ugly. Vanja often turned up wearing items of jewellery no customer would look at twice. Jewellery orphans, Vanja called them. Built like battleships and twice as durable.

"Nothing like that," Selena said. "Julie has a piece of jewellery she thinks might be valuable. I was wondering if we could get someone to look at it for her."

"What kind of a thing is it, then?"

"A necklace. A pendant, really. The frame is silver but the central stone is unusual. I thought at first it was an agate but now I'm not so sure."

"You're not sure? You know what an agate is. So what are you telling me?"

Selena sighed. This was the problem with Vanja – it was impossible to get one over on her. Living with Vasili would make that inevitable, she supposed. A baseline qualification. She had always admired Vanja's tenacity but that didn't stop it being damned inconvenient now and again.

"This is going to sound weird," she said.

"You've already told me you have a crazy sister. How weird can it be?"

"Julie's not crazy, she's just—"

"So now you're going to tell me she's *confused*."

"Yes," Selena said, then laughed. Not half as much as I

am, she thought. "The thing is, Julie thinks there's a chance that this pendant – well, that it might have come from somewhere else."

"Botswana, Bolivia, Birmingham? Where are we talking about?"

"Julie claims the pendant is of extraterrestrial origin." Amazing, Selena thought. I'm turning into Dad. Isn't that what people say happens when someone dies?

Vanja began to laugh, then abruptly ceased. "You're not joking, are you?"

Selena shook her head. "I'm afraid not. I know how it sounds but, I was wondering, aren't there tests you can do? That metallurgist you told me about, the one who was selling the silver that came from meteors – wouldn't she know?"

"You mean Nadine Akoujan?" She tapped her teeth with the end of a biro, something she only did when she was nonplussed, or as Vanja would put it, flummoxed. Vanja had once asked Selena if she thought she should get one of those diamond tooth studs. So I could flash it when I flummox, Vanja grinned. Think it would suit me?

No, Selena had said. Imagine what it would look like when you're seventy.

I had no idea you'd turned into my ma. Anyway, Vanja had insisted. I quite like the idea of being one of those mafia grannies. She hadn't mentioned the tooth stud since but Selena had the feeling she was still thinking about it.

"People bring Nadine all kinds of weird stuff," Vanja said finally. "She has some strange stories. Would you like me to call her?"

"How much would she charge?"

"Nadine does a lot of work for us. We pay her a salary. The money's no problem."

Julie's the problem, Selena thought. "Does she ever find anything? The kind of thing Julie is talking about, I mean?"

"What do you think? Most of these cases turn out to be a waste of time. Hoaxes, or else just mistakes. But every now and then." Vanja tapped her teeth again with the Bic. A black one, with a broken end. "Things come to light. Things that should not be here but are here anyway. Stuff, you know."

As in stuff you might find under the sofa. Alien artefacts.

"I don't know what's going on, Van." It was amazing, how much better she felt just by admitting it. Like a balloon rising upwards into clear air, its tether flapping behind it like a question mark.

Vanja rested her cheek on her hand, spun the Bic in a circle on the counter, making a rattling sound. "Understanding what's going on all the time is boring, don't you think? I hear your story and I remember how it feels to be excited about the world. I remember how the world is a mysterious place. I'd like to meet her, your Julie."

"She's just my sister." As if the word 'just' could ever apply to Julie. Where Julie was concerned, there were and always had been strings attached.

There were moments when Selena almost wished Julie had stayed missing. It was an awful thing to admit, even to herself, but she knew it was true.

"Thanks, Van," she said. She hoped the conversation would end there, but no such luck.

"You going to tell me what the deal is with her, or what?"

"What do you mean, what's the deal?"

"You tell me. For years there is no sister, no sister at all. Then you tell me you do have a sister, but she has been ill. Next time you mention her, she wasn't ill, she has been missing. Now you tell me she's been stealing shit from aliens. I know you, Selena, and you're not a bullshitter. So what's the deal?"

Selena pushed her hair back from her face, let it fall forward again. "All of it's true. Or none of it is. I honestly don't know any more." She sketched in the basics, beginning with Julie's first phone call and ending with Julie showing her the pendant. "She says it was given to her by this woman on the alien planet who took her in – Cally. It sounds mad, doesn't it? Now you can see why I had second thoughts about telling you. The thing is, if you met Julie on the street you wouldn't know there was anything wrong with her. I know it sounds crazy," she said, "but in some ways she hasn't changed at all. She's always been like this. Things were different with Dad – he really was very ill for a while. But Julie's still just Julie."

"It's as if this is what she was looking for all along," Vanja said, more to herself than to Selena.

"That's it – exactly. It's as if she's trying to put the world to the test in some way, seeing how far she can push things." She paused. "I suppose I've been thinking that if I can find proof – actual evidence – that the things she's been telling me aren't real – that they could never be real – that it might help her to start getting better. To come to terms with what really happened, I mean. That's why I want Nadine to examine the pendant. It's the only material evidence we have."

"Material evidence? You sound like a cop show."

"That's Dad's fault. He loved cop shows. You'd have thought they'd be the last thing he'd want to watch but he was addicted to them." She smiled. "I wish he were here now. I haven't a clue what he'd make of all this but I know he'd have a theory."

Vanja made a face, then crossed the shop floor to let down the shutters. "You are talking about trying to help your sister by proving her story isn't true. But what if it is true? Have you thought about that?"

"Oh God, Van. Don't you start."

"I'm serious. At the least, you shouldn't dismiss the possibility. The universe is weird shit. We're like ants. We don't know a thing."

"And don't I know it. I had enough of that from Dad."

"I'm just saying."

"You're the only person on the planet I could have had this conversation with, do you realise that?"

"What about Johnny?"

"Johnny would be hopeless. He'd believe the whole thing, just because he wanted it to be true. I haven't even told him Julie's back."

"He called you, then?"

"He did, actually."

Vanja grinned, and Selena could almost imagine she saw the flash of her hypothetical diamond tooth stud.

"Don't get started on that, either." She did her best to

sound irritated, although in fact she was feeling more relaxed than she had in days. Vanja had a way of making even the most insurmountable problem seem less than it was. It was a gift she had.

## 5

**[From Nadine Akoujan's diary]**

*When Vanja telephones to ask me if I'll meet the woman face to face, if I'll let her deliver the pendant by hand, I say yes because it is Vanja who's asking, even though I wouldn't agree to something like that normally. I'd be nervous of letting a stranger into my home. But Vanja is my friend, and she says the woman won't trust a courier company, not even one of the guaranteed ones like FedEx.*

*You don't mean she's coming all the way from Manchester? I ask, and Vanja says yes, that's right, she's travelling by train. She should be with you by about three o'clock. All right, then, I say. Tell her I'll be here.*

*I put down the phone and look out of the window at the van arriving to deliver groceries to the mini market opposite and think about the woman from Manchester who is going to be on my doorstep in a few hours' time. I realise I am interested at the thought of meeting her. I do not often get to see the owners of the objects I am paid to put a price on. A price, or in this case an origin, a provenance, a derivation. Usually objects come to me in packages, by courier, from men.*

*Almost always it is the men who organise the sending, even when the owner of the object is a woman. I wonder if this is because men still cannot bring themselves to trust women to look after their own interests, or whether it is simply that men are more obsessed with how much things cost.*

*There are times when I feel glad that Saira only gets to see her father every six weeks or so.*

*I know such feelings are unfair to Danny, who is a good man, most of the time anyway, but so what? I am not going to tell him I am glad he is so often away, or say things to Saira that might turn her against him, so it doesn't matter. These are just my own feelings, which I am entitled to. I don't have to excuse them. I feel that my daughter will not be harmed by the idea that women are complete beings, complete in themselves, that we will not collapse or die on account of not having a man stuffing his face at our table every night of the week.*

*Men sending packages and telephoning their questions, their concerns and their demands. So much manly noise. I realise I am eager to hear what this woman, this Julie Rouane, has to say for herself, why she feels it is important to bring the package herself. Why she will not trust a man to bring it for her.*

*I collect Saira from nursery just before one. She has a picture for me, a crayon and chalk drawing on white construction paper, a tottering, lopsided building sparkling with turrets and pointed windows and lacy balustrades. When I ask Saira what it's supposed to be, she tells me it's the castle of Boudicca, the English warrior queen who fought off the Romans. Gwen told us a story about Queen Boudicca, and then we drew pictures, she says. Gwen is Saira's nursery tutor.*

*I smile and hug her and tell her the picture is beautiful, which
it is, though it looks more like a palace from* The Arabian
Nights *than an English castle. We walk back across the
park, which is muddy from rain, and when we arrive home I
prepare lunch for us, some refried couscous with the remains
of the aubergine ratatouille we ate for supper the evening
before. Saira seems quieter than usual, absorbed in her own
thoughts. I hope there is nothing going on at nursery, although
I know it is more likely that Saira's introspection is a reaction
to my own inner preoccupation with the woman who is
coming, who should be arriving now in less than two hours.
Saira picks up on my moods so quickly. It is something I have
noticed, something I need to be careful of. Our two lives are
so intertwined, it is easy for me to forget she is not yet five
years old.*

*We have a visitor coming, I say to her. I am standing at
the sink with my back to her, washing the dishes.*

*What kind of a visitor? she asks.*

*Just a lady. She's to do with Mummy's work, OK?*

*OK, Saira says. She seems immediately more relaxed, less
pensive. I fetch her some drawing paper, and the tin box of
Daler-Rowney coloured pencils that Danny brought for her
last time he was here. He does love his daughter, I know that.
Within the next year or two they will be exchanging emails,
and there will be no more secure exclusion zone between
him and her. Perhaps this is for the best, after all. It could be
that I have already transferred too much caution, too much
prejudice around the subject of her father, matters that are my
concern, not hers.*

It is only now that I am in her position that I have begun to realise how terrified my mother was of losing me.

You can draw me another castle, if you like, I say to Saira. She gazes at me thoughtfully, her lips pursed. The castle might have a dragon in it, she says. Would that be all right?

Of course, sweetheart. I ruffle her hair, which is black and springy, just like Danny's. I love the feel of it under my hand and maybe a tiny part of that love is still love for Danny. Whatever went wrong between us, at least, thank God, there is Saira. I leave her to get on with her drawing and begin tidying up the living room. There are papers spread out over the coffee table, documentation from the last couple of jobs I picked up from Didier, sensitive information, if you know what you're looking for. I cannot imagine that Julie Rouane is an expert on the Amsterdam diamond market, but I tidy the papers away anyway, because you cannot be too careful. A mistake would do damage to my reputation and in the business I am in, reputation is everything.

I am paid to be invisible, a disagreeable necessity. I cannot afford to become visible suddenly. No one needs that.

Julie Rouane arrives at fourteen minutes past three. She is wearing a khaki-coloured parka over a shapeless woollen dress and Dunlop trainers. She has shoulder-length dark hair, a long face and a pale complexion. She seems nervous. I wonder what Vanja has said to her about me.

I am going to make some tea, I say to her. Or would you prefer coffee?

Tea would be lovely. Thank you, she says. She has a northern accent, like Danny's friend Ramez. She seems to add

the thank you as an afterthought, as if her real thoughts are
elsewhere. I show her through to the sitting room. As we pass
through the kitchen she stops still, looking across to where
Saira is seated at the table, intent on her drawing.

Saira looks up. Are you the lady? she says. She stares at
Julie Rouane with concentration, as if she is trying to work
out why she might be different from any of the other ladies
she knows.

I don't know about that, says Julie Rouane. I'm Julie.

Saira grins and then looks away, overwhelmed by shyness.

Julie Rouane hesitates, and for a moment I am convinced
she is going to ask Saira if she can look at her drawing. Then
she smiles in a distant way, and it is as if she has forgotten
Saira is even there. I ask her to excuse me while I put on the
kettle. Make yourself comfortable, I say. I see to the tea as
quickly as I can. When I return to the sitting room I find Julie
seated on the sofa, flicking through Saira's copy of Watership
Down. The book is too old for her really, but she kept on that
she wanted it and so I bought it for her. I don't know how she
came to hear about it – children are so mysterious.

This edition has beautiful illustrations, at any rate, which
Saira seems never to tire of looking at.

This book scared me to bits when I was a kid, Julie says.
I think it was because of the film, mostly. That bit where they
destroy the warren. She drops her voice when she says destroy,
as if she's afraid Saira might overhear her, and be frightened.

I've never seen the film, I say. I don't feel like telling her
that I've not read the book either, or not all the way through.
I had no idea it was so violent. I wonder briefly about

confiscating it, then decide that Saira would probably be more upset by that than by the book itself.

My father always used to say that books are their own censors, that a child will only understand when they are ready to. Anything else will pass them by, just a jumble of words.

I remember myself at twelve, clamouring for Dracula as if I would die without it, my disappointment and embarrassment when I discovered I could barely understand beyond the first page.

Then reading it again at seventeen and finding out it was magic.

Do you have children? I say to Julie. She shakes her head abruptly, as if she is trying to free herself of a fly that has become entangled in her hair. Is there pain in her denial, or simply annoyance that I dared to ask? I cannot tell. She adds sugar to her tea and stirs it around.

What has she told you? Julie says then. I am guessing she means Vanja.

She tells me you have an unusual piece of jewellery and that you would like me to examine it, I say. I feel it is best to be circumspect. It is Vanja who is paying me for my services, after all, not Julie Rouane. It could be that Julie is here unwillingly. And it is true that Vanja really did not tell me anything. I don't want to complicate matters, for any of us.

Julie laughs, without the smallest sign of being amused. She is a friend of yours, isn't she? My sister said. Did she forget to tell you I was mad?

Her directness surprises me. There is real anger in her voice, but I cannot yet tell where it is coming from, who it is *directed against. Perhaps Vanja, perhaps this sister, who I've not heard mentioned before. Perhaps myself, even. It is not as if I've never seen this kind of anger before. It is the anger of someone who has grown accustomed to not being believed.*

*It is only now that I begin to notice how tired she looks.*

*Vanja didn't say you were mad, I reply. She isn't like that. She didn't tell me anything about you, other than that you believe you are in possession of an alien artefact.*

*Did she tell you why I wouldn't send it to you?*

*She said you were afraid of losing it. I can understand that.*

*Julie shifts in her seat. I like your flat, she says. She looks about herself. It's not what I was expecting.*

*What were you expecting? She makes me feel nervous, a little, anyway, but this is probably only because she is not what I was expecting, either. Vanja told me she was uptight, and I suppose she is, but there is more to her strangeness than that.*

*I don't know, Julie says. She puts out a hand to touch one of the cushions on the sofa, the one with the large embroidered turtle that Saira has nicknamed Mr Biswas. It's just different. Warmer.*

*Thank you, I say. I am wondering if I should have offered her something to eat. If she has come here straight from the station she must be hungry. But maybe she has already eaten, on the train. I feel awkward, unsure of what to do. It is not my job to feed clients, but— Would you care for some lunch? I say in the end. Saira and I have already eaten, but I can fix you a sandwich? It would only take a moment.*

*That's kind, she says. But I'm really not hungry.*

*She pauses. She strokes Mr Biswas. Would you like to see the pendant?*

*I would, if that's all right? I am relieved that it is Julie who has brought up the subject, and not me. It is risky sometimes, to push people before they are ready. But I am uncomfortable with small talk and I sense that she is, too. I watch her carefully as she reaches into her bag – a canvas backpack – and brings out a small cardboard packing box.*

*I don't like to take it off, normally, she says. But then I thought that if I have to leave it here, it might be safer to put it in something. She hands me the carton. I weigh it carefully in my hand, trying to gain a sense of the mass it contains. The weight feels concentrated and distinct, what you might expect from a large crystal, for example, or from an ingot of precious metal.*

*As always at moments like this, I remember the first time I held the weight of gold in my hand, my mother's wedding ring. How powerful it felt, that weight, so much greater than I had expected, given its size.*

*It is interesting that Julie has spoken, so soon, about the possibility of leaving the pendant in my care. This must mean she has begun to trust me, at least a little.*

*Is it all right for me to open this? I ask. Julie nods. I flip open the lid of the box, which is secured by flaps, the same kind of carton you might use to transport watches, or computer hardware. On the top there is a wad of tissue paper, which I remove, laying it carefully aside on the coffee table. And now here is the pendant, the object this woman has travelled all this way to show me. My first thought is an echo* of Julie's own words to me about the flat – that it is not what I was expecting – but then also like Julie I do not know what I was expecting, either.

I suppose if I am honest I was expecting to be disappointed, to feel that feeling that sweeps over you when you understand in the first instant that the thing you are looking at is not the special object its owner believes it to be. Which is not to say that it is not beautiful or even valuable, just that it is ordinary, that it can be explained.

It is a familiar feeling, the most familiar in my line of business, probably, which when you start to think about it is what you would expect. You are not going to come upon alien artefacts every day. If you are lucky, and know what to look for, you might see one or two genuine examples in the course of a lifetime's study. You are more likely not to see any. Up until this moment I have seen two, possibly three. I say possibly because I still don't know if one of them was the real thing, or an exceptionally skilful fake.

Such fakes do exist, although the field we are talking about is so small, so specialised that hoaxes are almost as rare as the real thing. The convincing ones, I mean. What I encounter mostly are honest mistakes: rare jewellery from the Tang dynasty, African gold work, Roman hair ornaments and once a carved Egyptian figurine that dated from before the construction of the pyramids. All exceptional objects, all disappointing.

Even before I hold it in my hand I am in no doubt that Julie Rouane's pendant is no fake, that it is not a mistake either. You will ask me how I know this, how I can be so certain, and you are right to ask, right to be so sceptical, *especially when I have no proof to offer you, just my instinct, a feeling so strong it is as if every cell in my body is responding to the object's presence in my sitting room.*

*I am as sure as I have ever been sure of anything that Julie Rouane's pendant is the product of an alien civilization.*

*I glance towards the kitchen door, anxious in case Saira is feeling it too, but I can see she is still absorbed in her drawing and I am glad.*

*I am looking at a teardrop-shaped pendant. It is approximately two inches long, and one inch in diameter at its widest point. It has been manufactured from two distinct materials: a frame section which appears on cursory examination to be silver, and a semi-transparent, crystalline mineral at its centre. The central crystal is ovate, cut en cabochon and held in place by silver clips that are integral to the frame. The pendant is suspended on a silver chain formed of heavy grade, square-cut links of the same silver-type metal as the frame section.*

*The frame is exquisite, a richly worked mass of tiny forms – goblins, demons, homunculi? – intricately entwined with one another and yet each a separate and distinct entity. There is something about them, something ravishing, as fine as anything by Fabergé and yet with an energy and, dare I say, liveliness that sets them apart. I can say with certainty that I have never seen a piece of work like this, or by this maker, whoever they turn out to be.*

*The central crystal is a greenish-grey, similar in hue to tourmaline or even mutton fat jade, though it is obviously neither. When I touch my finger to the crystal's surface I feel a minute shudder, an immediate sensation of give, as if the crystal were not in fact crystal but some advanced organic polymer. Plastic, in other words, and yet it is cold to the touch, and dense, utterly unlike any plastic I have ever come across. I apply my finger again, this time more firmly, with the same resulting sensation, as if I were pressing against a meniscus of mercury, or resin. In spite of the substance's rubbery texture, the tip of my finger appears flattened, as it would do if I were pushing it against quartz crystal, or a sheet of glass.*

*In the following instant, the crystal clarifies and turns transparent. I draw in my breath, trying to control my startle reflex. Julie Rouane appears completely unsurprised. It's the heat of your hand, she says. You're lucky, though. It doesn't do that for everyone.*

*[A note for later: if the crystal does not behave in the same way for everyone who touches it, then there would seem to be some other factor in play and not just ordinary body heat. DNA? Blood type? These are conjectures only.]*

*I hold the pendant up to the light. There is something inside it, I see that immediately, embedded in the heart of the crystal like a fly in amber. A spindly-legged insect, with narrow, dart-shaped wings and a tapering body. It is a little like a daddy-long-legs, or crane fly. It appears to be moving, swimming almost, at the centre of its crystal prison. Its movements are repetitive, but captivating. The longer I keep watching the more I become convinced that the insect is caught in a repeat cycle, the same half-dozen movements endlessly repeated, like a living computer gif.*

*The creature itself is almost transparent, barely there.*

When I turn the pendant at a certain angle it disappears.

It's a silverwing, Julie says. They're very common in Fiby. Like mosquitoes. My friend Cally gave it to me. It's supposed to symbolise eternity.

I have heard many improbable stories in the course of my work. I would say that a good part of my work is about listening to these improbable stories and trying to decide if there might be any truth in them. I'm not talking about provable facts – it's more complicated than that. What interests me most, and what helps to bring me closer to discovering answers, is whether the person telling the story believes what they are saying.

Julie Rouane believes what she is saying. I am as certain of this as I am of the pendant's extraterrestrial origin. Partly this is because Julie makes no effort to convince me. She talks about the pendant as if it were a carton of milk, something she picked up at the corner shop on her way home from work. She doesn't seem to care if I believe her or not.

Do you know what these are called? I ask her. I point at the swarm of silver manikins that encircle the crystal.

They're glis, she says, without hesitation. They're a kind of monkey, or lemur, something like that. In the wild they live in the forests around Julippa but I saw some in the hothouse, in the zoological gardens. It's too cold for them in Fiby. To live outside, I mean.

She speaks in the same offhand way as when she was telling me about the silverwing. It is as if she is tired of telling her story, bored with it, almost. She is like a witness in a long-running court case. The facts of the matter are self-

*evident to her. She doesn't see why she should go over the whole thing again.*

*I ask her to tell me about Cally. How did she come to give you the pendant? I ask. Julie closes her eyes.*

*Can you imagine what it's like, being asked these questions? she says. I feel like a trained monkey. Everyone acts like it's a big deal when they see a chimpanzee pouring tea from the teapot but really what they want to see is the ape going ape and shitting on the carpet. She laughs softly to herself, then opens her eyes. I'm so tired, she says. My own sister doesn't believe me, why should you?*

*I do understand how you feel, I say. A little, anyway. It is difficult for people to accept ideas they are in no way prepared for. But I have seen an alien artefact. I know such things exist, and if they exist then so too must the civilisations that produced them.*

*You still don't believe me though, she says. Do you?*

*I don't know yet, I reply. But I would like to think I am capable of believing you.*

*I know things no one should know, she says, very quietly. She looks away from me and out of the window. Those things – they're a part of my life now, whether I like it or not. I know Selena would like me to pretend, to go back to how things were before, but I can't forget. It would be like trying to forget my own name.*

*Can you tell me anything more about the pendant? I say. I realise I am still holding it, the peculiar insect ticking back and forth against my palm. The crystal feels much warmer than it did before, and although I realise this is probably just* the warmth of my own hand I still feel uneasy. I lay it carefully back inside its cardboard carton.

Silver is common on Tristane, Julie says. As common as iron is here. It's not the silver that makes this pendant valuable, but the workmanship. This piece of jewellery was made by Aivon Ramera, who is a senior member of the Guild of Silversmiths in Fiby. Ramera's work is famous in all the six cities.

Is it actually made of silver, do you know? Or is it an analogue? An alien metal that looks and feels like silver?

I have no idea, Julie says. She looks surprised. I thought that was your department.

I will run all the standard tests for silver, of course, but I am already halfway convinced that the tests will come back negative, or inconclusive. The metal appears like silver when you first examine it, but look more closely and you begin to spot tiny differences. The surface sheen has a fuller glow, the underlying blue colour has a more intense resonance. The perfect outlines of the mouldings suggest that this metal, whatever it is, is denser than silver. Even the purest silver has a certain softness, a blurred quality. But the tiny monkeys – the glis – are sharply defined, as if they have been fashioned from glass.

I know better than to guess at such things, but I would lay money on the pendant being heavier than it should be. Heavier than the same object rendered in ordinary silver, I mean.

As for the crystalline substance containing the insect? For the moment I have no idea where I should begin.

*Do you have brothers or sisters? Julie asks me suddenly.*

*A younger brother, I reply. His name's Amir.*

*I was never close to my sister Selena, she says. I used to think I was, but I wasn't, not even when we were kids. There was always, I don't know, a gap. I used to think it was because she was younger than me, but now I understand it was because of Cally. I was still feeling the separation from her, even though I couldn't remember it. Even though I couldn't remember her, she was still in my life. I know all teenagers feel alienated, to an extent, but I felt as if part of my memory had been erased. You know, like when you tape some music off the radio and then later you decide to record something else over the top of it. Like with the Top 40. Selena and I used to record songs from the Top 40 every week.*

*And Cally is your friend, in the alien city?*

*It was Cally who knew where to find me when I got lost, out by Shoe Lake. If it hadn't been for Cally I would be dead now. Julie is silent for a moment. I saw Cally in Manchester once, on the street outside Allison's apartment. I mean Allison who was one of my college tutors. We watched a UFO together – Cally and I did, I mean. She looked after me when I was sick, after my father died. I've known Cally for as long as I can remember.*

*Were you and Cally lovers?*

*Julie shakes her head. It wasn't like that. And anyway, Cally has Noah.*

*Noah is Cally's partner?*

*He's her brother.*

*I wait for her to continue, to tell me more, but she says*

*nothing, just stares at me instead, as if she's waiting for me to do something stupid, like the chimpanzee she was talking about earlier, with its pot of tea.*

## 6

The trip to Amsterdam is Vanja's idea. The hotel's already booked, it's been booked for weeks, and there's a spare plane ticket. It would be a shame to waste it, Vanja says, and she can claim back the money anyway, because it's a business trip.

The spare plane ticket belongs to Vasili of course, but when Selena asks why he won't be going Vanja waves the question away as she so often waves away questions about Vasili.

He's busy, she says. Please say you'll come. It'll be hilarious. Amsterdam is so beautiful, you have to see it. And I want you to meet Nora. Nora is great.

It would be good to get away, Selena thinks. Away from Julie? Yes, probably. And it's just the two nights. Their hotel is in the city centre, one of the gracious old merchants' houses that flank the canals. This must be very expensive, Selena says to Vanja as they wait to check in. Are you sure I don't owe you anything?

Vasili is friends with the manager, Vanja says. We get discount rates. Don't worry about it. We can go shopping after lunch, she adds, but first we must see Nora. We'll take a taxi.

* * *

Nora is Nora Shah, who Selena likes immediately, even as she feels afraid of her. Nora is tiny but robust, with the compact, wiry physique of a long-distance runner. Her eyes are bright and skittish, like a robin's. It is impossible to tell how old she is. She has a youngish Dutch assistant, Peder, a po-faced, almost completely silent man with an old-fashioned jeweller's loupe on a leather thong around his neck. Each time Peder brings in a new tray of samples, Nora leaps off her chrome-legged stool and helps him to settle it securely on the examining table. When Vanja mentions that Nora was born in Kuala Lumpur, Selena's heart leaps up. She wonders how long it will be before Kuala Lumpur is translatable in her mind as anything but Johnny.

Before settling in Amsterdam, Nora Shah traded gemstones on the Asian markets for more than twenty years. Some of the older guys didn't like it, what a surprise, Vanja tells her later, when they are in the café. She rolls her eyes. Nora doesn't give a shit about those arseholes, or the arseholes here, either. Nora's a tiger.

The atmosphere of Nora Shah's office is curiously calm, more like a laboratory than a valuer's shop, the same gliding movements, the same ultra-clean surfaces and refined lighting. Nora wears dark trousers with a silk tunic. She looks like a government administrator, or the boss of an oil company. Each time she wants to examine a stone she takes off her glasses, squinting into the crystal as if she's convinced she'll find a message there. Selena longs to know more about her life in Kuala Lumpur but she's too shy to ask. She finds she can easily imagine Nora dressed in a T-shirt and messy combats, shifting and sluicing gem clay with her own bare hands. Nora and Vanja chat and make deadpan jokes together as if they've known one another half a lifetime, as Selena supposes they have.

Somehow, at some point, some kind of deal is concluded and the atmosphere changes again. Coffee is brought in, and amaretto biscuits. Afterwards Peder is dismissed, presumably on his lunch break. Nora asks Selena if she's ever considered studying for a qualification in gemmology. Selena blushes, says she's been thinking about it.

She has a very good eye, Vanja says. I've told her over and over she should go back to college. Not that she listens to me. I should fire her for obstinacy.

From the Latin verb *obstinare*, to persist, Nora says. She smiles at Selena, a gleaming, diamond-cut smile that is like the clouds opening. Persistence is more valuable than bravery, in my book. It is certainly more useful, in the long run.

Selena finds herself thinking, just for a moment, that the guy who just walked into the restaurant is Vanja's boyfriend. The man is in his late twenties perhaps, certainly no older, a lanky, loose-limbed individual with long mousy hair in a ponytail and a denim jacket. His eyebrows are darker than his hair, Selena notices. He's good-looking in a way, the kind of guy you don't always notice first off, but who sticks in your mind afterwards.

This is my son, Vanja explains as he approaches their table. Alexei.

Alex, says the guy. He puts out his hand. Good to meet you.

Selena shakes his hand and smiles. Good to meet you, too. She feels wide-eyed with surprise. The idea that Vanja has a child is startlingly new to her, although now she's been told who Alex is, it's completely obvious. They have the same hands, the same walk, the same smile, even. Alex has a vaguely American way of speaking, the rise and fall of his voice, like a guy in some movie about raising cattle in Arkansas.

Do you live in Amsterdam? Selena asks. It is the only thing she can think of to say without sounding stupid.

Alex laughs and says yes, he's Dutch now. Double Dutch, in fact, he adds, because I have two Dutch children.

Vanja grins and punches his arm. That makes you double *double* Dutch, then, she says. They really are very alike, Selena thinks. It is difficult to believe that up until five minutes ago she had no idea that Alex even existed.

Vanja orders more coffee and a plate of the small round honey cakes that seem to be everywhere in this city and they talk, Alex and Vanja, mostly in English but sometimes slipping over into Russian. Their pleasure in being in each other's company is obvious, and contagious. Selena feels it washing around her like a wave, like the wake from a ship. She sips coffee and listens. As so often with Vanja there seems to be a subtext to what is being said, a second, deeper level to the conversation she is aware of but can't quite interpret.

When Alex gets up to go to the toilet, Vanja puts a hand on her arm and asks her if it will be all right if she doesn't come back with her to the hotel tonight.

I'd like to spend some time with my grandkids, and Marieke, she says. Marieke must be Alex's girlfriend, Selena supposes, girlfriend or wife. I don't get to see them that often, Vanja is saying. Are you OK by yourself, just for this evening?

Selena says yes of course, without even thinking about it much, because what else can she say? The change of plan comes as a surprise to her, even as she realises that for Vanja there has been no change of plan, she has intended to spend the evening with Alex all along. Probably that's why Vanja invited her to come to Amsterdam in the first place, so she could cover for her. There will no doubt be a reason Vanja can only see her son intermittently, some beef with Vasili, presumably, and none of her business.

I'll be fine, she repeats.

You know how to get back to the hotel from here? Vanja asks. Just two stops on the metro and then turn right. She looks embarrassed.

I know where it is, Selena says, which she does, pretty much anyway, and she has the laminated fold-up map in her bag if she runs into problems. I think I'll stay here for a bit, though.

The pancakes here are great, Vanja says. Her face fills up with relief. You get loads for your money, too. Then Alex comes back from the toilet and they are gone. Their departure happens suddenly, in a whirlwind of bags and coats, as if now everything has been decided they can't wait to get out of there. Once she is sure they are out of sight, Selena drapes her jacket across the back of her seat to keep her place and goes up to the counter to order pancakes. They are Dutch pancakes, each one the size of a whole large dinner plate, with the filling cooked into the batter rather than rolled or folded inside the pancake itself. At the centre of each table there is a heavy brown earthenware pot of glistening syrup, which the Dutch like to eat with their pancakes, Vanja had explained, regardless of whether the filling is sweet or savoury.

The scent of the syrup, when you get close to it, is like black treacle: not sweet exactly, more spicy, with an undertone of something resinous, most likely tree bark.

Selena orders a ham and aubergine pancake with extra red onion then returns to her table. The little restaurant is filling up quickly now – students, mostly. The interior of the building is like a light box, replete with orange warmth and the combined aromas of candle wax and pancake batter and very strong coffee. Beyond the windows the streets are filling up, too, awash with bakers and hippies and grandmas, young men in designer shades with their hair slicked back. Selena presses her fingertips to the glass, letting the people spill through her hands like coloured beads as they flow past the windows of the coffee house, moving crowdwise, like a single-celled organism, nosing its way between the buildings and along the canal paths and over the bridges, seeking food, warmth, laughter, information, conversation – the life-giving sustenance it needs to get through this night, and begin another day.

The ghost in the machine, the beast in the cage, a behemoth of raw energy, an energy that sweeps down through the pavements and storm drains like excess rainwater, crackling in the briny air like free electricity.

Selena's pancakes arrive and she begins to eat. The texture of the cooked batter is softly luxuriant, the browned edges crisp, almost caramelised, the flavours of meat and vegetables smoky-buttery-peppery and delicious. She tries to imagine making her home here, in this city, blending in with the crowd the way Alex does, in his battered denim jacket and straggly ponytail. She tries to imagine working for Nora Shah, taking the place of her taciturn assistant with the antique loupe, fetching her coffee from the downstairs concession in between appointments, learning her habits and gaining her trust, taking on the attributes of the tiger.

A Sumatran tiger, Selena thinks, so rare they're close to extinction and yet they cling on anyway, prowling the forests, hiding their fires. The image shimmers before her like a projection, black-green-gold, like one of the coloured transparencies in Dad's old hand-held slide viewer, each photo in its own cardboard frame, each a single second's reminder of a world that has vanished, or of a future that can now never happen.

The idea that she could claim to belong here is an illusion, as ephemeral and deceptive as one of Dad's transparencies. Manchester is in her blood, like a build-up of tar or cholesterol. She is not like Nora Shah.

She finishes the last of her pancake then pays the bill. Outside on the street the air is warmer than it would be in Manchester at this time of year but still chilly enough to make her wish she'd brought a thicker jacket. She walks almost at random, wandering along thoroughfares that seem to her like aisles in a monster cathedral, away from the city centre towards the narrower canals, the murkier backstreets, the scratched and pockmarked doorways swathed in the liquid shadows of approaching night. Lights suspend themselves in the water, bobbing like oil spots. Selena tries to make a mental note of where she is going, counting the bridges, the cobbled courtyards, the gabled houses and concrete apartment blocks, the particular cant and angle of a particular street. It doesn't much matter where she ends up, she reminds herself. So long as she can locate a metro station she can find her way back to the hotel from anywhere in the city.

She takes the laminated map from her rucksack and unfolds it, just to try and gain a sense of where she is. She notices how the city is shaped like a hexagon, or like a snail shell, the streets and waterways like secret passages, tunnelling inward. Selena remembers something Julie said to her about one of the maps Cally had drawn, showing a section of an ancient city that was formed like a labyrinth.

Selena cannot remember the name of the city that Cally drew – the alien, imaginary city – but suddenly it is as if its buildings and piazzas and thoroughfares have been superimposed on to Amsterdam, or secreted within it, *something*. The result is that Amsterdam no longer feels quite real, or perhaps the alien city feels *more* real, and Amsterdam feels like a copy or a model, a child's version, a means of learning about the world, rather than the world itself.

It would be easy, Selena realises, to carry on with this train of thought, to keep picking away at the scab of normality until it flakes off. Like Dad did, and Julie too.

Staring the world in the face until quite ordinary objects begin to seem like forgeries of themselves, facsimiles – all surface, with nothing behind.

Selena realises she has barely thought of Julie all day until this moment. The novelty of being in Amsterdam has blanked her out.

Selena has not seen Julie or spoken to her since the Thursday of the week before, when Julie came back from London and they had that terrible row.

Julie called from the station, asking if she could come round. Selena was just leaving work. She almost said no, because she was tired, but in the end she said yes because it seemed easier to agree than to try and explain. Julie turned up less than five minutes after Selena arrived home. There was something different about her, Selena noticed that at once. She could not say what that difference was exactly, but it put her on edge nonetheless. She ordered takeaway from the Mogul Tandoori on Wilmslow Road and then went out to fetch it, glad to be in the open air again even though she'd only just come in. It was colder out, and spitting rain. Julie had offered to go to the restaurant with her but Selena had said no, it would only take five minutes, no point in both of them getting wet.

When she returned with the food, she found Julie sitting at the kitchen table with a bottle of Heineken. She looked up as Selena entered, coming to life with a jerk as if Selena's presence had triggered some kind of activation mechanism.

"Are you OK?" Selena asked. "How did you get on in London?"

Julie had been away for three days. She hadn't said where she was staying, and continued to be evasive when Selena asked her about it.

"With a friend," she said, then changed the subject. She seemed distracted, although when Selena dished up the curry she managed to clear her plate in under five minutes. "I haven't eaten all day," she said. She pushed her plate away from her towards the centre of the table and leaned back in her seat. "I saw Nadine," she said. "Do you want to know what she said?"

"Of course," Selena said. I thought you'd never ask, she thought. She felt anxious in spite of herself. She hoped Julie's visit to the – what was it? – *xenometallurgist* wouldn't turn out to have been a bad idea.

Too late now, she thought. Trust you, Vanja.

Julie didn't answer at first. She took a swig of her beer instead, drinking straight from the bottle in a way that for a second reminded Selena of Johnny.

"There are tests she has to do," Julie said at last. "But she says she's certain. As certain as she can be, anyway."

"Certain of what?" Selena said. She could feel her heart pounding, the insistent, uncomfortable pressure of the blood pulsing in her veins from the inside out. She scraped the remains of her curry noisily together with the edge of her fork.

"Nadine believes the pendant is of extraterrestrial origin," Julie said. "Or that the metals and minerals it's made of are, which is the same thing really, isn't it?"

Selena listened to her words, the sheer outlandishness of them, words that if you heard them anywhere but on *The X-Files* – on a TV chat show, say, or out of the mouth of a drunken pensioner shambling down the steps of their local off licence, or across the counter at Leggett's – you would dismiss on the spot as terminal confusion, as lunacy, as eccentricity maybe, but only if you were trying to be kind.

Selena sighed. For the first time almost, she feared she was running out of patience. She had been listening to this stuff for months now and she was sick of tiptoeing around Julie's feelings, treating her like an invalid, incapable of dealing with the truth unless it was broken down for her into bite-sized portions. I won't break, she remembered Julie saying. Well then, let's see. The idea of speaking her mind was like a drug, she found, a tablet of amphetamine, dissolving into her bloodstream, foaming inside her insides like a glass of champagne.

"Oh for God's sake, Julie," she said. The words were out before she could stop them. "Fuck this. I've had enough." Fuck *you*, she almost added, then managed not to, then wished she had. She could feel her self-control sliding away from her like a trap door opening. She realised she was smiling, the grin plastered across her face like someone painted it there, the garish, clownish colours, the paler highlights denoting moisture, the pigment still wet.

Julie was hunched up against the table, cowering like a wounded animal. Surprise, surprise. Precious Julie, so fragile you daren't speak a word. How convenient.

"You don't mean that," Julie said. "Not after everything

we've talked about." Her voice trembled, though her eyes looked frozen somehow, panicked, the eyes of someone who'd been running for hours and was all out of breath.

She's exhausted, Selena realised. Dead beat, and an image came to her then of her father: Ray after one of his marathon cross-country drives, eighteen hours at the wheel and then four hours of sleep snatched in a lay-by before struggling home from whichever random place he'd ended up in, Sheffield or Edinburgh or Slough or Virginia Water.

Unshaven and stinking of sweat, his brain in a state so different from what passed as normality he found himself losing the ability to travel between the two.

But what about the rest of us, Julie? You can call us cowards and normals and yes-men as much as you want, but that won't change a thing. People like me and Mum, we're stuck with the authorised version of life whether we like it or not, the boilerplate contract. You feel contempt for us and that's OK, that's your right, but we soldier on at least. Have you ever wondered what would happen to you if we didn't?

Selena felt her anger loping away like a stray dog, like an urban fox caught by the sunrise. Its red breath lingered maddeningly, a souvenir of transgression.

"Julie," she said. Her mouth felt parched. "I know something happened to you, something terrible. I want to help you, but we've got to stop pretending."

"You think I've been pretending?" Julie said. Her face was pale, greyish. She seemed close to tears.

"What else do you expect me to think? Honestly?"

Julie scraped her chair back from the table and stood

up. At least she's had something to eat, Selena found herself thinking. She must have been starving. "Don't go like this," she said. "Can't we at least talk about this like adults?"

Julie pulled on her coat and made for the door without saying a word. Selena heard a thump as the door slammed behind her and then she was gone.

The canals of Amsterdam are sparkling like dream roads. Selena thinks of those provincial English cities that become dead zones at night, their precincts and underpasses sinister suddenly, like sets from disaster movies, their pavements and car parks flyblown and rain-streaked. Industries laid to waste and workers demonised, history demolished. Racketeering and rent rises, unemployment and bomb damage, decade after decade after decade of governmental neglect. People cling on in such places, Selena thinks, but they don't flourish.

Amsterdam feels different to her, although she understands that this could be because she is a stranger here, and can only understand the city in a rough translation. Its internal rhythms and secret histories, its old enmities and inherent vices – these aspects of the city remain hidden from her, rendered invisible by the magnificent houses flanking the waterways, the picturesque barges cloaked in greenery, the ancient cobblestones. Those parts of history that insist that history is all in the past.

All cities are like Manchester under the skin, Selena thinks. Even the gorgeous ones, the favoured ones, the cities that ride like queens upon the tides of fortune. Opportunists, because they have to be. Change or die.

Xenometallurgy is really a thing, Selena has discovered, a discipline you can study at university. Meteorites, moon rock, other artefacts of unknown origin all contain trace metals – metals the xenometallurgist will offer assistance in identifying. It is a young science, and prone to being misunderstood, although in essence it is no different from any other branch of metallurgy as taught and researched and practised in every major scientific institution throughout the world.

The idea that Nadine Akoujan is part of a recognised scientific discipline is reassuring to Selena. No doubt Julie would mock her need for such reassurances as intellectual cowardice. *You're such a square, Selena.* She wishes now that she'd asked Julie some sensible questions about Nadine instead of just losing it. She had considered telephoning Julie, to apologise, then decided to leave it until after she returns from Amsterdam. They could both use the break, she reasoned. Then once she was actually on the plane, she wished she'd phoned anyway. She cannot even remember if she has told Julie she is going away. She texted Julie from the hotel just in case, soon after they arrived, but there has been no reply.

Two cyclists ride past on fluorescent bicycles, wearing identical silver eye make-up and pink feather boas. They look like twin brothers, twin angels, and part of the joy Selena feels in glimpsing them arises from the fact that here in the silvered darkness of Amsterdam, nobody is paying these men the slightest attention. It occurs to her that Julie's story about an alien encounter is just one story among many and not that unusual. In Amsterdam alone there would be dozens of them, thousands. Amsterdam could be twinned with an alien city for all I know. Something in the smoke.

Selena grins. She wonders how Vanja would react if she were to tell her she'd spent her free evening in one of the coffee shops on the Dwarsstraat, reclining on cushions and smoking a spliff with the rest of the tourists. Oh yeah? she would probably say. Which one did you go to? Not that Selena is seriously considering it, she would feel ridiculous. She has smoked pot precisely once, when she was nineteen. Even Johnny has given it up, more or less – he wouldn't do anything that might endanger his HGV licence.

There are rules for such things, no doubt, as there are for everything. Coffee shop etiquette. The concept makes Selena want to giggle. She wouldn't even know what to ask for.

Something to help me see the aliens, she thinks. She walks on, through narrower alleyways, beside lambent canals. A woman in a gold puffer jacket flashes past on roller blades. When Selena's phone goes and the caller is Julie, she isn't surprised.

```
I'm sorry, Selena. I shouldn't have left like
    that.
No, I'm sorry for going off at you. Are you all
    right?
I'm scared, Selena. I keep thinking I'm
    changing. I can't think properly. It's like
    my mind's gone cloudy.
```

Hang on a moment. What do you mean, you can't
   think properly?

I keep forgetting words.

Julie, that's normal, everyone gets like that
   sometimes. You're just tired.

But what if it's more than that? I don't feel
   right, Selena. I can't seem to get warm.

Didn't you tell me that Elina began to change
   less than six months after she became
   infected? You've been back here for ages,
   years. If anything was going to happen it
   would have happened by now. You've probably
   just got a cold or something.

I never thought of it like that. The time
   difference, I mean.

Well, you should. It's my fault, anyway. I
   knew you were upset. I should have taken
   more notice.

It's not your fault, Selena. I've been asking
   too much of you, I know that. I've been
   having nightmares recently. I spooked
   myself, that's all.

Nightmares about Elina?

About Steven Jimson.

You should have said.

I hate talking about him. What's it like
   there, anyway?

Amsterdam? It's great. We should come here
   together sometime.

```
I'd like that, I really would. Thanks for
   talking. I feel much better now.
Will you be OK until I get back?
Of course I will. I'm being an idiot. Don't
   worry about me.
```

I do believe you, Julie, she wants to say, but she doesn't, not quite, because Julie has rung off already and also because even now, just seconds after they terminate their phone call, she still has no idea what she believes, or thinks, or even wants to think. She is glad of her solitude, she realises, glad of Vanja's minor treachery in abandoning her, and when she arrives back in the hotel lobby, alive with warmth and the laughter of strangers, she is glad of that, too. She climbs the narrow stairway to her room in the eaves, wondering if it might be possible to find a house like this in Manchester, a tall house with gables and a wood stove, a house she could share with Julie that would make her feel safe.

The Dutch house creaks, as if in sympathy. It is almost midnight, Selena sees. Still no sign of Vanja. What a surprise.


Thanks for last night, Vanja says.

It is eleven o'clock the next morning and they are drinking coffee in one of the cafés along the Prinsengracht. There's still an hour before they have to leave for the airport. The sun comes out for ten minutes and then goes in again. Vanja looks pretty wrecked, although that might have something to do with the fact that she's not wearing make-up.

It's because of Vasili, you see, she says. He knows about Alex, but he doesn't like me to talk about him because of his father. Alex's dad was a friend of Vasili's, years ago, when we were all living in Berlin. It's complicated. But Alexei is my son and I need to see him. And the grandkids too. Look.

Vanja takes out her phone and scrolls through a series of photographs: herself, seated between two small children, a boy and a girl. In some they're on a sofa with big, brightly coloured cushions behind. In others they're at the breakfast table. Selena can see glasses of orange juice, a plate of cheese slices, seeded rolls. The kids look like Alex.

Where did you go, anyway? Selena asks. After you left the restaurant.

Oh, we went to The Bulldog. It's amazing there in the evenings. You should have come.

If you'd invited me I might have done, Selena thinks but does not say. The Bulldog is one of Amsterdam's oldest coffee shops – Selena knows this, because she's seen a reference to it in the guidebook she bought. She supposes it is Vanja's evening in The Bulldog, rather than her grandchildren, that is responsible for the dark circles beneath her eyes.

Did you have a good evening? Vanja asks.

Great, Selena says. Just walking around. It's a beautiful city.

You were OK, by yourself?

Selena nods. She remembers the two lovers? brothers? in their feather boas on their fluorescent bicycles. Pink ghosts in the night. It's a special place.

It occurs to her once more that she could decide to

stay here, disappear into the crowd, become someone else. Like Julie tried to, you mean? she thinks. By scoring a line through one life and beginning another?

If it didn't work for Julie then how could she even think that it could work for her?

When the time comes to go to the airport she feels almost relieved. The plane boards on time. Vanja falls asleep almost as soon as they're in their seats. She snores lightly, her head resting against the window, her hair askew on her cheek like strands of seaweed.

The sky remains clear until they begin their descent into Manchester. The rainclouds whip by the windows, bulky as puddings.

## 7

"I think we should go back," Selena said. "I don't know why you wanted to come out here in the first place."

"I've never experienced the English countryside," said Vanja. "I wanted to see what it was like." She lifted her head and sniffed the air. Making a joke of it, Selena thought, trying to make out she'd never ventured this far out of Manchester before, which perhaps she hadn't. She was wearing a ratty green parka, a garment Selena would not have imagined her owning in a million years, though in a weird way it suited her and for a moment Selena found herself imagining her as someone else: Vanja after the apocalypse, camping out in the hills, heating soup over an open fire and collecting rainwater in a plastic bucket.

Where had Vanja come from, exactly? What had her life been like, before she wound up in Manchester? Selena felt ashamed to admit she had no idea. She must think I'm pathetic, the way I hide from life, she thought. The way I back off from anything the moment it becomes remotely interesting.

It was raining, but only slightly. The surface of Hatchmere Lake was cloudy, burred all over with a fine mist, like a mirror coated in condensation. Selena hadn't been out here for years, not since Dad, not since forever. There were signs now, warning you about the dangers of unsupervised swimming, and the footpath that skirted the lake had been blocked off. Fishing was strictly prohibited. So much for those sneaky perverts with their mighty rods. She studied the information boards outside the Forestry Commission office, which gave details of how the unique and valuable landscape of peat bog was being restored. A good thing, probably, although there was something melancholy also in the way things were now, in the absence of people. She was surprised by how unfamiliar everything felt. It was almost as if the place as she had known it had been erased.

The village of Hatchmere was still the same, a cluster of disparate houses, a frowsy-looking pub. It crossed her mind that Brendan Conway might still be living in the village, in the bungalow he shared with his aunt, its yellow paint just starting to peel, its small front garden cordoned off from the road by a length of chain.

Selena couldn't remember the name of the aunt, though the bungalow itself she spotted at once, recognising it instantly from the newspaper photographs. It was white now instead of yellow, but otherwise the same. She thought of pointing it out to Vanja but didn't. What would be the point? It was just a building, the physical shell that gets left behind when a memory dies.

Could a story change a place? Selena wondered. It was almost as if Julie's version of Hatchmere – Shoe Lake, the Shuubseet – had contaminated the real one, bleeding into it through the rift to make it more like itself. The idea was ridiculous, she knew that, and yet that was how it felt to her, standing there at the side of the road where Julie had stood – perhaps – twenty years ago, balanced upon the hair's-breadth dividing line between one version of reality and another.

Walking up from the station, she had spotted a white Ford van in a lay-by, parked at a careless angle to the road, its front end half-hidden by brambles and other vegetation. A spray-painted logo identified it as the property of the Forestry Commission, yet Selena found the sight of it unsettling, nonetheless.

Could the scene of a crime be haunted by the crime itself? Jimson was in jail, his van sold for scrap, probably.

She was talking bollocks. All right then, *thinking* bollocks. What was the difference?

"There was a lake like this near home," Vanja said suddenly. Selena jumped. She'd been so caught up in thoughts of Jimson she'd more or less forgotten that Vanja was there. "Not Berlin. I mean our village, Vasili's and mine. It is called Bonfire Village, can you imagine? Kostër." She accented the second syllable, making a 'yo' sound. "It's in Ukraine."

"I thought you met Vasili in Berlin?"

"Uh-uh." She shook her head. "I've known him since we were kids. He was an arsehole then, too." She laughed. "We used to swim in the lake, after school. All of us did, except this one kid, Semyon Radich. He was so skinny, like a matchstick. I kind of liked him, actually, but he was so easily frightened. He had this terror of catfish and leeches, which is why he wouldn't go swimming with the rest of us. He believed there was a really big catfish in the lake, a monster, he said, although I'm certain he never saw anything of that sort. Some of the other kids used to tease him about it, try and force him to go in the water when he didn't want to. There was this other boy called Nika Belyushin who lost a foot from swimming in the lake. We tried to convince Semyon Radich it was a catfish that got him, but really it was because of an old car someone had thrown in there. Nika cut his foot on the metal and it became infected."

"We had stories like that, too," Selena said. "Dad said they were urban myths, that the catfish wouldn't grow that big here because the water's too cold. He told us the only place you get giant catfish is in the Mekong Delta."

"There are some huge ones in the Dnepr as well." Vanja sighed. "We used to have races. Swimming across to the island. It wasn't a real island, just a clump of trees on a patch of dirt, really. But it was our place, just like this was your place."

"It wasn't really our place," Selena said. "We came here because of Dad."

"I always think the only time you get to know a place properly is when you're a kid. You need to get down in the mud, you know? Get your hands dirty. Unless you've swum in this lake you can't know it. Did you ever swim here?"

Selena shook her head. "Dad wouldn't let us. We used to watch people fishing, though. Once there was this guy who tried to show us his cock."

Vanja started to laugh. "Was it a monster then, this cock?"

"Not really. It was just a cock. I'd rather have seen a catfish, quite honestly."

They both burst out laughing, doubling over at the

roadside, hugging their knees. Selena felt glad they'd come, after all, even though it was still raining and she was starting to feel cold.

WELS CATFISH (*Silurus glanis*) is a scaleless or true catfish that lives in slow-moving fresh or brackish water in a wide range of habitats throughout Western and Eastern Europe, and as far as Russia in the east and Greece in the south. Wels catfish live largely on invertebrates, although larger individuals will also eat rats, mice, pigeons and even aquatic birds such as coots and ducks. There have been reports of Wels catfish lunging out of the water in pursuit of prey. The Wels catfish is also known as the Sheatfish. They are long lived, commonly reaching thirty years of age and sometimes much longer. The largest recorded specimens are in the region of three metres long, although there have been isolated and thus far unproven reports of individuals reaching a full four metres in length. Wels catfish thrive in a warm climate. Po delta catfish commonly reach two metres or more in length, although the biggest specimens so far recorded have been in Ukraine. The fish is normally placid and slow-moving, although they will attack if provoked. A fisherman from the village of Győr in Hungary almost lost his life when a Danube catfish caught hold of his leg and attempted to pull him underwater. Incidents such as this one have encouraged a proliferation of urban myths relating to Wels catfish, although most of these are apocryphal. In the United Kingdom, where average temperatures fall below eighteen degrees centigrade, Wels catfish remain relatively small, a foot long and often less. They prefer deep water, with plenty of overhanging vegetation.

"Let's go back and find that café," Selena said at last. "I'm freezing."

"In a moment," Vanja said. She turned to face Selena. The edges of her hair were darkened with rain. "I looked up all the stuff about your sister on the Internet, did I tell you?"

"I knew you must have done. You wouldn't have wanted to come out here otherwise."

"Do you mind?"

Selena shrugged. "Why would I mind? It's all public knowledge. Anyone could look it up, if they wanted to."

"It is still painful for you to talk about, I can tell."

"Not really." She thought of telling Vanja that none of it felt real, not the parts of the story that were available through the news archives anyway: the police search, the arrests, the endless news reports. These things felt like common property, film of her life rather than her own lived memories of it, even more so now that Julie had returned. The official narrative was redundant. It no longer made sense.

She didn't say anything though, because what was the point? Everything you could read online about Julie's case was wrong, in any case, or at least partial, a version of history that had never happened. Most people wouldn't care, though. Most people preferred the movie version of life. It made a better story.

"You need to lay the ghosts," Vanja was saying. "That's what I think."

"Ghosts?"

"You know. The memories. That's all ghosts are, really, aren't they? Memories."

"I don't know. I think this is stupid. Coming out here, I mean."

"Tell me again, what Julie said. About the man who brought her in his van."

Selena wiped rain off her face. "Steven Jimson." I hate that creep, she thought. I could fucking kill him. She repeated to Vanja what Julie had told her, that night in Dido's Diner, about how Jimson had offered her a lift into Warrington then driven her out to Hatchmere Lake instead.

"She told him she wanted to go for a walk," she said. "It was the only way she could think of to make him stop the van."

Vanja whistled through her teeth. "She was brave, your sister," she said. "And she was what? Sixteen?"

"Seventeen," Selena corrected her. "But she was young for her age, in some ways. Young and old at the same time, if that makes sense."

"Yeah, it makes sense. Kids like that are always in trouble because they're not made for this world. They think about things too much. I would have kneed him in the balls, probably. But then he might have strangled me anyway, just for being such a bitch to him, so what do I know?"

"I think I'd have been too terrified to try anything," Selena said. "I don't like to imagine it."

"That's the point, though. You don't know what you'll do until it happens. No point worrying about it. Can you remember where she said he parked this van of his?"

"I'm not sure," Selena said, although she did know, more or less, because she'd looked it up on Google Maps, tracing the van's trajectory as it left the A556 at Delamere, heading north towards the forest boundary and to where it must eventually have ended up, in a lay-by just beyond the village and about ten minutes' walk from where they were currently standing. Less if you were running. From the lay-by there would be a pathway into the woods, she knew that because you could see it on the map, although she'd never been there to check for herself. "Does it matter?"

"I think it matters. I want to see where she went. Can we have a look?"

"If you like." Selena made a face, trying to convey how unnecessary and unpleasant she was finding it, this expedition, this pilgrimage, this wild goose chase, whatever you wanted to call it. The rain was seeping into her clothes now. She would rather be in the station café, drinking coffee, although she knew it was this – the rain, the dripping trees, the muddy pathway between the trees – that they had come for, and always had been.

Why had she never come here before, in all these years? It was as if the place was shrouded in time, surrounded by walls of time, the way the walls of Sleeping Beauty's castle were cloaked in briars. Was Julie like Sleeping Beauty? There were reams and reams of text written on fairy tales, Selena knew that, she had even read some of it – theories about the moon and Little Red Riding Hood and women's menstruation, the beast as hero and the hero as beast, Rapunzel and the myth of rescue. Selena had never found much point in any of them. A good story will survive, no matter what. Selena always thought *Sleeping Beauty* was a story about jealousy, about a thwarted, vengeful has-been who ruined everybody's lives in a fit of pique over not being invited to a stupid christening party, for goodness' sake. Now she realised it was really about forgetting. About a terrible thing happening, something so terrible you would shut down your whole mind rather than face the memory of it.

This is where it happened, Selena thought. We have to wake her up.

MEKONG GIANT CATFISH (*Pangasianodon gigas*) is a very large, very heavy member of the shark catfish family, a species of freshwater fish native to the Mekong basin in Thailand, Laos, Vietnam and China. In Thai it is called the pia buek, and is a sacred creature. In Thai and Lao culture, offerings of respect would traditionally be made to the fish prior to hunting it. The largest Mekong catfish grow up to three metres in length, over a period of six years. They have traditionally been fished for food for many centuries, although the past few decades have seen a disastrous drop in numbers, partly through overfishing but mainly due to water pollution and other threats to their natural habitat. The Mekong catfish is now on the critically endangered list. Various conservation initiatives have been implemented, along with programmes of captive breeding aimed both at restocking the Mekong river and providing alternative captive-bred sources of fish for sport and for food. The initiatives are promising, with Thai fishermen especially offering their support, but there is still a long way to go before the Mekong catfish's future is secure.

The path that led towards the lake had become overgrown, around its opening especially, and if Selena hadn't known it was there they might easily have missed it. At least the rain's stopped, she thought. She wondered how long it had been since the path was last used, then pushed the thought away. This is it, Selena thought. This is the place. She felt surprised at how difficult it was to finally be here, how upsetting, like being trapped in one of those found-footage horror movies in which teenagers with loud opinions go in search of a witch or the home of a maniac. All wobbly camera angles and indistinct dialogue, the inevitable fade to black. The lesson of films like these seemed to be that it was better to let things alone, that some secrets were not worth the risk of uncovering.

Julie must want to be found, though, or she would not have come home.

A breeze passed through the trees, showering them with raindrops. Not much further now. "What do you think happened?" she said to Vanja. "From what you've read, I mean?"

"It's obvious, isn't it?" Vanja stopped walking so suddenly that Selena almost ran into the back of her. "Your sister was kidnapped by this guy, this Jimson guy. He brought her here in his van, to the lake. Maybe he raped her, like he raped the other women he killed. Maybe he kept her prisoner in his garage or his cellar or something. At some point your sister escaped. We don't know exactly when, only that it must have been some time before this Jimson creep was arrested. Could be it was here at the lake, and she managed to persuade him to take her outside for a walk, just like she says. Could be that Julie doesn't know any more, that she doesn't remember.

These things happen. My grandmother told me a story about a guy in her village who forgot the whole of World War Two after his brother was killed. The mind is wild, you know, you can't always predict what it will do."

"But you said – you wanted Julie to go and see that woman in London. The metallurgist."

"Just covering all bases. Also I thought Nadine would be interested. She enjoys weird stories. She showed me an alien belt buckle once, you know."

"What on Earth are you talking about, Vanja?"

"What I say. A belt buckle, made from something like pewter, only it wasn't pewter. Nadine said the metal resisted analysis. Those were her exact words – resisted analysis. The buckle was found along with some Roman-era artefacts but it wasn't Roman. Nadine said it's like it was dropped here by mistake."

"Dropped here?"

"Yes. By someone passing through. You have to admit it's possible. But even if Julie's necklace does turn out to be alien I still don't think that has anything to do with what happened to her. The necklace is something she found, that's all. In a junk shop or somewhere."

"Did Nadine call you? After Julie went to see her, I mean."

"No, why? You think the aliens got to her as well?"

"I'm sick of aliens," Selena said. "Mostly I want to know what we're doing here, what we're supposed to be looking for. I still don't see the point."

"I don't know yet." Vanja turned back towards the path, continued pushing her way forward through the undergrowth. "I think the police must have missed something, though. They didn't know about this Jimson guy, not back then. So what else didn't they know?"

"But even if they did miss something—"

"It's ages ago. I know. I want to take a look, that's all. It won't take a moment."

"Fine."

"You sound pissed off."

"I am pissed off. You're worse than my dad."

"Your dad? I was thinking more Buffy."

"You keep right on thinking that. You realise we're going to have to walk all the way back to the station after this?"

"Do you think they do Irish coffee at that café place?"

"I don't know. Do you think there's a god?"

Vanja laughed. Selena made an annoyed sound, because she knew it was expected of her, part of the game they were playing, and yet she knew also that she would not turn back now, not if Vanja herself suggested it, nor for any other reason. She wanted to see the lay-by, the path running off it. Although she knew it was impossible, she found herself imagining that the tracks from Jimson's van tyres would still be there, imprinted in the dirt like a fossil record.

MOLOCH RAINFISH (Siak Thenh, Pearly Rainfish) is a medium-sized freshwater muriad common in the southern hemisphere wherever there are bodies of water large enough to accommodate an active population. Argent in colour, both males and females will usually develop large iridescent patches during the spring breeding season, and, more usually in the females, a fiery red striping through the dorsal and tail area prior to egg-laying. The fry are usually hatched following a rainstorm, a fact that has given rise to the common name of 'rainfish'. The Moloch is plentiful throughout the southern regions, and has always been a ready and popular food source, especially among the Noors, who traditionally keep large stores of the salted fillets to feed their families through the winter. The restaurant Siak Thenh in the Cam-Noor district of Fiby specialises in Noors cuisine, with the rainfish as a staple item on its menu. It can be cooked in a variety of ways, including the famous rainfish stew, with potato dumplings and seasonal herbs, which should preferably be freshly picked prior to cooking.

The lay-by was empty, windswept. Selena tried to remember what Julie had said about the other vehicles that had been there when Jimson pulled his van off the road. A Volkswagen camper, a motorbike? Julie hadn't said what kind of motorbike. Dad would have known, though, because he loved bikes. If Dad had been telling the story, that was the kind of detail he would have picked up on. Stories were odd like that. Even when the main facts were the same, different people noticed different things, according to what was important to them and what wasn't. With Julie it was all that stuff about music, Steven Jimson liking Marillion or whatever. With Dad it would have been the motorbike, only Dad would never have been kidnapped, would he? It was always women and girls, women and girls, with men rushing to find them because of course it was only men who could find them. The women had to stay at home in case they got hurt. *Picnic at Hanging Rock*, the filthy, agonised face of Michael Fitzhubert, the soiled scrap of lace clutched in his hand.

The rain had stopped, but still the sky was grey – grey like iron, grey like rainwater, like the ruffled, inscrutable surface of Hatchmere Lake. The ground was scuffed and bare, a mixture of sand and gravel, edged by the crumpled, broken kind of concrete you find at the margins of roads, and on the far sides of car parks. Leftovers and afterthoughts, make-do-and-mends. There were potholes filled with rainwater, a Sainsbury's carrier bag, also waterlogged, flapping its half-open mouth at the edge of the trees. There were car tracks in the mud, damp declivities in the gravel, but who knew what vehicles had made them or when they were made? The police would know, probably, or at least they could find out, if they had to, if they wanted to, if it seemed worth their while.

Such an ordinary place. If you were passing by in your car, or your father's car, or a car full of your mates on the way to Manchester, you wouldn't give it a thought or a second glance. If you were with your boyfriend or your girlfriend you might pull over, bring the car right up to the treeline and have a quick fuck. She and Johnny had done that once, in a lay-by near Macclesfield. No one had seen them, so far as she knew, and so what if they had? There was no law against it, or maybe there was now, like anyone gave a shit.

The lay-by was dank, greenish-grey, edged with trees. A nowhere place. If you didn't know the lake was nearby, you wouldn't think about pulling over here, because what would be the point? Even on a hot summer's day, what would be the point?

A Volkswagen camper van and a motorbike. Selena felt terrified suddenly, like an insect beneath the lens of a microscope, powerless and so acutely *observed* it was like being vivisected.

Her sister had been here. Julie had been here. This had happened to her.

"What a horrible place," Vanja said. "Desolate." She said the word slowly, separating the syllables. She was looking about herself, her wet hair flapping in the wind. A car flew past on the road, a blue Rover. "There's nothing here."

"I want to go back," Selena said.

"Sure," said Vanja. She sounded distracted. She was still looking around, scanning the road in both directions. "It really is creepy here, isn't it?"

"I'm getting cold, that's all," Selena said. She started walking towards the trees, towards the place where she knew the path would be. For a moment she couldn't see it, there was just a wall of green, all the trees identical-seeming, like in a child's drawing of a forest, each one straight as a matchstick, the branches set at right angles. Then as she drew closer the pathway appeared, as if out of nowhere, a narrow aperture shrouded with green, like the entrance to a labyrinth.

GREN-MOLOCH (Super Rainfish, Sanh Krenh). Not to be confused with the Pearly Rainfish, the Gren-Moloch or Greater Rainfish is a very large, carnivorous bony-fish, believed to be the last surviving species of a genus previously thought to be extinct. The Sanh Krenh is featured in many of the ancient Noors cave paintings at sites in the Mirkh Mountains and dating from several centuries before the founding of the city of Fiby. Unlike its distant cousin the Pearly Rainfish, the Sanh Krenh is a saltwater predator, indigenous to the northern coastal waters of the Marilly Sea. Sightings are most common during the winter months, when freezing temperatures drive the fish closer in towards the land. A well-documented mass beaching of Greater Rainfish occurred close to the coastal settlement of Serp. Thought to be a failed migration, the event forms the centrepiece of a long narrative poem, 'Rain', by the local poet and essayist Olla Wurock. The meat of the Gren-Moloch is a prized delicacy in southern cuisine, although the risks involved in capturing the fish make it prohibitively expensive. Noors tradition forbids the fishing and eating of the Gren-Moloch, except in times of famine, or when the fish has cast itself ashore and would be wasted otherwise. The Gren-Moloch is a fearless, rapacious predator and will take human prey where available and without hesitation. Gren-Moloch scrimshaw, or bone carving, is highly prized, and often intricate.

"Which way was it?" Vanja said. "I don't remember this other path. Was it here before?"

There was a fork in the pathway: the path they had entered by and another, sloping off to the right. Selena couldn't recall seeing it earlier but it was more likely they just hadn't noticed it. "I think it's this way," Selena said. She pointed to the lower path, the path they had come along, which was narrower but more distinct, a rift between the trees. She made as if to edge past Vanja, who was staring off down the other path as if she was hypnotised.

"Just a moment," said Vanja quietly. "What's that?" She was pointing into the bushes, where there was nothing to see of course, except more bushes, the odd toadstool possibly, fly agaric, *Amanita muscaria*, which was definitely eye-catching, spectacular even because of its iconic red cap and natty white spots, but this wasn't the season. Dad had known loads about fungi – he'd brought them here one autumn, shown them where to look, her and Julie. Dad had wanted to gather some mushrooms – boletus and chanterelles, which were plentiful in October – and take them home to eat, to have with a fry-up, but Julie had been scared, terrified really, convinced they'd all be poisoned and die in agony. She could be funny like that, Julie could, the way she took against things, took fright. Her mind was a mystery. But that was no reason for Vanja to go haring off after toadstools, or whatever it was she had spotted, something red, not worth the bother.

"You'll get your feet wet," Selena said, although the right-hand path was actually drier than the lower path, you could see that. The trees are thicker overhead, that's all, Selena thought. They keep the rain off.

"It's some sort of a maze," Vanja said, and laughed. With delight, it seemed to Selena, although her words, there was something about them, something chilling. Vanja made her way forward into the opening, brushing lightly against Selena's shoulder as she went. "How on Earth did we miss this?"

"Don't get lost," Selena said, in what she hoped was a

jokey tone of voice, although she didn't think she pulled that off, not quite, and it didn't matter in any case because Vanja was going to press on regardless, that was obvious. Selena kept her eyes on the back of her parka, striped with tree-shadow, more tree-shadow than there should have been maybe, as if there were more paths leading off from this one, more intersecting passageways that could not be seen from where she stood but that were there nonetheless. Selena took a step forward, thinking she might as well, what was the harm in taking a look at least? She thought of the remains of Beaudesert at Cannock Chase, which Julie didn't seem to think she would remember, although she did, just, a massive stone pillar with a globe on top, part of an entranceway, like this one, only crumbled to ruin.

*My name is Ozymandias, king of kings.*

She thought of Eduard and Elina Farsett amongst the ruins of Pakwa, heating soup and dumplings over an open fire.

Oh, Julie, she thought. She experienced a rush of love for her sister so intense it was almost anger. Where the hell did you go?

"Oh my God," Vanja was saying. "I think you should come and take a look at this. Don't touch," she added quickly. "I don't think we should touch this. Just look."

Selena hurried to her side. Leaves crunched and slithered under her feet. Her heart was pounding. Like Niagara, she thought, only that's not right, waterfalls don't pound. Thunder, then, roar. What exactly do they do?

There was something in the bushes. Something red,

or reddish, a rust colour, streaked with rain-dirt and leaf residue. Selena could see a tarnished metal buckle, a twisted leather strap, green with mildew.

This wasn't real, because it couldn't be. Things like this didn't happen in real life.

"It's a rucksack, I think. A backpack," Vanja said. "It looks like Julie's. I recognise it from the photographs. They did all those reconstructions, didn't they? Like on *Crimewatch*."

"Yes." Selena bent down to look, hunkered down. Her calves ached, the damp weather most likely, and the walking. They'd been walking for quite a while, all in all. She stretched out her hand, her fingers hovering just short of the thing in the bushes, the red rucksack. Selena understood that Vanja was right, they shouldn't touch it, but she needed to reach out, all the same, to *almost* touch it, to offer herself some proof it was really there.

This object, this artefact, this piece of the past that was now the present, this guarantee.

"I think I'm going to be sick," she said.

"Oh no you don't, *dushen'ka*, stand up." Vanja gripped her under the arms and tugged, hauling her to an upright position. "Rest here against this tree."

Vanja guided her to a twisty, rather narrow beech tree, and made her embrace its trunk with both her arms. How strong she is, Selena thought. She could feel the tree bark against her forehead, beneath her hands, she could smell its smell. It was as if the tree was holding her, rather than she it, the way Vanja had held her. It was as if Vanja was the tree, the tree Vanja. Both the tree and Vanja were stronger than she was.

"I'm going to call the police," Vanja said. "Are you OK with that?"

Selena nodded. "I can't stay here," she said. Her teeth were chattering audibly.

"I can deal with them. Can you find your way back to the station, if I stay here and wait for them to come?"

"I can't let you do that."

"Yes you can. This whole stupid thing was my idea, remember?"

Selena gazed at Vanja in her horrible green parka. She longed to say something that would make a difference, that would convey something of the gratitude she felt, the realisation that Vanja was one of the world's survivors. Vanja had true grit, like in the film, the film *True Grit*. Both she and Johnny had liked the Jeff Bridges version better. John Wayne was such a plonker, and anyway, Hailee Steinfeld's was one of the best screen performances ever. Vanja had true grit, like Hailee Steinfeld, like Mattie Ross, and if anything happened, anything awful, Vanja would have the grit to stand and fight. Whatever it was, she would fight, even if the outlook seemed hopeless, even if fighting seemed pointless, just another word for suicide.

Selena would not fight, probably, or in any case she would not fight hard enough. She was too tied to things as they were, too fearful of change.

She would go out like a light, like Shauna Macdonald at the end of *The Descent*. But Vanja would survive, and this tree would survive too, probably, so that was all right.

## 8

DESCRIPTION OF ITEM: a backpack or rucksack of canvas construction. Leather back-straps and trim, nickel-plated aluminium buckle and decorative eyelets. Manufacturer's label (sewn into inside seam) MIAMI, made in Singapore. Colour: beetroot. The backpack consists of one large main storage compartment, buckle-fastened, and two smaller, outer pocket compartments, zip-fastened. The canvas material is heavily soiled with mud, topsoil and other environmental contaminants. There is considerable weathering and water-damage, resulting in colour-fading, stiffening, and material deterioration caused by mildew fungus and general weather-exposure. There is little sign of deliberate or forceful damage. The overall condition of the backpack suggests gradual depreciation and decay as the result of prolonged exposure to weather. Invertebrate activity and vegetation growth in the area immediately surrounding the item at its point of discovery, together with the full contents inventory, suggest that the backpack had not been disturbed or examined for a period of some years.

CONTENTS OF THE RUCKSACK: books: The Science of Black Holes by Maria Chavez Healy, Becoming a Writer by Dorothea Brande, What Did You Do in the War, Granny? The Art and Science of Family Trees by Jodie Bissett, one ankle charm bracelet, with single heart-shaped lock charm, gold-plated 9ct, no hallmark, one pencil case, nylon fur fabric, green, (containing four Staedtler graphite pencils, HB, one green plastic pencil sharpener, one Pentel felt-tip thin-nibbed marker, red, two Bic ballpoints, black, one Bic ballpoint, blue, one plastic ruler, 6in, transparent, one pair compasses, chrome steel, one pair plastic flip-flops, one leather purse, red, containing £6.73 in notes and coins, one hair comb, plastic, tortoiseshell design, one 3oz bar Bourneville chocolate, one bottle Coty nail varnish, pigeon blue, one spectacles case, grey leather (empty), one Manchester Central Library lending card (Julie Fiona Amanda Ronane), one Warrington Libraries lending card (Julie F.

Rouane), one staple-bound A5 exercise book (J. Rouane), one pair of nail scissors, chrome steel, one pocket calculator, Sanyo, solar powered. It should be noted that two of the books (Healy, Bissett) were stamped internally as the property of Priestley College, Warrington. The condition of the remaining book (Brande) and the school exercise book is very poor owing to water damage over a long time period. It should further be noted that the buckle used as a fastening for the main body of the backpack had rusted shut and had to be chiselled open. Any earlier and previous attempts to gain access to the contents would therefore seem unlikely. Weight of rucksack (dry) without contents: 657 g.

## 'A Mother's Hope' by Stef Joby, *Warrington Guardian*, Saturday March 20th 2016

Margery Rouane is sixty-six. Only recently retired from her post as a medical practice manager in Warrington, she is an upright, neatly built woman with closely cropped grey hair and penetrating blue eyes. Perhaps appropriately for a mother who last Wednesday received definitive proof from Greater Manchester Police of the death of a daughter, she is soberly dressed. More unusually, Margery Rouane is a woman who seems happy to communicate, a circumstance best explained by the fact that she has been waiting for information about what happened to her daughter for more than twenty years. At this stage, Rouane explains, any news – even grim news – can feel like the lifting of a life sentence.

"Of course in the beginning this is the news you dread most," Rouane told me. "Suddenly, in an instant, your whole life becomes reduced to a process of waiting. You can't do anything, so you wait. I remember that for the whole of the first week I hardly dared go out of the house in case the phone rang. It became like a superstition. And yet at the same time you're terrified of the phone ringing because of what you might be told. While there's no news there's still hope. Nothing's happened, so maybe nothing's happened. It's like being on the run from an invisible enemy."

Of those who still remember the Rouane case, what they will recall most clearly is that it was never solved. Sometime during the afternoon of Saturday July 16th 1994, seventeen-year-old Julie Rouane opened the front door of her home in the village of Lymm, Cheshire, supposedly on the way to meet a friend. She was never to return, and no trace of Julie or of her body was ever found. Her disappearance sparked a massive police search, but following some early leads and two mistaken arrests, the trail went cold. There was no news from Julie, no evidence of what happened to her. Eventually the police stopped looking. Some have levelled the accusation that it was this seeming incompetence and apathy on the part of the police services that propelled Julie's father, Raymond Rouane, into the cycle of exhaustion and mental illness that eventually killed him.

"Ray was a quiet, stable, unassuming man," his wife remembers. "It doesn't sound romantic, I know, but one of the main reasons I married Ray was his fundamental decency. He was a very good father. I admired him even more than I loved him, if I'm honest. When Julie went missing he changed completely. It was as if he had a splinter lodged in his mind, turning it septic. No amount of talking or medication or even time passing could dislodge it. I know Ray felt powerless, but so did we all. I began to feel I couldn't get through to him any more, as if what I thought didn't count. This drove us apart eventually, as a couple I mean, although we stayed good friends. When he died I was heartbroken. Looking back on that time now, I regret not trying harder to accept the man he'd become, rather than doing what I did, which was to try and turn back the clock. People think differently, they react to tragedy differently. Ray needed answers. He wasn't about to stop looking for them just because the police insisted there weren't any. He was too stubborn for that. In a way I admire him."

Does Margery Rouane blame the police for what happened?

"Not in the slightest. I don't blame the doctors, either. I don't blame anyone, except the person who murdered Julie. It wasn't just her life he destroyed that day."

The more time passed, Rouane maintains, the more the agony surrounding Julie's disappearance evolved from a fear of what might have happened into the simple terror of not knowing. "It became a constant background noise, a wound that could never heal. In the beginning it's actually much easier. People are interested and sympathetic. The media attention is highly intrusive but on the other hand it gives you the sense that something is being done. When that attention disappears, you feel marooned. Every time you try to put pressure on the police, even just to keep looking, you're made to feel like a troublemaker, or ungrateful. There's a kind of unspoken consensus that you're never going to know now, so you'd best accept it. And as for Julie, so far as the outside world is concerned, she never existed. I made contact with several people, over the years, people who had been through a similar experience. All of them had had friends who would cross the street rather than speak to them, just to avoid hearing the name of the missing person. I suppose I'm lucky in that I never experienced anything that blatant, but I do know how those people felt. I felt like that every day. That's why it's such a relief to be able to think about having a proper funeral for Julie, a proper goodbye. In an odd way, it's as if she's finally come home."

Julie's homecoming is something of a miracle. In November of last year, a Manchester woman, Vanja Sukhanov, was walking in the Delamere Forest nature reserve when she happened upon the rucksack belonging to Julie Rouane just yards from a pathway leading directly to Hatchmere Lake, a beauty spot that became the focus of intense police activity immediately after Rouane went missing. "I go up there sometimes to think," Sukhanov said in a press release. "It's a peaceful place and I like it there, even when it's raining."

Sukhanov has lived in Manchester for twenty years. She and her husband came to Britain from Berlin, some eight years after the fall of the Berlin Wall and a full eighteen months after Julie Rouane's disappearance hit both local and national news headlines. Certainly Vanja Sukhanov knew nothing about the missing girl on the day she made her discovery at Hatchmere Lake. "I never became involved in a murder story before," she said. "So this feels very strange."

Sukhanov claims it was the rucksack's bright colour that drew her to investigate. "I saw something red, something large," she explained. "I was a bit scared, I think, a bit worried, anyway, because this was deep in the woods. Not many people go there, and it seemed unusual." When she finally saw the rucksack she said her immediate reaction was not to touch it, and to call the police. "It was as if something was telling me this isn't right. It was just a rucksack, I could see that, but I didn't like the look of it. Whenever I get these kinds of feelings I always obey. There are times when your body knows best, even before your mind. When your body speaks up it's time to listen."

What Sukhanov had discovered by chance was an item the police had spent days and weeks searching for in 1994, entirely without success: the cherry-coloured backpack Julie had been wearing when she went out on that fateful Saturday and which several witnesses clearly remembered seeing her carrying later on that same afternoon. The rucksack contained books and personal items belonging to Julie, as well as library cards and a college ID card – certainly enough to convince Greater Manchester Police to undertake a new search of the area, a full two decades after their colleagues – many of whom have since retired – gave up hope of ever uncovering the key to what had happened.

Three days after Sukhanov's discovery of the rucksack, police investigators unearthed human remains buried in a shallow grave less than twenty metres from where the backpack was found. DNA tests indicate a 98-percent probability that the remains are Julie's. Speculations that Julie Rouane was in fact the missing 'fourth victim' of Stockport serial murderer Steven Jimson remain unconfirmed, although an anonymous police source intimated that they were taking what has popularly become known as the 'Jimson theory' very seriously indeed.

For Margery Rouane, the identity of the killer is less important than the positive identification of her missing daughter. The DNA tests have acted like the lifting of a curse. "Before Julie was found, I could never entirely escape the feeling that she might still be alive somewhere, in terrible trouble or pain, and with no one to help her. Now I know that my daughter is dead, that she died a long time ago, I can begin to mourn for her. Most importantly I can begin to remember her the way she was. I've missed her so terribly. Now I feel as if my memories are my own again."

Unlike many who cope with the loss of a loved one by surrounding themselves with mementoes, Margery Rouane has not up until now felt comfortable displaying so much as a single photograph of Julie in her home. "It always seemed like a mockery, somehow," she says. Now this feeling also has changed. "It is as if I can hold her again," Rouane adds, and when she shows me the two framed photographs on her mantelpiece, one a posed studio portrait, the other of Julie during a family holiday in the Lake District, it is impossible to mistake the love and pride she feels in her daughter, finally restored.

[From Nadine Akoujan's diary]
[Sample: SG-357/21/3/16. Source: pendant with 16" chain.
Visual impressions: silver, high carat, no hallmark, hand/
studio manufacture, unusual stone, possibly fluorspar/
chalcedony/localised outcrop.]

*What I want to say first is that I believed Julie Rouane's story.
Or rather, I believed she believed it. She wasn't hoaxing, she
wasn't trying to con me, or to con Vanja or whoever had
sent her to Vanja, she didn't want money, she was for real,
as Danny would say, she was honest. These are not things
you can prove, they are just things you get to know. From
talking to people, from listening to their stories and to your
own reactions to those stories. And then there was Saira,
who never likes strangers, but she liked this woman, she
liked Julie. She even talked about her later, after she had
left. Is the lady coming back, Mummy? she said. She looked
disappointed when I said probably she wasn't, then asked
if she could draw her a picture. I said yes, we could send it
to her, couldn't we, that would be nice. She drew one, too,
one of her imaginary cities, and when I asked her what the
city was called, she was quiet for a minute then said the city
would have to have the same name as the lady, because it was
where the lady had come from. What, Manchester? I said,*

and laughed. Not Manchester, Saira said, in that funny voice she uses when she thinks I'm being really stupid. It's a bit like her teacher's voice, Gwen from the nursery. I don't think Saira is deliberately imitating her but hearing her speak like Gwen always makes me laugh. Not Manchester, silly, the other place. I didn't question her any more because I know she doesn't like it when I start getting too curious – she's a very private little person, like I was at her age – but it was odd, I thought, what she said. I hadn't left her alone with Julie Rouane, not even for a minute. Saira could have been listening in on our conversation, I suppose, that would make more sense. I haven't noticed her doing that before, but she is growing up so quickly, too quickly maybe. Dad would say that comes from her being an only child, though what he expects me to do about that right now I have no idea.

Believing Julie's own belief in her story is not the same as believing the story itself. My job is to test things, to find out what they are. There is no harm in having an opinion about something, but as a scientist especially it is unwise to let opinion take the place of fact. To say this looks like silver is not the same as saying this is silver, not until you've tested it, not until you know for a certainty what you are talking about. Until all the appropriate tests have proved positive, the identity of the substance you have in front of you remains open-ended, a series of probabilities. The greatest probability is that the substance is silver, but this is not the only outcome on the table. It is crucial to recognise this, to understand and believe it. If you want to be good at your job, I mean. Of all the things Zahar taught me, this is the most important.

*Most people, scientists included, would describe themselves as open-minded, but most of them are not. Most people with an opinion prefer to hang on to it, even to the point where proof to the contrary is staring them in the face, sometimes even beyond that. This is what I mean by not being open-minded. Even now, especially now, Zahar would say, there are some things that are acceptable to believe, and some that are not. So Julie Rouane believes she was transported to an alien city, on an alien planet, that she formed attachments there and that in the case of Cally the attachment was formed even before that. She claims she knew Cally in Manchester, that they had known one another as children. As a scientist, I have no way of proving or disproving these things. I have no idea of the current whereabouts of Cally, but not knowing where Cally is does not mean that Cally doesn't exist. All I have is the necklace, the pendant Julie says was given to her by Cally. She has given me permission to subject the metal to the appropriate tests, so that we can know for certain what it is made of. This report concerns the metallic components of the pendant only. Given the sensitivity of the material, my own ignorance as to its composition and the clear importance of the artefact to its owner I thought it unwise to attempt an analysis of the mineral component at the present time. (I didn't want to interfere with it, if I am honest.)*

## [Assay and results]

*To conduct the assay I removed a single link from the pendant's chain, which was then melted in a crucible. Simple magnet, electro-conductivity and heat conductivity tests proved positive. The nitric acid test yielded a strong (clear red) positive result. The water displacement test, which I carried out first with the single-link sample and later with the chain in its entirety, gave a heavier than normal result, suggesting either a greater than average purity or unknown anomaly. I conducted the weight test twenty-five times in all, each time with the same or very similar result. A full chemical analysis and isotope scan, which I booked with MaasLab and conducted myself, assisted by Heike Scheck, revealed a 98 percent 109 Ag to 1 percent 107 Ag, with the suggestion of an additional 1 percent 108m Ag. With Ag 107 being the more common isotope (to the value of 1.85 percent naturally occurring approximately) the heavily skewed 109 to 107 ratio would be highly unusual in any case. The presence of the meta-static isotope 108 would render the sample a logical improbability. Such anomalous composition is most commonly associated with ore samples taken from the Santa Clara meteorite (Mexico, 1976, in which the recorded samples indicated an anomaly in favour of 107 Ag).*

## [Conclusion]

*In the absence of more rigorous testing procedures, these results would seem to indicate that Julie Rouane's pendant is composed of particularly high-density argent silver with a 99.9 percentage purity and anomalous composition. I would go further in stating that because this present anomaly most closely accords with meteorite (extraterrestrial) rather than native ore samples, the silver used in the manufacture of the chain (and by probability the pendant also, although it should be noted this item was not sampled and so cannot be verified) is likely to be extraterrestrial in origin.*

*[NB] Just because a metal is extraterrestrial in origin, we cannot assume an extraterrestrial manufacture and it would be misleading and possibly harmful to do so in this case.*

*I was worried that Heike might give me aggro about the results – they were so unusual – but her mind must have been on something else that day because she disappeared as soon as we'd finished, more or less, and without a word. I thought about scrubbing the results from the system hard drive, then thought again. No one was going to give a shit about someone else's random isotope test. Any kind of data-scrubbing would be picked up immediately though, I knew that. If you're recruiting for a spying outfit you'd pick techies over chemists any time. Then I called up Julie Rouane and told her the pendant was alien. Probably alien. As close to one hundred percent as we can come without a provenance, I said. Or a photograph of the source site, I thought but didn't say. Things seemed weird enough without that. I thought Julie would sound excited but she barely reacted. I waited for her to say I told you so, but she didn't. What she said was, what do I do now? I couldn't think what to say to her. Whenever something like this happens, which isn't often, thank God, I always find myself wanting to check on Saira, to hold her tight and take her somewhere safe. There's nowhere to take* her of course, and she hates it when I hug her too tight, she wriggles to get free, which only upsets me more, so I try not to do it. I ask Julie if she wants to come and collect the pendant or if FedEx is OK this time. She says FedEx is fine. But only if you take it in yourself, she adds, which of course I will. I feel she's still expecting something. Sympathy? Advice? I don't really understand any of this, I say in the end. I'm just a metallurgist. She breathes in, sharply, I hear it clearly even at the end of the telephone line and it's as if I've punched her in the stomach. I got Saira's drawing, she says in the end. I'd like to send her some new colouring pencils, if that's all right. She'd like that, I say. I don't really want her near Saira, but I know Saira likes her. I add that she should come and see us, if she's in London. I spend the rest of the day worrying I've done the wrong thing, but what the heck, I like her too, and she seems so alone.

## 9

"Where have you been?" Selena said.

She had half expected Julie not to let her in. The flat was a mess. Books and papers covered the table under the window and there were more on the floor underneath. Three empty coffee cups on the windowsill and an air of general untidiness. Not dirty, just dishevelled, like a child that had been left too long to its own devices. It reminded her of Dad's place – because of course it did.

Julie's laptop was open and there was a video playing: images of outer space, covered with pulsing circles and darting red arrows. Julie was wearing black jeans and a baggy grey jumper. Her hair was snatched back off her face in an elastic band, to hide the fact that it needed washing, probably. Other than that she looked all right, which at least was something.

"Why didn't you answer your phone?" she added. Now that she knew Julie was safe, she was surprised by how angry she felt.

Julie looked at the ground. "I kept forgetting to charge it," she said. "And I've been out a lot. I probably wasn't here when you called."

"Yeah right. You didn't think I might be worried?"

"I wasn't sure you'd want to see me any more. I read what was in the papers. I kept expecting the police to show up."

"You thought I was going to call the police on you?"

"Not you. Mum."

"Mum wouldn't do that."

"You don't know that. You don't know what she might do."

"What is all this mess, anyway? You're not blaming Mum for that too, are you?"

Julie glanced at the overflowing table. "Nothing. Just some stuff I've been reading."

"Let's go and get something to eat."

"I don't feel like going out. What if someone recognises me, from the papers?"

"You seriously believe anyone's going to recognise you from an old school photo?"

"I don't know. They might."

"I hardly think so. Come on, Julie. You can't stay holed up in here forever. You'll go nuts. And you'll get fired."

"Is it cold out?"

"It's Manchester and it's March. What do you think?"

"I'll get my coat, then."

Selena waited, wondering how it was possible for them to be having this conversation, how it was possible for them to be together in the same space even, arguing over the weather and with all the deeper questions left unspoken.

It's because we're sisters, she thought. That's how sisters go on.

"Did you mean what you said on my voicemail?" Julie

asked later, when they were in the restaurant. "About not caring what the police said, about that girl they found. Did you mean that?"

"I said so, didn't I?"

"Who do you reckon she is, then? The woman they dug up, I mean?"

"How would I know? Someone else. Someone who died." It was strange, Selena thought, how little this question honestly bothered her. She cared that a woman had died, had been murdered, but that was all. Asking questions about who she had been felt risky to her, like prodding dynamite. She wasn't going to do it – she had decided not to. "I've been wondering what we should do about your name," she said instead. "I mean for work and everything."

What happens to a person officially, after they die? How long does it take for their existence to be scrubbed from the system? Selena recalled news stories about the families of pensioners who had died, and yet who still kept receiving telephone bills and council tax demands, months and sometimes years after the funeral. You couldn't stop these letters coming, not even if you produced a valid death certificate. It was harder to expunge an identity, apparently, than it was to create one.

The tax man cometh, Selena thought. Even unto the hereafter. Julie was different though, she'd been in the news. What would she do if the pen-pushers at the tax office tried to wipe her?

How can you prove you're alive once you're legally dead?

"That's one thing that isn't a problem, actually," Julie said.

For the first time that evening she laughed. "I changed my surname to Mum's maiden name. I did it years ago. It just seemed safer. In case anyone came asking questions, I mean."

"So you're Julie Hillson?"

Julie nodded.

"Suits you."

They carried on eating. People came and went at the front of the restaurant, collecting takeaways.

"I need to know what you're thinking, Selena," Julie said in the end. "What you're really thinking, I mean."

She seems calm, Selena thought. Calmer than when we first arrived here, anyway. She's ventured out of her hole and the world is still turning.

"I don't know." Selena sighed. "I don't think I'll ever know, to be honest. I don't understand any of it. All I know is that I believe you're my sister. You remembered Mr Rustbucket. The only person who would remember Mr Rustbucket is my sister Julie."

The police kept Selena updated on everything that was happening with Julie's remains. That was how the police worked these days, Selena supposed. Civilians were problem clients, liable to sue at the least provocation. Best to keep them onside.

The first police visit had been a shock, but only because she hadn't expected them to put the pieces together so quickly: twenty-four hours or even less, that was really quite something. The follow-up was more routine. DCI Schechter was nice:

a courteous, rather reticent man who said he'd been on the force at the time Julie went missing, that he remembered the case well. I was just a DCI then, he said. Green as pea soup. When he asked Selena if she'd like him to put her in touch with a victims' support counsellor, Selena said no.

I'm fine, she said. Honestly. She didn't say much else. Things seemed safer that way. She made DCI Schechter a cup of coffee and hoped that would be the end of it. I want to thank you for everything you're doing, she added.

I feel lucky to be working on this, to be honest, Schechter said. It's good to get closure on a case. Sometimes you don't. Sometimes. He stopped speaking abruptly. Clearly he thought he'd gone too far, been too candid. Selena smiled.

That's all right, she said. I understand. I'm glad it was you, she almost added, and then didn't. It seemed wrong somehow, disingenuous. She liked DCI Schechter and didn't want to lie to him any more than was necessary. It was all too easy to imagine him paging through Julie's back file, trying to work out where they'd gone wrong before, why their searching had failed to turn up anything of substance when presumably the evidence had been there all along. Had their methods fallen short somehow, or had the body simply been hidden somewhere else and then dumped back in the woods at a later date, after the search teams had given up and gone home? Selena guessed that Schechter was banking on it being the latter. She could almost hear the hum of his thoughts: the girl had been abducted and murdered, the killer must have decided to get rid of her rucksack along with the body.

Not that that explained everything, but it was a start. They'd find out the rest in due course, probably. No point in getting into details with the sister – best to spare her the worst of it. Civilians and death don't mix, *how many times have I had to tell you, DCI Schechter?*

Schechter shook his head as if to clear it. We should have the full forensics in a week or so, he said. He gave Selena his card. If there's anything I can do in the meantime, don't hesitate to call.

Thanks, Selena said. I won't. After he'd gone, Selena wondered why he hadn't asked her about her own movements on the day Julie's rucksack had been found, then supposed he hadn't seen much point in that, either. Schechter had no reason to investigate whether there was any connection between Selena and Vanja, and so he hadn't. No one had, and Selena wasn't about to bring it to anyone's attention. Even if Schechter or one of his colleagues eventually cottoned on to the fact that Vanja Sukhanov was Selena Rouane's boss, what did that prove? That Selena had told Vanja about her sister's long-ago disappearance, that Vanja had become curious and decided to have a nose around down by the lake?

It was hardly a crime. Selena came to the conclusion that what the police didn't know couldn't hurt them. As a general rule to live by, it was pretty much iron-cast.


Schechter brought round the forensics report himself. There's a lot of technical stuff, he said. But what it boils down to is that the remains are your sister's.

Definitely? Selena asked.

Almost certainly. There's a two percent margin of error, but that's so the lab guys can cover themselves, basically. Your sister is dead, I'm afraid. We're as certain of that as we are ever going to be.

When Selena phoned her mother later that evening, Margery made no mention of DCI Schechter, even in passing. She nattered on about her trip instead, the fly-drive expedition to the United States that she and Janice were planning for the following spring. Margery had seemed different since she came back from Janice's. Younger, more like the person she had been before the summer of her affair, although Selena's memories of that time were hazy, it seemed so long ago.

Julie's memories would be clearer, more accurate. The night after Schechter's second visit, Selena dreamed she was waiting for Julie outside her flat. It was the rush hour, and there were cars tailing back down the road all the way to the traffic lights. She pressed the bell push again, thinking Julie hadn't heard, and the button disappeared right back inside the little box. It's broken, Selena thought. It seemed like a disaster, and she began to cry. She awoke with a start, relieved to find the dream hadn't been real.

If she never called Julie again, no one would blame her. The DNA test said her sister was dead, she had Schechter's paperwork to prove it. So what was wrong, then, what was wrong?

Her sister was alone on an alien planet, and she had no one.

No one but me. So what if she isn't the same as she

was when she went missing? What difference does it make?

Whoever the hell she is, she's still my sister.

"I've been thinking," Selena said. "What if we bought a place together, the two of us? I saw one of those big three-storey houses just went up for sale, round on Parsonage Road? We could do it up."

Her voice trailed off. She had no idea how Julie might react to such a suggestion, whether she was moving too fast, whether the whole idea was madness anyway. There was also the question of Johnny, but they could cross that bridge when or if they ever came to it. If Johnny came marching home again, they'd have to see how things stood.

"You're trying to protect me," Julie said. "You think I'm like Dad, that I need looking after."

"Dad didn't need looking after," Selena said, and it wasn't until she spoke the words that she realised how true they were. Ray had been fine the way he was, he didn't need fixing. It was everyone else – the doctors especially – who kept insisting he was a problem.

Ray had always believed that Julie was alive. Which meant either that he'd never been crazy, or that she was crazy too.

Selena couldn't see that it mattered much, either way.

"He was lonely, that's all," she said. "He needed to talk, but no one would listen."

"And you think that's what I need – to talk?"

"I don't know what you need, Julie. I don't have a clue.

I just thought things might work out better for both of us if we stuck together."

"Two mad ladies?"

"Two bad ladies."

"That sounds OK to me." Julie put down her fork and reached across the table. She grabbed Selena's hand and held it tight.

The sky was covered with cloud and there were no stars visible. Before Julie came home, Selena hadn't taken much notice of the night sky, except to note if it was beautiful or sullen. In Manchester it was often difficult to see the stars in any case, there was too much artificial lighting.

These days, she found herself looking upwards more and more often. She did not know the names of any of the stars, or how to find the constellations. Dad had taught them a few once, when they were kids, but she had forgotten. Selena resolved to learn them again, properly this time. How hard could it be?

One afternoon in early April, Selena went with Julie to have a look at the house on Parsonage Road, a tall Victorian terrace with a narrow back garden and one off-road parking space. From the inside it looked as if nobody had touched it since the war.

"It wouldn't take much," Selena said. "Not once we get all this rubbish out." She hesitated. "We could strip the floors."

"We could convert the attic," Julie added. "We'd have even more space then."

Selena put her own house on the market the same afternoon. When she told Margery she was buying a place with a friend named Julie, her mother seemed happy to accept her decision. "It'll be nice for you to have some company," she said. "More secure."

When eventually she came to visit, she chatted away with Julie as if she'd never seen her before. "It's lovely to meet you at last," she said. "Selena's told me so much about you."

She admired the improvements they'd made to the house and then they ate supper, a lamb and apricot stew made to an Armenian recipe that Selena had prepared beforehand.

"If that's the way she wants to play it, I guess I can live with that," Julie said afterwards. "At least she seems to like me now. Better than she did before, anyway."

"I don't know how you can be so laid back about it," Selena said. "I'd be furious if it were me."

"No you wouldn't," Julie said. "Just think – she'll never be able to bitch on at me about what a ghastly teenager I was."

"There is that," Selena said. She laughed. "Kind of like a Get Out of Jail Free card."

When Selena typed *The Mind-Robbers of Pakwa* into Google Books it came back unrecognised. She tried other search engines, and other configurations of the title, but with the same result. She made a point of looking in second-hand bookshops instead. She felt certain the book would turn up one day, a nothing-looking volume with a scuffed cloth cover and no dust jacket, the kind that falls down the back of the shelf without you realising, that when you find it again by accident some years later, you can't remember how you came to have it in the first place.

Julie carried on with her job at the Christie and soon got promoted. She took up running again, and photography, and seemed much happier generally. She kept on at Selena about applying for the Open University.

"You could go part-time at work," she said. "We can afford it now, easily. It would be stupid not to."

"I'll think about it," Selena said. In the end they agreed she'd enrol for the following March.

## If I Could Tell You I Would
## Let You Know

In 1899, the Serbian experimental physicist Nikola Tesla built a radio transmitter and receiver at his laboratory in Colorado. The device intercepted radio signals of unknown origin. Tesla claimed they came from space, possibly from an alien craft that had been sent to gather information about the Earth and then report back.

Tesla thought the signals might be coming from Mars, but no one took Tesla seriously. He was everybody's tame mad scientist, a showman and an eccentric, brilliant but unreliable, running up massive electricity bills and then absconding with no forwarding address. How could anyone believe a man like that? Reports of the radio signals didn't stop though, and as the space race gathered momentum, sightings of the actual object began to filter through. It was a satellite, reporters claimed, an unidentified flying object, spinning about the Earth in a polar orbit. The object was first photographed in 1957 by Dr Luis Corralos of the Communications Ministry in Venezuela. Dr Corralos was attempting to track the progress of the newly launched Soviet satellite, *Sputnik 1*. This other object, its unidentified twin, appeared to be shadowing the Sputnik, although neither the Americans nor the Russians stepped forward to claim it. Nobody official was prepared to admit that it was even there.

A possible explanation was offered by space enthusiasts who suggested the UFO must be a piece of debris left over from the Black Knight missile testing programme, a series of dummy runs set up by the British in the mid-1950s. The theory was fatally flawed – the Black Knight scientists did not at that time have the technology to send a rocket into orbit – but it gave the still-unidentified object the name that it has been known by ever since.

The Black Knight satellite flies in a polar orbit, which space scientists agree is the kind of orbit most commonly used for the purposes of reconnaissance, or information-gathering. The satellite has been variously identified as space-station garbage, wreckage debris, an insulation blanket, an ejection seat, a rogue spy satellite. But still, no one seems to have a definitive answer as to what it is, or where it came from, or why it is there. Nobody seems able to track it properly, either. It has a habit of vanishing off radar screens, sometimes for years, only to reappear again just as mysteriously and without any warning. It has an orbit unlike any other man-made or natural object. The Black Knight satellite, named or otherwise, is still a UFO.

There have been theories, of course. Some have believed the signals could have been produced by an emissary probe from a distant star system, thousands of years ago. One particularly enthusiastic ufologist even extrapolated the signals into star charts. Other ufologists were enthralled.

Astronomers and physicists refused to give such lunatic propositions a second glance.

It's strange though, don't you think, that no one has ever really tried to track the thing, or get up close to it? It's almost as if people think it might be dangerous.

The satellite is still up there, Selena. God knows where it came from, or what's inside it. I wouldn't go near it, if it were me. I wouldn't touch it with a bargepole.

Most UFOs get identified pretty quickly. Nine times out of ten a UFO will end up being a weather balloon or a Chinese lantern or an albatross that's swallowed a radio transmitter or just a flock of geese. Every now and then there'll be an unidentified flying object that no one can immediately identify. Those are the ones that annoy people, because they leave room for doubt. I've read about scientists – astrophysicists and flight technicians and aeronautics engineers who've worked for NASA for twenty years – who have publicly denied UFO theory whilst admitting off the record that they just don't know. Any public statement suggesting they believed in flying saucers would be career suicide. Not worth risking their reputations over, anyway.

You remember that old Police song we used to love, 'Message in a Bottle'? We used to belt it out, didn't we, whenever we heard it come on the radio, singing at the tops of our voices, miming actions to the lyrics, pretending to search the horizon for rescue ships. There was something about that song that made us mad for it, something catchy and deadly serious and just a little bit frightening. Sting sung about a year passing since he wrote his note, but what if thirteen thousand years had passed, or more, and the message wasn't a message in a bottle but a series of radio transmissions, or an unidentified flying object? What if it came through the rift, that thing, that *repository*, whatever it is?

Even if the whole Black Knight satellite story turns out to be a fake, a hoax, that doesn't mean we're safe. That bottle, with its deadly message, could be hurtling towards us, even now. Even as we sit here talking over our day and putting wood on our lovely new stove and thinking about what film we're going to see at The Dancehouse on Saturday night. Even if it isn't us, it will be someone. It's like Noah said: the rift exists. Something is bound to come through it, sooner or later. I wish I could forget what happened to me and go back to normal. I wish I could tell you I made it all up, but that wouldn't be true.

*From the ruins of Pakwa you can see Tristane, huge and bright as a beacon, like a silver globe. Even in the daytime, you can see her, even when it's cloudy.* That's what Linus Quinn wrote in his memoir, and even though I was never on Dea I believe what he said.

End

# Acknowledgements

Huge thanks to Cath Trechman, Natalie Laverick, Chris Young, Lydia Gittins, Julia Lloyd and Ella Chappell of Titan Books for helping *The Rift* through to completion and getting it out there, and to all the wonderful friends and colleagues who offered encouragement and support along the way. In particular I would like to thank Anne Charnock, John Clute, Carole Johnstone, Vince Haig, Mike Harrison, Paul Kincaid, Maureen Kincaid Speller, Helen Marshall, Andre Paine, Cleaver Patterson, Cath Phillips, David Rix, Priya Sharma, Robert Shearman, Emma Swift and Douglas Thompson for their inspiring conversation and excellent company. Love and thanks as always to my mother, Monica Allan, and to my partner, Christopher Priest, for being the best.

## About the Author

Nina Allan's stories have appeared in numerous magazines and anthologies, including *Best Horror of the Year #6*, *The Year's Best Science Fiction and Fantasy 2013*, and *The Mammoth Book of Ghost Stories by Women*. Her novella *Spin*, a science fictional re-imagining of the Arachne myth, won the British Science Fiction Association Award in 2014, and her story-cycle *The Silver Wind* was awarded the Grand Prix de l'Imaginaire in the same year. *The Race* was a finalist for the 2015 BSFA Award, the Kitschies Red Tentacle and the John W. Campbell Memorial Award. Nina Allan lives and works on the Isle of Bute with her partner, the science fiction writer Christopher Priest. Find Nina's blog, The Spider's House, at www.ninaallan.co.uk

# The Race

## Nina Allan

A child is kidnapped with consequences that extend across worlds… A writer reaches into the past to discover the truth about a possible murder… Far away a young woman prepares for her mysterious future…

In a future scarred by fracking and ecological collapse, Jenna Hoolman lives in the coastal town of Sapphire. Her world is dominated by the illegal sport of smartdog racing: greyhounds genetically modified with human DNA. When her young niece goes missing that world implodes… Christy's life is dominated by fear of her brother, a man she knows capable of monstrous acts and suspects of hiding even darker ones. Desperate to learn the truth she contacts Alex, a stranger she knows only by name, and who has his own demons to fight… And Maree, a young woman undertaking a journey that will change her world forever.

*The Race* weaves together story threads and realities to take us on a gripping and spellbinding journey…

# The Rig

### Roger Levy

Humanity has spread across the depths of space but is connected by AfterLife – a vote made by every member of humanity on the worth of a life. Bale, a disillusioned policeman on the planet Bleak, is brutally attacked, leading writer Raisa on to a story spanning centuries of corruption. On Gehenna, the last religious planet, a hyperintelligent boy, Alef, meets psychopath Pellon Hoq, and so begins a rivalry and friendship to last an epoch.

"Levy is a writer of great talent and originality." SF Site

"Levy's writing is well-measured and thoughtful, multi-faceted and often totally gripping."
*Strange Horizons*

Available May 2018